*I hope you enjoy
in the Guardian —
took at least a year to write.
People ask me how I knew what
was going to happen. That's easy. It's
in the Bible.*
— Robin Helm
Phil. 4:13

Legacy

The Guardian Trilogy, Book 3

ROBIN HELM

Copyright © 2012 Robin Helm

All rights reserved.

ISBN: 1475137265
ISBN-13: 978-1475137262

Scripture quotations taken from the New American Standard Bible®, Copyright© 1960, 1962, 1963, 1968, 1971, 1972, 1973, 1975, 1977, 1995 by The LOCKMAN Foundation
Used by permission. (www.Lockman.org)

I CORINTHIANS 10:31

"Whether, then, you eat or drink or whatever you do, do all to the glory of God."

DEDICATION

Soli Deo gloria

ACKNOWLEDGMENTS

Thank you to my betas: Gayle Mills, Stephanie Hamm, Julianne Martin, Tiffany Colonna, Wendi Sotis, Betty Campbell Madden, Mia Carr, and Melanie Helm. As always, my husband, Larry, deserves my heartfelt gratitude for his patience and assistance. Wendi Sotis was tremendously helpful, as always, with the print cover.

Chapter 1

"Arise, cry aloud in the night at the beginning of the night watches; pour out your heart like water before the presence of the Lord."
Lamentations 2:19a

August 2008

Xander woke up Sunday morning, still kneeling on the floor by his bed. He had prayed for most of the night, thanking Jehovah-Jireh for another chance to talk with Elizabeth, and asking for wisdom in choosing the right words to say to her. Though God in His love and mercy had sent Gabriel to talk to Elizabeth during the night, and she had agreed to meet him at church this morning, he knew that she would have many questions concerning why he had never told her that he had been her guardian angel. When she had broken off their relationship, she had made it very clear to him that she felt he had betrayed her trust and deceived her in withholding the full truth.

He sighed heavily and rested his forehead against the side of his mattress as his mind ran through the terrible events of the previous day. Elizabeth had found out his secret in the worst possible way – from Gregory. Just as Xander had been about to reveal his dual nature to her, Gregory had dissolved the ropes holding the bridge on which they stood, and Elizabeth had fallen. Xander had been forced to reveal himself and save her or to watch her die on the rocks beneath them at the bottom of the gorge. After he had flown to rescue her in angelic form, in her anger she had left with Gregory,

Lucifer's son. Gregory had taken her to his home, drugging her with an intent to rape her, and though Xander had intervened in time to stop him, it had not erased his guilt from her mind.

Xander felt Michael's arm around his shoulders and turned his head to see the massive warrior on his knees beside him. *Michael? You spent the night kneeling on the floor with me? I remember that you comforted me while I prayed. I must have finally fallen asleep. Why did you not awaken me?*

You needed to sleep. Michael's voice was kind.

Xander suddenly understood, and his eyes widened. *You held me up. I would have fallen over, but you spent the night supporting me. I am humbled. Thank you.*

You are my brother. I was glad to be able to be of assistance in your time of need. You have done the same and more for so many others, Xander.. Your entire existence has been spent in the service of the Master, protecting and comforting His children. I know that the Almighty will be with you today. He heard your prayers, and He will answer them. Michael's thoughts were confident. He stood and extended his hand to Xander, helping him to stand.

Xander was stiff from having remained in one position without moving for such a long time, so he gratefully accepted Michael's assistance as he forced his legs to move. After rising awkwardly to his feet, he then released Michael's hand. Xander stretched, and then walked to his dresser, facing himself in the mirror, looking at the dark circles under his eyes from lack of sleep.

I think it is safe to say that if she takes me back today, it will not be because of my amazing good looks, he mused.

Michael stepped up behind him, smiling encouragement. *A shower will soon put you to rights. Remember that she thinks you are handsomer than I am. There is no accounting for the taste of some people, but it may work to your favor.*

Xander smiled crookedly and headed toward the bathroom. *I will need every advantage I can muster.* As he showered, his mind ran through all of Elizabeth's preferences for him – her favorite clothes, colors, scent, hairstyle, music – everything he could think of. He briefly wondered if he had time to get a haircut. Xander dismissed the idea and began to pray again.

~~oo~~

As he had nearly every Sunday morning since he had met Elizabeth in his human form in January, Xander drove to Tabernacle Church with Michael flying overhead. He remained silent, musing on the oddity that his thousands of years of existence had not prepared him for the ordeal which lay ahead. Facing the questions of the eighteen-year-old girl whom he loved with an intensity beyond anything he could ever have imagined made him extremely anxious, and knowing that she held his very heart in her hands and had the ability to crush it with a word was daunting beyond anything he had ever experienced. He realized that he had existed on the periphery of life, observing humans with very little actual interaction. Fighting on the behalf of others was not half so difficult as laying himself open before Elizabeth, trusting her to understand and accept what he was.

As he drove, he meditated on Psalm 37:4-5, *'Delight yourself in the Lord; and He will give you the desires of your heart. Commit your way to the Lord; trust also in Him, and He will do it.' Father, I know that You planted the desire for Elizabeth within my heart, and now I thank You for her, and I ask You to give her to me. Abba, please help her to understand, enable her to have confidence in me again, guide her questions, and help me to answer her in a way which pleases You. Calm my heart, Lord. Take my fear. I love you, Jehovah-Rophe.*

Xander parked at the church, put his forearms on the steering wheel, and rested his head on them with his eyes closed. He looked up when he heard a tapping on the window; he had been so focused on praying that he had failed to hear any human thoughts.

Elizabeth was watching him intently, her brown eyes serious. He rolled down the window.

Gabriel stood behind her, his lips upturned in a small smile, while Michael landed beside him and tucked his wings.

"Hi," she said. "Can we talk a minute?"

"Certainly. Where?"

Rather than answer, she walked around the car and got in. Her hands, holding her Bible, rested in her lap as she turned to him.

"Xander," she began, and then stopped to take a deep breath. "I know we don't have much time right now, but I want us to be comfortable with each other in church. Gabriel talked to me last night, and I have thought about everything he said. I am willing to listen to you, but I expect you to answer all my questions – fully and completely. Don't leave anything out this time. Don't edit or choose only what you think I need to hear. I want to know it all at once with no more surprises. If you can't do that, there is no more future for us. Will you do it?" She held his gaze with a raised eyebrow.

He was nearly giddy with relief, and it was only by great force of will that he did not envelop her in a hug to end all hugs. *Thank you, Father, that she came to me of her own free will. It sounds as if she is ready to listen to me and give our relationship another chance.* "I can answer your questions readily and without reservation, Elizabeth. Yes, I will. I absolutely promise to answer fully everything you ask me. I may actually add things you would not even think of asking because I want you to know everything about me. I have hated this secrecy, and I want everything to be out in the open finally. You may, in fact, have to ask me to be silent before I overwhelm you with information."

He wanted to take her hand, but he was afraid that she would think he was assuming too much; he would wait for her to make the first move.

"You look tired," Elizabeth said, her eyes showing her sympathy.

"I did not sleep well. May I make a request?" he asked hopefully.

Elizabeth's curiosity took the lead. "Of course, though it doesn't necessarily follow that I will agree, you know."

"I know, I know." He breathed deeply. "I love your family dearly, and I know that we always eat Sunday dinner with them, but would you mind if we went out for lunch today – just the two of us? I find that I am eager to talk to you, and I want to do it as soon as possible. My tenuous hold on my sanity may not last though Life Group, worship service, and dinner. I am actually anticipating being questioned for once. Can we make it sooner rather than later. Please?" Xander struggled to smile though his hands remained clenched into fists in his lap.

He is altogether adorable. She sighed.

"I'm sure you heard that," she said, a little sharply. He lowered his eyes and nodded.

Elizabeth bit her lip. "Mom would be disappointed. She and Dad have no idea what happened yesterday, and she still expects us to eat with them. She made most of your favorites – roast beef with homemade mashed potatoes, gravy, carrots, and green bean casserole, with banana pudding for dessert."

He very much appreciated the good will of Elizabeth's family, though he knew he would not be able to eat until after he and Elizabeth had talked. He looked up at her through his lashes. "I would not make her unhappy. Can we at least eat quickly, and then go somewhere quiet to talk? I cannot make polite conversation all afternoon while I worry about everything."

She smiled a little at the thought of imperturbable Xander in a state of high anxiety. "All right. We'll leave right after lunch, and you can choose a spot where we can talk. Let me rephrase that – I'll ask questions, you'll talk, and I'll listen."

"Yes, ma'am," he said, smiling broadly.

Ah, the dimples. Not fair, she thought.

I will warn you now. I plan to use every poor advantage that I have. The dimples will be on full display as often as I can manage it, he answered in her mind.

She looked him over in a frank appraisal. "I don't suppose it's an accident that you wore the blue shirt that matches your eyes along with my favorite jacket and pants, or that you're wearing Acqua Di Gio for the first time since the beginning of June."

Xander met her gaze levelly, aforementioned blue eyes serious and steadily focused on her. "No, ma'am. I would not deceive you; I admit that I have done everything humanly possible to advance my cause. Is it working?"

Elizabeth began to sing "Amazing Grace" loudly in her mind. Michael and Gabriel smiled. They recognized Elizabeth's way of blocking her thoughts from Xander.

~~oo~~

By the time Xander finally managed to get Elizabeth into his car four hours later, he had developed an entirely different view of eternity. He felt that he had already lived through it, and it was far too long a time. He was, however, glad that she had taken a few moments to change into comfortable clothing. Seeing her in her workout clothes lifted his spirits. It gave him hope that she might have plans for the two of them after their talk.

Michael, Gabriel, and Niall had spent the morning trying not to smile at his expense, and he knew it. He was aware that he was a source of amusement to them; however much they might sympathize with him, the knowledge stung.

"Where are we going?" asked Elizabeth, breaking into his thoughts.

"You have never been to my townhouse. Would you object to going there alone with me now? I want us to have absolute privacy with no chance of being overheard," Xander answered, glancing quickly at her as he backed out of the driveway.

Her eyes sparkled. "I'm going to the mysterious bachelor pad? No, I don't have a problem with it. You have always been a complete gentleman with me."

"Do not get overly excited. There is hardly any furniture, and the place is in desperate need of a feminine touch. However, it is quiet, and we can be assured of complete privacy."

She studied his profile for a few moments. "When you say 'complete privacy,' you aren't just talking about being away from humans, are you?"

He looked quickly at her, and then back at the road. "No, I am not. You know the Word very well. You know that holy angels are not the only ones who inhabit the spiritual dimension. Our talk should be done in a place that can be carefully monitored."

"I suppose that you are referring to Michael and Gabriel when you speak of monitors?" she asked.

Flying over the car, the angels glanced at each other, uncomfortable with her knowledge of them, and aware that her familiarity with everything in their world would soon be increased exponentially. Elizabeth would have more direct contact with them than any other human had ever had. Angels had made limited appearances to mortals throughout history, but no one had ever known them with the level of comfort that Elizabeth would require.

"Yes, I am. They will ensure that no spies eavesdrop on us." Xander felt strangely liberated. The topic of his true nature had been forbidden for so long that to talk about it now was a luxury. He had to make a conscious effort to be silent and allow her to direct the conversation.

"So they are with us now? Are they in the back seat?" Elizabeth looked back over her shoulder.

He chuckled and shook his head. "No, they are our protectors, remember? They are flying above the car so that they can watch for those who would harm us. They would not have a clear line of sight from the back seat."

"You are not allowed to laugh at my ignorance when you are the one responsible for it," Elizabeth said firmly, looking out her window.

"I am sorry, Elizabeth," Xander said contritely. "No angel has ever explained how our world works to a human before. Please remember that the angelic way of life is as common to me as is the human life to you. If I try not to laugh, may I at least smile from time to time?"

Elizabeth looked at her hands as she replied in exasperation, "By all means, show the dimples, but try to keep in mind that while many of my questions may seem foolish to you, I would not be asking the questions if I already knew the answers. You cannot expect me to automatically know what is not stated specifically in the Scriptures. You haven't told me anything, you know, except that you can read people's minds and speak into them. Can all angels do that?"

"All holy angels can hear human thoughts, but only guardians and archangels have the ability to speak into people's minds. Guardians who protect members of the same family share all of their own thoughts as well, though we can consciously think of something else in order to avoid revealing our thoughts to other guardians, and we cannot hear each other or communicate over great distances. Only Michael is unlimited by distance. He can hear all angels, and he can communicate with one or all at the same time. He can also summon the entire Host, which includes all holy angels, though we usually use that term to refer to warriors, within seconds. All holy angels can 'speak' while in angelic form so that other angels can 'hear.' I did that quite often as Chief of the Guardians."

Elizabeth tilted her head to see his face, and her hair fell across her shoulder. "Are you still Chief of the Guardians?"

"I am, and as such, I command all guardians, though Asim issues the assignments. If I need to call for a specific guardian or a group of them, I am unlimited by distance in that. I can also hear any of them that need to speak with me at any time, and I can call for scouts. If I require warriors, I speak with Michael." Xander concentrated on the road. He longed to tuck her hair behind her ear, to run his fingers through the curls, to smell her strawberry shampoo. He wanted to look at her face to judge how she was handling so much information at once, but he knew that it would be unsafe to watch her and ignore his driving. Privately, he wished that she would wait until they reached his townhouse to talk so that he could see her eyes.

You really should not be talking in the car. It is not so secure as is your townhouse, commented Michael.

"Elizabeth, the townhouse would be a more private setting for this conversation, but I would not have you think that I am putting off answering your questions." Xander refused to answer Michael in his thoughts because Elizabeth would be unable to hear him, and he was determined that he would be completely open with her.

In answer, she put in their CD of duets and settled back, bending her left arm across her stomach so that she could use it to prop her right elbow, resting her chin on her fist.

"I can wait; we aren't far from Spartanburg now," she said calmly.

Xander was greatly encouraged by her choice of music.

~~oo~~

As the couple entered the townhouse, Elizabeth noted that his living room contained only a grand piano and a computer desk with a chair. Once they were seated cross-legged on the floor of his living room facing each other, with Gabriel and Michael stationed at the windows looking for unusual activity, Xander smiled at Elizabeth, saying, "I apologize for the lack of furniture, but I never managed to purchase anything except what I required to live as a human. However, we did not come here to discuss my deficiencies in home decorating. I am sure that you have not exhausted your curiosity. Ask what you will."

"You mentioned 'holy angels' several times in the car. I assume the other angels are the fallen ones?" she asked.

"Yes. One third of the angels left heaven with Lucifer and were cast to Earth."

"Is Gregory one of those?" Elizabeth asked, looking him straight in the eyes.

"No, he is not. However, his father, Lucifer, is." Xander's voice was quiet and controlled.

Elizabeth's mouth dropped open. She finally regained her power of speech. "Gregory is the son of Lucifer? Satan himself?"

"Yes, Gregory is a halfling – a Nephilim. He was born of Lucifer and a human girl." Xander's eyes flashed, but he showed no other sign of emotion.

Elizabeth struggled for words. "He is a demon?"

He nodded.

"Is Cassandra a demon, too?"

He kept his voice carefully modulated. Elizabeth would not understand his satisfaction at the unbodying of Cassandra. "She was, but she no longer exists in this world."

"Where is she?" Elizabeth asked.

"When Gregory attacked you at his house, I fought him in human form. Michael and Gabriel were there in angelic form, fighting Cassandra and two other demons who guarded Gregory. Cassandra was sent to her final destination by Michael, though Gregory and the two others escaped."

"Cassandra is dead?"

Xander considered his words. "Not exactly. She has been unbodied and sent to the place prepared by God for Lucifer and his followers. She cannot come back to Earth."

To his surprise, Elizabeth showed no remorse for her erstwhile friend. "But Gregory escaped," was her comment.

"He escaped only because I thought that you had been through more than enough. I did not think that I should unbody him in front of you while we were in human form. You would have seen it, and you were already upset enough," Xander replied, watching her reaction carefully.

"Now I understand why you said that Gregory and Cassandra were beyond redemption. Demons have already made their choice, and it is unchangeable." She paused as she considered his words. "But what about Gregory? He is half human. Did he have a choice?" she asked.

"After what he did to you, you would defend him?" He was incredulous.

"He deserves to go to jail for attempted rape and for drugging me, but I do not wish everlasting torment on anyone."

Xander sighed. "You are so kind, Elizabeth, with so much more compassion than Gregory deserves. Gregory has been evil from his birth, and he likes being that way. He hates God and all good things. Lucifer and his son have been trying to destroy you from the time of your conception. They would gladly have killed your mother to prevent your birth."

"And you have been protecting me from them all this time," she stated.

"Yes, it has been my great privilege to guard you. I was the protector of Mary, Abraham, Moses, Daniel, Esther, David, and many others."

She sat up straight, her eyes wide open. "That is amazing!" She was having difficulty wrapping her mind around the idea that Xander, her guardian, had been the protector of such important people. He actually knew them. Furthermore, she realized that she was part of that select group. The thought was overwhelming. "Perhaps one day, we can spend hours talking about what that was like – to guard all those great people."

"I was a different creature then, Elizabeth. I felt no strong emotions, except on behalf of my charges. You are the first person I have ever loved. Angels do not love as humans do. We cannot be emotionally involved with our charges and do our jobs well."

"Ah, your job. Now there's the sticking place, isn't it?" she asked quietly, her eyes boring into his.

"Yes, Elizabeth, you were my charge. At first, I was able to maintain an emotional detachment from you, but as you grew, I loved you – first as a friend, then as a big brother, a father, and finally as a man loves a woman. Trust me when I say that my love for you caused quite a stir throughout the heavenly realm as well as the demonic one. We have been avidly watched since you were conceived." Xander grimaced slightly, remembering his embarrassment.

"What?" Elizabeth saw his fleeting expression.

He hesitated for a moment. "I did not enjoy being a spectacle for the spiritual realm. It was torture to guard you in your private moments, especially when I began to recognize my feelings for you. Finally, I could deny it no longer. It was apparent to your family's other guardians, as well as Michael and Gabriel, that I loved you. I turned my back when I had to be in the room while you bathed or changed. If we were alone in the house, I waited in the hallway outside your door, 'seeing' through your mind to make certain that you were safe, and hoping that you would not look in the mirror while you were unclothed. It had never bothered me to guard a woman before, but everything changed because of you. Yahweh gave me a dual nature, fully angel yet fully human, so that I might love you, Elizabeth. I am a new creature."

Elizabeth took his measure. He was physically beautiful, certainly, but he was even more wonderful in his spirit. He had not taken advantage of her, even though she would not have known it. If she chose not to trust and completely forgive such a man, she would be punishing herself.

She reached for his hands with both of hers, and he leaned over, took her hands, and kissed them gently.

"Elizabeth, I have seen the most beautiful women of the ages, and you outshine them all." He quoted freely from the Song of Solomon, "'How beautiful you are, my darling; how beautiful you are! You are altogether beautiful, my darling, and there is no blemish in you. Like a lily among the thorns, so is my darling among the maidens. You have made my heart beat faster with a single glance of your eyes.'"

Elizabeth surprised Xander by speaking from the same book, "'I am my beloved's, and my beloved is mine. His mouth is full of sweetness, and he is wholly desirable. This is my beloved and this, my friend. I am lovesick.'" She leaned closer to him and whispered into his ear, "'May he kiss me with the kisses of his mouth! For your love is better than wine.'"

Taking her words as the invitation he had awaited, Xander pulled her onto his lap and kissed her softly. He thought his heart would burst with the joy of it.

"I am your beloved?" he asked, nuzzling her neck as he held her in his arms, stroking her long hair.

"You are," she breathed. "I am spoiled for anyone else. No other man could match up to you."

She felt him smile against her neck and thought, *Don't waste the dimples. I can't see your face.*

I have many more smiles, Elizabeth, and you may have them whenever you want them. Do you forgive me?

I had already forgiven you, but I have decided that I must trust you again. Gabriel pointed out to me that God trusts you implicitly; I can do no less. However, I will have more questions, you know.

He continued to kiss the line of her jaw. *I hope that you never run out of questions for me, my love. Maybe I can manage to hold your interest if there are things that you want to know. I am a fairly boring man, I fear.*

Elizabeth laughed and drew back to look into his perfect face. "If you are boring, I don't want to meet anyone exciting. You are quite interesting enough for me."

"Elizabeth, will you excuse me for a moment?" he asked.

"Sure," she answered, puzzled.

He set her on the floor and hurried into his bedroom, returning almost instantly to kneel before her on one knee, taking her hand in his.

"Elizabeth, I wanted this moment to be special and memorable, and you nearly died. I do not want to take you back home without having this settled. When God made me into a dual natured being and told me that He wanted me to win your love, He said for me to use I Corinthians 13 and Ephesians 5:25-28 as guides. I have studied those Scriptures, and I truly do love you as Christ loved the church. I would be willing to die for you. I also know that love is greater than faith, hope, gifts, or knowledge. Without love, we are nothing. Without love, none of the rest means anything. Today, I am rejoicing in the truth, and I have learned that real love never fails. I know that you are young, but you are not like most eighteen-year-old girls. Elizabeth Faith, I love you with all that I am. You are a part of my heart which was missing for thousands of years, and I did not know it until I loved you. Will you marry me?"

Elizabeth stood to her feet and looked down into his eyes, shining with love for her. She thought of the sacrifices that he had made for her, and of how he always thought of her before anything or anyone else – including himself. He was the most unselfish person she had ever known, and she loved him with her whole self. He was her other half. She leaned toward him and held his dear face between her hands, kissing him gently, first on his lips and then on each eyelid.

"I will," she breathed softly.

He took the ring from his pants pocket and held out his hand. She gave him her left hand, and he slipped the ring on her finger, holding his breath in his excitement.

Xander stood and gathered her into his arms, lowering his face to hers for a deep kiss. He pulled away a few inches. "You are finally mine," he said with a broad smile.

Not yet, thought Michael.

Be quiet, answered Gabriel.

Xander easily ignored both of them, keeping all of his attention focused fully on his lady.

Chapter 2

"He who finds a wife finds a good thing, and obtains favor from the Lord."
Proverbs 18:22

Xander would have happily married Elizabeth the moment she agreed to be his wife, but he respected her and her family too much to suggest anything that might offend their sensibilities. He knew that David Bennet would expect his future son-in-law to talk with him, asking for his blessing on their marriage. He also realized that Lynne would take great joy in helping Elizabeth to plan her wedding. Having David and Lynne as in-laws would be the closest he would ever get to having actual human parents, and he wanted to please them. He wanted to love them and to be loved as their son in return. The thought of having an earthly family gave him great pleasure.

Holding Elizabeth in his arms, enjoying the perfect harmony of the moment, feeling the warmth of her body molded to his, Xander was perfectly contented. He fully intended to begin arranging the details of their marriage before the day was out, but there was something else he wanted to do first.

"Elizabeth," he said, turning his head to place his cheek on the top of her head.

"Hmmm?"

"I have a present for you." Xander's voice was husky with emotion.

"That's lovely, but I'm holding my favorite gift from you right now. The only thing I need is a date set for the unwrapping ceremony," she replied a bit dreamily.

Wonderful. It was difficult enough keeping Xander in line. Now we must deal with Elizabeth's passions as well. Michael sounded a little grumpy.

They are young and in love, thought Gabriel with a smile. *It is to be expected.*

Xander is not young, answered Michael quickly.

Michael, in the words of truly young humans, lighten up. Gabriel managed somehow to look angelic in spite of his words.

Looking over Elizabeth's head at Michael, Xander rolled his eyes a little. "We are in complete agreement about that, love, but actually, I found this particular present for you last week. Just stay here for a minute while I get it from my bedroom. I will be right back."

He released her reluctantly and strode toward his room. Elizabeth walked over to the piano and found a sheet of paper covered with words which had been crossed out and rewritten several times. She was reading when he came back into the room with a small box.

"What's this?" she asked, looking at the paper and then at him.

He grimaced as he walked to her and held his hand out for the sheet. "It is not finished yet."

"I think it's wonderful. Is it a song?" Elizabeth held the paper behind her back, smiling at him teasingly.

Xander held the box just out of her reach, smiling. "I will give you this box if you will let me have that sheet of paper."

"I'll give you the paper if you'll tell me about it later," she said playfully.

"Agreed," he answered, holding out the box in his left hand while reaching for the paper with his right.

Elizabeth handed him the sheet with one hand and held out her other hand, palm up. Xander took the paper and placed the box in her hand.

"More jewelry, Xander? You must stop buying things for me," she said with a slight frown.

"Elizabeth, I have noticed that you wear necklaces, charms, and rings that are special to you because they represent the people you love. You always have on something from your parents, and you usually wear jewelry that belonged to one of your grandmothers or your mother. I wanted to add something to your collection that will remind you of me." His face was earnest. "Please, open my gift."

She could not disappoint him, though she was already wearing an engagement ring from him, which certainly made her think of him and the promises which they had made to each other.

The moment she opened the box, a smile spread over her features. Elizabeth took the fine silver chain from the cotton and held it up to examine the charm – an angel fashioned of silver with golden wings.

"It's perfect. I love it, and I love you." She stood on her tiptoes to kiss his lips, and then handed the necklace to him, turning her back and pulling her hair over her shoulder so that he could fasten the chain around her neck.

"Ah, but I love you more," Xander replied as he helped her with the necklace, afterward bending to kiss her just below her ear.

Elizabeth turned to face him, mischief in her smile. "Now it's later. What is written on the paper?"

He sighed. "I have been working on something for you," he said, kissing her forehead. "It is not yet finished."

She looked up at him, her delight showing on her face. "Is it a song? For me? Let me hear what you have so far. Please, Xander?"

Xander could deny her nothing, so he sat on the piano bench and patted the space beside him. She sat down beside him, leaning into him to rest her head on his shoulder.

Elizabeth watched his long fingers caress the keys, playing a beautiful melody that she had never heard before. Then, Xander began to sing to her, his rich baritone singing words of love for her alone.

> *I thought that I had everything I needed.*
> *I thought I was complete all by myself.*
> *I thought that I was happy 'til I met you.*
> *You placed the missing piece within my heart.*
>
> *And then I thought that I had truly lost you.*
> *I learned the bitter meaning of "alone."*
> *I died a little when you turned and left me.*
> *I grieved each moment that we spent apart.*
>
> *But God heard my cries.*
> *He answered my prayers.*
> *He counted my tears.*
> *He spoke to your heart.*
> *You let me back in.*
>
> *And now I want to live forever,*
> *Always with you, together.*
> *You overwhelm me.*
> *I want to be the man you need.*
> *I want to be the one you love.*
> *I want to live forever*
> *With you.*

His expressive voice seemed to envelope her in his love. He soared on the final verse, declaring his heart's desire for them, and she heard the subtle ache in his words.

"That was beautiful, Xander. Thank you, my love. I do not deserve you, and I'm sorry I ever doubted you. I'm sorry that I ever believed anything Gregory said. I was childish and immature, yet you loved me through all of it. Until this moment, I never knew myself." She kissed his cheek, turned her face away to wipe her tears, and then fell silent.

With anguish, he heard her thoughts. He knew that Elizabeth understood his meaning. Xander put his arm around her, and stroking her shoulder with his fingers, he spoke softly.

"Elizabeth, my heart, I appreciate your apology, but it is truly unnecessary. You are everything that is lovely and good. It pains me to say it, but I do not know the answers to the questions in your mind. Only our Father knows what life holds for us. There is no one else like me, so I have no basis for comparison. I do not know if I am aging, though my hair and nails grow normally. I have no idea what will happen when I die, or even if I can die. My DNA is probably completely undamaged because I am a new kind of Adam of sorts."

As she looked back at him, she forced her eyes open in a way he remembered from her elementary and high school days, enabling her to hold her tears after her feelings had been hurt. Her eyes glistened as she put her arms around his neck. "You said you want us to be together forever – not that we would be. Please don't leave me to become an angel again. Even if you stay human, how can our marriage work? I am not Eve, and my DNA has been corrupted by thousands of years of human sin. I will do well if I live to be ninety, but Adam lived to be over six hundred years old."

He drew his brows together and embraced her. "I will never leave you, my love, though you may leave me. I do not wish to outlive you though. God Himself put us together, Elizabeth. He has a plan, and He will reveal it to us in His time. We must trust Him."

Elizabeth rested her head on his chest, listening to his strong heart beat. "What if I grow old, but you remain young? What if you are aging as slowly as the Old Testament saints did before the Flood? I will be like your grandmother. Will you leave me then?"

He held her shoulders and looked into her eyes. "Believe this, Elizabeth," Xander said firmly, fixing his blue eyes on her brown ones, "I will not leave you no matter what happens. Our wedding vows will include the words 'for eternity.' Even death will not part us. Our Father cannot be anything but good. We will do what He wants us to do, and He will take care of the rest. There is no mountain so big that He cannot move it. Nothing is too difficult for Him; nothing is impossible for Him."

His strength flowed into her, the force of his faith leading her to a fuller understanding of Jehovah Adonai.

He bent his face to hers, wrapping her in his arms as he kissed her. His intention was to comfort her, to tenderly show her how much he loved her, but she was consumed with need. Elizabeth entwined her fingers in his hair and pulled him to herself, conveying the depth of her feelings for him. He heard her thoughts of love and fear mingled together, and he kissed her more deeply, trying to erase her pain.

Knowing that his control was slipping, Xander broke the kiss and buried his face between her neck and her shoulder. He struggled to slow the beating of his heart and regulate his breathing, for he had never wanted her more than he did at that moment. Joining with her would make them one flesh; it would ease the uncertainty felt by both of them.

"Elizabeth," he whispered.

She kissed his ear. "Mmmm?"

His voice was deep when he spoke. "I was going to try to wait until next summer for our wedding. I know that you and your mother will want time to plan it, but this is torture. Would you consent to a Christmas wedding? Please?"

"Would you consider an elopement today? I am of legal age now," she whispered.

Are you serious? he asked, amazed.

You can read my mind. What do you think? she answered.

Xander knew that she meant what she had said, and the idea that her desires were as strong as his made his self-discipline even more difficult to maintain.

He groaned inwardly and released her. Standing rather abruptly, he took her hands and pulled her to her feet.

"I am extremely tempted, Elizabeth. You cannot imagine how much I wish that I could marry you tomorrow – today even, if the courthouse was not closed on Sunday. I am afraid, though, that your parents would not appreciate a rushed wedding with the two of us standing in front of a judge. Four months will pass by quickly while we find a house, go to school, and plan the wedding. It need not be an elaborate affair."

She sighed. "I really don't care about a fancy wedding, either, but you are probably right about Mom and Dad. A small church ceremony would please them. I can have Charlotte and Janna as bridesmaids. Oh, my!" Elizabeth stopped speaking, putting her hand over her mouth. Then she burst out laughing.

"What is funny? I hear your thoughts, but I do not see the humor," he said, puzzled.

"Think about it. Who will you have for your best man and groomsmen? Gabriel and Michael? Jonathan?" She dissolved into giggles.

Xander smiled at her. "Actually, Niall, your mother's guardian, should be my best man. Gabriel and Michael can be groomsmen. Would you like Josh Lucas and Chance Bingley to be ushers?" She nodded at him, and he continued, "Perhaps Jonathan could help your father perform the ceremony. After all, someone has to ask, 'Who gives this woman?' Your father could walk you down the aisle and answer the question, and then Jonathan could sit down and let your dad finish the ceremony."

Gabriel and Michael wore twin looks of amazement.

I have never been a groomsman, thought Michael with uncertainty.

You are never too old to learn, answered Xander.

You are the perfect example of that, my brother, added Gabriel, attempting to accept the idea of assuming human form in front of so many people and having to make conversation with them. *It will be well, Michael. We have four months to prepare for the wedding.*

He chuckled at the rapidly changing expressions on the faces of the archangels. *It is too bad that Elizabeth cannot see you. She would enjoy this.*

After Gabriel adjusted to the idea, he responded with aplomb. *I think I shall like wearing a tuxedo, and I think further that I might wear it rather well.*

When Elizabeth sees me in formal attire, she will no longer think you are the handsomest of the brothers, said Michael without any hint of humor.

"I hadn't thought of the other guardians. Won't we be rather decimating the ranks by using the three angels in the wedding?" she asked, genuinely curious.

"No, substitutes can be arranged for the day. Roark, Edward, Lexus, Alexis, and Hector will be there for your father, Charlotte, Jonathan, Janna, and Chance. There will also be guardians for every other believer there. Michael can assign warriors to guard us and your mother, or I can bring in guardians who are between assignments. There are hundreds of thousands of angels, Elizabeth, and all of them would like to be at our wedding. Unfortunately, that will not be possible. The rest of the world must be guarded while we marry." He smiled at her shocked expression.

She was silent a moment, mulling over what he had said. Then she looked at him in contemplation. "If you have two groomsmen and a best man, I must have two bridesmaids and a matron of honor. What would you think of Caroline Bingley being a bridesmaid with Charlotte?"

He raised a brow. "Would you want that, Elizabeth? I will accept whatever you decide, of course, but I know how much pain she caused you and others in your church. I was there, holding you while you cried. And think of the Williams family. They are your friends. How will Delores and Jim Williams feel? What about Richard?"

She hugged him to her and rested her cheek on his chest. "It was the worst thing that ever happened to me until yesterday. However, Caroline has truly demonstrated that she is sorry, and she is Chance's sister. We go to church together, and we're together all the time at family gatherings. It will seem odd if I don't ask her."

Xander's eyes hardened as he remembered Elizabeth's agony. He kissed the top of her head and rested his chin on her dark hair, blowing out his breath.

"God has forgiven me for so much. I forgave Caroline long ago because God demonstrated His forgiveness to me through Christ. If I ask her to be in our wedding, she'll know that I truly accept her into our family," said Elizabeth softly. "Perhaps, though, instead of asking her to be a bridesmaid, I could invite her to keep the guest book and greet people as they arrive. I think I should include her that much at least."

Xander held her more tightly. "Ask her only if you want to, my love. Do not have her in our wedding because you think you should."

She pulled back a little, looking up at him with a smile. "I will be marrying you, the most wonderful man in the world, while Caroline is still paying for her mistakes. Her past will always follow her. I can afford to be generous. I want to do this for her and for me."

He dipped his mouth to hers and kissed her lightly. "That is one of the reasons why I love you, Elizabeth. You are selfless and kind – and obviously blinded to my faults. If you want Caroline to keep the registry at our wedding, I will be pleased to welcome her. Who will you ask to be the third bridesmaid?"

Elizabeth thought a moment, and then her face brightened with a smile. "My cousin, Bethany Martin, of course. I should have thought of her first. She's Aunt Grace's daughter from her first marriage. I'm sure you already know that I was never around her as much as I wanted to be because she is four years older than I am – five years younger than Janna – and she had to split her time between Aunt Grace and Uncle Scott. I hope that she can do it. She lives in Lynchburg now, you know. After she graduated from Liberty University last spring she took a job teaching in the Academy there. I'll get her number from Mom later. I can't wait to call her!"

That problem solved, Elizabeth's mind then leapt in a different direction.

"If we are to live here, we need to do some serious shopping," she said with determination, looking around at the nearly empty room.

"Again, we are on the same wavelength. I was thinking of buying a couch immediately, and I would appreciate your input. Sitting on the floor is not very comfortable. However, as to where we will live, I was thinking of buying a house for us. We could pick it out together."

"Our own house. Happy thought indeed!" she exclaimed, genuinely pleased.

"Before we go house hunting, love, there is something else we must do," he said, holding out his hand for hers.

~~oo~~

Xander and Elizabeth were late to church that evening and slipped into a back pew just as the singing ended. He had taken her back to her house so that she could change her clothes, and she was so lovely to him that he had great difficulty in concentrating on her father's sermon. Xander held her hand in his, admiring the way that her engagement ring seemed to be perfect for her in every way, and he was pleased to see that she wore his necklace. He felt a sense of intense satisfaction that she was finally his, for he viewed their engagement as a betrothal in the Biblical sense. In his eyes, they were married already, merely awaiting the formality of a ceremony before consummating their vows. Any breach between them now would be a divorce in his mind.

He gazed at her profile with adoration, thinking back through the events of the afternoon, reliving each detail over and over in his thoughts. *How could twenty-four hours have made such a dramatic difference in my life?*

Gabriel glowed with happiness from his place behind Xander, while Michael smiled beside his fellow guardian. The other guardians in attendance noticed the happiness of the protectors and their charges, and they watched Xander and Elizabeth with interest. No one had ever before witnessed Xander daydreaming in church. As Elizabeth lifted her left hand to hide a smile at the blissfully unfocused expression on her fiancé's handsome face, the assembled angels saw the ring on her finger. They knew then that Elizabeth had agreed to be his bride.

Suddenly, he was called back to reality by the sound of David Bennet's voice saying, "Amen," at the end of the benediction. He shook his head to clear his mind and waited for Elizabeth's father to come down the aisle. When his future father-in-law was nearly even with his pew, Xander caught his eye and cleared his throat.

"Mr. Bennet?" Xander was struggling to keep a ridiculous grin from his face. *The man will think I am a lovestruck fool.*

David paused to recognize the younger man and his daughter.

"Yes?" David looked at Xander's face and noted that the young man looked much happier than he had when he and Elizabeth had left the Bennet home after lunch.

Xander continued. "When you are finished talking to the church members, might Elizabeth and I have a word with you and Mrs. Bennet?"

David nodded. "Certainly. Here in my office, or at the house?"

Xander looked at Elizabeth, and she smiled up at him. Then he turned his face back to David. "Elizabeth and I will go to your home to wait there for both of you, if that is agreeable."

"I'll see you there in a few minutes, then," answered David, continuing down the aisle, shaking hands and speaking to members of his flock. Roark nodded to Xander as he followed David.

Xander and Elizabeth spoke to a few people but managed to leave the building without revealing their engagement to anyone. They had talked in the car on the way back from Spartanburg and had agreed that Elizabeth's parents should be advised before anyone else was told. The couple had also agreed that they wanted to talk to David and Lynne together.

~~oo~~

About half an hour later, Xander and Elizabeth were comfortably ensconced on the couch in the Bennets' living room with her parents seated across from them on the loveseat. Michael and Gabriel faced Niall and Roark, forming a square with their charges. Four warriors stood at the corners of the room.

Niall had immediately looked for a ring on Elizabeth's hand, and he had not been disappointed. Grinning broadly, he had slapped Xander on the back when he entered the house.

Now, having read Niall's thoughts, Roark smiled as well, emitting a gentle glow along with the other three protectors. Happiness radiated throughout the room, though the warriors' faces remained neutral.

Xander held Elizabeth's hand on his thigh, and the ring was plainly visible. Lynne's eyes were drawn to it as Xander looked at her daughter's hand. An expression of sheer delight crossed her face, but she kept her silence.

"You wanted to talk with us?" asked David, maintaining a serious mien with difficulty. The ring was definitely the elephant in the room, and he had not missed it.

"Yes, Rev. Bennet," Xander paused to clear his throat. He glanced at Elizabeth and turned back to her father with a joyous smile. "I love your daughter with all my heart, and to my great happiness, she loves me, too. This afternoon I asked Elizabeth to be my wife, and she has accepted me. We wish to have your blessing, as well as Mrs. Bennet's."

David smiled. "Elizabeth, is this true?"

"Yes, Daddy. I love Xander, and he loves me. We want to be married before Christmas."

Lynne raised her eyebrows. "Before Christmas? That's barely four months!"

Xander nodded. "We know that it will be a relatively short engagement period, but both of us prefer a small, simple wedding at Tabernacle. Truly, I would not have you exhaust yourself planning a grand event, Mrs. Bennet, and we do not wish to burden you with an expensive affair. We would be happy to have a private ceremony, but we thought that you would want Elizabeth to have a wedding with a white dress, a few bridesmaids, and a couple of groomsmen."

Elizabeth spoke with conviction. "The only thing that is not negotiable is the date. We want to marry as soon as classes are out in December. That would make the date Saturday, December 13. Other than that, I'll do whatever you want, Mom, though I do want to pick out the dresses for me and the bridesmaids."

Lynne knew that specific tone of Elizabeth's voice, and she acceded to her daughter's request. "Four months will be plenty of time if we start right away. We can go shopping this week. I'll reserve the church and the fellowship hall tomorrow. The church will already be decorated for Christmas, and we can work out the details about the reception, flowers, musicians, invitations, a photographer, and a caterer this week. Christmas weddings are popular, so we need to line up those people right away." Lynne's mind was buzzing, making lists and organizing what had to be done.

Elizabeth smiled. *Mom will be in her element. She was made to plan things. She's been planning my wedding since I was ten.*

I know, answered Xander.

Smarty pants, thought Elizabeth.

The guardians smiled, enjoying the teasing exchange.

"Xander, I think it's time to stop calling us *Rev. and Mrs. Bennet*," said David, smiling at his future son-in-law.

He was confused. "Then what shall I call you?" he asked.

Lynne laughed. "*Mom and Dad*? Would you be comfortable with that?"

His delight showed in his display of dimples. "Mom and Dad? Really?"

"Really," answered David. "I always wanted sons in addition to my two beautiful daughters. Now I will have two whom I love and respect." He stood and extended his hand to his future son-in-law.

Xander got up and went to shake David's hand. "Does this mean that we have your blessing?"

"Do you need my blessing?" chuckled David.

"Actually, no, but we would like to have it just the same." Xander's blue eyes twinkled.

"Of course you have my blessing. Go to it." David embraced first Xander and then Elizabeth.

"I love you, Daddy," she whispered. He murmured, "I love you, too, my El. I could not have given you to anyone less worthy."

After Elizabeth had hugged her father, she reached for her mother, who had left the loveseat and stood before her.

Lynne clasped Elizabeth to her, hugging her fiercely. "I will always love you, El, my baby girl."

"I love you, too, Mom."

Lynne turned to Xander, and for the first time, he extended his arms to her before she did so to him. "I love you, Mom."

Though Lynne had controlled her emotions very well to that point, his declaration broke through her resolve, and her eyes filled with tears. "As I love you," she choked out. "I'm so silly," she said as everyone laughed with her.

Lynne reached for her daughter's hand to admire her ring.

"He designed it himself," Elizabeth said, looking up at her intended with justifiable pride. "He truly is the best man I have ever known." She turned her head to wink at her father, "Except for you, of course, Daddy."

"That goes without saying," replied David, trying to hide his pleasure at her declaration of his status. "Xander, we'll have to call Chance and do some male bonding."

Elizabeth hit her forehead with the palm of her hand. "I should call Char and Janna. And, Mom, I need Bethany's number. I want her to be a bridesmaid."

"And I will let my brothers and the ushers know. I already have a tuxedo, but they will need to be fitted. Dad, I do not think you have met my three brothers."

Three? asked Niall.

You are my best man, answered Xander.

Cool, replied Niall with a grin.

"I look forward to it. Maybe we can meet for lunch soon," said David.

"Oh, yes. They would enjoy that," Xander replied with a huge smile.

Eat? Michael's face reflected his shock.

Get used to it, smirked Xander.

Order something very plain, Michael. It will be well. We will practice eating ahead of time. Gabriel thought, stoically.

Piece of cake, added Niall.

Have you ever eaten? asked Michael, looking at Niall a little sternly.

No, but how hard can it be? Xander does it all the time. Niall feigned nonchalance.

True. I can do anything he can do. Well, almost, answered Michael, thinking of Xander kissing Elizabeth.

Xander laughed and immediately coughed into his hand to cover it up. The sound was strangled.

"Are you all right?" asked Lynne with concern.

What's up? thought Elizabeth. *What are the other angels saying?*

I will tell you later. He nodded at Lynne and kept coughing.

"Let's go to the kitchen, and I'll fix us something to eat and drink," said Lynne, leading the way.

The others followed her as the light beings floated through the walls.

Xander and David sat at the kitchen table as Lynne served them leftovers from Sunday dinner and Elizabeth got out glasses and poured their drinks.

The conversation continued long after they had finished eating. Lynne and David told Xander stories from Elizabeth's childhood, never realizing that he already knew all about her life. After all, he had been present for nearly every moment of it.

Fitting into their family was as easy for him as flying. It was second nature to him. He was content.

Chapter 3

"And he causes all, the small and the great, and the rich and the poor, and the free men and the slaves, to be given a mark on their right hand, or on their forehead, and he provides that no one should be able to buy or to sell, except the one who has the mark, either the name of the beast or the number of his name. Here is wisdom. Let him who has understanding calculate the number of the beast, for the number is that of a man; and his number is six hundred and sixty-six."
Revelation 13:16-18

August 2008

On their first day back at Converse, Xander and Elizabeth arrived together and held hands as they walked to their first class, flanked by Michael and Gabriel.

Elizabeth's mouth was set in a grim line. "I really am not looking forward to seeing Gregory. The idea actually turns my stomach."

He squeezed her hand. "Do not worry, love. I doubt that he will acknowledge either of us. I am certain that Gregory dreads this meeting as much as you do."

She turned her head quickly and looked up at him. "You do not seem apprehensive about seeing him again."

He smiled at her. "Why should I be? Gregory knows who won that fight and which of us flew away, running like a frightened child. He was humiliated in front of all the dark forces." He paused, and then continued to hold her eyes with no trace of his smile remaining.

His voice was low and terse as he spoke again. "He will not wish to engage me again so soon, and he will never be allowed to touch you or harm you in any way while I exist. Believe this – the next time I have just cause as well as an opportunity, I will unbody him, and he knows it. I will chase him to the very gates of hell."

Elizabeth felt a distinct chill at the words coming from her fiancé; she knew that he meant every syllable he spoke. His pronouncement seemed prophetic to her, and as much as she knew that Gregory deserved his sentence, she could not be happy about Xander having to be the one to mete out justice to their enemy.

As they approached the door to their first class of the morning, Xander stepped slightly in front of her. She thought it was odd for him to behave in such a way until she observed him pausing in the entry, scanning the room. *You are looking for Gregory,* she thought. *Are Michael and Gabriel with us?*

Always, was his short reply.

He is not here, Xander said into Elizabeth's mind as he stepped aside and allowed her to precede him into the room, following her and taking a seat beside her. Michael and Gabriel, unsmiling, remained within an arm's length of them at all times.

As the day continued, they were somewhat surprised that Gregory was absent from all of their classes, though as Xander thought at length about it, he realized that he should have expected it.

During the last class of the day, he spoke with Gabriel and Michael about Gregory's absence. *What is your opinion of this business with Gregory?* he asked.

Michael observed, *For one thing, the halfling is probably still recuperating from the beating he suffered at your hands scarcely a week ago, brother.*

Gabriel nodded and commented further, *Now that we know Lucifer's ultimate plans for Gregory, it is obvious that the only reason Gregory has been at Converse was to destroy Elizabeth. Since he failed in his attempts, both on her life and her virtue, it seems reasonable to assume that he will regroup and approach his goals from another direction.*

He knew that his brothers were likely right, yet it bothered him not to know where Gregory was or what he was doing. As unpleasant as Gregory's company had been, as long as he had been attending classes, Xander had known of his whereabouts and movements.

During the day, Michael had sent out angelic scouts who had reported back to him that Gregory had put his house in Spartanburg up for sale and departed from the area. Beyond that, there was no information available. The Captain of the Host put the entire angelic realm on alert, though he felt that it was only a matter of time until Gregory would be located.

Xander agreed, for he knew that Gregory would not hide, licking his wounds, indefinitely. His enormous ego would demand retribution.

~~oo~~

The SoulFire rallies of the past June and July had sparked revivals across the country as the team had traveled to eight major cities spread from coast to coast. More than fifty thousand souls had joined the kingdom during the series of week-long meetings, and God had revealed Himself in ways rivaling the days of the early church. The gifts which He had bestowed on the SoulFire team members had been used mightily: Jonathan had preached the Word and cast out demons, Elizabeth had spoken to diverse multitudes through her gift of tongues, Xander had healed hundreds of sicknesses and injuries, and Charlotte had used her discernment to unite the team and help to direct the ministry. He and Elizabeth had also developed their musical gifts even further, taking the crowds to new heights of worship, showing the people God as they saw Him in all His glory, displaying His love and forgiveness to a world which thirsted for Him.

Jonathan and Dave Branard, the manager of SoulFire Ministries, had arranged Saturday night rallies in Charlotte, North Carolina, and Jacksonville, Florida, for September and October. After Xander and Elizabeth's wedding in December, they planned to tour with SoulFire two weekends per month from January through April, complete their graduate degrees from Converse and Liberty in early May, and embark on a global ministry tour with the team in June. The couple, along with Jonathan, had decided to do their doctoral work online in order to accommodate their tour schedules. Charlotte would complete her bachelor's degree from Converse in May and begin her studies for her graduate degree in theology using Liberty University's online program so that she could travel as well. Jonathan's plans were to use Xander, Elizabeth, and Charlotte more in speaking capacities on the global tour. He wanted to break the extended meetings into smaller groups led by the four of them during the afternoons and continue the nightly rallies. Elizabeth and Xander would continue to lead the music during the evening meetings.

On a September Saturday, Xander and Elizabeth arrived at the arena in Charlotte, North Carolina, in the early afternoon. They met Jonathan, Charlotte, Thorncrown band members, and the rest of their crew there. It was the first time the entire crew had been back together since the end of July. Everyone was already in a flurry of activity, preparing for the night's rally, efficiently going through the motions of setting up, as they had done all summer. The arena had been fully booked for a capacity crowd of twenty thousand people for months, and the SoulFire team wanted to be certain that everything went smoothly.

Thorncrown took the stage to rehearse and do a sound check as soon as the setup was complete, and technicians scurried to make last-minute adjustments to the lighting and sound as well as the timing of the video feed and the cameras.

As the band and the crew worked, Xander, Elizabeth, Jonathan, and Charlotte met to go over details for the night and to pray as their guardians surrounded them. They were comfortable together, like a family. By the time they were finished, the crew was ready for Elizabeth and Xander to rehearse and do their sound and lighting check.

Catching Elizabeth completely by surprise, he smiled at her and put a finger to his lips as he held a microphone and cleared his throat. The normally reserved Xander had rarely called attention to himself in such a way; consequently, everyone stopped and turned toward him to listen.

His smile was fully dimpled as he reached out to take Elizabeth's left hand, lifting it with his so that everyone could see her fingers.

"Many of you probably already know this, but I wanted to be sure that all of you, our very good friends, were aware that last Sunday this beautiful, unbelievably wonderful woman agreed to make me the happiest of men and become my wife in December." As he kissed her hand and she blushed, the SoulFire crew and team erupted in applause and cheers.

Elizabeth impulsively took her own wireless mike from the stand in front of her. "Our church is too small to hold everyone we want to invite to the wedding, but there will be no restrictions on the number we can invite for the reception. We hope that all of you will be able to join our celebration. It's not every day that you get to see a woman marry an absolute angel." It was Xander's turn to blush as she stood on her tiptoes to kiss his cheek. More applause followed, accompanied by loud whoops and whistles. Losing all of his shyness, he embraced a squealing Elizabeth, lifting her from the floor and twirling her with joy as everyone joined in their laughter. As he set her back on her feet, she noticed a man in what appeared to be a military uniform standing just beyond the edge of the stage lights. He waved at her tentatively, and Elizabeth shaded her eyes, trying to see his face.

It is Richard, said Xander quietly into her mind. Garnet, standing beside Richard, saluted his Chief and the archangels, and Xander nodded very slightly in return. Michael and Gabriel acknowledged Garnet openly.

Elizabeth's mind rapidly scrolled through memories of her time with Richard – going on the summer youth trip, watching movies with his family, running through the house with him following her dad's scavenger hunt clues, dancing at the prom, kissing for the first time in her driveway, being embarrassed in front of him because of Caroline's comments and subsequently punching her in the nose at church, reacting the first time he told her that he loved her, breaking up at the end of that awful weekend when he had slept with Caroline, and living in the terrible darkness that followed for months afterward. They had loved each other as innocents. Though she had never felt for Richard the deep, abiding love that she had for Xander, he had been her first and only boyfriend until she had met her fiancé. He had been the center of her life, her hopes, and her dreams during the dullness of her young teen years. He had rescued her from being relegated to the oblivion of the exclusion of the girls at her school, and then he had shattered her heart.

Xander kept his own counsel as he listened to her thoughts reliving both the joys and the pain associated with the young man who stood before them.

Richard stepped into the light so that Elizabeth could see him, and she could see by his face that he had heard Xander's announcement. Because she knew him so well, his struggle to wear a smile was obvious to her. Elizabeth quickly left the stage by the side steps and ran to him, reaching her arms out for a hug.

Charlotte whispered in Jonathan's ear, and he went to the stage microphone to alleviate the awkward silence. Everyone was still watching Xander and Elizabeth, transfixed by the events playing out before them.

Jonathan said pleasantly, but authoritatively, "I think we're ready for tonight, folks. Take a dinner break and be back in an hour."

Xander smiled at him in appreciation, and then followed Elizabeth, standing back to give her and Richard relative privacy. Gabriel and Michael stood by their charges. Xander turned his face away from Elizabeth and Richard, flinching a little at the young man's pain.

"Richard, it's so good to see you. I'm so glad that you came," Elizabeth said as he enveloped her in an embrace. *I'm sorry, Xander. I'm sure you know who Richard is.*

Do not worry, Elizabeth. I know that you love me; I am not jealous. His voice was calm and gentle.

After a few long moments, she stepped back to look at him. "The military has agreed with you, Richard. You are certainly no longer a boy," she said with a smile. "How much have you grown?"

Richard had always been unusually handsome, but now he was tall and muscular as well. He laughed lightly. "I had a growth spurt – about four inches, I guess. I just got off a plane at the Charlotte airport. Because I'm in uniform, I got free bags and first boarding privileges. Mom and Dad picked me up; they're waiting for me in the car. Mom told me that you were doing a rally here tonight. I've kept up with all your travels and concerts. I've missed you so much, El." He paused, and then his words came out in a rush. "Thank you for writing to me, El. Some days, your letters were all that kept me going. I know that I've said this before, but I want you to know how sorry I am for what happened. You can't possibly know how much I regret it." He looked away.

Elizabeth, the drinking was his fault, but the rest was not, Xander thought to her.

What do you mean? she questioned.

Caroline planned it all. She drugged him with something she stole from her father's medicine cabinet. She never told anyone, so even he does not know. He was not in control of himself any more than you were when Gregory slipped a drug into your drink. Xander was aware of how Elizabeth would react to his words, but Richard needed to know the truth, and it appeared that Caroline would never tell him willingly.

Elizabeth's eyes widened with the knowledge, and she remembered how devastated she and Richard had been, how much their families had been hurt, and she was angry with Caroline for her selfishness. *If I had known that he had been drugged, I might have felt differently. He has suffered so much. Thank you for trusting me with this information.* She began to cry quietly, covering her face with her hands. Michael placed his hand on her back.

"El, why are you crying?" asked Richard earnestly, putting his hands on her shoulders. Hearing his thoughts, Xander knew that he still loved Elizabeth and had hoped that she would take him back. The announcement of her engagement had staggered him, laying waste to all his dreams.

"Richard, it wasn't your fault, truly," she choked out, lowering her hands to look at him. "Caroline slipped something into your drink. You were drugged. She planned it all, even down to having Lydia ready to take the pictures."

Garnet stepped to his side as Richard stood frozen; he thought that his chest would explode. Elizabeth's words echoed through his brain, and all of the old wounds burst open. For the past half year, Caroline had written to him, all the while letting him believe that he had slept with her willingly. He could not help himself; he despised her, and he was glad that she was not there to receive the full force of his anger. He wanted to hurt her like she had made him hurt, and had she been standing in front of him, he would have made sure of it.

His clenched hands dropped to his sides, and he spoke through gritted teeth. "If only I had never gone to that blasted party. She set me up, asking me to Grant's house and getting me drunk. I was so stupid that I let her do it. I was an idiot." Richard's voice softened, "El, I still love you. I always have, and now it's too late."

Elizabeth carefully considered her words. "Richard, I know what it feels like to be drugged and taken advantage of, and I know that you must resent Caroline right now. Fortunately for me, Xander was there to help me before it went too far." She put her hand on his arm. "You have to let it go. It will eat away at you. It will hurt you and make you bitter, and that's not the Richard I know. Forgive her, Richard, even if she never asks for it. You can't heal if you don't forgive her. All of that took place more than two years ago, and so much has happened since then. I am happy, and I want you to be happy, too. I still love you, too, though not in the same way. Xander is God's choice for me, Richard, and I know that God has someone – some very lucky girl – for you, too."

He grinned crookedly, though it did not reach his glistening eyes. "I'll work on that, but I hope you'll understand if I don't agree with you right now." While he said the words, his mind screamed, *There will never be anyone else for me, but I won't let you see how much it hurts. I won't spoil your joy.* "So, aren't you going to introduce me to your fiancé?"

Xander walked up beside Elizabeth and extended his hand to Richard. Elizabeth smiled at Richard, and then at Xander, moving her hand from Richard's arm to Xander's back. "Richard, this is Xander Darcy. Xander, Richard is a very good friend of mine from my high school days."

Richard shook Xander's hand as he thought unhappily, *I am only 'a very good friend' from her high school days. Here is a man who actually deserves her. I certainly don't,* but he smiled and said, "So you're the lucky guy who has captured El's heart. I wish you two all the best."

"We hope that you'll come to our wedding. Both of us would love to have you there," said Xander sincerely.

"December, right?" he asked. Elizabeth nodded.

I can't stand to see her marry someone else, and Caroline will probably be there. She's Chance's sister, and she goes to Tabernacle Church, he thought. *I'll have to forgive her someday, I know, but it won't be that soon.*

Richard cleared his throat and continued, "I'm using up most of my leave now, and I'll be in San Diego by then. I may come home for a few days at Christmas, but you'll probably already be married by that time." *You will be happy, and I'm glad about that, but, God help me, I can't stand it. You will be his in every way.* His insides knotted painfully at the thought.

"The wedding date is December 13, but we should be back in town for Christmas. I hope we'll see you," Elizabeth replied.

"If I'm home, I'll be at Tabernacle with my parents, and I'll see you two there. I've been seeing stories on the news about the wonderful work you guys have been doing. I'm so proud of you, El. I always knew that you were meant for great things." He struggled to keep his mind from thinking about her being married to the tall, handsome man by her side.

"Thanks, Richard. We'll look for you at Tabernacle. Will you be there tomorrow?" she asked.

I'm not ready to see Caroline yet, he thought. "I doubt it. I really need to visit some relatives out of state before I report back. You look busy, and the preacher said this is your dinner break. I need to go anyway. I'm going out to eat right now with Mom and Dad. It was great meeting you, Xander."

"Nice to meet you, too, Richard. Be safe," said Xander.

"I'm going to hug your fiancée goodbye, if you don't mind," said Richard, glancing at Xander, and then smiling sadly at Elizabeth.

"Permission granted," answered Xander, trying to sound lighthearted. He knew the pain that Richard was suffering, and he was not insensible to it. The memories of the weekend before were still very fresh and sharp in his mind. When he had thought he had lost Elizabeth, he wanted to die. *After two and a half years of longing for Elizabeth, he knows for certain that he will never have her love again. How does he bear it? Seeing her with me, knowing that we will marry, must be excruciating for him.*

As Garnet touched his shoulders, Richard took Elizabeth tenderly into his arms one last time, kissed her hair, and released her, turning quickly to walk away so that she would not see his tears. *Goodbye, my El.*

"Goodbye, Richard," she called to his retreating back.

He lifted his hand in a wave, but did not look at her. Garnet walked beside Richard, speaking peace into his tortured mind.

~~oo~~

Lucifer's minions, both human and demon, had been busy throughout the world, tirelessly adjusting the dates on all of Gregory's personal information. Many articles and videos of Gregory simply disappeared; some were altered to make him appear older. His college records were adjusted, as well as his birth certificate, driver's license, and social security card. All of Gregory's paperwork reflected that he was thirty-four years old and had lived in Boston for the past sixteen years. A deceased human father was also created for him, because, in order to one day be President of the United States, the Constitution required him to be a natural born citizen – born to citizens of the United States. Though there was an ongoing discussion in legal circles concerning whether or not both parents had to be United States citizens, obviously Lucifer, as a non-human, did not meet the requirement, and the lack of a father on the birth certificate would have raised questions. Any paperwork that would prove those records to be false was either mysteriously missing or sealed.

Popular cable news anchorman, Dirk Horne, had gone to the Betty Ford Clinic in mid-June to be treated for his alcoholism and had returned to work a new man. His changed behavior amazed his co-workers and impressed the owners of the network. Within six weeks, he had his own show in a prime slot, and his popularity soared throughout the country. Dirk Horne was on his way to becoming the most trusted newsman on television. One by one, his enemies conveniently disappeared, succumbing to illnesses, car wrecks, or fatal accidents. A few committed suicide under dubious circumstances. Because of the aura of evil surrounding him, before too much time had passed, people began to feel that it was very unwise to disagree with Horne even privately. He exuded confidence and power, and when he spoke, most people believed whatever he said.

Everyone who remembered Gregory was surprised when Dirk Horne announced the young man's candidacy in the 2008 Massachusetts Senate election on the night of the Charlotte rally. However, within minutes of Horne's announcement, most of the populace had forgotten that Gregory had missed the June filing deadline. The memories of believers were still intact, however, and many of them wondered how he had qualified to be on the ballot in the first place. Those who had followed his career knew that he was too young and that he lived in Charlotte, North Carolina, not Massachusetts.

Because of Dirk Horne's obvious support of Gregory Wickham, the candidate received inordinate amounts of positive air time. Only the Christian community seemed to have a problem with Gregory, and they had become so marginalized politically because of their objections to him that their opinions were of no concern to those making the executive decisions.

The majority of students who had known him at Converse remembered him no longer, and those who had been at Harvard thirteen years earlier suddenly knew him very well, though oddly enough, no one remembered being in classes with him. The few believers on the Converse faculty were quite confused when they researched Gregory's time at Converse, and though Christian students spoke out against the travesty being perpetrated on the people of the United States, no one wanted to listen to them. Dirk Horne labeled the dissenters "terrorists" and "religious activists," and the labels stuck fast. They became the butt of jokes on late night shows and in national news magazines.

Harvard confirmed that Gregory Wickham had completed his bachelor's degree as well as a JD/MBA program in Harvard Law School, and public records indicated that he had passed the bar and had practiced law for several years.

While they were initially shocked by the information, Elizabeth, Charlotte, and Jonathan were not surprised in the least about the deception after Xander told them about Gregory's 666 tattoo hidden underneath his hair.

Jonathan immediately thought of Revelation 13:18, '*Let him who has understanding calculate the number of the beast, for the number is that of a man; and his number is six hundred and sixty-six.*' *Gregory is the beast. The end of the age is approaching.*

Elizabeth was quiet and kept her head lowered during his narrative. Xander did not tell the others that he had seen the incriminating evidence of

Lucifer's plans during Gregory's attack on Elizabeth in August when he had prevented the halfling from raping her, but Charlotte had eyed her sharply.

So, Gregory is being set up to be the Anti-Christ. The Senate now, the Presidency in 2012. No big surprises, I suppose, but there is something Xander is leaving out, thought Charlotte. *Elizabeth will tell me when she's ready.*

They discussed the matter in depth and prayed about it before deciding to hold their counsel for the time being. Now more than ever, they were convinced that their focus should be to reach as many souls for God as quickly as possible.

Time was running out.

Chapter 4

"But God demonstrates His own love toward us, in that while we were yet sinners, Christ died for us."
Romans 5:8

September 2008

At first, Xander was amused by the flurry of activity in the Bennet household; however, his amusement was soon turned to distress by the dwindling amount of time left in Elizabeth's days for him. Each time he was there – which was nearly every day – Elizabeth, her mother, and usually Janna were tending to more wedding details. Whenever he was allowed to do so, he helped with the plans. He and Elizabeth had put an engagement announcement in the local papers, using a favorite photograph taken for publicity purposes before the SoulFire rallies, and the two of them had made arrangements for the rehearsal dinner to be catered at the local country club, but Xander soon realized that there was a myriad of things to be done with which he could not assist Elizabeth.

After selecting her wedding dress, Elizabeth had pleased her mother by following a Southern tradition and having her wedding portrait made, to be unveiled at their reception. Lynne had engaged the same photographer to take pictures at the wedding while his assistant shot video. In addition, Lynne had reserved the church and the fellowship hall, selected a florist, and, along with her daughters, chosen the flowers. A lady from the church who had directed Janna's wedding had agreed to direct Elizabeth and Xander's as well. Elizabeth and her mother had met with the caterer and discussed the wedding cake, the menu, and the table settings. Elizabeth, Lynne, and the bridesmaids had spent a pleasant Saturday shopping for the bridesmaids' dresses and having lunch together. Lynne's niece, Bethany, had come from Virginia for the weekend, and she and her mother, Grace, had joined the Bennet ladies for the day.

Xander and Elizabeth had ordered their invitations and drawn up a list of wedding guests together. Because Xander had no one to add to the list other than those people both he and Elizabeth knew, he had already told the Bennets that his brothers would be his groomsmen, but his Father would not be able to attend as He was quite old and rarely left His home.

Speaking with David and Lynne, Xander explained, "My Father wishes you to know that He will be with us in Spirit, though not in flesh. He regrets that He will not meet you at our happy occasion, but He wants me to assure you that He will meet you in Person sometime in the future. He says that He knows you already through my eyes, and He is very happy that I am marrying your daughter. In fact, I have spoken to Him so often in such glowing terms about your family and Elizabeth that He has told me we were meant to be together. He knew that I loved her before I was aware of it myself."

David was puzzled by Xander's manner of speaking and asked, "How old is your Father? Perhaps we should go see Him if He cannot travel here."

Roark put his hands on David's shoulders and spoke into his mind, *Do not be anxious, David. All is well with Xander's Father.*

Xander smiled. "My Father would seem ancient to you, but He does not seem old to me. He is so full of life and power that He is ageless in my eyes. He does not receive guests, however."

Lynne looked confused by his statement, and Niall whispered to her, *Lynne, Xander is trustworthy. Be at peace.*

Privately, David and Lynne thought Xander's Father must be rather eccentric and likely very wealthy, but they talked of it only between themselves. Niall and Roark smiled knowingly at each other whenever their charges discussed their Master.

The only part of the engagement period that Xander was not enjoying was the time he had to spend apart from Elizabeth while she did things in which he was not allowed to participate – such as choosing her dress, shopping with the bridesmaids, and having her wedding portrait made. He was not supposed to see her dress before she walked down the aisle as his bride, and she was adhering rigidly to the rules on that point. He could somewhat understand her desire to see his face when he saw her in the dress for the first time, coming down the aisle toward him, but he did not comprehend why he was left out of all of the other outings.

Xander had barely arrived at her house on Saturday morning when he found to his chagrin that she was going shopping with her mother yet again.

I find it difficult to believe that there is anything left to buy in Spartanburg, he groused to his brothers.

Elizabeth does not really enjoy shopping. You know that, Gabriel said quietly.

"Elizabeth, why can I not go with you this time? I miss you. I hardly see you anymore. Our lack of time together has become so stressful to me that I am actually grateful when we have classes. At least I am with you there. Will you let me come?" asked Xander, kissing her goodbye at her door. Elizabeth had told him that he would spend the day with her father until she returned.

Elizabeth chuckled, "This will be a good time for some 'male bonding' between you and Dad."

He pouted. "I much prefer to spend the time bonding with you instead."

She shook her head with a smile, and Xander held her as he asked, "Why not, love?"

Elizabeth blushed and answered, "Because we are going to buy something for me to wear as a surprise for you."

He frowned a little. "I think there will be enough surprises already. If it is for me, why can I not have a say in it? I am getting to know the words of 'Amazing Grace' extremely well, for you use it continually to block your thoughts from me."

She hesitated, and then smiled shyly. "We're going to Victoria's Secret. Now do you understand?"

"No," he answered. "Who is Victoria? And why would you prefer to spend time with her rather than with me? I am more confused than I was before."

Niall, standing behind Lynne, snorted.

Xander, it is a lingerie store. Elizabeth and her mother are going to select what she will wear on your wedding night.

Oh... Oh! His eyes lit with understanding.

Elizabeth saw awareness dawn in his eyes. "I know neither Gabriel nor Michael enlightened you, so who is your informant?" she asked in a low voice, looking toward her mother to see if she was listening.

"My best man," he whispered in her ear.

Their whispering had caught Lynne's attention, and she grabbed her purse as she headed toward them, Niall following behind her.

"Let's go, El." Smiling at Xander, Lynne said, "You guys have fun. Lunch is in the 'fridge for you. We'll be back in a couple of hours." Lynne walked between Elizabeth and Xander as she headed out the door.

Michael and I are really looking forward to this. Are we not, Michael? teased Niall.

Michael glared at him. *I truly dislike shopping. Especially for clothing. And looking at lingerie has to be the worst type of shopping possible.*

That reminds me, thought Xander. *My groomsmen, future father-in-law, ushers, and I have an appointment early next month for fittings for our tuxes. Elizabeth wants them to match, so she is coming along to help us pick them out. My tux will not do after all, so I will have to be fitted as well. The three of you can 'meet' us at the store. Michael, Niall will need a warrior to guard Lynne while we are gone unless she decides to come with Elizabeth.*

More clothing! muttered Michael while Gabriel smiled beatifically.

At least you are not having to eat – yet, thought Xander.

Michael's face assumed a glum expression at the idea.

Elizabeth stood on her tiptoes to kiss her fiancé goodbye. "We won't be gone any longer than necessary. You'll thank me later. I promise."

He surprised her by kissing her soundly in front of her mother. At Lynne's amused look, he grinned. "Just practicing, Mom. Only two months until the big day, and I want to be sure to get this part right."

She raised an eyebrow. "Somehow, I have no worries on that score. The rest of the day may collapse around our ears, but you will get that right, I have no doubt." Lynne grabbed her daughter's hand and pulled her to the car, chuckling.

Their angelic escort was right behind them.

~~oo~~

It was a cool, late September Monday, and Xander left his townhouse in Spartanburg early, anticipating having breakfast with Elizabeth before they went to classes. Gabriel flew over his Escalade as they wove through the morning traffic.

Lynne had taken the day off work to see to some wedding details, and Elizabeth was waiting for Xander in the parking lot at Converse when he arrived. She was driving her own car – a white Toyota Rav4 they had picked out together the previous weekend. Michael stood beside the car, waiting for her to get out. Instead, she lowered her window and smiled at him in excitement. He got out of his car, followed by Gabriel, and walked to her car, leaning over to kiss her through the open window.

"Hi, handsome," she said as he broke the kiss. "Charlotte rode with me, but she's already gone to an early class. Let me take you to breakfast this morning. You always drive."

"Yes, I do, because I like to get to my destination in one piece. You drive entirely too fast, you know," he replied with a stern look.

"Ah, but I have my own personal guardian angel – two in fact – to make sure that I'm safe. If I promise to slow down to your granny speed, will you agree to ride with me?" she asked, tilting her head to look up at him.

He thought a moment. "There will be a price to be paid."

She laughed. "I'm betting that I can pay it fairly easily. What's your price? Name it."

"Two kisses, and an 'I love you,'" he answered looking very serious.

"Well, come around and get in the passenger seat, and I'll work on that," she teased.

She watched him in the rearview mirror as he walked around the car. *I am a lucky woman, and I don't care if you hear me.* She saw him smile as he heard her thoughts, and her stomach did a little flip.

He opened the door and settled himself in the seat. "Pay up, and I will not accept short, perfunctory kisses. I want real kisses if I am to risk my life."

"Happy to oblige," she said, turning toward him and leaning to take his face between her hands. Elizabeth kissed him eagerly, and pulled back a few inches. "That's one."

"Say it," he whispered.

"Say what?" she asked innocently.

"You know what I want to hear, and you promised. Say it," he insisted in a low voice.

"I love you." Elizabeth moved toward him for the second kiss, but Xander held her back for a moment.

"I love you more. I win," he said just before he took her into his arms.

That was tricky. You know I let you win, she thought as she kissed him.

I know you did, but I still love you more, he answered, enjoying his prize.

~~oo~~

The morning news was on the television in the restaurant, droning in the background as Xander and Elizabeth slid into their booth, Michael and Gabriel following them to stand beside their charges. They had been at the diner fairly regularly for the last two months, and it was only a moment before a waitress appeared to fill their coffee cups and take their orders. They wished her a smiling "good morning" and ordered their usual meals.

"I have a surprise for you this afternoon," he said once they were again alone at the table, his blue eyes twinkling.

"Oh, I love surprises. What is it?" Elizabeth asked, leaning toward him, her face wreathed in delight.

"If I told you it would not be a surprise. At least that is what you have been telling me over and over for the past two months. I need your cooperation, however, so I will have to tell you, I suppose," said Xander with an exaggerated sigh.

Elizabeth raised her eyebrows. "So…tell me."

After a pause for effect, he showed his excitement in his reply, "I have several houses for us to look at this afternoon. I have taken into consideration all the things we have been talking about, and I contacted a real estate agent to line up showings for us. I hope that we can find something we both like fairly quickly. I want us to have a real house when we are married – not my small townhouse."

"I'm assuming you scheduled the appointments for after classes today?" she asked.

"Yes. Is that all right?" He suddenly realized that he should have asked her about her plans before he made the appointments.

He was relieved when she smiled and replied, "Luckily for you, I have the afternoon free. I'll text Mom and let her know what we're doing. She'll be ecstatic."

"I hope so. Charlotte can drive your car home, and I will take you back to Bethel after we look at the houses, if that is all right with you," Xander said.

"Charlotte is on the short 'approved' list to drive my car, so I suppose that will work," she replied.

Looking over Elizabeth's shoulder, Xander's attention was drawn to the face on the screen. Gregory Wickham was with a lovely woman, holding her arm possessively. He was amazed to hear the lady being presented as the wife of his nemesis.

"Have you heard that Gregory is married?" he asked Elizabeth, nodding at the screen.

She turned quickly to look at the couple, dressed to the nines for a charity function and pausing to talk to reporters before they walked into Lincoln Center.

"Married? You're kidding! When did that happen?" she asked, stunned.

"According to the report, they married quietly last week after a long courtship," Xander answered.

They fell silent, riveted to the television, watching a much more mature Gregory than they had known as he smiled at his blonde, blue-eyed wife while they charmed the nation together.

~~oo~~

Each day seemed to bring a new revelation concerning Gregory Wickham, and Elizabeth, Xander, Jonathan, and Charlotte were frankly astounded at the false life he had built in a few months. In fact, Xander suspected that his plans had been laid for years, and Lucifer had waited only for the right time to implement them. Lucifer's human servants must have had everything in place, ready for his commands.

It seemed that Gregory had been the darling of the media from the moment he had burst onto the scene, garnering national attention in every major news outlet – both in print and on the small screen. He had gone from political obscurity to having the star status of a savior virtually overnight, and it was a foregone conclusion that he would be the next senator from Massachusetts. Gregory Wickham was well-educated, brilliant, talented, knowledgeable, extremely wealthy, and extraordinarily handsome with a beautiful, intelligent wife who added the full support of her well-connected family. He had absolutely no baggage, for reporters could not find a single woman who had ever dated him, except for his wife. He had no friends from college and no record of saying or doing anything controversial, and his oratorical skills were unmatched. His ability to mesmerize an audience was remarkable; he was universally hailed as the only answer to the country's problems and possibly the best hope for the future of the world.

The Wickhams traveled in the highest circles of society, though they were very active in work for the homeless and other charitable endeavors. Mrs. Wickham, formerly Anne De Bourgh, handled their obligations to the less fortunate by hosting fundraisers and serving as the head of The De Bourgh Foundation, a non-profit organization which awarded grants to charities and individuals who sought to improve the living standards and promote the health of the poverty stricken peoples of the world.

Gregory's political platform was deliberately vague – a blend of promises of peace, equality and fair treatment for all people, and economic security for the masses. He received the unqualified support of the wealthiest as well as the poorest in society, for both stood to benefit greatly from his election. The financial burden of implementing Gregory's proposed "New Order" would fall on the middle class, though he never presented a plan showing that particular aspect of his program. His smiling, beautiful face was on the cover of nearly every magazine, and people believed all the lies he uttered. He was a great favorite on the west coast and was heavily funded by the elite of the entertainment industry. Friendships with the rich and famous came easily to him, and pictures of the Wickhams with celebrities were commonplace in various media outlets as they attended charity fundraisers, premiers, galas, and sporting events.

The people of the United States were very impressed with Gregory Wickham.

~~oo~~

Xander and Elizabeth picked up take-out to eat at his townhouse after viewing several suitable homes in the Spartanburg area. They had prayed about it together and decided to hold off on a decision until they looked at a few available houses in Bethel. Because they expected to be traveling most of the time, both of them felt that it would be pleasant to live closer to Elizabeth's parents so that they could spend time with them more easily on the rare occasions when they were home. The realtor had promised to set up showings for them within the next few days.

They sat together on his new couch and placed their food on the matching coffee table. In the previous week, he and Elizabeth had done a little shopping of their own, and he was very pleased with their purchases. The idea of making a home with Elizabeth was already quite appealing to him, and it seemed to get better the more she was involved in his life.

After they had finished eating, they gathered up the containers, took them to the kitchen, and disposed of them in the trashcan under the sink.

Michael and Gabriel stood against the wall between the two rooms which were separated by a bar.

Elizabeth's face took on a dreamy quality when she turned to face Xander in the small kitchen, and he smiled when he heard the words of "Amazing Grace" being sung in her mind.

He smiled, pulling her into his arms, and asked, "What are you blocking from me, love? You know that you can tell me anything."

"I've been thinking of something for a while, and it's a little embarrassing," she said, putting her cheek against his chest and looking down so that he could not see her face.

"I hope that you can share it with me. I particularly like that expression on your face, and I would love to know the thoughts that put it there," said Xander, holding her close.

Her voice was so low that he barely caught the words. "I want to be kissed by an angel."

He pulled back a few inches and used one of his hands to tilt her face up to his. "You have been kissed by an angel many times. What do you mean?"

"I mean, I want you to be an angel when you kiss me. I want to know what it's like to kiss the angel that saved my life by flying me out of the gorge. I was angry with you, but I still recognized that you were beautiful in an otherworldly way," she said as she blushed furiously.

Xander was surprised at her admission. "You really want to see me in my other form? You were not frightened?"

She laughed a little nervously as she said, "I have dreamed of it. I know Michael must think I'm weird when he watches those dreams in my mind. Will you let me see you? Is it allowed?"

"Really?" He was ridiculously pleased. "For as long as I have loved you, I have wanted you to know all of me and accept me as I am. I will happily morph for you. And Elizabeth – remember that I have never kissed anyone while in that form. I wonder what it will be like as much as you do."

He released her and stepped back a few feet before assuming solid angelic form, never taking his eyes from hers. The transformation was accomplished in less than a second. Xander had never willingly let a human being see him in the form in which he had lived in for ten millennia, and he had no idea what Elizabeth's reaction would be. He smiled as she looked at him, hoping to ease the shock she likely would experience upon seeing him as an angel, but he could not know that the radiance of his face would further stun her. The light he exuded chased the darkness from every corner of the room and reflected back to him from her glittering eyes.

Xander heard her mind go completely blank as her eyes widened and her mouth formed an "O." Elizabeth moved further back so that she could see all of him in his glorious form. He glowed softly, his arms bulging from his sleeveless tunic. His golden armor gleamed under the kitchen light as he watched her eyes move from his feet slowly up to his face, taking in his muscular legs and molded breastplate. Because he was not in battle, his helmet had not appeared, and his shining hair fell in loose curls around his neck. His shield and sword hung at his waist, and his translucent, shimmery wings were pulled close to his back. He suddenly realized that Elizabeth had never seen him so unclothed; he had neither completely removed his shirt around her nor worn shorts above his knees, and now he stood before her in a short, guardian tunic.

He could tell that she was breathing faster even as he heard her heart rate quicken. The flush across her skin was lovely, but he was unable to read her jumbled thoughts.

After a few long moments, he began to worry. *Why is she not speaking? Have I frightened her?*

Gabriel reassured him. *Give her some time, my brother. To her knowledge, she has met Xander only once, and the circumstances were not pleasant. Let her adjust in her own way.*

I have seen her dreaming of you in this form over and over again, brother, thought Michael. *Trust me on this. She is not frightened of you, although perhaps she is overwhelmed at this time by her own feelings. Not many humans are able to live out their fantasies, but she is living one of hers now. She likes your angelic form – very much.* Michael chuckled. *Expect her to ask you to change into this form often.*

I certainly hope you are right, thought Xander as he watched her, waiting for her to move. *She has yet to even blink her eyes!*

"Elizabeth?" Xander extended his hand to her.

She was still unable to speak, though he stepped closer to take her hand and held it in his, lightly stroking it with his fingers. When he touched her, he was surprised to find that her hands were moist. As he stroked her hand, her breathing became even faster and shallower, and she glanced around the small room as if she did not know where to look.

"Are you afraid of me?" he asked, concerned.

Elizabeth cleared her throat, glanced into his eyes, and quickly looked away. "No, not at all. I just don't know what to do. You are so beautiful that I don't know how I should act." She turned her eyes back to his. "Can I touch you? You are holy, and I am not. When I look at you, I am confronted by my own sin. Can you ever forgive me?" Her voice broke on the last word, and she caught her breath, looking at the floor.

He was thoroughly confused by her question. "Forgive you for what, Elizabeth?" he asked, stepping closer to cup her face with his hand. She caught her breath, lowering her eyes to avoid looking into his face.

"When I fell and you caught me, I was so angry with you. I never really thanked you for saving my life. I am so full of sin that I actually turned from God – and from you – to go with Gregory, and you rescued me again, knowing that I would still reject you. I remember how you begged me to let you drive me home, promising that you would not talk to me – 'bother' me, as you said. How can you stand me? I acted like a spoiled child. How can God forgive me for doubting Him?" Elizabeth tried to turn her face away, but he held her chin firmly, forcing her to face him. She slowly raised her eyes to his, and his heart broke to see them filled with unshed tears.

Xander's voice was soft and low as he said, "Oh, my love. I was glad that I was there to help you, even if it parted us. I wanted to tell you the truth about me, but the timing was never right. I knew that you had every right to be angry with me because I was there when Richard hid the truth from you, and

I knew how you would feel. Please believe me when I say that losing you for a short time only made me value you more when you accepted my love again. Elizabeth, I am not perfect, and neither are you, but we are both forgiven by God through Christ. We love because He first loved us. We forgive because He forgave us. You know that He has forgiven you for your short crisis of faith. Our Father understands our frailties." He bent his head to kiss her tears away, and after he had feathered her eyelids with his lips, she lifted her face to his. The glory of his countenance was reflected in her eyes.

He kissed her gently, pouring his soul into his touch, and she put her arms around his waist, feeling his wings for the first time. Though she was greatly enjoying his kisses, she was momentarily distracted.

What is that? she asked, moving her hands gently up and down his back, barely touching him.

Those are my wings. Do you want to see them?

Do we have to stop kissing? Elizabeth queried.

Yes. His answer was short.

I can wait until later, then. She reached further around him to explore his wings with her hands, and his mind emptied of coherent thought.

Your wings are muscular, strong, and much thinner than I imagined – yet there is a softness and warmth, like a baby's skin, Elizabeth thought.

He pulled away, turning his face so that she could not see his expression.

"Did I do something wrong?" Elizabeth was slightly alarmed.

His voice was ragged. "No, it is just that…no one has ever touched me there before. I was not expecting it. I did not know how it would feel."

"Did I hurt you?" she asked, more urgently.

"No. Quite the opposite." He lowered his lashes against his reddened cheeks in embarrassment.

Michael snorted.

Gabriel glared at Michael.

"Oh," she said slowly, with understanding. "Then I won't do that again – at least until after we are married."

"That would probably be for the best. I did not expect them to be so – sensitive. All of my ideas about physical intimacy are based on my observations of human males, and none of them have wings." Xander was silent while he struggled for control. After a moment he looked at her and asked, "Would you still like to see them?"

"Do you mind?" she asked.

Xander could feel the curiosity flowing from her in waves.

"Not at all." He turned to stride into the living room, relieved to leave the small space.

"Where are you going?" Elizabeth asked as she followed him.

"There is insufficient room in the kitchen," he answered.

Xander stood in the center of the living room and faced her, unfurling his silvery wings and holding them out so that she could see them. His wingspan was at least ten feet across; he was awe-inspiring. He watched her as she walked around him, ducking carefully under his spread wings. Xander knew from her thoughts that she wanted to touch him, but she held herself back, concentrating on how his wings looked rather than how they felt.

When she was in front of him again, she seemed puzzled. "There are no feathers."

His laughter came out like a bark. "Feathers?"

"Birds have feathers," she said reasonably.

"Bats, flying fish, and penguins do not. All wings are not feathered. Our wings are layered with feather-shaped membrane which is more responsive to touch than feathers are, I suppose. There are nerve endings and muscles throughout my wings so that I can adjust them as needed in order to fly in different ways," He drew his wings back to mold against his body, and the movement of the air caused her hair to ruffle a bit.

"Your wings are beautiful – not at all like the wings of bats or penguins, but they are not how I thought they would be. Their structure seems to resemble the more rounded wings of birds rather than the sharp, bony wings of bats, though they are featherless and more flexible than any wings I have ever seen. Did I offend you?" she asked.

"No, I was unprepared for your question. That is all." He smiled broadly.

"Angel wings have feathers in all the pictures," she pointed out.

"You mean 'paintings,' not 'pictures,'" he corrected.

"So the artists are wrong. Interesting. Why are there no pictures?" she asked. Her thoughts betrayed how badly she wanted to explore his wings with her fingers, and he concluded that she kept questioning him to keep herself distracted.

"My, you are inquisitive tonight. I suppose because angels cannot be photographed well in angelic form, and we have not often appeared to artists or anyone else." His handsome face showed his amusement.

"Yes, the glowing would not look right in a picture," she mused.

"I sense that there is something else you want to know," he stated.

"Well…" she said uncertainly.

"You have officially kissed an angel and seen my wings. How else can I satisfy your curiosity, my love?" he asked as he stepped even closer to her.

She put her hands on his chest and looked up at him shyly. "I dream about you – quite often – and in those dreams, you are holding me against you, and we are – could you take me flying?"

"I have flown with you twice, you know," he replied with a grin.

"I know you flew with me at the lodge. What other time have we flown together?" Elizabeth drew her brows together, frowning slightly.

"I flew you to the hospital after your four-wheeler accident. You were unconscious," Xander answered, watching her face.

Her surprise was evident. "Really? I wish I had been awake. Why didn't anyone see you?"

"I kept to the treetops, and then changed into human form after I landed in the woods behind the hospital. I carried you into the emergency room myself," he said. "To be solid enough to carry you, I have to stay at the edge of visibility. Invisible flight is faster, however."

"You have degrees of solidity?" she asked in fascination.

"Yes. I can be so invisible that everything passes through me, just solid enough to stop cars and other things while remaining unseen, or completely solid like I am now. You would not be able to touch me in any form other than this one, though you could feel the peace and comfort of God being relayed to you if I touched you or spoke to you." Xander tried to keep his explanations simple. He had a lifetime to tell her things, and he did not want to overload her with too much information at once.

"Hmmm…You were with me when evil was in my room, when I had the chicken pox and was in the hospital, when I left church and hid in the bushes at my house, and when I looked at the pictures of Richard and Caroline, weren't you? I remember God's comfort at those times," she said, smiling.

"Yes, I was there, holding you and whispering to you. I already had begun to love you, and it was agonizing to watch you suffer. I loved you long before you met me," he said softly, taking her into his arms and kissing her again.

After a few moments, he lifted his head and kissed her forehead. "I have to take you home now, but in ten weeks, you will stay with me."

His voice held such joy that she looked up at him and was amazed at his radiance. He seemed to glow even more brightly, and he vibrated slightly with his emotion.

She held her breath. *You literally take my breath away. You are glorious, my love,* she thought.

You do not know how you affect me, Elizabeth. You have been stunning me, innocently torturing me, since you were fourteen.

"I take it that you shine more brilliantly when you are happy?" she asked, smiling.

"Yes. I will have to take care on our wedding day to keep my angelic nature firmly under regulation. It would not do for me to blur all of the pictures," he stated solemnly.

"Could that really happen?" she asked, a little worried.

He laughed. "No. I can easily control my forms. I do not change without wishing to do so, unless I have a head injury apparently."

She remembered how he had appeared to glimmer following his bicycle accident. "So my eyes weren't playing tricks on me the day you had a concussion?"

"You really did see me in this form. I had my brothers quite worried for a while," he said as he smiled at Michael and Gabriel. They shifted uneasily, unused to being exposed.

"So they are over there?" she asked, following his eyes.

"Yes. They are always with us, but do not think of it unless you need them. They are not comfortable with your knowledge yet," he explained.

"That makes three of us," she said in a wry tone.

"You are not comfortable with your awareness of my nature?" he asked.

"I am perfectly comfortable with you. It's knowing that Michael and Gabriel are there watching us all the time that requires some attitude adjustment on my part. If I have to get used to knowing about them, I suppose that they will have to adjust to my knowledge of them as well." She looked in the general direction of Michael and Gabriel and spoke again, "I'm sorry, guys. That's just how it is."

Xander smiled at his brothers. "I think she summarized it well, gentlemen." Looking back at Elizabeth, he said, "And with that, I must take you home before your father changes his mind about me."

He changed back into human form and took her hand, pulling her toward the door.

"But I have more questions, and I want to fly," she protested, tugging gently against his hand.

He chuckled. "You will always have more questions, love, and I will answer them. And I will certainly take you flying soon. I have wanted to do that for a long time now. We do not have to do everything today. We have the rest of our lives."

She nodded her head in agreement, smiling as she allowed him to lead her from his home.

After they had driven to her house, while they sat in his car with the moonlight playing on her curls, Xander looked at her beloved face with his heart in his eyes and asked, "Well, what was it like to kiss an angel, my love?"

Her eyes were dreamy again as she answered with a sigh, "Heavenly. Just heavenly."

Chapter 5

*" '... God sees not as man sees, for man looks at the outward appearance,
but the Lord looks at the heart.'"*
I Samuel 16:7

On the first Monday in October after classes were over for the day, Xander and Elizabeth drove to Thomas & Sons Formal Wear in Spartanburg to select tuxedos for the groomsmen and ushers. David and Lynne Bennet, Charlotte and her brother Joshua, and Chance and Janna were meeting them there. Anne Bingley, Chance's mother, was going to Chance and Janna's house to babysit her grandson, Matthew, while her son and daughter-in-law were out for the evening.

The Bennets felt that it would be a good opportunity to become better acquainted with their future son-in-law's family and had invited everyone to dinner at a nearby restaurant after the fitting. Xander also thought it was a good idea, for it gave his "brothers" an opportunity to acclimate themselves to conversing and eating with humans before the rehearsal dinner and the wedding.

While Niall thought of the outing as an adventure, Michael and Gabriel were not so sanguine. The idea of appearing in human form while being fitted for clothing, and then eating a meal in front of five guardians and ten warriors did not appeal to them, though Gabriel was his usual diplomatic, unruffled self.

After everyone had arrived, Michael, Gabriel, and Niall flew to the back of the store where the tuxedos were stored and exited through the rear wall of the building. In the secluded area, they took human forms dressed in business casual clothing and walked back around the store, through the parking lot, to the front door. As they entered the building, a sales clerk behind the counter caught sight of them and stood frozen to the spot, her amazement written plainly across her face.

Her thoughts were loud. *I wondered how we would find one tuxedo large enough for the six foot nine inch groom. I suppose the three giants will need to buy tuxes and have them altered. I'm estimating seven feet for the green-eyed blonde and nearly that for blue-eyed one. The dark-haired man looks small in comparison, but he must be at least six feet two inches. We can fit him, I think. They are all built like Olympic athletes, too – and gorgeous! I have never seen anyone like them around here. Where are they all coming from? I wonder if they have girlfriends or wives.* She glanced quickly at their hands. *No wedding bands!*

Hurrying from the fitting area, the store manager looked at the clerk in mild irritation and walked quickly toward the men, reaching out her hand to shake theirs. "Hello. You must be here with the Bennet party."

Xander, standing to the right by the fitting rooms, watched Michael scowl as he shook the woman's hand. *Michael, smile. She thinks that you are angry with the sales clerk. She has no way of knowing that you simply hate the idea of trying on clothes.*

Michael immediately smiled, and the sales clerk nearly fainted. *Great idea, brother. If her heart rate goes up any more, she may have a heart attack,* thought Michael as his green eyes flashed. *I will try to be pleasant, though this gives me little pleasure.*

Gabriel and Niall shook the lady's hand while smiling at her and introducing themselves.

While the manager looked the men up and down, professionally estimating their measurements, Elizabeth stood up and, with Xander, walked over to greet them, accompanied by her parents and Roark. Janna and Charlotte remained seated in the area to the right of the front door, and Josh and Chance waited by them. Alexis, Hector, Edward, and Skylar stood by their charges while ten stalwart, unsmiling warriors stationed themselves along the perimeters of the room.

As the introductions were being made, the manager and the clerk went to find the correct style of tuxedos in sizes which they thought would fit the men.

Elizabeth greeted Xander's "brothers" warmly, surprising Michael by reaching up to hug him. "Michael, it's so good to see you again." He recovered and returned her light embrace. She stepped back and gestured toward her father and mother. "These are my parents, Lynne and David Bennet. Mom, Dad, this is Michael, Xander's big brother, and this paragon of good manners is Gabriel."

Gabriel did not wait for Elizabeth to hug him; instead, he surprised her by leaning over to initiate the gesture of affection himself. "It is always good to see you, Elizabeth. My brother has done well to secure you. 'He who finds a wife finds a good thing, and obtains favor from the Lord.'"

Elizabeth laughed lightly, "Proverbs 18:22. You just keep telling Xander that, Gabriel."

As Lynne and David shook hands with Michael and Gabriel, Elizabeth turned her attention to Niall, putting out her hand to him. "You must be Niall. Xander has told me about you. He said that you're his best friend as well as his brother."

Niall's dark eyes sparkled with good humor. "Elizabeth, you cannot hug Michael and Gabriel, yet give me only a hand shake. Where is the fairness in that?" Xander smiled broadly as Niall ignored Elizabeth's hand and wrapped her in a quick, friendly hug instead.

"Hey, careful there, brother. Elizabeth is my fiancée, and do not forget it," said Xander, smiling.

Niall smirked at Xander over Elizabeth's shoulder.

David and Lynne watched, delighted with the way Elizabeth was being received by Xander's brothers.

After Niall stepped back from Elizabeth, he turned to Lynne and David, saying with a smile, "I feel that I have always known you."

As Lynne shook his hand, she tilted her head and looked at him quizzically. "And I feel the same about you. Strange, isn't it?" Her mind went back nearly ten years before to Janna's car accident her senior year of high school. She could vaguely remember the young man who helped her, and the man before her seemed startlingly like him. *This man is too young to be the same guy.* "Your name is Niall? You look very much like someone I remember. Have we met before?"

He smiled, and his dark eyes twinkled. "Anything is possible, but I am not originally from this area. Yes, I am Niall. It means 'champion.' And you are Lynne? May I call you Lynne? Mrs. Bennet sounds too formal for a lovely lady like you."

"Oh, you are a charmer! Of course, all of you must call me Lynne, and my husband is David. We don't stand on ceremony," she said, looking up at each of the brothers in turn.

David looked closely at the imposing, handsome men. He put his hand out to clasp each of theirs in turn, sensing a connection as he did so. David knew that he had never met them before, but he felt that he should know them. There was something very familiar about them; it was almost as if his spiritual self reached out to them, very much like meeting another believer. *That must be it. The Spirit in me witnesses to the Spirit in them, but it is somehow more than that. They are like Xander to me. There is a family connection of some sort.*

Standing beside Elizabeth, Xander could tell that David's feelings only became stronger as both Michael and Gabriel smiled at him.

Elizabeth, accompanied by Xander, then led the angels to her sister, brother-in-law, and friends. "This is my sister, Janna Bingley, her husband, Chance, my friend Charlotte Lucas, and her brother, Joshua. Michael, I'm sure you and Gabriel remember meeting Charlotte in San Diego when Xander had his biking accident."

As both Michael and Gabriel smiled at Charlotte and nodded, they heard her thoughts. *My future children will definitely be taking piano lessons, or voice, or something artistic. Elizabeth has met the most interesting, beautiful people through her music. Jon. Remember that you love Jon, Charlotte. Well, I can admire the wrapping without opening the gift.*

Elizabeth continued, "And this is Niall, Xander's best man."

Xander and the other men stepped back as the manager and sales clerk returned with the tuxedos. Based on her estimates of their sizes, she handed each man a tux. Because there were only four fitting rooms, Chance, Joshua, David, and Niall took their suits to try them on first, leaving the three larger, harder-to-fit men for last.

Elizabeth nodded her approval as the men emerged from the rooms dressed in her choice: black, traditional, one button, satin shawl lapel tuxedos, vented, with satin beasom pockets, vests, black bow ties, and white tux shirts.

"Very nice," she said, looking to the other ladies who were smiling in agreement.

The manager made notes concerning whose pants needed to be lengthened or shortened on the orders for Chance, Joshua, and David, but frowned when she looked at Niall.

"This won't do. We can work with the pants, but the jacket is too tight across the shoulders. Let me get a larger one," she said, hurrying away while Niall shrugged out of his coat, and the other men went back into the rooms to change back into their own clothes.

Chance, Joshua, and David returned to the group, handing their tuxedos, hung back on the hangers, to the sales clerk as Michael, Gabriel, and Xander took their tuxes into the vacant fitting rooms.

The manager returned with another jacket for Niall just as Xander, Michael, and Gabriel were emerging from the fitting rooms. She went behind Niall and helped him into the jacket, and then came around the group of men to face them, shaking her head in dismay.

"Gentlemen, we have a problem," she said grimly. "We can make the pants long enough, and take in the waists on them, but even if we lengthen the sleeves on the jackets, they will never fit you as they should."

The four angels looked distinctly unhappy. While they had managed to stuff themselves into the jackets, none of them could move their arms, and the garments hung loosely around their waists.

Xander said, "I have to have my dress clothes tailor-made. Nothing off-the-rack has ever fit properly."

She nodded. "I can certainly see why, though I can hardly believe that all four of you have the same problem. Your shoulders are unusually wide in proportion to your waists and hips."

Michael looked especially displeased, and even Gabriel and Niall showed disappointment.

Elizabeth thought quickly. "Is there not anything you can do? We understand that we may have to pay more in order to get something that fits well."

The manager's face brightened at once. "In that case, I think I have an idea. We have a warehouse here in Spartanburg. I can have larger jackets sent over immediately. If we can fit the shoulders properly, I have seamstresses who can alter the waists and hips to fit perfectly. The only catch is that you will have to buy the jackets. I won't be able to rent them once they are fitted to each of you, because no one else in this area would ever be able to wear them."

Gabriel was happy with the solution and spoke quickly, "Can the jackets be sent over right now? We are not in this area very often, and we really need to handle this today if possible."

Michael added, "We will be happy to pay any extra expenses you incur for your trouble."

"Excellent," replied the manager, happy to have found an answer to the dilemma. "I'll call the warehouse now so that they'll have several jackets in this style ready for each of you. If the warehouse can't deliver them right now, my assistant can go pick them up while I phone a few of my seamstresses. I want them to do the actual pinning, because this job is beyond my skills. We can probably have your jackets and the seamstresses here in half an hour. Would that suit?"

"Absolutely. Thank you for your trouble," answered Xander, smiling at her as he wriggled out of the ill-fitting jacket. His brothers followed his example and took the coats off, handing them to the manager.

The lady took the coats, handed them to the clerk to put away, and hurried to the counter to make her calls. After the first call, she confirmed to the group that the warehouse would send the jackets to the store immediately.

They all moved to the couches at the front of the store to wait until the clothing and seamstresses arrived.

Niall looked around at the group and spoke brightly, "I suggest that we make the most of the situation and use this time to get to know each other better."

Just what I was hoping for – an extra half hour in which I can make a mistake, grumbled Michael.

There is a scowl on your face. Think about your expression and remember that everyone can see it, thought Gabriel.

I will get right on that. Thank you, Miss Manners, returned Michael, refraining from glaring at him only with great effort. He looked at the floor in an effort to hide his face.

Michael, with the utmost respect, lighten up, thought Niall.

Roark and the other guardians were grinning openly, though the warriors never changed their expressions.

Xander noticed Michael's rigid posture and searched his mind for a topic that might distract him.

David unintentionally came to the rescue. "Xander is something of a martial arts expert and has been training El. Do the rest of you know his style of fighting?"

Xander smiled as he released his breath. "Michael taught me a great deal of what I know," he said, nodding toward his brother.

"How very interesting," said David, looking at the tallest of the brothers. "Who taught you, Michael?"

Michael lifted his head and fixed the older man with his gaze. "I developed my methods myself a long time ago. There has never been a time when I did not use my skills and seek to improve them. And my brother is being modest. He was already a master when I began to help him hone his skills; I merely added to his knowledge of the art."

"And what about you, Gabriel?" asked David. Everyone looked at Gabriel awaiting his reply.

"I practice so that my technique does not suffer. I am always ready to do whatever is needed, though I rarely use my skills to fight. I find that the discipline required to maintain my fighting form helps me to control myself in other ways as well. Conflict distresses me, so I make peace whenever it is possible," Gabriel replied. His sincerity shone from his azure eyes.

Lynne raised a brow in surprise. "You have actually fought then?" she asked.

Gabriel leveled a tranquil gaze at her. "Oh, yes. Sometimes it is unavoidable."

Xander interjected, "Mom, you must understand that because we are unusually large, others sometimes test themselves against us, trying to prove their superiority. We defend ourselves as well as others, but none of us prefers to fight. We would all rather live in harmony."

Speak for yourself, thought Michael. *I would cheerfully unbody every demon in the universes.*

His warriors nodded and rumbled in agreement.

Niall spoke softly. "Our Father wants us to live in peace, but He understands that fighting is necessary at times. We are careful to please Him before we please ourselves."

With that I will agree, praise His holy name, thought Michael.

Praise His holy name, thought every light being present in agreement.

"The respect with which you speak of your Father is commendable," said David smiling gently. "He must be very special to command such love and loyalty in His children."

"He is," replied Xander. "He truly is."

There was a lull in the conversation until Elizabeth spoke up.

"Where do you want to eat tonight?" she asked, addressing the group.

Chance spoke up. "There's a Longhorn Steakhouse, a Red Lobster seafood restaurant, and an O'Charley's nearby. At O'Charley's, you can order steak, seafood, pasta, burgers, or salads. Janna and I like all of them. Do you guys prefer steak, seafood, or something ethnic? We also have Chinese, Japanese, Thai, and Mexican restaurants."

Janna added, "We really enjoy O'Charley's, and they have a wider selection."

"Elizabeth and I have been there many times, and we've always enjoyed it," said Xander, reaching for Elizabeth's hand.

"The food was good, but the company was even better," Elizabeth said, smiling at him.

Charlotte laughed, "Ah, young love! We like to eat there, too. Don't we, Josh?" she asked, ruffling his hair.

"Well, if you gentlemen agree, I believe we have a consensus. O'Charley's it is," said David.

It matters not to me. Unfortunately, food will be served at all of those places, thought Michael.

If no food were served, it would be of little use to go there with the intention of eating, said Gabriel reasonably. *We shall be fine, brother.*

Niall spoke for the group. "O'Charley's is fine with us." *Step out of your box, Michael. Come out of that comfort zone and embrace the experience.*

Michael's grunt was imperceptible to everyone except the angels.

Charlotte looked sharply from one angel to another, and they all heard her thought. *I could swear that there is a conversation going on that we can't hear.*

Fortunately, the manager returned at that time. "If you will follow me back to the fitting area, the jackets and seamstresses are here."

Chance, David, Joshua, Janna, and Charlotte remained on the couches as the four brothers, Elizabeth, and Lynne did as she asked. With very little delay, the four angels were in coats that fit them through the shoulders while they hung loosely at the waists. Four seamstresses busily pinned the garments to ensure that they fit perfectly, checking the pants as well.

Michael held himself erect, keeping his expression neutral while the woman touched him, pinning and prodding him. He had never before allowed anyone such liberties with his person. *I am doing this for Xander and Elizabeth,* he kept reminding himself.

Xander smiled into the mirror, *I used to feel the same way every time I visited my tailor,* he thought. *You become accustomed to it.*

I will not, replied Michael.

You do not have to, brother, said Gabriel with patience.

I doubt that we will be in any more weddings, Michael, added Niall.

Elizabeth and Lynne closely watched the process, and at last proclaimed themselves to be satisfied.

~~oo~~

Xander and Elizabeth took Charlotte and Joshua with them to the restaurant, while Janna and Chance rode with her parents. Niall, Michael, and Gabriel had promised to meet them at the restaurant.

After Xander and David had parked the cars, everyone walked together to the front door, closely followed by their invisible contingent of guardians and warriors. Michael and Gabriel walked up to join them as they entered the restaurant. The group waited as David went to the hostess and asked for a table for eleven. After a few minutes, a waitress came and led them to their table.

Once they were all seated, the waitress took their drink orders, eight iced teas and three waters, and left them to peruse their menus.

"What do you recommend?" asked David, looking at his daughters, Chance, and Xander.

"Their baked potato soup is the absolute best, Dad," replied Elizabeth.

Janna added, "Mom, you'd probably like the California chicken salad. I usually order the ribs, but they're too messy to eat in front of so many people." Everyone laughed at her shy smile.

Xander said, "I like the shrimp scampi, and the spinach and artichoke dip appetizer is excellent. Elizabeth and I share that when we come here."

"I always go for a juicy steak," Chance said, grinning.

It all sounds like a gigantic stomach problem to me, thought Michael.

Try the soup and a salad, Michael. Stay away from anything too heavy – like meat or fried foods, replied Niall.

I think you must be right, Niall, said Gabriel. *I think I will order the baked potato soup with a side salad.*

By the time the waitress came back with their drinks and served them, everyone was ready to order. Xander watched his brothers in case he needed to help them, but soon saw that they had matters well in hand.

As long as you eat slowly, you will have no problems, thought Xander. *You have watched Elizabeth and me long enough to know how to use your utensils. I will be listening for you if you have any questions.*

Do not worry. We can do this, Michael answered, his natural confidence reasserting itself.

I know that you can, replied Xander, pleased with Michael's change of attitude.

As her parents chatted with Janna, Chance, Charlotte, and Joshua, Elizabeth took Xander's hand under the table and pulled it onto her lap. *What are they thinking?* she asked.

They are nervous about eating, but they will be fine. They have done very well so far. Xander spoke with pride, and his brothers, hearing his thoughts, smiled.

Yes, they have been impressive. I am marrying into a very distinguished family. She squeezed his hand and winked at Niall.

Charlotte, seeing Elizabeth wink, tilted her head and watched her friend closely. *One day, I will know what is going on with them. I can just feel the undercurrent. Fascinating.*

Xander, listening carefully to Charlotte, began to talk aloud with Elizabeth about the upcoming rally in Jacksonville.

Though the two of them put on a convincing show, he knew that Charlotte was not fooled. She continued to gaze at them with a small smile.

Go ahead. Try to divert me, Charlotte thought. *I know when I am not hearing the whole story. Don't I, Xander?*

He looked quickly at her when he heard his name. Too late, he realized his mistake and returned his attention to Elizabeth.

Charlotte smiled enigmatically. *I knew it! You can hear me. You can hear all of us, can't you? Elizabeth knows it, too. But how does she hear you? I will know the answers to my questions eventually, Xander. Don't worry, though, my friend. Your secret is safe with me.*

Chapter 6

"I, Jesus, have sent My angel to testify to you these things for the churches."
Revelation 22:16

Wednesday dawned, and Xander was glad to have the last weekend in October coming up, because SoulFire Ministries was scheduled to be in Jacksonville for their final rally of the year. Both he and Elizabeth needed a respite from the constant wedding planning, and the additional sight of Gregory all over the television news had made the two of them uncharacteristically edgy.

Since they could not escape Gregory's image whenever they were in public, Xander had finally decided that rather than trying to avoid seeing his enemy, it would be better to use the media feeding frenzy to follow the halfling's activities. With that in mind, he did something that he had never intended to do: he bought a television for his townhouse.

As he and Elizabeth watched live coverage of Gregory giving a speech on a cable news station one evening while they ate dinner together, Xander commented, "The only thing that is growing faster than Gregory's reputation is his ego. Every time he speaks, I have a mental image of his father, Lucifer, saying his five famous 'I will' statements just before Jehovah ejected him from heaven. It appears that the son is definitely following in his father's footsteps. Next, he'll be saying that he is greater than God. Maybe he will invite me to join him, as his father once did."

Elizabeth looked at him in amazement. "Lucifer asked you to join him?"

He raised one perfect brow. "Oh, yes. He wanted Michael, Gabriel, and me to rebel against Jehovah with him. Lucifer thought that together, we could draw enough followers to overpower God Himself. He wanted us to rule the universes with him."

Elizabeth stared at him. "How could he have ever thought you and your brothers would do such a thing?"

Xander chuckled darkly. "Lucifer is very good at deceiving himself. He actually believes that he will defeat the Almighty Himself in the end. He truly thinks that he will unseat Him and take His place. Lucifer has obviously convinced Gregory to join him in his quest against Jehovah, and Gregory is vain enough to think that they can dethrone the Ancient of Days. He believes his own press releases."

Michael glared at the television. *Can we never be free from the image of that preening fool?*

Gabriel was listening intently to Gregory's speech. *It is a shame that so much talent and beauty should be wasted.*

Elizabeth grinned and answered, "Yes, as much as the general public and the media are impressed with Gregory, I believe that he is actually even more impressed with himself. He always was rather proud and cocky."

Xander arched an eyebrow. "Rather proud and cocky? He is full of pride and conceit. He has no thought beyond advancing himself and his own agenda. Lucifer may think that he can control Gregory, but I have my doubts."

Elizabeth looked surprised. "But aren't their goals the same?"

"For right now, they are. However, if a moment comes in which Gregory must choose between what he wants and what Lucifer wishes, Gregory will choose what he thinks is best for himself." Xander spoke with confidence.

"And how will Lucifer respond to that betrayal?" asked Elizabeth.

"Only God Himself knows the answer to that question," he answered.

And He will tell us what we need to know when the time is right, thought Michael.

~~oo~~

Xander and Elizabeth left immediately after classes were over on Friday to join the rest of the SoulFire team in the caravan to Jacksonville, Florida, with Michael and Gabriel flying overhead. Xander had driven to Elizabeth's house the evening before so that they could pack their things in his Escalade, wanting to be on the road as soon as possible. They knew that they had a long ride before them if they were to reach Jacksonville and their hotel before eleven o'clock. Though it would be an extremely busy weekend, both he and Elizabeth saw it as a welcome time of spiritual refreshment, as well as an opportunity to spend some time alone together before the final flurry of wedding activities. They realized that they would also be busy with their final required projects due and comprehensive exams administered at the rapidly approaching end of the school semester. Free time would be at a premium. Xander actually looked forward to the drive, because he would have Elizabeth all to himself for at least six glorious hours, traveling both to and from the rally.

They had taken the exit to I-95 and merged with weekend traffic when Elizabeth stopped humming, looked at her fiancé's relaxed profile, and spoke hesitantly. "We need to talk about something."

He glanced at her, and then looked back at the road. "This sounds serious, Elizabeth. I know that you have been keeping your thoughts from me by humming. What do you wish to discuss?"

He noticed the color rise in her cheeks and smiled. "Elizabeth, are you embarrassed? We will be married before long. There is nothing which you cannot tell me, surely."

Gabriel asked Michael, *Has she been worried about something?*

Michael laughed easily. *Yes, but Xander will soon put her mind at ease.*

Xander heard the exchange and relaxed, waiting for her to speak.

"I wondered how you feel about birth control," she said quietly.

Birth control? "I have not thought of it. What are your feelings?" he asked.

"Do you want to have children immediately, or do you wish to wait for a year or two?" she asked.

Xander was flummoxed. He had never thought about controlling such a thing. His mind raced through the years of her lifetime, and he remembered that Elizabeth's mother, Lynne, had used a birth control method called "the pill," so he supposed it was acceptable to her parents; however, he did not want to prevent the conception of his children. *But I will not be the one carrying the children or giving birth. We should talk about it.*

"Elizabeth, I need to know your thoughts before I answer your question. I would like for us to discuss this without your being influenced by my ideas before we even begin," he said.

"Lucifer intends for Gregory to be the Anti-Christ, doesn't he?" she queried.

"Yes, he does, but I do not understand what that has to do with our use of birth control," he answered.

"If Lucifer is successful, we will be raptured soon, leaving this earth to meet Jesus in the air, and then the tribulation will come, followed by the Millennium," she said, referring to her theological belief, supported by I Thessalonians 4:13-17, that believers would be taken from the earth and transported to heaven before the time of tribulation foretold by Jesus in Matthew 24 and seen by John in the book of Revelation. "According to my understanding of dispensational theology, the seven year tribulation, foretold by the prophet Daniel, will be followed by the Second Coming of Christ to the earth, the Battle of Armageddon, and the Millennium, or the thousand year reign of Christ on Earth from the New Jerusalem."

He was puzzled by the direction of her thoughts. "Yes, your theology is sound, but God has said that He will not allow Lucifer to force His hand."

"Are you sure that God was talking about the end times when He said that?" She looked at him, her eyes piercing and bright.

Intuitive, thought Gabriel.

"I assume that is what He was referring to, but it is possible that He was speaking of something else. 'His thoughts are not our thoughts and His ways are not our ways,'" Xander answered, still puzzled.

"Xander, I know that I am only eighteen, but the end of this age could be very near, and I have always wanted to marry and have a child before I depart this life and receive my glorified body." She paused a moment, and then drawing a deep breath, exhaled her next words in a rushed, but very determined manner. "I want to have your baby now because I will be unable to have children in heaven. Is that wrong of me? Am I selfish to be worried about what I want instead of what will happen to the world if Lucifer succeeds? Our children would go to heaven with us, so would it be wrong to bear children so near to what could be the end of the world as we know it?" she asked, her sincerity ringing in every syllable.

He smiled broadly. "Elizabeth, you always thrill and amaze me. If you are selfish, then so am I, for I want us to have children together, too. I want us to have all the children that God chooses to give us whenever He sends them. Becoming parents will not stop us from serving Jehovah Adonai. In fact, I think that loving our children will make our passion for serving God and bringing souls into His kingdom even more urgent. Children will enhance our ministry and our marriage. We will want to fight evil even more, to make the world a better place for them."

"That's true, but I will become heavy and awkward, with swollen feet and a puffy face. Will you still love me when I'm nine months pregnant and no longer pretty?" she teased, stroking his jaw line with her fingers.

He turned his head to kiss her fingers. "My love, there will never be a time when you are not beautiful to me. 'Pretty' will always be inadequate to describe you, in my opinion. And once I marry you, 'what God has joined together, let no man put asunder.' You will be *mine*, and nothing will ever stop me from loving you or take you from me, in this life." Xander spoke each word with great satisfaction and conviction.

"I think you enjoyed saying that, and I like the way you said 'mine,'" she said, smiling. "You will be *mine*, too. I Corinthians 7:4 says, 'The wife does not have authority over her own body, but the husband does; and likewise also the husband does not have authority over his own body, but the wife does.'"

"Actually, I greatly look forward to being yours in every way, Elizabeth," Xander replied, the corners of his mouth twitching in amusement.

"Just six more weeks. It doesn't seem possible, does it?" Her eyes were dreamy.

"At this moment, six weeks seems an eternity. But, the time will pass, and we will enjoy our honeymoon away from everyone who knows us. Forty-two days to go," he said, getting a little dreamy himself.

Watch the road, thought Michael.

She sat up. "Speaking of our honeymoon, I am really curious about this surprise trip you have planned. Can't you give me just a hint of where we're going? I need to know what kind of clothes to pack, after all."

He laughed at her. "Your mom, Janna, and Charlotte will handle your packing. This is going to be a surprise. If I start giving hints, you will soon guess our destination. You have your secrets and surprises, and I have mine."

Gabriel smiled. *She will love it.*

She leaned over to kiss his ear. "Can't I convince you to tell me even one tiny thing about our trip? Just one? Please?"

He turned his face and caught her lips in a quick kiss, keeping his eyes on the highway. "You can possibly cause me to run off the road if you do not stop, but I will give you no information. Having you kiss me like *that* is a sweet torture – not the most effective means of making me yield this particular secret to you."

Elizabeth settled back into her seat with a smug expression, one hand twirling a long curl. "I have forty-two days in which to wear you down, Xander. That's over one thousand hours. Never underestimate the power of a determined woman."

"I would never do that with you, Elizabeth. I well know your power over me and respect it. You are formidable, and I recognize that, which is why you will not succeed in getting our destination out of me," he replied with a laugh.

"How do you do that?" she asked in exasperation.

"Do what, love?" he returned with a raised eyebrow.

"How do you succeed in making whatever you say about me sound like a compliment?" Her smile belied her accusation.

His reply was simple. "Because I love everything about you."

She threw her hands in the air. "You win. I surrender. There's no way I can top that. The honeymoon will be your secret and my surprise."

He smiled and remained quiet, graciously accepting his victory as he reached for her hand.

They drove for a few minutes in companionable silence. When Xander spoke again, his voice was grave.

"Elizabeth, Charlotte has discovered that I can read minds," he said.

"What?!" exclaimed Elizabeth, quickly turning her face toward him. "When did she figure that out? Not that I'm really all that surprised. Char has always been very perceptive, and she seems to have grown even more discerning in the past year. I never could keep a secret from her for very long."

"She has suspected it for some time now, but she tricked me when we were having dinner after the tux fitting. Charlotte called my name in her mind, and I looked at her before I thought about it. It was only for a second, but that was long enough for her to know that I could 'hear' her. She has noticed our silent communication in the past, and she rightly concluded that I was the one hearing everyone's thoughts. It is now one of her goals to determine how you know what I am thinking. She does not yet understand that I can speak into the minds of others," he said.

Elizabeth looked at the passing scenery and smiled as she thought of her friend. "She will eventually come to that conclusion on her own. At the very least she will conclude that you can speak into my mind. Why haven't you told me this earlier?"

"We have had very little time together alone," he replied with a grimace. "I have not wanted to spend the short time that we have had discussing Charlotte," he added with a sheepish smile, and then continued with his former solemnity. "In addition, I had to pray about the best course of action to take. This is a serious matter, not to be dealt with lightly."

"I don't like the idea that you are keeping things from me. Could we not have prayed together?" she asked, looking back at him to see his slight frown.

He breathed deeply. "Yes, normally I would have shared this with you for us to pray about during our devotional times, and after we are married, I hope that we will be as one in all things. But this matter goes beyond us; it was not my decision to make. Just as I could not reveal myself as an angel to you until I was sure that the time was right, I cannot tell anyone else anything that might cause them to wonder whether or not I am a normal human. I am convinced that neither Charlotte nor anyone else should be told that I am a dual nature. That information would lead to more questions, and I am not at liberty to give anyone except for you those answers.

"In II Corinthians 12:1-4, Paul talks of a man who 'was caught up into Paradise, and heard inexpressible words, which a man is not permitted to speak.' In Revelation 10:4, John reveals that he was instructed thus, 'Seal up the things which the seven peals of thunder have spoken, and do not write them.' There are certain things that should not be spoken of until God chooses to reveal them Himself. People know that there are angels around them, and they even know that spiritual warfare is waged constantly. The Scriptures tell them that. But they do not really think of it in the same terms as we do – as a reality that is dangerous to them. Angels fight on the behalf of believers, but we do not show ourselves as angels during this period of time. If humans truly knew what was happening around them, they would have no rest, they would never sleep, and they would be anxious constantly. God keeps this information from people for their own peace of mind."

Elizabeth nodded her understanding. "You're right. I have seen enough myself to know that the knowledge must be carefully guarded. Had I known that Gregory and Cassandra were demons, I could not have acted normally around them. Had I known that you were an angel, I would have been afraid of you as well. Humans fear what they do not understand, and some things are best left unsaid. If God had wanted humans to be aware of angels and demons, He would have made you visible to us at all times."

Exactly, thought Michael.

Gabriel looked at him. *I told you she was very astute. Charlotte is not the only one who is discerning, though she is particularly gifted in that area.*

Xander smiled gratefully, glancing quickly at her. "It would also be very difficult for me to do the work that God has planned for me if people knew what I am. I would become a sideshow and would distract people from God rather than point them to Him."

"That's true, too. Back to the original question. What do you want to do about Char?" asked Elizabeth.

"I think that if we do not answer this question of Charlotte's, her mind will naturally leap to her own conclusions. She may end up with even more questions if we are evasive," he answered.

"You seem to know her very well," Elizabeth said with a laugh. "Trying to keep a secret from Char just makes her dig harder for her own answers. What are your plans?"

"I feel the Spirit leading me to talk to Charlotte and Jonathan together. You and I will tell them that I can read the thoughts of those around me, and that I can speak my thoughts into the minds of others. All four of us have been gifted in unusual ways by God, so I think they will accept what I plan to tell them and ask no further questions. God is very good at preparing people for what He wants them to know. I believe that, like you, they will use the information to communicate privately. Though I have had no need to tell you before this time, you may be surprised to know that I can 'speak' into all of your minds together at once, just as I can 'speak' to all angels present or all guardians at the same time, or I can 'speak' to one or two angels without the others hearing. This actually may be a very useful tool for us. Demons can hear us, both angels and humans, when we speak aloud, but they cannot hear our thoughts. If I know demons are present, including Gregory or Lucifer, I can 'speak' into your minds, and they will not know what we are saying. What is your opinion?" he asked.

"I think your idea is brilliant and inspired by God Himself. The truth is always the best option," Elizabeth replied.

"Good. It is settled then," he answered with satisfaction.

I cannot like this, but I know that you are right, Xander, thought Michael.

It will be well, replied Gabriel.

~~oo~~

The caravan pulled into the parking lot of the Wyndham Jacksonville Riverwalk around 10:30 Friday evening. The hotel had been chosen because it was less than a mile from the Veterans Memorial Arena, which was the venue for the rally. Crew members in vans followed the semis to the arena so that they could bring the drivers back to the hotel after they parked the vehicles for the night.

Because it was fairly early, Xander asked Jonathan and Charlotte if he and Elizabeth could talk to them privately. Jonathan offered the use of his suite, and after putting their luggage into their rooms, the four of them, accompanied by their guardians and warriors, assembled in his room.

They pulled chairs around the small table in the room and seated themselves while Lexus, Edward, Michael, and Gabriel took stances behind their charges. The warriors stationed themselves at the windows, constantly scanning for demonic spies.

After Jonathan led the group in prayer, he lifted his head and looked at Xander expectantly. "Xander, you wanted to talk to us?"

"Yes, Jonathan. Charlotte, as you know, is very observant. She has the gift of discernment, and she has noticed something about Elizabeth and me that we think should be made open in this group only. No one else can know about this except the four of us. Agreed?" asked Xander.

Lexus turned his face to Michael. *Are you certain that this is the correct course of action?*

Michael looked at him steadily. *I believe that Xander is being led by the Almighty in this.*

Lexus nodded, his expression carefully neutral.

Jonathan smiled, "Usually I don't like to agree to anything without knowing what it is beforehand; however, I think in this case, I will. Whatever you say will be held in the strictest confidentiality."

Xander looked at Charlotte. She smiled. "I knew I was right. You can hear all of our thoughts, can't you, Xander?"

Jonathan looked at him in surprise. "What? Is Charlotte right?"

Xander kept his gaze level. "She is, and she knows that there is more, though she hasn't quite figured it all out yet. Rather than play games with the two of you, I think that I will share the information so that we can use it in our ministry."

"Good, because I have been thinking of this for months," answered Charlotte, eyes bright with curiosity. "I know that you can hear all of our minds, but how do you communicate with Elizabeth without speaking? I have known her well enough and long enough that I would have noticed if she could read my mind. Can you project your thoughts into her mind?"

Elizabeth smiled. "Very good, Char. We have tried to be careful and discreet, but you are too savvy for us."

Jonathan shifted in his chair uncomfortably, remembering how often he had thought of Charlotte around Xander.

Xander smiled at him, saying, "Jonathan, your mind is godly and pure. You have nothing to be embarrassed about."

"But I am human, with human desires and thoughts. This is too much to think about so quickly. How far does your gift extend?" asked Jonathan.

Xander was silent for a moment, organizing his thoughts. "I can read the minds of all people who are within a few miles of me, though I am well-practiced at choosing what is important and blocking the rest. As far as speaking into minds, I can speak into the minds of everyone at once, one person only, or any number of people with whom I choose to speak." *I can 'speak' so that the three of you can hear it, but no other people can.*

Shock registered on the faces of Jonathan and Charlotte, though Elizabeth only smiled at the demonstration.

"Wow!" Charlotte's eyes were wide. *I know that you've heard me think all kinds of things, but I'm cool with that. I usually say whatever I think anyway.*

Michael snorted. *She is priceless.*

Edward grinned. *I have enjoyed being her guardian. Her mind is lively and quick, and she is unusually honest.*

Xander laughed softly. "Charlotte, I know that to be true of you. That's why I have never felt that I was violating your privacy by 'hearing' you."

Jonathan looked at her, uncertainty in his expression, and then he returned his attention to Xander. "How can we use your gift in our ministry?"

"When it is needed, we can 'converse' silently, as Elizabeth and I have been doing for months. If there is anything that you need to know, I will 'speak' to you, and if you would like me to relay a message to Charlotte or Elizabeth, I will tell them for you. I think we should agree that I will usually communicate with all of you at once. Elizabeth and I will, of course, continue to 'speak' privately, but I would rather that anything concerning the ministry would be shared among all of us," Xander said.

Jonathan's face showed his resolve. "I will not pretend that I am comfortable with the idea of your knowing my mind, Xander, but I know that it is a gift from God and something which you cannot help. You have always been trustworthy and steady in His work, and although you could have used your ability for your own gain, you have not. Though I don't know right now how your gift will be useful, I have no doubt that it will be. God never wastes anything, and He doesn't do things without a reason. I am eager to see how He uses this to further accomplish His will."

"Thank you, Jonathan. I had confidence that you would see His wisdom and realize that He has a purpose in this. Now, it is getting late, and we have much to do tomorrow. Will you lead us in prayer again before we go to our rooms, Jonathan?" Xander asked.

"Of course." They bowed their heads and Jonathan prayed, "Father, thank you for Xander, our brother in ministry. Thank you for his gifts and his willingness to use them for You. Please give us a good night's rest and bless the rally tomorrow. Help us to harvest souls for Your kingdom. We are your servants. In Jesus' name, amen."

The guardians and warriors followed as Jonathan left his room with Xander, Elizabeth, and Charlotte, walking his girlfriend to her door and kissing her goodnight before he returned to his own room.

Xander and Elizabeth paused a moment outside her door.

"How do you think it went?" she whispered.

"It was a shock for him, but he will be comforted tonight, and by the morning, he will have accepted it completely," answered Xander. He stepped closer to her, drew her into his embrace, and kissed her.

"Everything will be fine by tomorrow, Elizabeth," he said.

She opened her door and turned to watch him leave. *I love you.*

He looked back with a smile as he walked down the hall. *I love you more. I win.*

You always win!

I know, Xander chuckled. *Sweet dreams, love. Only forty-two more days.*

Chapter 7

"And the two shall become one flesh; consequently they are no longer two, but one flesh. What therefore God has joined together, let no man separate."
Mark 10:8-9

November 2008

Lucifer sat regally on his throne, the air electric with excitement, as he, Gregory, and Dirk Horne met with the assembled demonic underprinces in the still dark early morning hours of Wednesday, November 12. While the underprinces of the global dominions knelt before their masters in the abandoned warehouse, their captains prostrated themselves on the floor behind them.

The unholy trinity basked in the worship and awe of the second tier of rulers in the demonic underworld. Gregory sat to Lucifer's right and Dirk Horne to his left, surveying with satisfaction some of the most powerful dark beings in all of the fallen ranks bowing before them in total subjection.

On national television, Horne had declared Gregory to be the next U.S. Senator from Massachusetts an hour after the polls had closed on the previous evening and had returned to his penthouse apartment for a few hours of sleep before boarding a private jet to attend the meeting. Gregory had celebrated the rest of the night with his wife, their political cronies, and people who had worked tirelessly on his campaign. Though he had not yet been to bed, he showed no signs of fatigue. The adulation of his followers had been more than sufficient to keep him energized.

Lucifer stood, resplendent in his black robes, lifted his chin, and spoke slowly and deliberately with hauteur, "Behold your king, your prince, and your prophet."

A rumbling began from the back of the building and grew in intensity until the rafters shook with shouts and cheers of the hundreds of howling fiends. They leapt to their feet, fists raised, and cadenced in unison, "Praise them! Praise them! Praise them!"

After allowing himself a full five minutes of their adoration, Lucifer raised a hand to silence his followers. "We are closer to realizing our goals than ever before, my subjects. This time, our prize will not be denied us. We will ascend to heaven, we will raise these thrones before you above the stars of God, we will sit on the mount of assembly in the recesses of the north, and we will ascend above the heights of the clouds. I will make myself like the Most High. When that is accomplished, we will cast God and His angels to this dismal planet, and we will take our rightful place, ruling the universes."

He paused, allowing the darkness to flow from him and fill the place, and after a moment of total silence greeted his terrible words, the demonic throng began to scream, "Our king! Our prince! Our prophet!" over and over again, stomping their feet and dancing in their frenzy, until their voices reached the throne room of Jehovah-Elyon and resounded through the halls of heaven.

Light beings throughout all of creation covered themselves with their wings, grieving at the blasphemy and crying out against it, until the bright, warm light of Jehovah-'Ori flooded the spiritual plane and penetrated their wings with His presence. They folded their wings and turned their faces in worship toward the Light which obliterated all darkness.

Until that moment, the warehouse had been shrouded in thick blackness, though the day had dawned. As Jehovah-Helech 'Olam's light grew, the darkness fled, and the assembly of evil quieted to a fearful hush. They knew that Light and shrank from It in utter terror.

LEGACY

In the brightness of His light, the warehouse was shown as it truly was – no longer a throne room, but a filthy, run-down building, condemned and fit only for a wrecking crew. The Light then disappeared as quickly as it had come.

Lucifer frowned as his minions cowered before him, dreading his anger.

From Dirk Horne, Dark Spirit's low voice began to speak persuasively, creeping into their minds. "We still have much to do before we prevail – and prevail we shall. Have no doubt of it."

Gregory smiled easily as he shifted forward on his throne, leaning toward the audience with his arm on his knee, allowing his beauty to mesmerize the demonic force before him. "Dark Spirit is right, my friends and colleagues. Send out your underlings to whisper into the ears of the easily lead humans. Our power grows day by day, and in four or five earth years, the time will be right."

Lucifer glanced at Gregory, narrowing his fiery eyes, and then back at his minions. "Wait no longer. Go and do our will."

The demons fled into the light of the morning, scrambling to escape, preferring the light of the sun to the scalding holy Light which had briefly invaded the warehouse.

~~oo~~

Xander smiled in satisfaction as he finished his last exam, put down his pencil, and turned the test over on his desk at Converse on Thursday, December 11. He gazed at Elizabeth beside him, her head bent over her work, dark hair held back by her left hand as her right hand busily scribbled. She chewed her bottom lip and wrinkled her brow in concentration. *The day after tomorrow, she will be my wife,* he thought in wonder and exultation. *In fewer than forty-eight hours, she will be mine.*

From beside him, Michael rolled his eyes.

Gabriel, on the other side of Elizabeth, smiled at Xander, full of joy for his brother.

Though Xander had looked forward to his wedding day with great anticipation since the moment God had revealed his plans concerning him and Elizabeth, he could hardly believe it was nearly upon him. He was going to be married in two days, assuming all the joys, responsibilities, and privileges that came with the title "husband." Xander was fully ready for marriage, but he was sobered by the knowledge that Elizabeth would trust him to care for her financially and emotionally, and that she would look to him to be their family's spiritual leader. He had absolutely no fear of the total commitment required; he could, however, now better understand the men who did.

Mr. and Mrs. Xander Darcy . . . I like that. I will be her husband, and she will be my wife.

He sighed in contentment, and Elizabeth turned toward the sound as she flipped the paper over on her desk, finished at last. When she smiled at him crookedly, he realized that he must have a rather silly expression on his face. *Yes, I was thinking of your becoming Mrs. Xander Darcy in two days. So shoot me,* he thought into her mind.

We are a pair. The thought is never very far from my mind. How could it be with my wedding dress hanging up in my room, gifts piled in the den, and a list of errands in my purse that must all be done today? she mused.

Is there any way I can help you? he asked. *All I need to do today is pick up the tuxes for my brothers and me. Otherwise, I am fully at your service.* Xander had arranged all the details for the rehearsal dinner weeks before.

Oh, yes, my love, there is. You can 'Feed me, Seymour!' and then drive me around, pleasantly distracting me while I complete my list. Then we can go to my house, open presents, write thank you notes, and help Mom and the others decorate the fellowship hall. We can also take the gifts from Mom and Dad's to our house and unpack some more things. I don't want to come back from our honeymoon to a war zone, though I suppose it will have to do as it is for our wedding night, she thought, gathering her things. Because Xander absolutely refused to spend their first night together in a hotel or on an airplane, they had decided to stay in their home for that night and fly out the next morning.

Xander and Elizabeth had bought an older two-story, four bedroom house just outside of Bethel in a beautiful wooded area only two miles from her parents' home. He had moved into it the week before, loading what furniture he had from his townhouse into a U-Haul for the thirty minute drive. Several college students who attended Tabernacle had been happy to earn extra money by helping him to move the items. His custom-made bed took up more than half of the master bedroom in their "new" house, but he could not part with it. The couch and occasional tables were new. He and Elizabeth had decided to wait until after they returned from their wedding trip to shop together for the rest of their furnishings.

Hmmm...our honeymoon. His thoughts drifted.

Focus, Xander. Today – lunch, the list, presents, thank you notes, helping Mom decorate, and unpacking. Tomorrow – decorating the hall for the reception, and then attending the rehearsal and rehearsal dinner. Saturday – the wedding and reception. Then, the honeymoon. She smiled at him.

As long as we eventually get to the honeymoon, he answered.

Oh, yes. I promise to happily give you my full and undivided attention for ten glorious days in – where will we be again? she questioned innocently.

Good try, he chuckled.

It was worth a shot. Elizabeth laughed lightly, stood, pulled her purse over her shoulder, and picked up her exam. As she walked to the professor's desk and left her paper, Xander strode behind her, put his exam on the desk, and joined her in wishing the professor a "Merry Christmas" before he took Elizabeth's hand and led her to the door, followed by Michael and Gabriel.

~~oo~~

Xander woke up early on his wedding day, and his first thoughts were of Elizabeth. *This is the last time I shall awake alone.* She was still asleep in her own bed only two miles away – close enough for him to 'see' her dreams; he closed his eyes and allowed himself the luxury of sharing her unconscious mind. They were flying together, and she dreamed that she had wings like his. *If only that were so.*

The thought saddened him, but he refused to allow anything to spoil the day. He sat up and swung his legs over the side of the bed, looking at his brother. *Gabriel, will you work out with me?*

Of course. Your preferred form or mine? he asked.

Human form. You need the practice, Xander stated.

I do, and you need the distraction, replied Gabriel, morphing into human form.

True. It is unfortunate that Michael cannot join us. He would love a hard training session, thought Xander, rising from the bed and pulling on his sweatpants.

When you and Elizabeth are married, we three will be together all the time. Since she knows about us, we can train whenever we wish. I must say that I am glad I am with you today, Gabriel thought.

Really? I appreciate the sentiment, but why? asked Xander, walking toward the bathroom.

Michael will spend this entire day with five women preparing for a wedding. They will be getting their hair done, having manicures, doing their makeup, and getting dressed. It will be a time of talking and giggling, crying, and sharing memories. Gabriel smiled. *Does that sound like an enjoyable day for Michael?*

Xander laughed aloud. *It is fortunate that you thought of having a contingent of warriors relieve him and Niall at two o'clock so that they can be here to dress for the ceremony and ride with us to the church. You will have to speak peace into his mind to cheer him. He must not be glaring in all of the pictures.*

We will lift his spirits together, thought Gabriel. *It will probably take both of us.*

There may not be sufficient time, brother. We will have only two hours. Grinning, Xander picked up his sword and led Gabriel to an empty bedroom.

Michael heard them from two miles away in Elizabeth's bedroom. *We can spend one of those hours training. I will be in extreme need of exercise and diversion by the time I have spent six hours with the ladies. In fact, I think I will call in the warriors at one o'clock. Roark, Edward, Alexis, Hector, Duarte, and Sender will be here. I can have the house surrounded by a phalanx if necessary.*

Xander smiled compassionately at the note of desperation in his "big" brother's voice. *We will expect to see you and Niall at one o'clock then.*

~~oo~~

The wedding party had been at the church for the past two hours while the photographers took all the wedding pictures which did not require the bride and groom to be together, and they, along with the videographer, had stationed themselves in inconspicuous places in the church sanctuary.

Finally the time for the actual wedding had arrived, and Xander, with his groomsmen and Jonathan, waited nervously in the hallway which ran by the right side entrance of the Tabernacle church sanctuary. He checked his watch again as he listened to the string quintet from Converse College playing Handel's "Water Music Suite." He had fought his urge to listen to Elizabeth's mind all day, fearing that he might catch a glimpse of her in her wedding dress before a mirror. He could not bear to disappoint her, but his patience was nearly at an end. Jonathan, Lexus at his side, put a hand on Xander's arm and chuckled.

"The next song should be 'Jesu, Joy of Man's Desiring,' Xander. That's our cue. Relax," Jonathan whispered as he patted the groom's shoulder affectionately, checked his white rose boutonniere, and straightened his bowtie.

As the words left Jonathan's mouth, the familiar strains of Bach's masterpiece began. Niall, Gabriel, and Michael stepped up behind Xander, placed their hands on his shoulders and back, and bowed their heads, silently speaking peace into his mind.

When they lifted their heads, Jonathan opened the door and walked to his assigned spot at the front of the church, followed closely by Lexus. The previous morning, Xander, Chance, and David had removed the pulpit from the front center of the stage and placed steps on the floor leading up to the area it vacated. Jonathan now stood in front of those steps and faced the assembly. Xander, Niall, Gabriel, and Michael followed closely behind the evangelist, found their proper places, and turned to face the double doors at the end of the aisle.

The whispering began as soon as the men entered the sanctuary. While the church family had grown used to Xander's unusual height and physical beauty, only those at the rehearsal dinner had met his brothers. Gabriel's blond hair, dark blue eyes, and serene countenance were angelic, while Michael's towering height and emerald green eyes commanded attention. Niall, though six foot two inches, looked almost short beside the archangels and the Chief Guardian, but his dark hair and laughing deep brown eyes won the hearts and attention of every female under the age of twenty-five. The men were the handsomest group of groomsmen ever assembled; their immaculate tuxes were perfectly fitted, their postures and bearing regal in appearance.

Xander looked anxiously down the aisle, not noticing the pink and white poinsettias or the twin Christmas trees – covered in white lights and decorated in ivory, dark green, and gold – which stood on either side of the flower-trimmed arch, flanked by candles on the raised stage. He gazed past the carriage lamps tied with hunter green bows affixed to the ends of each pew, completely filled with friends of the couple and relatives of her family. His arm twitched with the effort to keep himself from looking at his watch again. *Surely it is time. What could be taking so long?*

Women are always late, Xander. Get used to it, thought Niall. Then he added softly, *Elizabeth is well worth waiting for, is she not?*

Xander smile in response, deliberately releasing the tension in his shoulders. *Do you have the ring?*

The ring? I thought you were supposed to have it, answered Niall.

Xander turned his head to glare at him, and Niall winked. *Gotcha!*

Conscious of the hundreds of eyes, human and angelic, trained upon him, Xander refrained from rolling his eyes. *Very funny. Again, do not quit your day job.*

Again, I am wounded by your lack of appreciation for my sparkling wit, returned Niall.

Guardians and warriors stood thickly around the perimeters of the auditorium, honored to be present at an event so highly anticipated, and Xander was aware that they watched his every move. He raised his chin slightly and trained his eyes on the doors through which his bride would walk for the last time as Elizabeth Bennet.

The doors opened, and Bethany Martin walked slowly down the aisle, her petite figure shown to advantage in the floor-length, hunter green, sleeveless, silk bridesmaid dress. A wide, stiff sash of the same fabric circled her just above the waist of the sheath dress, coming to a large bow in the back which fell to a train following the hemline of the skirt. She and the other bridesmaids carried a bouquet of small white calla lilies, edged in pink, and tied with a light green bow. Sender walked solemnly beside her, looking squarely before him.

After Bethany had taken her place to the left of the steps, Charlotte began her slow walk down the aisle with Edward at her side. Xander noticed the moment when her eyes met Jonathan's, for he saw her expression brighten as she smiled for him. Though Xander did not look at Jonathan, he heard his friend's thought of appreciation for Charlotte's appearance.

Once Charlotte had taken her place, Janna, Alexis by her side, stepped forward from the back, her lovely face full of joy for her sister. As she passed her mother's pew, she turned her head to smile at Lynne and Chance.

Baby Matthew had been left in the church nursery with a babysitter but would join them for the reception, freeing Chance to escort his mother-in-law and sit with her.

Xander saw the affectionate display between Janna and Lynne and looked at the empty pew where his mother would have been seated, if he had ever had a mother. Lynne had left the pew empty in honor of his mother, even though, to her understanding, she had given her son up for adoption. His heart swelled as he thought of Lynne, soon to be the only mother he would ever know, and David, who would become his earthly father.

Two small flower girls, daughters of the church's minister of music, came next in matching light pink dresses accented with green bows, strewing the petals of sweetheart roses down the aisle as they giggled, their guardians trailing them. Janna took the hand of one child, and Charlotte reached for the other as they arrived at the front, turning them to face the audience.

The wedding director closed the back doors, and a trumpeter stood, beginning the strains of Jeremiah Clarke's "Trumpet Voluntary," accompanied by the string ensemble. After a few moments, the director re-opened the doors to reveal Elizabeth and her father waiting in the doorway, and every head turned to see the bride. Then, all movement stopped until her mother stood and faced them.

Xander had always considered Elizabeth to be the most beautiful woman of his acquaintance, both past and present, but as he beheld her radiance on this special day, he thought that she was even more magnificent than she ever had been before. He forgot to breathe as she started slowly down the aisle toward him on the arm of her father, Roark and two warriors walking behind them.

Elizabeth's ivory silk gown, covered in lace, fit her slender, willowy figure perfectly, dropping from her waist straight to the floor. The gown was tiered;

the scalloped edges of the lace overdress covered the area above her bust left bare by the strapless silk slip-dress and continued in wide straps over her shoulders. Her figure was defined by a wide ivory silk sash which hugged her just above her waist, covering her torso until it met the gentle swells of her bosom. Elizabeth's back was bare, as the lace capping her shoulders continued in a V pattern until, above her waist, it met a squared bow made from the sash. From there, folds of lace covered silk fell in a graceful train. Rather than a veil, her dark curls were caught up by several ringlets of pearls which held it loosely, allowing tendrils to escape, framing her face and wandering down her back. She wore no jewelry except for her engagement ring and her grandmother's pearl earrings. The effect was, at the same time, innocent yet alluring.

Xander was enchanted, and his perfect face displayed his emotions for all to see. *She was, and is, worth waiting for. She is everything that is beautiful.* The idea that she had arrayed herself for him was nearly overwhelming, and his eyes spoke the words to her that he could not say aloud.

She seemed to float down the aisle toward him as in a dream, stopping by her mother to hand her a white rose which she had held under her bouquet of calla lilies and roses, and he shivered slightly when she and her father finally stood beside him. The groomsmen and bridesmaids turned to face the couple as Lynne took her seat, signaling the guests to sit down as well.

Elizabeth, still holding her father's arm, tilted her face up to his and smiled, and he forgot for a moment that anyone else was in the room. Xander knew that Jonathan was talking, and he knew that the evangelist prayed, but his voice sounded like a faint buzz in the background. All he could see was Elizabeth, and all he could hear was his own heartbeat thundering in his head.

"Who gives this woman to be wed?" asked Jonathan.

"Her mother and I," answered David. Elizabeth broke her gaze from Xander and looked at her father. David kissed her cheek, and moved her left hand from his arm. She lifted her right hand so that her father could place it in Xander's hand, but Xander remained motionless.

"Take her hand, son," whispered David, smiling as he looked at Xander's expression.

Xander shook his head slightly and lifted his left hand to take her slender fingers in his. Hearing Niall chuckle behind him, he remembered to breathe.

Jonathan stepped from his spot to the seat left vacant for Xander's mother, and David moved to the position Jonathan had held, continuing up the steps to stand behind the flowered arch. Xander led Elizabeth up the steps, and Janna adjusted her train before she, Niall, and the rest of the wedding party followed them. Once the bride and groom stood under the arch, Janna stood to Elizabeth's left and Niall took the position by Xander's right. The other bridesmaids, flower girls, and groomsmen walked to their assigned spots, and the ceremony began.

After David gave the charge to the bride and groom, speaking about the sanctity of marriage and the relationship of Christ to His bride, the church, a pianist began to play, joined by the strings, while Xander sang "Forever" to Elizabeth in his wonderful baritone, as she had requested. She looked into his beautiful eyes as he sang to her, and he nearly forgot the words he had written himself.

The women in the audience tried unsuccessfully to hold back their tears at such an open display of love from the normally reserved young man, and some of the men surreptitiously wiped their eyes.

As soon as Xander finished singing, David continued the traditional ceremony with the pledges, Xander and Elizabeth each answering "I will" at the appropriate moments.

Xander thought that they were then ready for the vows and the exchanging of their rings, but Elizabeth turned her body to fully face him, smiled a heart-stopping smile, and whispered, "I have a surprise for you."

A CD began to play through the sound system, and he was stunned when he recognized her piano styling on the recording and realized that she had actually found the time to record the track. Xander was further astonished when Elizabeth began to sing to him, a song which he had never heard before, "My Angel's Kiss." Her clear soprano softly caressed the words describing how special he was to her and how deeply she loved him. The song was a pledge in itself, a vow that she was his and his alone. Her words spoke of their love for God, and her gratitude that God had brought them together, choosing each of them for the other.

More tears flowed freely down her mother's face as Elizabeth sang, and even her usually imperturbable father choked back a sob. Sniffles were heard throughout the congregation.

Xander gazed at her glowing face and knew that everything he had suffered was worth it to have a lifetime with her. His love for her was a living entity, burning his soul with her brand. He would spend the rest of his own life trying to be worthy of her love.

There was silence as she sang the final notes, and then one of the flower girls tugged on Elizabeth's gown, pointed her little index finger at Xander, and solemnly intoned, loudly enough for everyone to hear, "He looks like an angel. Is he really one?"

The titters of the crowd broke the emotion of the moment, enabling the service to continue without the threat of tears from the wedding party, but not before Elizabeth looked down at the child, whispering softly, "Yes, he is. He is my angel."

Her words brought smiles to the faces of the groomsmen as well as the hundreds of guardians present. Even the warriors wore small grins which they quickly extinguished, resuming their proper stoicism.

David asked Xander and Elizabeth to face each other and hold hands. After they had turned in full profile to the wedding guests, David began to read the familiar words of the vows in a steady voice, pausing at intervals for Xander to repeat the words. Xander spoke loudly enough for everyone to hear, his deep voice full of conviction as he recited the vows which would bind him to Elizabeth forever. "I, Xander Darcy, take you, Elizabeth Faith Bennet, to be my wedded wife, to have and to hold from this day forward, for better, for worse, for richer, for poorer, in sickness and in health, to love and to cherish, as long as we both shall live, for all eternity, according to God's holy ordinance, and thereto I pledge you my love and faithfulness."

David then directed his attention toward his daughter, and she also repeated her vows, looking into Xander's eyes and speaking in an unwavering voice. When Elizabeth spoke her final pledge, he smiled at her, his countenance so achingly radiant that she nearly gasped aloud.

As she finished speaking, beams of light shot through the stained glassed windows though it was already past sundown. The sanctuary was illuminated with the dancing colors, and Xander and Elizabeth were bathed in a golden aura. Xander knew that his Father was blessing his wedding and showing His approval, and he spoke into Elizabeth's mind, *Our Father is here today, Elizabeth. Jehovah-'Ori is pleased with our union.*

She prayed with her eyes focused on the light beams, *I love you, Jehovah Adonai. Thank you for your blessing.*

The assembled angels glowed with the light and hummed their praise to Almighty God. Michael, Gabriel, and Niall smiled and praised Him in their minds.

David had always known that Xander was full of the Spirit and different from anyone he had ever met, and, while he did not recognize the full significance of the light, he correctly surmised that God was present in the little church in a special way at that moment. He felt that God Himself had planned the marriage of his daughter to this man of God.

Lynne's thoughts were similar to those of her husband, and she watched in awe as her daughter and son-in-law were surrounded by the light of God. Though she and David had privately talked of how God had worked through the couple in marvelous ways, she had not expected to see God manifest Himself in such a way at the wedding, and she was humbled and filled with praise.

The rest of the wedding party as well as the congregation saw the light and felt the presence of God, and they were hushed. Jonathan and Charlotte looked at each other in full understanding. They had spoken often of how God had brought Xander and Elizabeth together.

The dark ones fled for miles around the area, for darkness and the pure light of God Himself could not exist together in the same place.

After a moment, David looked first at the couple and then at the assembled wedding party and guests, saying, "I feel led to pray. Please bow your heads. Father, I sense Your presence, and It is glorious. Thank You for our children who stand before You. Thank You for bringing them together, and I pray that they will always serve You as one. Please bless their union, Lord. In Jesus' name. Amen."

David then raised his head and continued the ceremony. At his direction Janna and Niall handed the rings to Elizabeth and Xander, and Janna took Elizabeth's bouquet. The congregation bowed their heads as he prayed, "Father, bless these rings which Xander and Elizabeth have set apart to be visible signs of the inward and spiritual bond which unites their hearts. As they give and receive these rings, may they testify to the world of the covenant made between them here."

As everyone lifted their heads, Xander placed the slender wedding band on Elizabeth's finger, saying, "Receive and wear this ring as a symbol of my trust, my respect, and my love for you."

Her eyes full of love for him, she in turn slid his solid platinum band on his finger, repeating, "Receive and wear this ring as a symbol of my trust, my respect, and my love for you."

Together they pledged, "This circle will now seal the vows of our marriage and will symbolize the purity and endlessness of our love."

David finished the simple ceremony by saying, "By the power vested in me by the state of South Carolina, I now pronounce you husband and wife. What God has joined together let no man put asunder. Son, you may kiss your bride."

Xander wasted no time in leaning down to draw his wife into his embrace, taking the liberty of kissing her fully and soundly. Behind him, Niall cleared his throat. *I think that is enough for now, Xander.. The natives are restless. You have all night, you know.*

David spoke the moment Xander broke the kiss. "I now present to you Mr. and Mrs. Xander Darcy."

Seraphim flooded the building by the hundreds, spinning and dipping in a kaleidoscopic dance of joy in the air above the people.

Immediately, the string ensemble began playing Handel's "Arrival of the Queen of Sheba," Elizabeth received her bouquet back from her sister, and the happy couple walked down the steps, leading the recessional. As they left the sanctuary, the Light disappeared, and the seraphim followed It back to the throne room of heaven.

As soon as they cleared the church doors and stood in the foyer guarded by warriors, Xander swept his bride back into his arms and kissed her as he had longed to kiss her throughout the whole interminable day of separation. Though the wedding party quickly arrived and surrounded them, speaking of the Light, he did not let her go. He knew that hours of pictures, receiving guests, and attending the reception remained before he would have her to himself again, and he did not release her until the groomsmen and ushers began to escort the guests out of the sanctuary and into the foyer.

I liked the appetizer, she thought as they returned to the sanctuary to finish having their pictures taken.

Then you will love the full course I have planned for later, he answered, favoring her with a fully dimpled smile.

Her only answer was a quick peck on his cheek and a mysterious smile of her own.

Chapter 8

" ... behold you have sinned against the Lord, and be sure your sin will find you out."
Numbers 32:23

After the final pictures had been taken, the bride and groom entered the church's fellowship hall hand-in-hand for their reception, and a cheer went up from the crowd of well-wishers already helping themselves to food and beverages. The DJ stopped the music long enough to announce the arrival of Mr. and Mrs. Xander Darcy and the rest of the wedding party.

By Michael's command, warriors surrounded the church grounds and stood around the edges of each room being used. Xander had assigned extra guardians to Lynne and Elizabeth, though there was little likelihood of their being needed. He knew that Lucifer himself would not dare to enter a place so heavily fortified. However, he would take no chances with the safety of his bride, her mother, or any of their guests, so guardians shadowed their charges as they moved from place to place.

Though it was mid-December, the weather was unseasonably warm, and a large, enclosed, white tent had been set up outside, attaching to a side exit of the fellowship hall, in order to increase the capacity of the building. Because of the great number of guests for the event, only food and drink buffet tables had been set up in the main hall. Seating was provided around the perimeter of the room, but most people stood to chat, holding their plates and setting their punch cups on them. Tables were provided in the heated tent for those who wished to sit and eat. Speakers had been set up so that the music flowed through both the hall and the tent.

Xander and Elizabeth had been busy on Thursday evening and all day Friday helping David, Lynne, Janna, Chance, Grace, Charlotte, Jonathan, and Bethany decorate the areas, and they were all quite pleased with the results. Because Xander had arranged for the rehearsal dinner to be catered at the local country club, the fellowship hall had been free since the missions groups had met there on Wednesday, and there had been time to do everything without the pressure of being rushed.

The men, under the direction of Lynne and Grace, had strung grapevines just below the ceiling connecting the twin rows of columns that ran down the center of the hall. Looped through the vines were white Christmas lights under white netting, silk ivy, and pink and white silk flowers. The food tables were covered with white cloths overlaid with hunter green netting, and white bows caught up the netting in scallops around the tables. White and pink poinsettias were arranged in groups throughout the hall and the tent, and each window was decorated with candles under globes, greenery, and ribbon. The tables in the tent repeated the theme of the food tables, and each featured a centerpiece of a large crystal globe over white candles nestled in pearlescent stones. The globes were surrounded by silk ivy vines and their light cast a warm glow over the room. To further light the tent, white Christmas icicle lights outlined the ceiling and dripped down the walls, giving a fairy tale appearance to the place.

After greeting their guests, Xander led Elizabeth to the wedding cake, topped whimsically by two angels rather than a bride and groom. As cameras flashed, he cut a piece and fed it to her, being careful not to spoil her make-up, and then she cut a piece for him. While he was eating the piece she was feeding him, Xander noticed a commotion behind her. Elizabeth heard the noise and turned to see Richard Williams shaking hands with the other guests and smiling. He broke from the group and walked to the table, waiting for the photographer to finish.

As soon as Xander and Elizabeth received a nod from the photographer, they went to Richard. Xander shook his hand, saying, "We are very pleased you came, Richard."

Elizabeth opened her arms to him, smiling. "I'm so glad you changed your mind, Richard. We're so happy to see you." He hugged her, and then stepped back to admire her, still holding her hands.

Richard smiled at both of them, and returned his gaze to Elizabeth. "You are absolutely beautiful, as always, El. I saved some leave time. After I thought about it, I decided that I couldn't miss your wedding. This will be one of the happiest days of your life, and I wanted to share it with you. We grew up together, and I hope that we'll always be good friends."

Xander, hearing his thoughts, knew that what Richard was saying was true, but it was not the only reason he had come. Garnet stood behind Richard, and his face was serious. *I have been speaking peace to him, but he is determined on this course of action. He has spent much time thinking about it and feels strongly that this is something that he needs to do.*

There comes a time when people have to take responsibility for their actions. This needs to be done. It will help them both to let go of the past, answered Xander. *Michael, would you, Gabriel, and Niall watch the situation, please? You can step in if necessary.*

The three groomsmen, who were standing with Charlotte and Jonathan near the punch table, looked at Xander and smiled.

Depend upon it, thought Michael.

There will be no problem, added Gabriel.

Niall, who had actually been present during the terrible ordeal concerning Elizabeth, Richard, and Caroline had a slightly different viewpoint from that of his brothers. *Richard deserves the opportunity to confront Caroline, and she needs to understand the gravity of her actions. She must face the consequences so that she sees how her sin affected everyone around her. I will interrupt them, however, if it starts to get out of hand.*

Across the room, Caroline stood with her parents, Anne and Donald Bingley. Xander saw her scan the room, and he knew the moment that she saw Richard holding Elizabeth's hands. Her smile had been genuine, but it became forced, her face frozen in a mask. Caroline had not known until that moment that Richard was at the wedding; he had entered a side door to the sanctuary in order to avoid her at the guest registry. Behind Caroline, Ros met Xander's eyes and nodded solemnly in greeting.

One of the caterers came up to Xander and Elizabeth, asking if they were ready for her to begin serving the cake. Xander answered her in the affirmative, and he took Elizabeth's elbow, speaking to her in a low voice, "We need to move so that she can serve the guests. I think the photographer wants us at the punch table. He is there now, motioning for us to come over."

Elizabeth smiled up at her husband, releasing Richard's hands and promising to talk to him later. Xander guided her through the crowd, both of them smiling and chatting to guests as they made their way to the photographer.

Xander glanced at Richard just as the young soldier looked across the room and caught Caroline watching him. Richard's mouth was set in a grim line as he made his way through the throng, greeting friends while he continued doggedly on his way. Finally he stood before her and the Bingleys.

Michael, Gabriel, and Niall made their excuses to Jonathan and Charlotte, leaving them in order to move closer to Richard and the Bingley family.

"Hello, Mr. and Mrs. Bingley. It's good to see you again," Richard said, making a great effort to put a smile on his face.

Donald grunted in acknowledgement as Anne smiled nervously and said, "It's wonderful to see you, too, Richard. How have you been?"

"Good, thanks, and you?" Richard answered, holding his irritation at the small talk.

"Fine, thank you. Will you be home for very long?" Anne asked.

"I'm just home for the week. I came especially for the wedding." He turned his head to look at Caroline who had remained silent throughout the banal exchange. "Caroline, we have some catching up to do, but it's very crowded in here. I see an empty corner over there by the kitchen door. Would you join me?"

Caroline swallowed hard and nodded. Richard smiled at Anne and Donald before he turned on his heel and strode toward the area, Caroline following close behind him.

Xander spoke to Garnet and Ros, *I do not wish to have a scene at our wedding. If you cannot keep peace between them, try to get them to go outside.*

I think being surrounded by people may keep them from raising their voices. Richard does not intend to cause a problem for you and Elizabeth, thought Garnet, following his charge closely.

The last thing Caroline wants is for anyone to hear this conversation. She saw his expression, and she knows that all is not well, added Ros, close on Caroline's heels.

All the same, we will monitor their conversation, answered Michael.

Gabriel, Michael, and Niall watched Richard and Caroline cross the room, waited a few moments, and then began to move casually in their direction.

Xander watched their procession and carefully monitored their progress. He listened to both Richard's and Caroline's thoughts as he smiled for the photographer.

Richard stepped into the empty corner behind a conveniently placed Christmas tree and leaned on the wall, waiting for Caroline.

She stopped short of walking behind the tree, trying to compose herself. When she finally approached him, her face was serene.

Richard leveled a cool stare at her, and she had the grace to blush.

Michael positioned himself on one side of the tree, facing the guests and drinking a cup of punch. Gabriel and Niall stood on the other side, talking to each other quietly. They effectively blocked anyone else from seeing the couple or accidentally coming upon them.

Caroline looked beautiful in her fitted red dress, her caramel colored hair cascading down her back and her makeup perfectly accenting her green eyes and fair skin.

She's wearing red. That's perfect, Richard thought cynically. *What a waste. Going to all that trouble to make the outside attractive when the inside is rotten.*

Caroline straightened her spine and waited for him to speak. *I deserve whatever he says,* she thought. *I have dreaded this for more than two years. I wonder exactly what he knows. Now it's time to face the music for what I've done.*

"I've enjoyed your letters, Caroline. Thanks for writing me while I was overseas and for continuing after I came back to the States," said Richard smoothly.

"Yes, it was the least I could do. It was my fault that you left, and I have felt terrible about it," she replied.

Niall frowned. Gabriel smiled at him, reminding him that others might be watching them.

"You have? Here's a news flash – this isn't about you, Caroline. The world does not revolve around you. I actually thought you meant it when you apologized in your letters. I was stupid enough to believe that a girl who could get me drunk, do me, and plaster pictures of it all over MySpace could get right with God and be sorry for what she had done. I have always been an idiot. Nothing has changed, has it? You're the same, and I'm the same," he said bitterly, his handsome features marred by his frown.

She lowered her head. "I did mean it. I have rededicated my life to God, and I am sorry for what I did. I don't hang out with that crowd any more, and I go to church and read my Bible regularly. I'm trying to be a better person."

"Well, that makes me feel all warm inside. You basically ruined my life – with my help, I admit – and now everyone has forgiven you for the despicable things you did. I forgave you, too, until I found out that you didn't tell the whole truth," he spat out in a low voice.

She looked up at him quickly. "What do you mean? I admitted that I planned the whole thing and set you up." *How could he know? Nobody knew it but me. Even Lydia and Grant never knew.*

He stood up straight before he spoke. "I mean that you made it so that I couldn't help myself. You drugged me. What you did was rape, Caroline. I was stupid to go to that party and get drunk, but I wouldn't have slept with you if you hadn't put something in my drink. I had no control over myself, and you knew it." He kept his voice low, but his hands were clenched with the effort.

"How do you know that?" she asked in a whisper.

The Word says, 'Be sure your sin will find you out,' thought Niall.

"What does it matter how I found out? It's true, isn't it?" he demanded curtly, his brown eyes blazing.

She looked up at him with tears in her eyes and said, "Yes, it's true."

"For two and a half years I've thought everything was my fault; part of it was, but the major part of it was yours. For nearly a year you've been writing me, and you still never came clean. You made yourself feel better, and you relieved your guilt, but you never helped me to get past what happened. The course of my life was changed that night, and nothing will ever be the same for me again. I might have been the one marrying the woman I love today if you hadn't set me up. El forgave me for getting drunk; she couldn't get past my lying about sleeping with you. I lied because it was so horrible that I thought she would never forgive me if she knew. If I had known that you drugged me, I would have told her about it. I would have told her that you drugged me and took advantage of me. She would have understood that, Caroline, and she wouldn't have broken up with me."

Richard's voice had become a little louder, and Michael turned as if to go behind the tree and stop the conversation, but Niall lifted his cup to catch his attention and shook his head a little. *Let him finish. The music is loud enough that no one has noticed.*

Michael remained where he was. *If anyone looks in this direction, I am putting a stop to this.*

Agreed, thought Niall.

Richard continued, "But you already knew that, and that's why you never told me. You wanted to hurt her because she punched you in the nose, and you wanted to hurt me because I never wanted you. You just couldn't stand it that we were happy, and you weren't. When you wrote me, you said that you wanted to make things right between us, but you still let me believe that I slept with you willingly. How could you do that, Caroline?"

Richard was angry, but his military training had taught him to control himself under any circumstances.

Garnet put his hands on Richard's back, speaking peace to him. Some of the tension left Richard's shoulders.

The tears rolled down Caroline's face as she listened to him. She knew that every word he said was true, and she had never felt so worthless in her life.

Ros placed his hand on her shoulder and spoke into her mind. *You are not worthless. Christ died for you, and He loves you. You are precious to Him.*

She lifted her chin a little. "Richard, I know what I did was wrong, and I know that my actions have greatly impacted your life. I'm so sorry for that; I wish that I could change things and make it all right for you, but we both know that I can't. I wish that I could go back in time and stop myself from doing what I did to you, but I can't do that either, so I'm asking for your forgiveness. Being bitter and angry won't help you in the long run. It may feel good for a while, but I know from experience that you won't be able to move on until you let this go. Until then, you'll be miserable. Forgiving me is part of that process. I will always regret what I have done, but we both need to move forward with our lives now. Can you forgive me, Richard? Can you put this behind you?"

Richard looked at her tear-streaked face, and he knew that she was right. Suddenly, he was very tired, and all he wanted was for the pain to stop. *Lord, I have hurt for so long. I can't stand it anymore. If forgiving Caroline is the only way for me to stop this agony, please help me to do it. And, Lord, please take away my love for El. Help me to see other women, and not just her. She is lost to me forever, Lord, and I must not love her in that way anymore.*

Gabriel smiled. *The Spirit is at work here.*

Garnet rubbed Richard's back. *You must do this, Richard. You must forgive her. She is truly sorry. Remember that you are not blameless in this.*

Richard gazed at her for a long moment, and then he spoke slowly and deliberately.

"I am trying very hard to forgive you, Caroline, and I know that I'll get there eventually, but it won't be tonight. I also want to believe that you have changed. I wish that you had told me the whole truth before I found it out, but I can sort of understand why you didn't. I didn't tell El the whole truth either when the whole mess happened. I hoped she would never find out that I slept with you. I was just too humiliated and embarrassed, and I was afraid of losing her." He paused for a moment, and then released a heavy sigh. "I think that it will be best if we don't talk for a while. Give me a chance to deal with this in my own way, and I'll let you know when I'm ready to be your friend again. Please pray for me."

Caroline managed a small smile. "Thank you, Richard. I can't expect any more than that. I will certainly pray for you, and I know that God will help you, just as He has helped me. I'll wait to hear from you. I really hope that we can be friends."

Michael thought, *They have been back here long enough. People are starting to miss them.*

Do whatever you think is best. They are finished, answered Niall.

Michael walked around the tree and smiled at them. "Is everything all right? Is there anything that I can do to help you?"

Richard spoke up quickly, "Everything is fine. We're just catching up. We'll be out in a minute."

Caroline added, "There's no problem, Michael." She had been introduced to Xander's brothers at the rehearsal dinner the night before, and she looked from Michael to Richard. "Have you two met?"

"No, I have not had that pleasure," Michael answered, extending his hand to Richard. "I am Michael, Xander's brother. Come and meet our other two brothers."

They shook hands as Richard said, "I am Richard Williams, a long-time friend of El. We grew up together."

"Wonderful to meet you, Richard. I know Gabriel and Niall would want to be introduced to you, too. Come with me."

Caroline spoke softly, "I need to go to the ladies' room. I'll be right back."

"I'll see you later, then," said Richard over his shoulder as he walked out from behind the tree, following Michael. Caroline left in the opposite direction.

Michael and Richard stopped in front of the tree, and Niall extended his hand, saying, "Hello, my name is Niall, and this is my brother, Gabriel."

"I'm Richard. It's nice to meet you," said Richard, shaking Niall's hand, and then Gabriel's.

Elizabeth spotted them and smiled, waving her hand. "Richard, come over here. There's someone that I want you to meet."

"It seems that I'm in demand this evening. Maybe I can talk more with you in a little while, but I have to do as the bride says, I think," said Richard, laughing a little halfheartedly.

"Of course," said Gabriel, as Richard strode to Elizabeth.

Richard stopped short when he saw the beautiful young woman standing by Elizabeth at the punch table. He recognized her as one of the bridesmaids, but he had watched Elizabeth during the ceremony, never sparing a glance for anyone else. He could see a faint family resemblance in their features, but the woman was probably five inches shorter than Elizabeth, blonde, and green-eyed. For the first time in more than three years, he felt an attraction for a woman other than Elizabeth, and he knew that God had answered his prayer.

Elizabeth smiled when she saw his expression. "Richard, this is my cousin, Bethany Martin. She teaches at Liberty Academy in Lynchburg."

Richard could be charming when he wished to be, and when Bethany smiled at him in greeting, he very much wanted to be attractive to her.

As Bethany shook his hand, Richard's face lit up with a wonderful smile, and he said, "El, where have you been hiding her? I thought I had met all of your family."

"She's my Aunt Grace's daughter from her first marriage, so she traveled back and forth between Aunt Grace and Uncle Scott quite a bit. Also, Bethany is four years older than I am, so we never really got to spend much time together when we were younger. She's become one of my closest friends in recent years, though," Elizabeth replied, grinning and giving her cousin a warm side-hug. "We've been burning up the phone lines between here and Virginia."

Richard did the mental math. *Bethany is not quite two years older than I am, then. I've just turned twenty-one and she's twenty-two. That's not bad.*

"El told me that you're a Marine, Richard. Where are you stationed?" asked Bethany, releasing his hand.

"I'm in San Diego right now. How do you like teaching school?" he asked, reaching for a cup of punch.

They rapidly became so engrossed in their conversation that neither of them noticed when Xander stepped to Elizabeth's side and claimed her for a picture of him removing her garter.

Elizabeth sat in a chair provided for her in the center of the room. She had placed the blue garter just above her knee, and there was much good-natured laughter as Xander carefully slid her dress up her leg to find it. Finally, he slipped it off her leg and stood, calling for all the single men to stand in front of him. After the young men were in place, Xander turned his back and shot the garter – straight into Richard's hands.

Xander moved the chair, and Lynne handed Elizabeth a separate arrangement of flowers, tied with a green silk ribbon which had been specially set aside for the bouquet toss. Elizabeth gaily asked for all the single women to gather, and the married women helped her by pulling the unwilling ones to the middle of the room with much giggling.

Elizabeth turned and tossed her bouquet over her head. When she heard a squeal, she whirled around to see it in the hands of her cousin, Bethany Martin.

"Now we have to have a shot of the two of you," Elizabeth said, calling for the photographer.

As Richard and Bethany stood together, smiling for the camera, Elizabeth returned to her husband's side.

"I think that was a good day's work," she said a little smugly.

"I think you may be right," he replied, kissing her cheek as Lynne, Grace, and Delores grabbed their cameras to take pictures of the couple.

"Shall we leave now, Mrs. Xander?" he asked, smiling at his lovely wife.

"I do believe we can, Mr. Xander. Mom packed a hamper for us and put it in your car, and I think we have talked to everyone and had all the pictures made that anyone could possibly want. I'm ready to go spend our first night together in our home. I'm very tired, you know. I'm looking forward to a good night's sleep before we head out to – where is it we're going in the morning?" she asked innocently, her brown eyes wide and merry.

"That is still a surprise, and I think we must do something to wake you up as it is much too early to think of sleep," he whispered in her ear.

"I know! We could do a training session! That always raises my energy level," she teased.

"Oh, yes. A training session. That is exactly what I have in mind," he answered, bending to kiss her lips quickly.

Michael, Gabriel, and Niall walked up behind them.

Michael cleared his throat.

Do not say a word, Michael. They are married before God and man. They have taken vows and signed the marriage license, thought Gabriel.

This will take some adjustment on my part, thought Michael.

I hope you are able to adjust quickly, chuckled Niall.

Just remember that you agreed to turn your back and be very, very quiet, answered Xander.

That will not be a problem. I plan to spend at least a week with my back turned, said Michael.

Make it two, answered Xander.

Agreed, replied Gabriel.

Elizabeth spoke to her mother and father, kissing them goodbye, and David had the DJ announce that the couple was leaving. Everyone gathered outside to toss the birdseed that had been handed out at the reception by the flower girls.

Joshua Lucas drove Xander's Escalade up to the door, and Xander raised his eyebrows. His car was decorated with signs, and there were old shoes tied to the bumper. Their status as newlyweds would certainly be no secret.

The freshly minted Mr. and Mrs. Xander ran from the building to the car through a shower of birdseed. Xander opened the door for his bride, being careful of her train, and then walked rapidly around to get in himself. The happy couple waved to their family and friends as they drove away.

Xander and Elizabeth left with substitute guardians and warriors flying overhead. Michael, Niall, and Gabriel had arranged for Jonathan to drive them to the only hotel in town. From there they would change forms and fly back to guard their charges. Until that time, Michael had assigned a full contingent of warriors to surround Xander's house while the guardians would station themselves inside the house.

For all his bluster, Michael was determined that nothing would disturb the happiness of his brother and sister on their wedding night.

Chapter 9

"So the Lord God caused a deep sleep to fall upon the man, and he slept; then He took one of his ribs, and closed up the flesh at that place. And the Lord God fashioned into a woman the rib which He had taken from the man, and brought her to the man. And the man said, 'This is now bone of my bones, and flesh of my flesh; she shall be called Woman, because she was taken out of Man.' For this cause a man shall leave his father and his mother, and shall cleave to his wife; and they shall become one flesh. And the man and his wife were both naked and were not ashamed."
Genesis 2:21-25

The happy couple left their reception under a heavy angelic escort and drove straight to their house only a couple of miles away. When they arrived, Xander got out and came around to open the door for his bride. She took his hand and stepped carefully from the car, taking care to retrieve the train of her wedding dress so that it would not be caught in the door. Hand-in-hand they walked up the steps to their home, pausing on the wrap-around porch so he could unlock the door. He pushed the door open, and then turned and caught Elizabeth up in his arms.

As warriors quickly surrounded the outside of the house and guardians preceded them into the hallway, Elizabeth giggled a little in surprise at Xanders's actions. She graced him with a lovely smile. "Such a superstitious groom!"

"I will carry my bride over the threshold as is the custom. All of the traditions have been observed so far, and this one will be as well," he replied, smiling.

"By all means. Let it not be said that we did not do everything properly and in order," she teased in return.

"While I do not believe in bad luck, I will acknowledge that having you trip over the door sill in that gown could put a damper on our honeymoon," he replied, still holding his bride.

"You have a point, my husband," she laughed.

"I also will make certain that my bride is not kidnapped by anyone other than her lawful husband – namely me. I like the idea that we are now a family, starting a new life together," said Xander as he took her into the house.

He pushed the door closed with his foot and kissed her hungrily, still holding her tightly in his arms at the foot of the stairs.

When they were both out of breath, he lifted his head and whispered into her ear, "I have wanted to do that all day. Now I can kiss you as much as I want, any time I want. I can relate to the man in *Sweet Home, Alabama.* You are finally *mine.*"

She brushed his cheek with her lips. "And you are mine. As much as I am enjoying this, are you ever going to put me down? I would like to change, and you could bring in my luggage and the hamper. Aren't you hungry?"

Xander's smile was a little crooked. He pursed his lips and said, "Oh, I am hungry. But if you want your bags and the food, I suppose we could eat." He placed her on her feet and drew her to him. "You asked me for something a little while ago, and I did as you wished. I changed forms for you. Will you now do something for me?"

Her head was nestled under his chin. She took a step back and looked up at him, smiling. "You have a fantasy? Tell me about it. This is fascinating."

He lifted her chin with his fingers and kissed her lightly on the lips. "I have a whole host of fantasies, Elizabeth, and you are featured in all of them. But I have a special one right now. The idea took root when I saw you walking down the aisle toward me, and it has grown over the course of the evening."

"I have complete confidence in you, my love. I know that whatever you want would never hurt me. Name it, and I will do my best to fulfill it," she replied, looking him full in the eyes. "This is ... new territory for both of us," Elizabeth whispered shyly, as he drew her close. "But my mother –"

He nibbled her ear. "Yes, love?" he murmured. "What about your mother?"

"She has told me about … you know. This."

Xander pulled back, smiling. "Elizabeth," he said, with mock severity. "I seem to recall your watching *The Notebook* with Charlotte. That movie was fairly explicit."

"Yes, but you have guarded so many people," she said. "And even though you're a –"

Elizabeth hesitated, humming to guard her thoughts. She dipped her head coyly, but there was laughter in her eyes.

"What," he said, completely hooked. "Go on. I am a – what exactly am I?"

Smiling, she spread her hands. "You always bring up movies."

"And –" he prompted.

"And it occurred to me that, well ... even though you're a 'ten thousand year old virgin,' you certainly have more knowledge than I."

"There is a way to remedy our deficiencies, Elizabeth," he said, blue eyes twinkling. "We must practice until we are proficient."

"Oh, that's a good point."

"Then, do you agree it is time to begin to address our education?" he asked, smiling.

"I place myself in your capable hands," she said, looking up at him.

He took her shoulders and turned her toward the stairs. Red rose petals were scattered up the steps.

"We shall follow the trail, then," he said, scooping her up into his arms again.

Elizabeth chuckled as he carried her up the stairs. "I'm beginning to think I may never have to walk anywhere again." She began to kiss his neck, and he stopped on the landing.

Xander's voice was low. "Unless you want my fantasy to be lived out right here, you may want to stop kissing me until I get you upstairs."

"You have iron control; I am not worried," Elizabeth said, though she resorted to leaning her head on his shoulder rather than kissing him.

The rose petal trail continued through an open door, and he carried her into the room. She looked around, amazed. The room was in perfect order. His massive bed stood against one wall, the covers turned down to reveal the sheets strewn with rose petals as well. Music played softly through speakers mounted behind an antique screen which had belonged to her grandmother.

He lowered her gently to her feet, and she turned in a slow circle. "You've hung the curtains and cleared away all the boxes. It's wonderful, Xander! When did you do all this?" Her enchantment was obvious.

"My brothers and I put all of the boxes in one of the downstairs bedrooms. We cleaned up the house earlier today so that you would not be coming into a mess tonight. I did not want you to be distracted or feeling that you needed to work," he said, smiling at her.

She saw her luggage by the closet door and the hamper on a small round table beside the bed. The table was covered with a lovely embroidered tablecloth and bore an old-fashioned lamp which glowed softly. "I assumed my things were in your car. How did you manage this?" she asked, gesturing to the luggage and hamper.

"Chance and Janna brought the luggage and hamper over while we were having the last of the pictures made. Living so close to the church and your parents has its advantages," he answered.

"You, Xander Darcy, love of my life, are amazing," she said, stepping to him and reaching up to put her arms around his neck.

"My strategy appears to be working already," he replied, exploring the back of her dress with his hands.

Michael and Gabriel arrived, floating through the walls, settling to the floor, and tucking their wings. They immediately separated, walking to the two windows and facing them to look outside through the sheer curtains. The guardians they replaced flew through the ceiling, back to heaven to receive their next assignments from Asim.

"What are you doing?" she asked with curiosity.

"Trying to figure out how to take your wedding dress off you without destroying it in the process. I thought that you might want to keep it," he answered. "I have been looking at it for the last several hours, attempting to see how it fastens, but it seems to be quite intricate. We should have worn simpler clothing," he said.

"Oh," she answered. *I think I am beginning to understand at least part of your fantasy.*

It is not very complicated, love. I have not seen you unclothed since you were quite young, at which point I determined, even then as your guardian, not to allow myself to look on you when you were undressed. Now that you are finally my wife, I want to undress you myself the first time.

I would have needed your help in any case. I could never get out of this dress by myself, she thought.

Xander answered, *I have made every effort over this long, wonderful day not to think of undressing you. I did not know how you would feel about it since I have not even seen you in a swimsuit since I assumed human form. Had I realized that you already knew that you would need my help in removing your dress, it would have been very difficult to control my thoughts all day.*

I never thought about it because it was a foregone conclusion. She turned her back to him. "There are snaps and fasteners under the bow. The train lifts away to expose the zipper." She looked back over her shoulder. "You know, I *do* have an absolutely beautiful nightgown."

He was already through all of the snaps and working on the fasteners. The zipper quickly followed. "I am sure that you will look stunning in it, too, love. Later, though. Much later."

Xander kissed her neck, turned her to face him, and softly guided the dress off her shoulders. He watched as it fell to the floor. Elizabeth stepped out of the dress and stood before her husband, clad only in her under garments. He stood silently in awe, unable to speak, and his chest tightened as he looked at his beautiful wife. He had known she was perfection, and that her form would please him, but nothing could have prepared him for the glorious sight before him. He reached out and embraced her, hoping she felt all the love he had to give her in that moment. *You are altogether beautiful, my love. Words are not enough.*

After a few moments, Elizabeth pulled back and looked up at him with a slight frown on her lovely face.

"Xander," she said in a slightly petulant voice.

"Hmmm?" he answered, leaning in to kiss her neck while removing the pins from her hair.

"This is not fair," she replied as her hair fell in curls around her shoulders.

Using all of his considerable willpower, he stopped kissing her long enough to look into her face. Her expression was not happy, but her pout was adorable.

"What is the matter, Elizabeth? Have I done something wrong?" He drew his brows together and forced himself to look no lower than her eyes. He quoted from I Corinthians 13 in his mind, *'Love is patient, love is kind ... does not seek its own ... love never fails.'* Patience, patience.

"Well – it's just that – one of us is overdressed, and it can't possibly be me," she said, a small wrinkle appearing between her brows. "I hope this wasn't your fantasy – you in a tux and me in – very little."

Xander smiled in understanding, showing both dimples. "I never thought about myself much in the fantasy, Elizabeth." He began to remove his jacket. *You cannot be embarrassed, Elizabeth. You are exquisite.*

She stopped his hands. "Oh, no, you don't. Turnabout is fair play. I have been cooperative while you lived out one of your dreams. Shouldn't I get to live one of mine, too?"

"By all means, love. What shall I do?" he asked, smiling as he dropped his arms to his sides.

"Turn around," she commanded. "I'm going to unwrap my present now."

"Do you need any help?" he asked, giving her his broad back.

"You'll be the first to know if I do," she promised, reaching up to pull his coat from his shoulders.

She walked around him to face him and started unbuttoning his vest and his shirt. "You know, Xander, I've worked out with you for six months while you wore that tank top and sweatpants. I'm sure that I didn't control my thoughts all the time, especially before I knew that you could read my mind. What was I trying not to think? You must remember."

Xander did remember, and she was working much too slowly to suit him. He moved his hands to his chest to help her with the buttons, and she batted them away.

"I told you that I would ask for help when I needed it. I think I can handle a few buttons," she teased. When she finished removing his shirt and vest, she bit her lip. She had seen him in a tank top, but never without a shirt of any sort. *Good grief, you are beautiful.* Another thought escaped. *You are perfect.* She looked at his muscled, sculpted chest, and her eyes dropped to his well-defined torso. Her hands covered her mouth, and her heart thudded as her courage deserted her. *Okay. I think I need help now.*

Are you sure? he asked, standing motionless, careful not to smile. *Because I thought you were doing a fine job. Please continue. I would by no means suspend any pleasure of yours.*

No, I think I'll just wait for you over here. She dove for the bed and pulled up the covers, watching him.

He took off his shoes and socks, walked to the bed, and sat on his side of it, looking into her sparkling eyes as they peeped at him over the comforter.

"That bed looks so much better with you in it," Xander said, thinking of all the times he had imagined her there. "May I join you?"

"Nope," she said in a small voice.

"No?" he asked, drawing out the single syllable as he raised his eyebrows in surprise. "Why not?"

"You are still overdressed," she said. *Have mercy, Xander. Please don't make me spell it out for you. Help me – please. Just because I could not yet undress you fully myself...it doesn't mean that I don't want you to be...oh, you know what I want. Stop teasing me!*

"Ah, now you have fulfilled another part of *my* fantasy," he replied as he removed his trousers.

She pulled the comforter down under her chin and turned toward him. Her eyes widened in wonder as she watched her husband get into bed and under the covers with her. *You really are magnificent,* she thought.

Abruptly, Elizabeth's thoughts jerked back to his statement, and she blurted out, "Really? You wanted me to chicken out?"

Xander laughed a little as he reached for her and pulled her to his side. "No, love. I wanted you to ask me to disrobe. I wanted you to desire to see me as much as I have wanted to see you. You have been … upsetting my equilibrium … for so many years, Elizabeth. It is unbelievably satisfying to know that I finally have the same effect on you."

"I haven't disappointed you, then?" she asked, placing her hands in his hair and drawing his face to hers.

"Not possible, love," he said as he kissed her, stroking her back, delighting in her soft, bare skin, and in the feeling of her relaxing in his arms.

Elizabeth found many things for which to be thankful in the next few hours, and she discovered, to her husband's delight, that she especially liked his gift of mental telepathy. What she could not put into words concerning their connection, he was able to know from her thoughts. Xander, in turn, shared more of his mind with her than he ever had before. When he thought, *With my body, I thee worship*, she knew that he meant it.

You truly complete me, Elizabeth, he thought. *You understand me as no one else ever has. Only God could love you more than I do.*

Michael and Gabriel were so still and silent that Xander was almost able to forget that they were there.

~~oo~~

Just before dawn, while the room was still in darkness, Xander watched his wife sleep. He had never known such complete contentment in all of his long existence. She was everything he had ever dreamed she would be and more. Her eyelids fluttered open as if she felt his gaze upon her, and she awakened, feeling his warmth in the last hour of the night.

Mmmm…I'm not at my best in the morning. It's a good thing you can't see me now, or you would take back all those complimentary things you said last night about how beautiful I am, she thought as she stretched.

You are just as breathtaking on the wings of the dawn as you are at any other time. Your hair is tousled around your face, and your eyes are sleepy. You have never been more alluring to me than you are at this moment, Xander replied.

You are saying that only because you can't see what a mess I look, she answered.

"I can see you perfectly, Elizabeth," he said, lifting her hair with his hand and watching it slide through his fingers like curled silk.

"What? You can see in the dark?" she asked, lifting her head to look in the direction of his voice.

"Psalm 139:12 says, 'Even the darkness is not dark to Thee, and the night is as bright as the day. Darkness and light are alike to Thee.' God can see in the dark, and so can His angels," he said, as if it were nothing to be surprised about.

She was quiet a moment. "That does make perfect sense. How could you guard people at night if you couldn't see them? I wonder if I'll ever know all there is to know about you."

"We have at least two hours before we have to leave for the airport. You could spend part of that time getting to know me better." He smiled at his wife through the darkness. "I am a little tired, but I am willing to sacrifice myself for the greater good, and we can sleep on the plane," he answered her, pulling her into his arms again.

She grinned a little. "That's my angel. Always willing to put me first, never thinking of himself, wearing himself out in my pursuit of knowledge. I think I could get used to waking up this way."

"I keep hoping that as long as there are new things for you to know about me, I will never become boring to you," he replied, laying her back on her pillow to kiss her more fully.

Not possible, love, she thought.

I may have my back turned for years at this rate, grumbled Michael.

Be quiet, admonished Gabriel.

Do something useful. Send some warriors to take the signs and shoes off my car while it is still dark and no one can see them, thought Xander.

Done, answered Michael, glad to have some occupation to take his attention.

~~oo~~

Xander was amused to watch the excitement of his new wife as they boarded the plane. She continued to pepper him with questions regarding their destination, and he was enjoying giving her outlandish answers.

He was unable to fly coach comfortably because of his size, so the couple had opted to fly first class. Michael and Gabriel stood beside them as they settled into their seats.

Elizabeth knew from the flight arrival and departure screens in their gate that they were going to Fort Lauderdale, but beyond that, her guesses had been wide of the mark.

"The Miami Seaquarium? A condo on the beach? A drive to Key West? Scuba diving lessons? Splitting our time between the beach and Disney World?" Her guesses ranged from the sublime to the ridiculous.

About halfway to Florida, she hit closer to the answer. "A cruise? I know that cruise ships leave Port Everglades."

Xander made no answer, and that told her that she was on the right track.

"Lucky for me that you cannot lie," she laughed.

"I wanted to surprise you," he said, looking at her with puppy dog eyes which melted her heart.

"Then I will stop guessing. That way, our destination will be a secret until we board the ship. I'm so excited, Xander. I've never been on a cruise before, and I've always wanted to go on one!" She then paused a moment, thinking.

"But aren't the rooms sort of small for you? Will you be comfortable?" she asked in genuine concern.

He chuckled. "Elizabeth, we are cruising in the off-season. Deluxe suites are very reasonable at this time of year, and they are quite luxurious. The beds are queen-sized, not so big as mine, but I think I will be able to adjust and suffer through the ordeal."

"A suite! It probably has a balcony, too. Oh, I've planned my dream vacation online and looked at the ships!" She looked at him with sudden comprehension. "You knew that, didn't you? You're taking me on my winter cruise to someplace warm – the vacation I've always wanted!" Unheeding of the crowded plane, Elizabeth threw her arms around his neck and kissed him enthusiastically.

He was glad for the relative privacy of first class. The flight attendant raised an eyebrow as she watched them from the front of the aisle, stopping beside them with the drink cart.

"We are newlyweds," said Xander quietly to her, blushing.

I don't think I've ever seen a man blush – and so becomingly. I can't say I blame his new wife for staking her claim publicly. He is absolutely gorgeous, she thought, smiling at the couple.

"Would you like anything to drink?" she asked.

"Water for me," answered Elizabeth, settling back in her seat, returning the woman's smile and holding his hand in her lap. *She's thinking I've caught myself a handsome husband, isn't she? She's right, but she can't know that you're even more amazing on the inside. I love you so much.*

He blushed again, though he knew the attendant could not hear Elizabeth's thoughts. "Water for me, too," he said politely. *You are bold when we are in public, and I cannot do anything in response.*

I think you will find that I am over my embarrassment of last night, my love. Her expression was a little smug.

Xander handed her the water bottle and plastic cup. *I thought you were charming, Elizabeth, though I have no doubt that I will enjoy all of your changing moods when we are alone.*

~~oo~~

Xander and Elizabeth did everything together that she had imagined doing on a cruise to the Bahamas. They swam in the ship's heated pool, snorkeled among the tropical fish, relaxed in the hot tub, danced every night, ate at a secluded table each evening, explored the open markets, took a tour of the island, rented jet skis, and even tried their hands at playing steel drums with a local band. Elizabeth kept her curls under a floppy hat most of the time, and Xander dressed down in jeans and cotton shirts during the day. When they weren't busy with some outdoor activity, they kept to themselves in their suite, enjoying their hours alone with each other.

It was a carefree time, full of the joy of new love, which they would remember often in the years to come.

Chapter 10

"Therefore be careful how you walk, not as unwise men, but as wise, making the most of your time, because the days are evil."
Ephesians 5:15-16

February 2009

Xander and Elizabeth watched a cable news channel one night as Gregory Wickham, junior Senator from Massachusetts, was being interviewed by Dirk Horne. Michael and Gabriel stood behind the couch where their charges sat, intensely interested in what their enemy had to say.

Horne asked Senator Wickham what he saw as the most pressing problem in the United States, and the handsome Senator began his answer with a treatise on the abundance of poverty, hunger, and sickness throughout the country, quoting statistics, demographics, and individuals he had met while touring the heartland recently. Charts and pictures flashed on the right of the screen while the camera focused on his face, filling the other half. The subtle aging of his features had only improved his looks, making him seem more intelligent, mature, and thoughtful rather than youthful and impulsive. Though he represented Massachusetts in the Senate, Senator Wickham made it quite clear that he saw his role as one who sought what was best for the entire country and ultimately, the world.

As the cameras panned to capture both men seated comfortably in a living room setting, Senator Wickham continued to speak earnestly, his eyes full of compassion for the suffering of his countrymen.

"Dirk, people are hurting. Gas prices are sky high, unemployment is at record numbers, and businesses are fleeing the country, going overseas to take advantage of cheap labor and low taxes. Something must be done quickly; people are losing hope."

Dirk Horne looked suitably concerned in his expensive suit, every hair in its proper place. "What do you propose, Senator?"

Senator Wickham leaned forward, emphasizing his eagerness to solve the problems facing his nation. "I am introducing a bill that will virtually eliminate poverty, hunger, unemployment, and sickness in the United States. Desperate times call for desperate measures, and this bill will address a badly needed overhaul of the way our government operates. It is too complicated to explain in full during the short time that we have, Dirk, but people need to understand that help is on the way. We will provide jobs and healthcare for all of our citizens. Emergency measures will be put in place to distribute food and clothing to the needy; shelters will be provided for the homeless in every city; free clinics will be multiplied."

"What are the chances of actually passing this controversial bill, Senator?" asked Dirk, drawing his brows together.

Gregory's eyes narrowed just the tiniest bit. "The odds are excellent that the bill will pass on the first vote, Dirk. Some very powerful people have joined with me, and a twin bill is being introduced simultaneously by my colleagues in the House. Opposing this bill will mean political suicide for any who try to stand against it."

Xander grimaced and said tersely, "The suicide would be more than political, I would think."

Elizabeth's responding laugh held no mirth. "I wonder if the opposition already understands that they have no chance of defeating Gregory. Could they possibly know how much power he has?"

"If they do not know it now, they soon will. A few of the Senators and Congressmen have powerful guardians, and they will survive this, but most of our political leaders are non-believers. They turned their backs on the Almighty long ago, thinking that they could handle everything on their own. They will soon find how unwise a thing it was to reject the only source of help Who could defeat Lucifer," replied Xander.

Michael immediately dispatched extra warriors to protect the Senators and Representatives who were believers. The warriors would fight alongside the politicians' guardians.

Dirk directed another question to Gregory. "You mentioned providing jobs, Senator. Could you tell us a little about that part of your plan?"

"Certainly, Dirk," answered Gregory. "We intend to require two years of military or humanitarian service from every high school graduate who chooses not to attend college. College graduates who are unable to find work within six months of their graduation will submit to the same requirement. There will be no more gangs of unemployed young people causing havoc in our cities, stressing both our public safety net and our public defenders. So you see, the benefits both to them and to our country will be great – we will have the strongest military in the world, and these young Americans will have meaningful employment. Humanitarian service is an option for those who conscientiously oppose military service. Those young people can choose to serve in organizations such as the Peace Corps or the domestic equivalent, Peace U.S.A. By taking these young people out of the job market, we will greatly increase the availability of jobs for others seeking work. These are only the first steps in our push toward sustainable employment."

"That sounds wonderful, Senator. Thank you for being with us tonight and sharing this good news," said Dirk as both men rose and shook hands. The camera zoomed in on Dirk Horne's face as he announced the next segment of the program and went to a commercial.

Xander pointed the remote toward the television and turned it off.

"In other words," he said, "the government plans to take more and more control of people's lives under the guise of taking care of them. Citizens will give up the right to make their own decisions in exchange for a promise of security and happiness."

"And anyone who stands in Gregory's way will be eliminated or rendered powerless," added Elizabeth.

"Exactly. And this is only the beginning," replied Xander.

"How much time do you think we have?" asked Elizabeth.

"As much as God chooses to grant us. He said that He would not allow Lucifer to force His hand before the time is full. Gregory is still building his power base. It is obvious that he plans to run for President in 2012, unless he can aim even higher than that. If he can manage to convince the nations to come together in a global government with him at the head of it, he will. I expect that we have four or five years until we will have to act," answered Xander, taking Elizabeth into his arms.

"Why do we have to wait? Why can we not stop him now?" she asked, snuggling onto his lap.

"Because it is not God's plan for us to intervene at this time. For whatever reason, He is choosing to let this play out, and we must trust Him," he replied.

"What should we do?" Elizabeth turned her face up to her husband's, looking into his eyes.

"We shall do what He has told us to do. We will continue with the rallies as planned while we still have religious freedom. We must bring all the souls to our Father that we can. Even if Gregory's bills are passed, it will take a couple of years for the changes to be fully implemented. The machinery of government moves slowly. I suspect that he will not suspend the Bill of Rights completely until he sets up a world government. We must continue in God's work as long as we can do so freely. We must work even harder. In a few years, we may have to meet secretly, or we may even face persecution." Xander drew Elizabeth to his chest, resting his chin on her head.

She was very quiet. *I want to have children before we die or are raptured. Am I selfish?*

He gently turned her face up to his with his fingers. "You are not selfish, my love. God wants us to have a child. Our child will be very special, and I suspect that he or she will be quite important in His plan." He kissed her lips gently. "We are very serious tonight, and the sky is too beautiful for us to brood. You should dress in warm clothes; I have an idea." He kissed her again, and then stood with her cradled in his arms. She put her arms around his neck as he carried her to their bedroom.

Michael and Gabriel followed closely behind them.

He placed her on her feet before her dresser, and she looked up at him with a question in her eyes. "What is your idea? How should I dress?"

"You told me before we married that there was something you wanted us to do. There is almost no moon tonight, and because of the cloud cover, it is very dark. I think it is a good time to fulfill your wish, so wear a sweatshirt and sweatpants. Put on your Under Armor ColdGear first, because it is very cold outside," he answered, smiling.

"Are you taking me flying?" she asked, excited.

"Would you like to fly tonight? It really is cold," he answered.

Is this a good plan, Xander? What if she sickens? You have a rally this coming weekend, thought Michael.

"Yes, yes, yes! I'll get my warmest things and dress in layers," Elizabeth said, starting to rummage through her drawers.

"Good, because your guardian thinks that it is too cold, and that I should not risk your health. He is a mother hen," laughed Xander.

I am not. It is my job to watch over my charge. Michael looked very stern.

We will fly with them, Michael, thought Gabriel. *You will know if she is cold, and we can quickly return.*

That is true, Michael answered.

"Michael, I will be fine. I'll put on so many layers that Xander will have trouble finding me under all the clothing," Elizabeth said, pulling on her sweats as she spoke. "Besides, all three of you will be with me. I will have the most powerful protection imaginable, and if I so much as shiver, I'm sure you will all make certain that we return immediately."

She understands the situation, Michael, thought Gabriel. *She will agree to come back here without any argument if the need arises.*

I still think it would be a good idea to wait until the weather is warmer, Michael answered. *However, I see that I am the only one who thinks so.*

Xander chuckled, and Elizabeth turned to look at him.

"Do I look funny, love?" she asked, making a face. "I think I have on four or five layers."

"No, you are always beautiful. I am laughing at Michael. He worries more than Mom, and that is saying a great deal," he answered.

He took her hand and led her down the stairs and out the back door, Michael and Gabriel following them. Xander became concerned when Elizabeth exhaled and he could see her breath.

"Perhaps Michael has a point," he said. "We could wait a few months until it is warmer. We will have to fly above the clouds to avoid being seen, and the temperatures are even lower at that altitude."

"Oh, no, you don't. I'm warm to the point of a meltdown. I want to fly. I promise not to block my thoughts – no 'Amazing Grace' concert. You'll know if I'm cold," she answered adamantly.

You will never deny her anything she wants as long as it is in your power to grant it, thought Michael.

I would if it was best for her, answered Xander. *She is being reasonable. We will all be able to read her thoughts.*

Holding hands, they walked further from the house into a grove of trees. Xander released Elizabeth's hand, took a step back from her, and transformed.

"I will never get used to seeing you as an angel," she whispered, reaching out to touch his radiant face. "You are so beautiful that my heart aches."

"I can change forms inside where it is warm if you wish when we return. However, if we are to fly tonight, we should leave now. I will not keep you out long in this weather." Xander quickly unfurled his wings and gathered her into his arms, taking flight with Michael and Gabriel on either side of them.

They streaked to an altitude just above the clouds, careful to remain low enough so that Elizabeth could breathe easily. She clung to her husband, turning her head to look beneath them, catching glimpses of ground through breaks in the clouds. Looking above them, she could see stars twinkling like diamonds in the blackness of the moonless night.

Is that Spartanburg already? How fast are we flying? Elizabeth asked.

I have no idea. Speed means very little to us. We can fly as fast as is required by any given circumstances. For instance, if we are summoned to heaven, we cover the distance in a few seconds. We are flying rather slowly now so that you can see. Your eyes would perceive only a blur if we increased our velocity much more than this, he answered.

It would not be blurred to your eyes? she asked.

No. We always see with minute detail, no matter how fast we fly. That is Charlotte, North Carolina, below us now, said Xander.

Elizabeth looked at the city lights, recognizing the downtown area by the distinctive pattern of the intersecting freeways, and then she was distracted by the sight of her husband's wings moving to a streamlined position behind him. They dove for a few seconds, and then he began to glide just beneath the clouds.

The lights of the city keep anyone from seeing us, he thought to her.

Do you see that black area? asked Gabriel.

Demons. There must be hundreds of them to create an absence of light covering that much space, answered Michael.

The darkness is spreading rapidly. We have stumbled upon a meeting in a new place, said Xander to his brothers. He banked quickly to fly in the opposite direction, hugging his wife more closely to him. The guardian pulled up short, hovering in the air when he saw a dark army advancing rapidly upon them. *We are too late to avoid a confrontation, Michael.*

It would appear so, answered Michael curtly, positioning himself in front of Xander and Elizabeth.

Gabriel remained behind them, facing away from them to see any demons approaching from the rear.

Michael immediately summoned a phalanx of warriors. Within a second, the battle lines were drawn. The light faced the darkness.

Why have we stopped, Xander? What is happening? asked Elizabeth, seeing the deep blackness, but not understanding it. Then suddenly, she felt the overpowering evil, one hundred times worse than what she had known in her room two years before. It crept around her, smothering her; she could not breathe. Her mind refused to function as the terror enveloped her.

Xander heard her mind scream. He knew that she was senseless with fear, and he was horrified that he had exposed her to the evil. *Elizabeth, there are demons, but you are safe. Michael has called out the warriors, and you are in no danger. Believe me, my love, and have no fear. They mean to frighten you; they feed on your feelings of helplessness. Trust in Jehovah, Elizabeth. There is no death angel here; it is not your time.*

She turned her face into his chest and began to pray. *Lord, I believe. Please help my unbelief. Help me not to fear.* She remembered Isaiah 35:4 and quoted it in her mind, *'Say to those with palpitating heart, Take courage, fear not. Behold, your God will come with vengeance; the recompense of God will come, but He will save you.'* More boldly she said to God, *Father, Isaiah 43:1 says, 'Do not fear, for I have redeemed you; I have called you by name; you are Mine!' Heavenly Father, you know my name! I am yours! Thank you for restoring my joy and taking away my fear.*

Every holy angel heard her mind, and they smiled as they faced the enemy.

Let us pass, commanded Michael, *or we will unbody you.*

You are in our territory. We want the girl, spoke Ryu, underprince of the southeastern United States. His voice was harsh and guttural, and his eyes blazed with fury as his long red hair flowed down his back. Tala, his captain, sneered from beside the underprince.

The air is claimed by no one, and you have changed your meeting place. We were not aware that you had taken any new part of the city. We are over the downtown area, not the lost neighborhoods, answered Michael, his green eyes piercing the demon while his hand moved to grasp the hilt of his sword. Every warrior replicated his action.

Ryu laughed derisively, and his laughter was repeated throughout his ranks. *We own all of Charlotte now, and the Dark Lord is the Prince of the Power of the Air. You will give us the girl and leave this area.*

Michael did not flinch. *Lucifer is the god of this world, but the airspace has always been free for both light and dark beings. You do not set the rules. The Creator of the Universes decides what will be. You will not touch Elizabeth, for she belongs to Him. Move from our path, and we will leave. If you do not move, we will cut our way through you.* Michael smiled as if the thought pleased him exceedingly.

The Captain of the Host flew forward slightly, and his entire front line advanced with him. Ranks closed in around Xander and Elizabeth, and Gabriel was joined by a line in the rear.

Think, Ryu, though I know that takes a great effort on your part. I have three times more warriors at my disposal than does Lucifer, and I can call all of them if necessary. You do not command all of Satan's troops. I would think that every demon available to you is with you now.

Michael issued a silent command and another phalanx appeared, doubling his army.

Michael sighed. *I grow weary of this. Draw your swords, or part your ranks and let us pass. I will give you five earth seconds to make a decision.*

Ryu glared at him with hatred burning from his eyes.

Four… three… two, counted Michael slowly as the tension mounted.

We will have the girl! shouted Ryu, shaking his fists.

You will not! And that was a threat to my charge. I now have just cause to attack, replied Michael, drawing his sword. The hiss of angelic weapons being unsheathed filled the air. Elizabeth lifted her head at the sound, looking toward Michael, though she could not see him.

Ryu cursed, drew his weapon, and lunged forward. Michael immediately matched his move, blocking the demon's sword with his shield as he sliced the underprince in two. As Ryu disintegrated, Tala held up both of his hands, and Michael halted, as did the Host.

What is that putrid smell? It reminds me of the stench in Gregory's house after he tried to attack me, thought Elizabeth, shivering.

Michael just put some garbage out, my love. All is well, answered Xander, though he drew her closer to him. *She is freezing,* he thought impatiently to Michael. *Let us finish this and get her home. We have been out far too long.*

Agreed, thought Gabriel.

Michael stared at Ryu's captain. *Tala, it seems that you are now underprince of this dominion. Are you willing to leave this airspace and allow us to depart without a fight? Consider your next words well, or they may be your last in this world.*

Tala grimaced. *We will save this battle for another day, Michael.*

With those words, the demons dipped to fly straight down into the city, leaving the path clear before Michael and his forces.

As one, the entire light force flew quickly back to Xander's and Elizabeth's house, staying just above the cloud cover.

Elizabeth's teeth chattered as the wind blew in her face, and she tucked herself more tightly into her husband's arms, reaching around him for warmth as the muscles of his torso pumped, shooting them through the air.

His face was grim, and she could feel the tightness throughout him.

When they reached the grove of trees, the warriors remained in the air while Michael and Gabriel joined Xander and Elizabeth on the ground. Michael dismissed the warriors, and they flew upwards, quickly disappearing into the night.

As soon as he landed, Xander took human form and began to run toward the house with Elizabeth, Michael and Gabriel close behind them. Gabriel flew around in front of them and entered the house first, checking it rapidly.

Slowing slightly, Xander threw open the door and carried her through the house, up the stairs to their rooms. He took her into the bathroom and set her on the floor while he turned on the water, testing it with his hand to make certain that it would not burn her. As the tub filled, he undressed her, knowing that her hands were too cold to work the buttons, snaps, and zippers of the layers of clothing.

Michael and Gabriel stood in the corners of the room, wearing twin expressions of displeasure.

Mentally, Xander berated himself for his own idiocy. His face plainly displayed his disquiet.

Knowing that her husband would be upset if he heard her teeth chattering while she tried to speak, Elizabeth thought instead, *My love, I am fine. Please do not be upset.*

His breath exploded from him. "You are *not* fine! You are frozen, and you were in danger. It was my fault, my arrogance, that did this."

He picked her up and gently placed her in the tub of water, reaching to turn up the thermostat, and then looking back at her, worry written on his features. "You are blue, Elizabeth. What if you get sick?"

He started chaffing her legs to warm her.

Xander, calm down. I am fine, really. I'm just cold. I'll be warm soon enough, she thought.

"If you are so *fine*, why are you thinking instead of speaking? You are unable to speak because you are so cold your teeth are chattering, and you know that I will hear it and feel worse. Please do not say that you are *fine* again, or I may lose my control." He paused a moment in his ministrations and hung his head. "Tonight I have been neither a good husband nor a good guardian," he said bitterly.

The tears began to roll down Elizabeth's face. *Please don't say that. Don't ever say that. You were trying to please me. If you have any fault at all, it's that you try to make me happy all of the time. I loved flying with you, and now you will never take me again. This is my fault. I should have listened when you said Michael thought it was too cold. Michael doesn't love me like you do. He thinks very rationally of what is best, not always what I want.*

As Xander cupped her face with his hands and wiped her tears away with his thumbs, Michael folded his arms and turned to look out of the small window. The Captain's voice was gruff when he spoke into Elizabeth's mind. *We will send scouts ahead the next time we take you flying, but you will fly again.*

Gabriel smiled.

She looked at Xander in wonder. *That was not you.* She paused. *That was Michael, wasn't it?*

Xander's smile was small. "Yes, that was Michael. He does care for you, you know, in the same way that he loves me. You are his sister, and he wants you to be happy, too, though perhaps his judgment where you are concerned is a little clearer than mine. Are you warmer now?"

She smiled broadly. "I am in a perfect state of … warmness. If I get any warmer, I may go up in flames. You are the best husband and guardian in the world, and you're my best friend. I love you with all my heart."

He reached in the cabinet under the sink to retrieve one of his extra large towels, pulled her to her feet, and wrapped her snugly in the softness. And suddenly she was being lifted again as Xander headed toward their bedroom, Gabriel and Michael walking behind them.

She chuckled. "I really can walk, Xander, though I must admit that I enjoy being carried."

He held her in one arm as he turned down the covers on their bed with his other hand. Gently tucking her between the sheets, he whispered, "Before I took you flying, I told you that I would change forms when we returned to our house if you wished. Do you want me to do so, Elizabeth?"

"I love you in either form, as you well know, but I will never turn down the opportunity to be kissed by my angel," she replied, looking lovingly into his summer sky eyes.

"Well," he said, finally allowing himself to smile, "I will kiss you as an angel, and then love you as a man." He grinned. "Otherwise, my wings would get in the way."

"It doesn't matter to me which form you take, for you are always an angel and always a man," Elizabeth replied, reaching up to draw him down to her lips.

He kissed her deeply, then drew back and smiled again. "You are correct, my love. No matter which form I assume, I am fully human yet fully angel. I am glad you understand that. I would not have you to think my natures are separate, or to prefer one form to the other."

She laughed lightly. "Choices, choices. Do I wish to see my magnificent, beautiful human husband, or my gloriously radiant, angelic husband? There is no bad option where you are concerned."

He took her into his arms and showed her his appreciation by his actions.

Michael and Gabriel dutifully turned to look out the windows.

I think I know the trees by name, thought Michael, sighing.

Be quiet, answered Gabriel, chuckling.

Chapter 11

"Then I heard the voice of the Lord, saying, 'Whom shall I send, and who will go for Us?' Then I said, 'Here am I. Send me!'"
Isaiah 6:8

2009

Throughout the spring months, the SoulFire team traveled every other weekend, flying to some of the more distant locations. On those occasions, the trucks and tech crew would leave earlier in the week in order to arrive and set up before the team flew in on Friday nights. Ten three-day meetings were held during those months, beginning on Friday nights and ending on Sunday afternoons, focusing on areas of the United States which were not reached during the previous summer. Xander, Elizabeth, Charlotte, and Jonathan would return on Sunday nights, tired but rejoicing in the harvest of thousands of souls for the kingdom. Jonathan continued to preach in churches in the southeastern United States throughout the weeks while the others finished their graduate and undergraduate degrees.

In mid-April, Xander and Elizabeth had performed a final concert together on twin grand pianos in Twichell Auditorium, presenting a program of classical and sacred music in appreciation for the scholarships extended to them during their years at the college. The couple had agreed to allow Converse to record the concert and sell the CDs in order to continue to fund the scholarship program.

The seats had been sold out for nearly a year in advance, and the stellar performance of the gifted pair did not disappoint. All proceeds were placed into scholarship funds for the musically gifted who had chosen to attend Converse.

Michael and Gabriel stood beside them as they took their final bows before their professors, state dignitaries, and friends, and, as she looked over the audience, Elizabeth reflected on all that had happened to her in the past four years. She clasped her husband's hand and looked up into his eyes as she smiled at him. *You are so handsome in your tux, my love, and you are even more beautiful on the inside. Apart from my salvation, you are the best gift that has ever been given to me. I thank God for you every day.*

Xander returned his wife's smile as he admired her and squeezed her hand gently. Elizabeth was resplendent in a brilliant white chiffon gown, rhinestones glittering at her waist and throughout her dark brown curls which flowed from a loose knot on the back of her head. *You take my breath away, Elizabeth. You have bewitched me, body and soul, and I love you with all of my heart. I never wish to be parted from you for all of eternity.*

From their seats on the front row, Jonathan and Charlotte held hands and smiled brightly at their co-workers, recognizing the small signs of mental telepathy. Jonathan watched his beloved Charlotte as she looked at her left hand, admiring the ring which he had placed there a few hours earlier as they had dined together in a small, romantic restaurant before the concert. They had not yet talked to her parents or Xander and Elizabeth, but she was unable to bear the thought of removing the ring until they could do so later in the evening.

Auburn-haired Edward, standing beside the immense, regal Lexus, smiled at Charlotte's thoughts. The dark-skinned Lexus, his bald head gleaming as brightly as Michael's golden hair, displayed an expression in his brown eyes that betrayed his pleasure at his charge's betrothal.

Michael and Gabriel observed the interaction from the stage.

Jonathan has chosen well, said Michael to Lexus and Edward. *Charlotte will be an asset to him in his ministry, as well as a wonderful wife and mother.*

Gabriel added, *Our Father brought them together in His wisdom. There will be rejoicing in heaven over this match.*

Lexus and Edward nodded in response.

~~oo~~

David, conscious of the expanded role which his son-in-law would be assuming in the ministry, suggested to his son-in-law that he be ordained, and Xander had submitted to David, Jonathan, and the committee of deacons at Tabernacle Church for questioning the week after the concert in April. After meeting with the men, he had been approved and was to be duly ordained as a minister of the gospel at Tabernacle Church the following Sunday.

At the ordination service, during his charge before the church, David spoke about the qualifications of a minister, quoting I Timothy 3:2-7, "An overseer, then, must be above reproach, the husband of one wife, temperate, prudent, respectable, hospitable, able to teach, not addicted to wine or pugnacious, but gentle, uncontentious, free from the love of money. He must be one who manages his own household well, keeping his children under control with all dignity (but if a man does not know how to manage his own household, how will he take care of the church of God?); and not a new convert, lest he become conceited and fall into the condemnation incurred by the devil. And he must have a good reputation with those outside the church, so that he may not fall into reproach and the snare of the devil."

David, with Roark behind him, stood before his daughter and son-in-law, who were seated on the front row along with Jonathan and Charlotte, and smiled at them, saying, "Xander fulfills all of these qualifications, except for one, and I am certain that he will make an exemplary father when the time is right."

Michael, Gabriel, Lexus, and Edward smiled at David's comment. They all knew that Xander and Elizabeth hoped to be parents within the next year.

Xander squeezed Elizabeth's hand. *Maybe we can have some happy news for them before the summer is out,* he thought into her mind.

Though it might be difficult to travel if I were pregnant, I know that you would help me. Our own child! She sighed and traced the letters "I LOVE YOU" in the palm of his hand.

Xander looked up at David as he began to speak again.

"This service is twofold: first, we are ordaining Xander Darcy into the gospel ministry, and second, we are commissioning him and the others in SoulFire Ministries as they make final preparations to leave on a world tour two months from now. We are partnering with that team in prayer and support, pledging that we as a church will help them in any way that we can as they fulfill the Great Commission given by our Lord in Matthew 28:19-20, 'Go therefore and make disciples of all the nations, baptizing them in the name of the Father and the Son and the Holy Spirit, teaching them to observe all that I commanded you; and lo, I am with you always, even to the end of the age.'

"I believe that God has chosen this team for a special purpose which is only just beginning to be revealed," David continued, looking first on the four on the front row, and then across the congregation. "I cannot help but think of the words our Lord spoke, just before He ascended into heaven, as recorded in Acts 1:7-8, 'It is not for you to know times or epochs which the Father has fixed by His own authority; but you shall receive power when the Holy Spirit has come upon you; and you shall be My witnesses both in Jerusalem, and in all Judea, and in Samaria, and even to the remotest part of the earth.'

"I have seen firsthand the powerful way that God works through SoulFire. I have seen different members of this team cast out demons, heal the sick and injured, speak in tongues, and display remarkable discernment. As I watched, I was reminded of the words of Christ spoken in Mark 16:15-18, 'Go into all the world and preach the gospel to all creation. He who has believed and has been baptized shall be saved; but he who has disbelieved shall be condemned. And these signs will accompany those who have believed: in My name they will cast out demons, they will speak with new tongues; they will pick up serpents, and if they drink any deadly poison, it shall not hurt them; they will lay hands on the sick, and they will recover.'

"I have not yet seen them drink poison, but I have been present when they defeated a serpent and rescued a young man from his grip."

From the second seat, just behind Xander and Elizabeth, Mark Goodman raised his hand.

David nodded to him and smiled. "If you don't believe me, just ask Mark to tell you his testimony."

The congregation, well aware of the young man's salvation experience because he had shared it with them, laughed.

David, his face assuming a serious expression, said, "A few years ago, I would have said that those gifts belonged to the early church alone, but now I think that God may have gifted this team in a similar way because we are nearing the end of this age. I think He has a divine purpose for them, and I feel privileged to have a small part in His plan. If I am needed during the five months that they are traveling, I hope that you as a church will support Lynne and me as we join them. Wherever they are, whenever they call, we will go to Jonathan, Xander, Elizabeth, and Charlotte as soon as we are able. I don't know what God is doing, but it is something mighty and wonderful, and if He needs me, I must answer with the prophet Isaiah, 'Here am I. Send me!'"

In response, the people stood to their feet and applauded, giving their pastor their unqualified approval.

The following week, the deacons formed a search committee to seek a qualified young man who would serve as David's Associate Pastor. In the event that David and Lynne needed to take a leave of absence, the pulpit would be filled and the flock would be shepherded. The church had grown considerably in the past few years, adding a minister of music three years prior, and the people knew that they needed a third minister to work with the youth and the children in any event.

~~oo~~

Xander and Elizabeth completed their Master's degrees while Charlotte completed her B.S., and the three of them graduated from Converse with highest honors on May 16. The Darcys also finished their graduate degrees at Liberty University, but elected not to march in the commencement ceremonies due to time constraints.

Charlotte had already begun her Master's work on her theology degree through Liberty's online program, and she planned to use the long hours in the air to do her class work.

Because the SoulFire global tour would begin in mid-June, Charlotte and Jonathan had elected to marry at the end of May. Tim and Laura Lucas had understood the desire of the young couple to be wed before they left for a five month long series of meetings, and they had agreed, to Jonathan's profound relief, to help the young couple plan a small wedding for May 23. Jonathan's elderly parents, located in Columbia, South Carolina, had met Charlotte several times and already loved her, and they were likewise pleased to have the ceremony sooner rather than later. Jonathan, at thirty years old, was their youngest child, born to them in their forties, and they were overjoyed to see him so happily settled with a godly young woman.

Lynne, Elizabeth, and Janna also offered their help to Charlotte and Laura, and the plans were quickly made. Elizabeth was Charlotte's matron of honor, and Xander was a groomsman, along with Joshua Lucas. Jonathan's oldest brother, a pastor in Virginia, attended the wedding with his family and served as Jonathan's best man. David performed the ceremony before a church filled with people who dearly loved Charlotte and her "young preacher," as well as a full complement of guardians and warriors, including Michael, Gabriel, Lexus, and Edward.

Xander and Elizabeth sang several songs requested by the bride and groom. In addition to those requests, Charlotte had gladly given the responsibility of procuring the musicians to Elizabeth and Xander who had arranged for several of their classmates to play piano and strings for the wedding. Six busy weeks had been sufficient to arrange a beautiful day of celebration for the partners in ministry.

~~oo~~

After a week-long honeymoon in Florida, Rev. and Mrs. Jonathan Edwards, accompanied by Lexus and Edward, returned to the house they had rented in Columbia near his parents. The evening after the couple came home, Dave Branard and his assistant, Amy Michaels, as well as Xander and Elizabeth, met them for dinner at California Dreaming to finalize details for the tour to begin the following week. Michael, Gabriel, and Hector joined Lexus, Edward, and Esmund behind their charges, who were seated at the table. Warriors stood along walls.

Dave introduced Amy, a travel specialist he and Jonathan had hired several months earlier, and she handed out itineraries to the team and answered questions along with Dave. Xander, Elizabeth, and Charlotte had received many e-mails from Amy as the tour had been planned, but they had not yet met her in person.

"Amy, I'm so glad that we have you to handle all these details," said Elizabeth, smiling as the young woman took a seat across from her at the table.

Charlotte added, "It will be great to have another woman on the team. I hope that we will all be good friends."

Amy, a petite brunette of twenty-eight, nodded and smiled. "I'm looking forward to it. I've enjoyed my work as a travel agent for the past seven years, but I couldn't pass up this opportunity to combine my vocation with my faith. I'm really excited about the tour. Details are my specialty. Dave tells me that you and your husband are gifted in languages," she said to Elizabeth with interest.

"Yes. Xander speaks many languages, and I understand any language that is spoken to me. People understand what I'm saying no matter what language they speak," Elizabeth replied, a little embarrassed.

"Dave explained the gifts of the different team members to me, Elizabeth. I think it's wonderful. I may have to call on you or your husband if we have any difficulties. I speak Spanish and French, but in several of the cities, I will probably need help from time to time. I hope you don't mind," said Amy.

Elizabeth smiled. "Not at all, Amy. Please ask us any time you need help. Char is our human lie detector. You can always trust her judgment."

Charlotte laughed at the humorous description of her gift, but Amy surveyed her seriously.

"Charlotte, that is an extremely useful ability. Please tell me anytime there is something I need to know."

Xander's low voice startled the women. "You can depend on that, Amy. Charlotte knows the truth when she hears it, and she does not hesitate to speak it in love."

Jonathan smiled at his wife as Michael chuckled from behind Xander.

"I hope that's a good thing, Xander," said Charlotte.

He smiled crookedly. "I have always thought it was, Charlotte. Do I speak the truth?" he asked, teasing her.

"You always have," she answered, suddenly serious. "You and Elizabeth are two of the most truthful people whom I have ever known. You both abhor deceit, though you are very good at keeping secrets when you must. Even then, you do not lie."

~~oo~~

The opening rallies of the tour would take place in Vancouver, and they would travel from there to Mexico City. Also to be included during the months of travel were Kiev, London, Paris, Stockholm, São Paulo, Manila, Kuala Lumpur, Jakarta, Johannesburg, Cape Town, Seoul, Tokyo, Hong Kong, Sydney, Kigali City, Soweto, and Kampala. The mechanics of such an undertaking limited their time in each city to four days so that the following three days could be spent traveling to the next location, setting up, and resting. Equipment would be transported to airports by rented trucks, shipped to the next city, and driven by more hired trucks to the city's arena or largest meeting area.

Whenever possible, Jonathan had included local pastors in the process, arranging to meet them as soon as the team arrived in each city. Ministers had been invited to follow the pattern begun in Atlanta by having daily mission activities arranged and using the nightly meetings as rallies for a spiritual retreat. Every effort had been made to contact spiritual leaders in the host cities and to coordinate efforts between the SoulFire team and the churches. Jonathan had been very successful in forming these partnerships, and the team looked forward to meeting fellow believers who would help them reach the unchurched in their cities.

Mark Goodman, SoulFire's publicist, had also worked on the tour arrangements with Dave, and they had bought airtime on television and radio stations, using clips from the previous summer and spring to publicize the tour.

Mark's connections to important people in the cable news industry in the States stood them in good stead. One cable network was so interested in the global tour that they arranged for Mark to make regular reports on their progress via satellite.

~~oo~~

Lucifer, Gregory, and Dirk Horne sat in the living room of Gregory's home in Boston, celebrating the passage of Gregory's bill through both Houses of Congress. It had been signed by the President earlier in the week. The full effects of the change in the law would not be felt for four years, after the next election cycle.

The guards stood rigidly behind the chairs of their masters while Aborian, a medium-sized demon of the upper ranks knelt before the three.

Lucifer gazed at the dark one for a moment, and then called his name. "Aborian, what have you to report?"

"All has been done as the Dark Prince requested, my master," answered Aborian in a gruff voice.

"Lift your head and tell me about it, Aborian," said Gregory, leaning forward in his chair.

Aborian lifted his head and looked into the glowing amber eyes of the Dark Prince. "We have successfully hacked into the computer used by Amy Michaels. We have all of the travel information for the upcoming SoulFire tour, just as you ordered." With a grimace serving as the approximation of a smile, Aborian continued, "As an added gift for you, Master, we have cloned her cell phone which has a GPS capability programmed into it. We can monitor all of her conversations and movements. We will know where the team is at all times."

Gregory laughed, "I just love modern technology. Smart phones! Brilliant. Good work, Aborian. Have you covered your tracks?"

Aborian's grin was evil. "Of course. She will never know that she is taking us everywhere she goes. We can listen in to every word she says and read each text that she sends or receives. It is child's play, Master."

Gregory stood, walked to the bar, picked up a glass, and poured another drink. He returned to his seat, handing the drink to an astonished Aborian.

Gregory smiled at him. "Sit with us, Aborian, and we will congratulate you on your good work."

Lucifer's head swiveled quickly toward his son, a frown marring his beautiful face.

Aborian's eyes shifted to Lucifer's face, and seeing his expression, Aborian stood quickly, threw back the drink, and bowed from the waist to the unholy trinity.

"Thank you for your recognition and your invitation, but I am unworthy to sit in your presence," said Aborian.

Lucifer spoke in carefully modulated tones. "Your good judgment is noted, Aborian. You may return to your duties."

Aborian carefully backed from the room, placed the glass on a table, and flew from the house through the ceiling, returning to his rented office space and beloved computers.

ROBIN HELM

Chapter 12

"Be anxious for nothing, but in everything by prayer and supplication with thanksgiving let your requests be made known to God. And the peace of God, which surpasses all comprehension, shall guard your hearts and your minds in Christ Jesus."
Philippians 4:6-7

Xander stood stiffly, resisting the urge to stretch his large frame in the confined space of the Boeing 737. *Airplane seats were definitely not designed for comfort,* he thought.

His wife still slept, and her lashes made dark crescents on her cheeks. *My wife.* He sighed in contentment, and then, unable to resist, he sat back down beside her, leaning over to place tiny kisses over her face.

Gabriel looked at the two with amusement.

It is difficult to believe that our brother has adapted to being human with so little trouble, thought Michael.

Elizabeth smiled, and he kissed her double-dimple. "Time to wake up, my love," he whispered. "We are making our approach to Vancouver and will be landing soon."

Elizabeth put her arms around his neck, her eyes still closed. "Just a few more minutes," she said in a sleepy voice.

He chuckled deeply, and his lips vibrated against her cheek.

"That tickles," said Elizabeth, pulling him even closer. She turned her head and fluttered her lashes against his skin, giving him butterfly kisses on his face.

"Elizabeth, you know that I am ticklish, and I know that you are even more so. Do you want me to embarrass you in front of everyone?" he asked, smiling and reaching for the area under her arms.

"No, no! I'm awake. No need to resort to such drastic measures," she replied, sitting up and pushing his hands away with a giggle.

It was early morning, and the other passengers began to stir. They had flown through the night, but the dawn was just breaking, and people began to raise their shades to watch the sunrise.

"I must look terrible," she said, yawning and stretching. She put her hand over her mouth. "Yuck. Morning breath. How can you stand me?"

"Elizabeth, you know that you are always beautiful to me," he answered.

Lynne had taught him to French braid Elizabeth's long, thick hair, and it remained in a heavy queue down her back, though a few curls had escaped around her face and at her neck. To him, she was never more lovely than when she first awoke. He always tried to awaken before she did, so that he could see the last few remnants of her dreams and watch her as she came to consciousness.

She reached into the backpack at her feet. "We don't have time to brush our teeth. Do you want some gum?"

"You have taught me never to refuse anything offered to me for my breath, so, yes," he said grinning crookedly and reaching out his hand.

Elizabeth popped a piece into her mouth and bypassed his hand, saying, "Open wide."

Xander obediently opened his mouth, but she pulled the gum back, laughing at him. He grabbed her hand and brought it to his mouth, snapping the gum from between her fingers with his teeth.

Newlyweds! sighed Michael, though he smiled.

You mistake the matter, replied Gabriel. *Our brother and sister have been married for six months. Those are the newlyweds.* He pointed to Charlotte and Jonathan who sat in the seats across the aisle from Xander and Elizabeth.

Charlotte was curled under a blanket with her head in Jonathan's lap. He stroked her hair as he looked at her, the adoration showing on his face, and then he leaned over to whisper, "Charlotte, the seatbelt light has come on. We're about to land. Wake up, honey." She snuggled closer to him, so he gently rubbed her shoulders. "Wake up, sleepyhead. We're in Vancouver."

Lexus towered in the aisle by their seats, and Edward hovered above them.

Dave, Amy, and Mark sat in the seats behind the two couples, their guardians as close to them as they could get.

The flight attendant's voice came through the speakers, advising everyone to put on their seatbelts and prepare for the landing.

The SoulFire Global Tour 2009 would begin in two days.

~~oo~~

After an hour had passed, with Amy and Dave handling all the details, the SoulFire team had arrived at their hotel in a car rented for the five days they would be in Vancouver. They all agreed to leave their luggage in their rooms and meet in the hotel restaurant for breakfast.

The tech crew had flown in a day earlier, and they were already busily setting up at the arena for the afternoon rehearsals. Thorncrown had also signed on for the tour, and as they were nearby for another engagement, they elected to meet the team at the arena. The meetings would not begin until the following day, but no one wanted to leave anything to chance. They all thought that two rehearsals would be better than one.

Xander and Elizabeth were the first to enter the restaurant, so they went through the breakfast buffet line and secured a table for their party of seven. Michael and Gabriel followed.

Xander held Elizabeth's seat for her, and after they were both seated, they bowed their heads together as he thanked God for their food. When he lifted his head, he noticed that Elizabeth's nose was wrinkled as if she smelled something unpleasant. He looked at her plate and saw that there was nothing unusual in her choices.

"Is anything wrong, Elizabeth?" he asked, concerned.

"Something doesn't smell right to me. It makes me feel a little nauseated," she answered, turning her head away.

Michael watched her closely.

"Elizabeth, you have oatmeal and toast. There is no way that it can be spoiled. Is it perhaps something on my plate?" Xander queried.

She leaned over and sniffed delicately.

"Ugh!" she said, sitting up quickly. "It's your sausage. Maybe you shouldn't eat it."

I have always thought sausage was nasty stuff. Do you know how it is made? Disgusting, thought Michael.

You feel that way about nearly all food, Michael, thought Gabriel.

True, he answered. *But sausage is particularly offensive.*

Xander lifted the offending sausage patty to his nose with his fork and smelled it. "It seems fine to me, but if the odor bothers you, I'll throw it away. I probably shouldn't eat it anyway. Too much fat." He motioned to a passing waiter and asked him to remove the plate. Then he went back through the buffet line, filling his plate with fruit and waffles.

As he sat back down, he smiled at his wife. "Is this better?"

"Yes," Elizabeth answered, though she still had not eaten anything. She sipped at her coffee.

Xander watched her as he slowly ate, his concern mounting.

Michael and Gabriel stood protectively at her shoulders.

The rest of the party entered the room with their guardians, went through the line, and joined the couple at the table. As they all sat down and Jonathan led them in blessing the food, Elizabeth put her elbows on the table and placed her head into her hands.

Are you ill? Xander asked.

I don't know. I think I'm going to throw up if I don't leave right now, she thought.

He glanced at their plates and saw sausage, bacon, and ham. *Is it the meat again?*

I think so. I've got to go! she answered.

As Elizabeth fled the room, Michael and Gabriel raced after her. Xander paused just long enough to say that Elizabeth felt sick, and then he quickly followed them.

She was leaning on the wall in the hallway just outside the dining room, breathing deeply. "I'm sorry. I feel better away from all those smells. You should go back in and finish your breakfast."

"Absolutely not, Elizabeth. Wait right here, and I will go handle everything. We will eat in our room." He spoke firmly.

She nodded at him, and he strode back into the restaurant, told the others where he and Elizabeth were going, and arranged to have room service deliver their breakfast to their room.

As Xander approached her, he noticed that she had both hands on her stomach. It made other memories come to his mind.

Impossible, thought Michael. *There would be another guardian here.*

Normally there would be, answered Xander, *but we are not normal.*

That is true enough, said Gabriel, wrinkling his brow.

Xander led his wife to the elevator, barely able to contain his excitement. He wanted to tell her his suspicions, but he did not wish to disappoint her if he was not right.

He held her hand as they exited the elevator and made their way to the room. As soon as they were inside, she went to the bed and stretched out on it. Michael and Gabriel stood on one side of the bed, looking down at her, and, after closing the curtains, Xander lay down beside her, turning on his side and propping his head on his elbow.

After thinking for a moment, he sat up and shifted his position, and then he leaned over her and put his ear against her stomach. Xander smiled as he heard it – a faint, rapid thudding.

Elizabeth drew her brows together and watched him. "What are you doing?"

"I am listening," he answered, turning his head to see her face and grinning widely. "You are not ill, Elizabeth."

"Really? I feel sick. How do you know?" she asked.

"You are with child. I am listening to the heartbeat of our baby," he said, and his smile was glorious. He radiated joy.

She leaned her head back on the pillow, stunned into silence for a moment. Then she sat straight up and held her husband's head against her stomach.

"How can you hear that? Even a doctor probably wouldn't pick it up this early. I've missed only one period," she said, her eyes beginning to brim with tears of joy.

"All of my senses are much stronger than a normal human's. I can also reach out to the child's mind. Why did you not tell me that you had missed your period?" he asked.

"Because it's happened occasionally before, and I didn't want to raise your hopes only to disappoint you later. Now, please let me hear what you're hearing. Put it in my mind," she whispered.

"I have never tried to do that, but I suppose if I let the sound into my thoughts it will work. Be very still." He concentrated on hearing the heartbeat and thinking about it, projecting it all into her mind.

Amazing, thought Gabriel. *I can hear it through your mind, too.*

Her brown eyes widened. "It's true! I'm pregnant! Oh, Xander, this is wonderful!" she said, both crying and laughing at the same time.

Xander sat up, puzzled, bending his knees and crossing his legs, and drew her into his lap, holding her against his chest. "Why are you crying, my love? Are you not happy?"

She laughed and sobbed at the same time. "I am deliriously happy. But how have you not known this earlier? Doesn't our baby have a guardian?"

He considered her question, and then spoke. "From the moment you were conceived, I joined your family as your guardian. When Lucifer's demons saw me with your mother, they began to attack immediately because they knew you were important. I think that Jehovah might be avoiding that as long as possible with our child. As soon as another guardian joins us, the entire spiritual realm will know that you are pregnant. Perhaps our Father will have Asim send our child's guardian when He is ready, and if He chooses to do so. Michael can call for extra warriors if he thinks they are required."

She will have a phalanx at all times if she needs it, thought Michael.

Xander stroked her hair absently as another idea occurred to him.

Elizabeth looked at his face. "I know that expression. What are you thinking?"

"That there is another possibility," he answered.

Interesting, thought Gabriel.

"Another possibility?" she asked, turning his face towards hers with her fingertips.

"Perhaps I am our child's guardian – at least for right now. I am still Chief of Guardians, you know. I can protect you and our child without raising the suspicions of Lucifer or Gregory. No one will know until you begin to increase, and by that time we will be nearly through with the tour," he said, and then looked sharply at her face, his eyes focused on her like lasers.

"What now?" she said, a little alarmed.

"Maybe we should return home. Perhaps you should not overtax yourself, Elizabeth. We should not risk your health or that of our child." His eyes held worry.

Elizabeth smiled. "You know you shouldn't be anxious; it is a sin. I'm young and healthy. I promise to rest all that I can and try to eat, but I really should see a doctor and start taking pre-natal vitamins. Maybe Amy could find a doctor for me."

He cradled her more closely to himself. "I am not certain that we should tell Amy. After you see a doctor, we can share the news with Charlotte, Jonathan, your parents, Janna, and Charles, asking them to keep our secret, but we risk letting the whole world know if we expand that circle of trust."

"You don't trust Amy, Dave, and Mark?" Elizabeth asked.

"Yes, I do, but the more people we tell, the more likely it is that the news will become common knowledge. I cannot forget that there is a reason why our child has no guardian yet. God has a purpose in that," Xander replied somberly. "I will ask one of the local pastors to recommend a gynecologist for you. He must be a believer in whom we can confide. I remember the doctor who tried to get Mom to have a test which could have caused her to miscarry you. Demons followed him around. I will not have that with our child," he said with determination.

Michael took human form and spoke aloud so that Elizabeth could hear him. "Why not let me ask the guardian of a pastor for the name of the doctor who attends the pastor's wife? No human has to be involved in this."

Elizabeth showed surprise at Michael's gesture, but she remained silent.

A knock sounded on the door.

"It must be room service. I will answer it," said Xander, beginning to move Elizabeth from his lap.

"No, brother," said Michael. "Allow me. Hold your wife."

Michael opened the door, startling the waiter who stood behind the cart. Michael accepted the bill from him, signed Xander's name to it. Adding a tip, he handed it back, saying, "I can take the cart. We will leave it outside the door when we are finished. Thank you."

As soon as the cart was in the room and Michael had closed the door, Gabriel also took human form. He wheeled the cart across the room and moved the covered plates from the cart to the table. "Come and eat," he said, looking at Elizabeth and Xander with kind eyes.

Xander gently moved her from his lap, slid from the bed, and stood before her with his hand extended. "Let me help you up."

Elizabeth laughed lightly. "I am not made of porcelain, guys. Millions of women are pregnant and doing very well." Even as she said the words, she gave her hand to her husband and allowed him to assist her to her feet.

As they ate, Gabriel spoke again. "Xander, we could send scouts to find a Christian gynecologist right now. Elizabeth could go this afternoon. Would it not be better if she did not wait until tomorrow? The meetings start tomorrow night, and she should see a doctor before she overexerts herself."

"Agreed," said Michael.

Xander wanted to agree as well, but he knew his wife. Looking at her, he asked, "Elizabeth, what do you think?"

"I was beginning to wonder if I would be allowed to say anything about what I will and won't do during this pregnancy. However, I think Gabriel has a good idea. No one has to know what kind of a doctor I'm going to see, and they all knew that I was sick at breakfast. They will not question it if I see a doctor this afternoon. We can rehearse tomorrow. All we really need is a sound check; everything is ready."

As soon as Elizabeth agreed, Michael dispatched scouts throughout Vancouver, and within minutes, they were reporting back to him. He took the yellow pages from the bedside table, opened the book to "Gynecologists," and began to mark names in the listing. He then directed the scouts to speak with the guardians of the doctors, asking questions to ascertain their level of commitment to the Father as well as their trustworthiness and skill level. Within an hour, a doctor named Scott Sanders was selected, and Xander had his private cell phone number.

Xander called the doctor, identified himself, and explained that he had obtained his number from a mutual friend. He then continued, "My wife and I are here in Vancouver for the SoulFire rallies, and she is unwell this morning. We have good reason to suspect that she may be pregnant. Could you see her privately today? We wish to keep the pregnancy a secret as long as possible."

The doctor thought a moment, and then replied, "I know who you and your wife are, Mr. Xander. I was there for your wife's classical concert in Toronto as well as your rallies in Chicago. Come to my office at 12:10. All of us normally go to lunch at noon, but I'll have something brought in today. Knock on the office door, and I'll let you in. There will be no one else in the office."

Relief showed on Xander's face. "Thank you so much, Dr. Sanders. Please call us Xander and Elizabeth. We really appreciate your help. If Elizabeth is pregnant, she will need to see a doctor every four weeks. At those times, we will be in London, Manila, Cape Town, and Sydney. Is there any way that you can help us?"

Dr. Sanders answered, "Let me think about it. I have many contacts, and I'll see what I can do. I look forward to seeing you and your wife at 12:10."

"Again, thank you. We will be there."

As Xander hung up and sat down heavily at the table, Michael spoke. "He is a very good man, and he is active in his church. The scout said that he travels nearly every year with Doctors Without Borders and that he has been on several mission trips. His practice is quite successful because he is an excellent physician."

Elizabeth smiled at her husband and reached across the table to take his hand. "Everything will be fine, my love. Though the timing may seem inconvenient for us, God's timing is always perfect. I'm sure that my biggest problem will be finding the time to shop for larger clothing on our tight schedule. In three more months, my fitted jeans may show the baby bump too much. I'll need loser clothing that will hide the presence of our child. If I'm extremely lucky, I won't be big enough for real maternity clothes until we're back home. Then we can go to my own doctor, buy clothes, and get everything else ready for the baby."

He returned her smile and stroked her hand. "If all is as we think it to be, you will deliver in January. We will be home by mid-November, and I should have plenty of time to prepare the nursery. I know that your parents and our friends will help us. As for shopping for your clothes, we will make time for whatever you need. If you are too tired to go to every rehearsal, you will remain at the hotels, and I will cover for you. The rallies are more important." Xander's mind was spinning with organizational details.

Elizabeth knew him too well to miss the signs of his stress. She leaned over, cupped his face in her hand, and kissed him gently on the lips. "This pregnancy will be a time of joy for the two of us. There will never be a nine-month stretch in which we aren't traveling. This will be a trial run for us. By the time we have our second child, all of this will come naturally to us, and we'll have contacts all around the world."

He searched her mind. "You are not afraid. I should be the strong one, yet I am drawing strength from you." Xander had seen thousands of pregnancies, and he knew how many things could go wrong. He worried that she would need medical attention, and that they would be unable to find it in a foreign country, but he would not burden her with his concerns.

He heard a familiar Voice in his mind, saying, *Cast all your cares upon Me, because I care for you.*

He took both of Elizabeth's hands in his, bowed his head and prayed aloud, "Father, I know that You love Elizabeth, and You love our child. I know that You will take care of us. Please forgive my lack of faith. I ask You for guidance, deliverance, and wisdom. Please show me the way, Lord. Teach me to love my wife and child as You love them. Help me to trust You for all things. Thank you for Your love, and thank You for our child. Your ways are perfect, and Your timing is always right. I love you, Lord. In Jesus' name. Amen."

He stood and leaned over his beautiful wife, took her face between his hands, and kissed her with passion, putting all of his love for her in his kiss. Pulling away just enough to rest his forehead on hers, he said, "I am a father, and you are the mother of our child. It is nearly beyond my understanding, but I know that God will lead me when I need to know what to do."

Xander stood, dialed Jonathan's number, and told him that Elizabeth had a doctor's appointment at noon, promising that he and Elizabeth would meet them at the arena in the afternoon if she felt up to doing so.

~~oo~~

Because Dr. Sanders had sent his nurses to lunch, Xander was in the room while the doctor examined Elizabeth, performing a transvaginal ultrasound to check the baby's heartbeat. Xander was fascinated, watching the images on the computer screen, Michael and Gabriel on either side of him. Branko, the doctor's guardian who stood behind him, acknowledged the archangels with a palm forward. They nodded in response. When Dr. Sanders finished, he and Branko left the room so that Elizabeth could dress, saying that he would return promptly.

After Elizabeth was fully clothed, Xander opened the door slightly, letting the doctor know they were ready.

Dr. Sanders, followed by his guardian, re-entered the room with a huge smile. "Congratulations. You were correct. I estimate that Elizabeth is about six weeks into her pregnancy, and everything is normal. Because you are asking for complete secrecy, and I know who you are, I am not putting this on our books or in our computers. So many people have access to those records that there would be no way to guarantee absolute privacy. This is unorthodox, to say the least, so I ask that you don't tell anyone that you came to me. I am giving you a six month's supply of pre-natal vitamins so that you won't have a prescription which can be tracked. Fortunately, we have plenty of sample packs. You haven't told me why you require secrecy, but I have traveled and seen enough to be a strong believer in spiritual warfare."

Branko smiled as his charge spoke.

Xander nodded at the doctor. "The longer we can keep Elizabeth's pregnancy a secret, the better for all three of us. The attacks against her would fail, but it would be preferable not to have to deal with them while we are touring. In short, we do not wish to draw attention when there is no need to do so. Thank you for your understanding."

Elizabeth smiled at the young doctor. "Since you are not billing us, will you let us repay you in some other way? Is there anything we can do for you?"

Dr. Sanders laughed. "Actually, there is. The rallies have been sold out for at least six months, and I was out of the country at the time the tickets were available."

Xander held up his hand. "Say no more. There will be tickets for you and your family for the entire week of the rally delivered here today. Will five be enough?"

Dr. Sanders tilted his head, a question in his eyes. "That's exactly the number I had in mind. Five is perfect for me, my wife, and our three children." He reached in his pocket and drew out a paper. "Before you leave, here is a list with the names of specific Christian OB/GYNs, one each in London, Manila, Cape Town, and Sydney. They all belong to Doctors Without Borders, just as I do. I have already called them and left messages, telling them only that a well-known couple will be contacting them. Now I will write to them, giving them your identities and telling them to expect your calls. I will also send them hand-written records of this visit. Computers and cell phones are not secure, as I have learned from experience.

Elizabeth stepped forward and put out her hand. "Thank you so much for everything, Dr. Sanders. We hope to see you tomorrow night and meet your family."

The doctor shook her hand, and then Xander's. "I'll be praying for you and tracking your progress across the globe. God bless you."

~~oo~~

"And then that lawless one will be revealed whom the Lord will slay with the breath of His mouth and bring to an end by the appearance of His coming; that is, the one whose coming is in accord with the activity of Satan, with all power and signs and false wonders."
II Thessalonians 2:8-9

The group of powerful Congressmen and Senators sat around the conference table, all of them wondering why this particular group of people had been invited to a power luncheon given by the junior Senator from Massachusetts. The mixed group of twenty-five Democrats, Independents, and Republicans made uncomfortable conversation until Gregory entered the room, taking the seat at the head of the table.

Gregory's secretary handed out bound folders of papers as his personal caterers served the meal. The men and women scanned the documents as they ate and drank, talking quietly among themselves. The more they read, the louder the conversation became.

Gregory remained silent, observing them through narrowed eyes. His invisible guards stood behind him, eager for their master to show his power. There were no guardians present.

When everyone had finished, they looked toward him expectantly.

"Has everyone had enough to eat?" Gregory asked.

His question was met with a mixture of curt nods and curious stares.

Their plates and utensils immediately disappeared into thin air. A gasp of surprise went up from the assembly.

"What is this? Some sort of a parlor trick? Is that why you called us here, upstart? To show off?" asked one of the Senators belligerently.

Gregory closed his eyes as they briefly flared red, and then opened them when they had returned to their normal amber color. The outspoken Senator grabbed his chest and fell forward, his head hitting the table with a thud. The people seated on each side of him jumped to their feet, looking at the man with horror. One of the Senators, a doctor, rushed to his fallen colleague and checked his pulse at his carotid artery.

He looked at Gregory grimly, "He's dead. I need to perform CPR immediately."

Gregory looked at his fingernails, and then at the doctor. "If you wish, but it will do no good," he said calmly.

The doctor and a few of the men placed the stricken man on the floor, and the doctor began to administer CPR. "Call 911," he ordered.

As one of the Representatives took his cell phone from his pocket, Gregory fixed him with a steely stare. "Belay that."

"But we must do something to help him," said the Congressman.

"No one can help him now," answered Gregory in a low growl.

"Did you kill him?" asked the doctor, ceasing his ministrations.

"You all saw me sitting here ten feet away from him when he collapsed. He was overweight with high blood pressure and diabetes. The Senator never exercised and did not watch his diet, so he died of a heart attack," said Gregory nonchalantly.

"We can't just sit here having a meeting with a dead man on the floor," said the Congressman.

"I agree with that," replied Gregory. "Take your folders with you and read them carefully. They outline the plans which I want implemented within the next three years. I will introduce bills, and you will co-sponsor them with me. If a bill has to do with appropriations, one of you Representatives will have to introduce it to the House."

"Why us?" asked one of the women. "Why are we being singled out?"

Gregory looked at her appraisingly. "You have all been chosen because of your service to your country and your voting records. These plans are the natural extensions of what you have already put into place. You are getting exactly what you have been asking for: redistribution of wealth, control of the citizenry from the cradle to the grave, power in the hands of a few, the growth of government, and the stringent limitations of personal freedoms. After all of these things are achieved, we will institute a state church, curtailing freedom of religion, and we will take our place in the global community. There will be one religion, one language, world citizenship, and a mandatory identification chip to be accepted for implantation by all world citizens. During these three years, we will build a massive military which will control the people of this country by force if necessary."

There was shocked silence.

Finally, one Senator cleared his throat and asked what the others were thinking. "And what will happen if we choose to decline your invitation to join this august group?"

"Oh, my. This is awkward," replied Gregory, leaning forward and looking at each person in turn. "I don't remember giving you a choice; I will do so now. Join me and increase your power, or join your friend on the floor. He should be splitting hell wide open as we speak."

No one moved.

"Would anyone like to leave?" Gregory asked. "All you have to do to refuse my requests is to stand and walk toward the door."

He waited a long minute while each one deliberated.

"If you are with me, raise your hand," he said.

One by one, every hand in the room went up.

"Excellent," said Gregory, smiling wickedly.

Chapter 13

"Behold, I send you out as sheep in the midst of wolves; therefore be shrewd as serpents, and innocent as doves."
Matthew 10:16

Xander watched his wife carefully on the drive back to the hotel from the doctor's office. Her color had returned, and she appeared to feel much better. He reached for her hand and held it lightly, stroking the top of it with his thumb.

Michael and Gabriel flew above the rental car, constantly scanning for spies. Though Xander and Elizabeth had been very careful, their caution would be useless if they were seen leaving the office of an OB/GYN.

"Are you feeling better, love?" Xander asked, keeping his eyes on the traffic and listening for the directions from the GPS.

"Xander, please don't worry about me. Morning sickness is normal, and mine is actually very mild compared to what I've heard described by other women. If I avoid the smell of meat, I think I probably won't be sick at all. I'm a very healthy, young woman. And, yes, I feel quite well now. We can go to rehearsal with everyone else."

He glanced at her, his brows drawn together. "We do not have to rehearse today. You should not overdo. After the long plane trip, do you not think you should rest?"

She smiled and looked at his perfect profile. "My sweet husband, pregnancy is a normal condition, not a sickness. There is nothing wrong with me. We're going to be traveling for the next five months, and I likely will tire more easily as I get bigger, but right now, I'm feeling well. Let's keep things as normal as possible for as long as we can; otherwise, all this secrecy has been for nothing. People will ask questions if we start skipping rehearsals and acting differently. You can't treat me like I'm made of glass. Everyone will notice and wonder what's wrong with me, and it won't take them long to come to the correct conclusion." She lifted his hand and kissed it.

She makes sense – as usual, Xander, thought Michael while his keen eyes searched every alley and doorway.

I think you must take her feelings into consideration, brother, added Gabriel gently. *Elizabeth does not wish to be viewed as sickly, and, in truth, she is not.*

Xander sighed. "I am outnumbered, it seems. We will go to rehearsal if you feel well after eating a healthy lunch."

"Actually, I'm hungry now. If we go straight to the arena, we can eat with everyone else. You can fill a plate for me, avoiding meat or anything fried. If I stay away from the smells, I think I'll be able to eat," she answered.

He took his phone from his pocket and handed it to her, sighing as he did so. "I give up. Pull up the arena address so that we can program it into the GPS. I know that it is not far from the hotel, and we are almost there."

Elizabeth leaned over and kissed her husband's cheek. "I know that was hard for you. Thank you." She pulled up the information and tapped it into the rental car's navigation system. "We'll just tell everyone that the doctor said I am fine, and that I'm feeling better now. We can talk to Jonathan and Charlotte after rehearsal when we get back to the hotel."

Xander was silent.

"I love you," said Elizabeth, stroking his cheek.

He turned his head and kissed the palm of her hand, keeping his eyes on the road. "I love you more. I win."

~~oo~~

Xander noticed that Charlotte was watching him closely as he took Elizabeth a glass of water and bowl of soup. He could tell by her thoughts that she knew they had not heard the whole story about his wife's trip to the doctor, but he could not risk telling her, even by telepathy, because of her possible reaction to their news. Charlotte would probably be overjoyed, and her squeals of delight would draw attention.

Elizabeth sat at a table well away from the others, and Charlotte, followed by Jonathan, took her plate and walked over to sit with her. Michael stood behind Elizabeth, and Lexus and Edward accompanied their charges as they joined her.

Xander made a quick decision. Speaking into the minds of Jonathan, Charlotte, and Elizabeth at the same time, he thought, *Charlotte, you are right; there is more to tell. Come to our room when we get back to the hotel, and we will talk together. We need to keep this a private matter as long as we can.*

Jonathan's eyes showed his concern. *Is everything all right? Is Elizabeth sick?*

Xander smiled as he walked over to them holding his own plate and drink, Gabriel by his side. He again spoke into their minds. *Everything is fine, Jonathan. Do not worry. The news is good, actually, but we must not talk about it now.*

Charlotte suppressed a smile and squeezed Elizabeth's hand. *I knew it.*

Elizabeth smiled reassuringly at Charlotte and Jonathan, and then noted the foods on their plates. Jonathan was eating a grilled chicken salad, and Charlotte was indulging in a cheeseburger. *Xander, the chicken and beef don't seem to bother me. This morning, you had sausage, and the others had bacon and ham. Maybe pork products are the only meats that make me feel sick, or perhaps the smells upset my stomach only in the morning. This may be easier to control than we think.*

Xander sat beside Elizabeth, putting his bowl on the table. *Do you think you could eat more than the potato soup I brought you?*

She eyed Jonathan's plate. *Jonathan's lunch looks good to me. Would you mind getting me a little of what he has? Please get something else for yourself, too. You can't go the rest of the day with fruit for breakfast and a bowl of soup for lunch. You have to eat, whether I can or not.*

He leaned over and kissed her cheek, whispering, "I love you." He then went back to the buffet, returning shortly with two grilled chicken salads.

Elizabeth took a few tentative bites, smiled at her husband, and continued to eat.

Nobody noticed Amy as she watched them, smiling sweetly at the scene, or observed her as she pulled out her cell phone and began to text.

~~oo~~

The rest of the afternoon was spent in rehearsals, and everyone returned to the hotel by six for a relaxing evening and a good night's sleep. Jonathan had made arrangements for Charlotte, Xander, Elizabeth, and him to meet with local pastors after breakfast on the following day concerning counselors for the rallies. Material to be used in training sessions for volunteers had been sent ahead to each location months in advance, and nearly a thousand people had taken the classes in every city.

As the four of them exited the hotel, followed by their guardians, they were greeted by photographers angling to get a picture of Xander and Elizabeth. The presence of the press was not unusual; they had become well-known figures over the years. The couple had even graciously released some photographs of their wedding to several newspapers, magazines, and television networks. In doing so, they had hoped to maintain some control over which pictures were publicized. Their latest CD of solos, instrumentals, and duets including "Forever" and "My Angel's Kiss" was topping the charts in Christian music and was receiving attention on secular radio stations as well. The two solos from their wedding were being sung at weddings throughout the United States and Canada, and they were consistently in the top ten on Billboard's Hot 100 list.

Photographers were to be expected, but their questions were not. "Are the rumors that Elizabeth is pregnant true?" asked one. "How far along is she? Will she be able to complete the tour?" asked another.

Xander held up his hand and said, "We have no comment at this time. Please allow us our privacy. We will issue a statement later, but for now, you may say that Elizabeth is well, and that we have no intentions of leaving the tour."

He put his arm around Elizabeth, and they hurried to the car, sliding into the back seat. Jonathan and Charlotte got into the front seat, and he started the engine. The photographers stepped away from the car when they saw his reverse lights come on.

Elizabeth looked at Xander with shock apparent in her eyes. "How could they know so quickly? We took every precaution, and we found out only yesterday ourselves."

Xander knew from Charlotte's and Jonathan's thoughts that they had told no one, nor had they talked about it outside of their room.

He breathed deeply to calm himself. "Someone on the tour with us must have speculated about your condition when you were sick in the morning, went to a doctor, and seemed fine after we arrived at the arena. Even if they did so, I cannot imagine that anyone would have alerted the press."

I have not sensed anyone having any animosity toward the two of you, thought Michael, flying with the other guardians above the car.

The only one who even thought you could possibly be pregnant was Amy, added Gabriel. *She would not have told the news people, but she may have told a friend or relative. Even if she did, how could the media know so quickly?*

Lexus and Edward remained silent, but they frowned at the thought of betrayal.

"Jonathan, we need to meet with Dave, Mark, and Amy as soon as we return to the hotel," said Xander, laying his hand on his friend's shoulder.

"I'll call them and set it up," answered Jonathan, looking at Xander in the rearview mirror.

"No, don't call them," said Xander quickly. "We will go to their rooms in person and ask them to come to our room for a quick meeting."

Charlotte raised an eyebrow and looked over her seat at Xander. "You suspect that one of them told the press that Elizabeth is pregnant? They don't even know about the baby themselves."

"They wouldn't have done it on purpose," answered Elizabeth, chewing her lower lip, deep in thought.

"No, they would not have; however, Amy, being a woman, may have suspected that Elizabeth had morning sickness. She may have mentioned it to a friend or family member in a text or phone call," replied Xander.

"You think whomever she talked to, if she did that, alerted the media? I can't imagine that. Too many dots have to connect very rapidly," said Jonathan.

Could Gregory have some way to monitor her phone? asked Michael.

Anything is possible with him, thought Gabriel.

"Before we jump to any conclusions, we need to talk to both of them," said Xander firmly.

Elizabeth took her cell phone from her purse and pulled up a number.

"You're calling Mom?" Xander asked. *Ah, now I understand.*

"Yes. She and Dad are going to hear this from us before they read about it in the paper, hear it on the radio, or see it on the news. There is no need for secrecy any longer, and I'm calling Janna after I tell Mom and Dad," Elizabeth answered.

"Maybe secrecy was not the best route anyway. Mom and Dad can activate the Tabernacle prayer chain, and we can ask for prayer worldwide as we travel," said Xander. "We will put on the whole armor of God instead of hiding."

Above the car, four angels smiled widely.

I love playing offense, thought Michael.

You love playing defense, too, thought Gabriel, chuckling.

Michael grinned. *True.*

~~oo~~

As soon as they returned to the hotel, Charlotte went to Amy's room and Jonathan went to Dave's and Mark's, asking them to join them for a meeting in Xander and Elizabeth's room. Hector, Custodio, and Esmund joined Edward and Lexus, following their charges to the Xander's room. Esmund's eyes widened in surprise as they entered the room to find it lined with inscrutable, brawny warriors.

Xander stood behind Elizabeth with his arms crossed; Charlotte, Amy, Mark, and Dave joined Elizabeth at the table, and Jonathan stood by the window, close to Charlotte's chair. Xander heard him wondering why their curtains were always closed.

When Xander cleared his throat, everyone looked at him.

"My wife, Elizabeth, is indeed pregnant. Did any of you tell anyone that you suspected that she was with child?" His face was somber.

Amy, Mark, and Dave looked at each other, puzzled.

Dave spoke at once. "I had no idea that she was pregnant, but you have my heartiest congratulations." He smiled and reached across the table to shake first Elizabeth's hand and then Xander's.

Mark smiled, also shaking their hands. "That's wonderful news, but I had no clue either."

Amy thought a moment longer, distress evident in her expression.

Jonathan took a step closer to the table, watching her carefully.

Esmund thought, *She did not know it was a secret, and neither did I. None of you spoke it to me, and you know that I cannot hear thoughts of guardians who are not in my family unit unless they are spoken.*

"I'm so sorry," said Amy, her eyes filling with tears as she looked from Xander to Elizabeth. "My sister, Julie, is such a huge fan of the two of you, and she was disabled in a car accident a few years ago. She's paralyzed from the waist down and lives with Mom and Dad, hardly ever leaving the house. I texted her yesterday, telling her what hotel we were in, and that I thought you might be pregnant and not even know it yourself yet, Elizabeth. She wouldn't have told anyone. Why are you asking?"

Xander's face was grim, so Jonathan spoke immediately, "When we tried to leave the hotel this morning, we were greeted by photographers snapping pictures and asking questions about her pregnancy. We're just trying to figure out how they knew."

The tears overflowed Amy's eyes. "I try to talk to Julie everyday to keep her spirits up. She was so excited that I was traveling with you on this tour; she has all of your CDs and plays them constantly. Do you want me to ask her if she told anyone?"

"No," said Xander, a little too quickly.

Elizabeth glanced at him, and then smiled at Amy. "It's all right, Amy. We're sure she didn't tell anyone. In fact, Xander and I would like to send Julie some autographed CDs and pictures. When we get back to the States, we want to meet her. Right, my love?" Elizabeth lifted her soulful eyes to his, and his expression softened in response.

Xander made a concerted effort to smile at their newest staff member, handing her a box of tissues from the dresser. "Of course, Amy. I'll get those to you this afternoon so that you can mail them to her. Do not worry yourself about this. Everyone would have known eventually, and there is no harm done. However, since we do not know how this news became available to the press, we are going to have to ask you not to give out any more information to anyone unless Mark has already used it in a press release."

Mark nodded. "No one needs to know our travel arrangements or specific locations. We do not release the names of our hotels or anything about our daily schedules. What we do on our personal time is also private. That falls under the heading of 'need to know,' and no one outside of this room needs to know. It's a security issue."

Dave agreed. "I'm concerned about that, too, Mark. This appears to be a security breach of some sort. Could someone have access to our cell phones?"

Is that possible? asked Michael, speaking aloud so that all the angels could hear.

Dr. Sanders made a point that computers and cell phones are not secure, replied Gabriel.

Xander said, "Yesterday, Dr. Sanders said that he would not use cell phones or computers to communicate about Elizabeth's pregnancy with the doctors in other countries. He would not even enter our visit into his computer for fear that someone would get the information. It is possible that Amy's phone was hacked in some way. I have seen movies in which they cloned cell phones using some sort of a device. From now on, none of us should say anything by text messaging, e-mailing, or speaking on our cell phones that we do not want others outside of our circle to know. We can be fairly certain that someone has found a way to read Amy's text messages; it could be true of all of our electronic devices."

"I agree," said Jonathan.

"Why would anyone want to do that?" asked Amy, shock registering on her face.

Xander looked at her calmly. "Amy, we are in spiritual warfare with a devious enemy. If he can find a way to stop us or hinder us, he will. Satan will use anything at his disposal to disrupt this trip and distract us from our mission, and we must not allow him to do that. We cannot lower our guards for a moment. In the past, there have been attempts on Elizabeth's life as well as mine, and I cannot stress enough how serious this situation could become."

Elizabeth's eyes began to sparkle, and she glanced up at her husband. "This reminds me of a spy movie. There may be a way to use this against Satan."

Xander read her mind, and his eyes lit with understanding. "Very clever, my love. Instead of being on the defensive, as we have been for years, perhaps we should play a little offense."

He looked at the others, remembering that Mark, David, and Amy did not know he could read Elizabeth's mind. "Elizabeth and I like to watch movies to relax. We watched one not so long ago with a plot similar to what we are experiencing. Rather than let whomever Satan is using know that we have figured out his scheme, we should use his own device against him. We will plant information in Amy's text messages, giving him confidence that his plan is working. Everything that she says will be true and will come to pass. We will, of course, make sure that she gives away nothing that is important. Eventually, we may be able to control the source by giving him incorrect information or only what we want him to know."

Brilliant, said Michael with admiration.

Amy's tears dried on her cheeks. "That sounds like a plan. Just tell me what to say."

Xander smiled at her. "I will let you know exactly what to say and when to say it. We will beat him at his own game. This will not be a short term plan,

Amy. It may take years for it to come to fruition. We will not spring the trap until the time is right."

"I'm in it for the long haul – as long as you guys will have me," she answered.

"I like it," said Charlotte chuckling, "a lot."

Jonathan smiled at her. "Dropping the bits of insider information will also let us know if we are correct in our assumption that Amy's text was hacked. Each of us can send text messages about different things to people who are not in this room and see whose texts are being intercepted."

Elizabeth added, "Exactly. We can test our theory tomorrow by having Amy tell her sister where we'll be in the morning or where we'll eat lunch. Each of us can text someone outside of this circle with a message about something else – what time we're going to the arena or what we will be doing in the afternoon. If we control what the hacker knows, we can be prepared for the response of the media."

"Or anyone else," added Xander. He looked at the faces of the assembled SoulFire team. "I will write down the messages you are to send and give them to you in the morning. Text your message to a family member or friend not on this trip. We will see which message is acted upon."

Excellent, commented Gabriel.

Lucifer – 'hoist with his own petard.' I love it, thought Michael, his green eyes gleaming.

This is important. I am certain of it, answered Xander. *This is our way in to whatever Gregory has planned, for this has his stamp on it, not Lucifer's.*

Jonathan reached out both of his hands, holding Charlotte's on one side and Dave's on the other. Following his example, everyone joined hands, and Jonathan bowed his head to pray. "Thank you, Father, for showing us this chink in the enemy's armor. Show us the way to use it, Lord, and guide us to do Your perfect will. In Jesus' name. Amen."

~~oo~~

Mid-morning of the next day, Aborian cackled as he read Amy's text to her sister, Julie. He e-mailed Gregory and his media contacts the information immediately.

Xander and Elizabeth will be eating lunch away from the arena today at a Quiznos on Abbott Street. The team usually breaks for lunch around 1:00.

The demon looked around at his human and demonic team members, saying proudly, "That is how it's done. *Bon appétit*, SoulFire. Right now we are only irritating the couple, throwing them off their game. Later, we will find them in a more vulnerable place, and we will eliminate the entire team. From *bon appétit* to *bon voyage*."

High fives and laughter met Aborian's statement, and he basked in the warmth of their attention. His lack of strength in battle or useful gifts had been a disadvantage to him throughout his long existence, but he was thoroughly enjoying the new technological age. He had finally found something important at which he was supreme among his brothers. His name was now being spoken in the highest circles, and he would do anything to elevate himself even further.

Chapter 14

"'No weapon that is formed against you shall prosper; and every tongue that accuses you in judgment you will condemn. This is the heritage of the servants of the Lord, and their vindication is from Me,' declares the Lord."
Isaiah 54:17

Their plan had worked perfectly. Amy's text was the only one which had produced a response. As the SoulFire team stepped from their rental van at Quiznos for lunch, they were surrounded by photographers and reporters.

Michael took umbrage when one of them shoved a microphone in front of Elizabeth's face, the demon behind the man whispering encouragement in his ear.

The archangel glowered at the dark one, his hand on his sword and fire in his eyes. *You will answer for it if he harms her in any way,* said Michael with menace.

The demon smirked, but he stepped back and ceased speaking to the newsman.

"Are the rumors true, El? Are you pregnant? Will you and your husband leave the tour? Who will replace you?" the reporter asked loudly, crowding Elizabeth as she turned her body to her husband for protection.

Xander gently moved his wife behind him and stood towering over the man, Gabriel by his side. Glaring at the man fiercely, he struggled to calm himself. The clicking of cameras was heard as the questioning stopped.

Calm yourself. He will not harm Elizabeth or the child, thought Gabriel, placing his hand on Xander's shoulder.

Be assured of that, brother, growled Michael.

Mark Goodman, followed by Custodio, hurried to place himself between the Darcys and the media.

"Yes," Mark answered calmly, "we will confirm that Elizabeth Darcy is in the very early stages of pregnancy. She is doing well and does not anticipate any problems. She has already seen a doctor who has cleared her to travel. The Darcys have no plans to leave the tour. Now, please step aside and let us have our lunch."

Mark and Dave walked in front of Xander, Elizabeth, and Charlotte while Jonathan and Amy stepped in closely behind them, moving quickly to the door of the small restaurant. Their guardians surrounded them, forming an impenetrable shield.

They went quickly through the line, ordering their food as takeout and returning with it to the van. Jonathan took the driver's seat, looked in the rearview mirror, and asked, "Shall we return to the arena to eat, or would you rather go to a park or back to the hotel?"

When the others were silent, Xander spoke up. "I would like to return to the hotel for a couple of hours. We can eat in peace, and Elizabeth will have an opportunity to rest." He took her hand in his.

She looked at him gratefully. *Sometimes I love that you can read my thoughts. I am a little freaked out by the idea that we are being tracked so closely. I have known it for a long time, but I kept it in the back of my mind. Now I can't do that anymore. And now, there's the baby. What if they try to hurt our baby?*

The guardians flew over the van, as well as on either side of it, and Michael dipped through the roof of the vehicle, placing his hand gently on Elizabeth's head, speaking into her mind. *Isaiah 41:10 says, 'Do not fear, for I am with you; do not anxiously look about you, for I am your God. I will strengthen you, surely I will help you, Surely I will uphold you with My righteous right hand.'*

Thank you, Michael, she thought, releasing a sigh. *I need to be reminded of that from time to time.*

Is she upset? asked Jonathan, navigating the streets efficiently as they returned to the hotel with their lunch.

Yes, she is. She needs this time to get her mind off the idea that we are being monitored. She fears for the baby. We will eat in our room, but all of us need to do another test, answered Xander.

He looked at Amy. "I think we have established that your cell phone is compromised. Now we need to know if they have accessed your computer as well." He looked around at the other team members. "We will all send e-mails from our laptops tonight. I will write out the messages and give them to all of you after we return from the rally. So far, the enemy has not been bold with the information they have retrieved, but Satan will harm all of us if given the chance. We must be on guard at all times."

~~oo~~

"And I saw one of his heads as if it had been slain, and his fatal wound was healed. And the whole earth was amazed and followed after the beast."
Revelation 13:3

Senator Gregory Wickham descended the steps of the Capitol building, his personal guards close on his heels. As his agenda was advancing rapidly, he was much in demand, so it was no surprise when a crowd of reporters met the handsome Senator there, shouting questions with cameras rolling. The surprise was the young man who stepped up to Gregory, pulled a gun from his waistband, and shot him through the heart before he could be stopped.

Two of Gregory's guards immediately grabbed the criminal, jumping on him and throwing him to the steps, placing him in a chokehold. Policemen were on the scene nearly immediately, taking charge of the perpetrator and controlling the growing crowd.

Three of the Senator's guards hunched over him protectively, watching the blood pour from the wound and down the steps. Before more than a few minutes had passed, a doctor arrived, and one of the guards moved to allow him access to his master.

Gregory was pale, and his breathing was labored and shallow. He moaned, and then he was silent. The doctor checked for a heartbeat and felt for a pulse, but the Senator was dead. He began CPR, and soon the wail of a siren heralded the arrival of an ambulance.

The people parted to let the paramedics through, and a boom mike caught the doctor telling one of them that there was no pulse or heartbeat. Whispers of, "He's dead," ran through the shocked crowd. The paramedics started to lift the stricken man onto the gurney, but stopped short when he raised his head, fixing them with a stare.

"What are you doing?" asked Gregory, trying to sit up.

The doctor's eyes were round with astonishment, and he spoke with difficulty. "Please lie down on the gurney, Senator. You have been badly wounded," said the doctor, placing his hand on Gregory's arm.

"I feel fine. What happened?" demanded Gregory, shaking off the doctor's hand and looking at one of his guards.

"A man came out of the crowd and shot you through the heart," he answered, lowering his eyes.

Gregory sat up, glanced down at his chest, and saw the blood. He touched the hole in his suit jacket. "Help me take this off," he said to the guard, standing up and turning his back to the guard for his assistance.

"Senator, I must insist that you let us examine you," said one of the paramedics.

"You may examine me in a moment," Gregory answered tersely.

The guard held the coat as Gregory pulled his arms from it. "Ruined one of my favorite suits," muttered Gregory, adding an oath. The people gasped at the sight of his blood-soaked shirt. He quickly unbuttoned it and pulled it from his pants, opening it so that his chest was visible.

"Wash away the blood," Gregory instructed one of the paramedics.

"But, sir –" the man began.

"Wash it away!" ordered Gregory, amber eyes flashing. "Now!" Gregory closed his eyes as they glowed red. He breathed deeply, and then opened his eyes, looking at the EMT. "Hand me a cloth so that I can wipe it off."

Gregory reached out his hand, and the paramedic put a towel into it.

The doctor tried to reason with Gregory. "Senator, touching the wound is a bad idea. If somehow the blood has clotted, you could start the bleeding again. Besides, it must hurt."

Gregory swabbed at his chest until he had cleared away most of the blood. "I feel no pain at all," he replied. "You may examine the wound now."

The doctor bent to lean his face closer to Gregory's chest, and then straightened up with a puzzled look. "There is no sign of a gunshot wound at all! Not the tiniest scratch!" He looked at Gregory's shirt and saw the hole, squarely over the area which would have covered his heart. He checked Gregory's pulse. "His heartbeat is strong and steady. I can't explain it."

Gregory laughed lightly.

"You were dead," the doctor insisted.

Gregory fixed him with a level gaze. "Yes, doctor, I was. However, I am no longer dead, and I have a busy day scheduled, so you must excuse me."

He waved to the amazed, silent crowd and walked to his car, which had pulled up to the curb. After he was seated and the car had pulled into traffic, Gregory turned to his guards. "That went rather well," he said. "We should make the evening news easily."

They smirked in answer.

A few hours later, in a holding cell not far away, a man faded to nothingness, and then walked through the walls, flying away to freedom. The camera trained on him caught his disappearance, but when the technicians tried to view his escape, the screen showed nothing but static.

On the evening news, Dirk Horne reported on the incident, showing the riveting footage of the attempted assassination and blaming the attack on fringe extremists who were opposed to the good Senator's ideas for helping the poor and rescuing the economy. He showed his outrage that the shooter had escaped and said that he must have been allowed to do so by a guard who disagreed with the Senator's politics, vowing that the investigation would continue until the guilty party was exposed.

Senator Wickham's amazing resurrection was shown around the globe, and his face became a well-known symbol of a man who risked his own life in the service of his people. The miracle of his restored life was the stuff of legends, and Gregory Wickham's power and prestige grew.

~~oo~~

"And as He was sitting on the Mount of Olives, the disciples came to Him privately, saying, 'Tell us, when will these things be, and what will be the sign of Your coming, and of the end of the age?'"
Matthew 24:3

The Vancouver rally was successful beyond any expectations. Xander and Elizabeth had written new music expressly for the tour, and they sang and played those songs for the first time in Vancouver. The theme, The Globe for God, was woven like a thread throughout their music, tying it all together, and the urgency of the message was clearly expressed.

Ethnic groups from throughout the city flocked to hear the gospel in their own languages through Elizabeth's amazing gift as she sang and spoke of God's love and forgiveness.

Michael stood close to her at all times, scanning the audience constantly. He had stationed warriors throughout the arena, and their armor gleamed alongside the white tunics of the thousands of guardians present with their charges.

Xander, Gabriel beside him, began a series of talks about spiritual warfare which would continue throughout the four days of meetings, punctuating his main points by speaking in the different languages of the people present while the screens behind him displayed his words in English. As he heard the people's questions through their thoughts, he worked the answers into his presentation.

Jonathan spoke last, Lexus behind him, beginning a fascinating four sermon series about the end times, showing from Scripture, particularly Matthew 24, the evidence that some of the prophecies had already been fulfilled and other prophetic events were in the process of happening, taking place in the present. Off stage, Elizabeth repeated his words into a microphone which fed into a system set up with ear buds available for those who did not speak English.

As Jonathan bowed his head to pray, Thorncrown took the stage, playing "For You" softly. When Jonathan opened the altar, inviting people to come, more than a thousand counselors walked down the aisles to receive the crowd flooding the front of the arena, the mass of their guardians creating a gentle glow around them

While the band sang, "He came for you. He died for you. He lives for you," the counselors took groups of people seeking salvation into areas set aside for the purpose of prayer and counsel, and new guardians joined their charges.

Finally, Xander, Elizabeth, Charlotte, and Jonathan were left at the edge of the stage, waiting to see if any others needed counseling.

Xander then saw a sight which chilled him – hundreds of demons swarmed the building, heading at them from all directions. He immediately issued a summons to all available guardians, and they flooded in behind the demons within a few seconds.

Elizabeth's breath quickened as she sensed the oppression of the evil ones. Xander instinctively stepped in front of her while Michael and Gabriel formed a shield before them.

Jonathan and Charlotte clasped their hands together, feeling the very air change around them. They knelt to pray as Lexus and Edward joined Michael and Gabriel, forming a line between their charges and the shrieking denizens of hell.

Thorncrown's guardians closed ranks in front of them, and the people left in the audience moved toward the center, huddling together as their guardians whispered directions into their minds. Non-believers followed them, feeling the emptiness which had invaded the building. Guardians and warriors met in a circle of protection around the gathered mass of people.

A huge demon settled in front of Michael, throwing back his raven hair and lifting his chin arrogantly. His troops landed around him, filling the front of the arena.

Michael narrowed his eyes and spoke, "What do you want here, Abigor? Do you seek a battle today?"

The demonic warrior, commander of sixty legions, laughed.

Elizabeth shivered and stepped closer into her husband's back, putting her arms about his waist and peeking around his arm. *I can see something, but I don't know what it is.*

What do you see? asked Xander.

Many dark forms like large men with wings, she answered. *The biggest one stands in front of Michael. I heard him laugh just now.*

Michael and Gabriel also heard her thoughts but made no reaction.

Abigor spoke in a rough voice, "We have come for the child. We wish to know what Xander has spawned with the human woman. Give her to us, or let us take the child from her, and we will leave. If you refuse, we will fight to take her."

Elizabeth's hold on her husband tightened, and she struggled to contain her fear, knowing that the evil ones would feed off her terror.

"You fear the power of an infant?" Michael chuckled ominously. In his mind, the Captain of the Host called for fifty thousand warriors, and they were stationed around the demons before Abigor could speak again.

"When did you become so weak, Abigor? The child is not yet born, and you quake before a babe which cannot yet survive outside the womb. Do you also fear the child's mother? You are pathetic," said Michael.

Abigor roared. "I fear neither the child nor the mother! My master has need of the child, and I obey his commands."

Michael laughed aloud. "So Lucifer is frightened of the babe? How ashamed you must be to serve such a weakling."

Elizabeth felt the truth of Michael's words, and his strength flowed into her. She released her hold on Xander and stood tall, stepping to his side and staring straight at Abigor.

Xander immediately knew the difference in her mind, and the change was exhilarating to him. *You are no longer afraid of them. You know that you are safe, and that our Father will not let them harm you or our child.*

She smiled, never releasing Abigor's eyes. *I do. I think I could drink poison now, and it would not affect me.*

Elizabeth began to quote II Chronicles 20:15, 17 aloud, the words ringing throughout the building as she spoke in a strong voice. "Thus said the Lord to you, 'Do not fear or be dismayed because of this great multitude, for the battle is not yours but God's. You need not fight in this battle; station yourselves, stand and see the salvation of the Lord on your behalf… Do not fear or be dismayed…for the Lord is with you.'"

Xander's joy was boundless; he wanted to soar to the heavens with her. Instead he began to sing praises to God, just as Jehoshaphat and his men had done in the same chapter of Scripture Elizabeth had quoted. His strong, rich baritone rang out with the words of "The Battle Belongs to the Lord." Elizabeth's sweet soprano lifted in harmony with his song.

Jonathan and Charlotte rose to their feet singing with Xander and Elizabeth, and when Thorncrown heard their voices, they began to play. Before long, everyone remaining in the arena was singing as loudly as they could.

The demons put their hands over their ears and writhed in agony while Michael, Gabriel, and the other angels glowed more brightly and hummed in praise to the One who could inspire such fearlessness in His followers.

When Xander finished singing the first song, he transitioned into "Amazing Grace (My Chains Are Gone)," and the band as well as the other people followed. As the saints worshipped, a holy Light permeated the building, and the demons could not stay in Its blinding purity. Cursing, they fled, flying in all directions, scrambling into each other in their haste to leave.

As the last strains of the song faded, the beams of Light withdrew from the arena, and an awed silence settled over the people. After a moment, the ones who were not yet believers ran down the aisles toward salvation. Xander,

Elizabeth, Jonathan, and Charlotte divided them into four groups, took them to different parts of the arena, and ushered them into the family of God.

Gabriel looked across the arena at Michael and thought, *'And the Lord was adding to their number day by day those who were being saved.'*

Michael smiled and returned, *Acts 2:47. It is almost as if we are living the days of the early church again.*

Chapter 15

"For man does not originate from woman, but woman from man; for indeed man was not created for the woman's sake, but woman for the man's sake. Therefore, the woman ought to have a symbol of authority on her head, because of the angels. However, in the Lord, neither is woman independent of man, nor is man independent of woman. For as the woman originates from the man, so also the man has his birth through the woman; and all things originate from God."
I Corinthians 11:8-12

Late January 2010

Xander watched Elizabeth as she moved slowly around their baby's nursery in the late afternoon light, her right hand cradling her nine-months pregnant belly tenderly as she smoothed the blankets in the crib with her left. Her face was serene, and though she was unwieldy and a little awkward with the extra weight of their son, he thought she was the most beautiful sight he had ever beheld.

Michael and Gabriel moved to either end of the crib as Xander quickly crossed the room to stand behind his wife, pulling her against his chest and placing his hands over hers as they rubbed her stomach together.

"I will do whatever needs to be done, my love. Please sit in the rocking chair; you must be tired," he said softly. "You have not rested today. Shall we take a nap together before dinner?"

She laid her head back on his chest and drew his hands closer about her, hugging herself with his arms. "I am a little tired, but I don't think I can sleep. I just keep seeing things that need to be done before the baby comes."

"Then tell me what to do, Elizabeth," Xander said as he rocked her gently, swaying from side to side. "I am your obedient servant."

Elizabeth lifted his arm across her chest and turned the palm of his hand against her cheek. She looked around at the lovely room, painted a light yellow with white crown moulding. The curtains were hung at the bay windows, and the white furniture was in place. She and Xander had shopped for the furnishings as soon as they had returned from the tour in November, and her parents had been delighted to help with the painting. Elizabeth had actually done very little.

David and Lynne had joined the tour for the final month. Because of the overwhelming response in the rallies, they had been needed to help with counseling, and Lynne wanted to be with Elizabeth as she increased. She had helped her daughter shop for much-needed maternity clothes, and while they all traveled together, they had been able to plan the nursery.

"Love, you are so good to me. You have already done everything, and it's wonderful. There really isn't anything left to do, but I am restless. I'm so heavy that I waddle everywhere, and I can't get comfortable." *I feel so fat and ugly.* She sighed.

He lifted her into his arms and carefully made his way down the stairs, sitting on the couch with her in his lap, stroking her poor swollen feet with one hand as he held her with the other.

Michael and Gabriel positioned themselves at the ends of the sofa. Elizabeth could see their outlines, glowing faintly, and she took comfort in knowing that her baby was so well protected.

Xander gazed into her eyes and spoke firmly. "You have never been ugly for even one second of your life, and I have been with you for all of it, so I would know. Gaining twenty-five pounds hardly qualifies you as being fat, either. You grow more radiant every day, and you have never been more beautiful to me. You could never be anything but lovely in my eyes." He then lowered his face to hers and kissed her in a way that proved how attractive she still was to him.

Elizabeth turned her body into his and put her arms around his neck, nuzzling her face into the soft place under his jaw. He rubbed her back slowly, seeking out the sore spots and knots, listening to her thoughts directing him when to use more pressure.

She kissed his neck. "You always know what to say to make me feel better. I love you so much," she said, her words slow and sluggish.

Xander replied gently, "I love you, too." He continued to massage her back even after he felt her relax in sleep. As she cuddled against him, warm and soft, his hand slowed and his head rested on her shoulder as their eyes closed. Their dreams mingled, both envisioning a dark-haired child laughing and dancing.

Michael looked at Gabriel with a smile, thinking, *As Proverbs 30:18-19 says, 'There are three things which are too wonderful for me, four which I do not understand; the way of an eagle in the sky, the way of a serpent on a rock, the way of a ship in the middle of the sea, and the way of a man with a maid.'*

Gabriel mused, *The writer, Agur, was wise to recognize that it was beyond him to understand those things which left no trails and had no recognizable mode of action that would determine their courses. Even twenty years ago, we could never have predicted the growth of love between our brother and our sister. I have to agree that it is wonderful.*

Michael thought a moment, and then answered in contemplation, *She truly completes him. In the beginning, God did not create a woman and say that she needed a man; rather, he created a man and said that he needed a* woman. In their case, it is literally true as well. Xander was created thousands of years before Elizabeth was born.

Gabriel replied, *And our brother acted in a manner toward his virgin as God would have him behave. In doing so, he won her love and devotion. It is sad that today, most young men do not realize that the responsibility for behavior before marriage lies with them. Their unions, based on a faulty premise, often do not survive.*

Michael watched Xander and Elizabeth sleep. *It was not easy for him, but he pleased God with his actions. I have never thought much about marriage before, but our brother studied the Scriptures, obeyed Jehovah, and built a strong relationship with his beloved based on a pure love for each other and shared devotion to God rather than a purely physical attraction. His wise decisions will bring them both much joy, and a union that glorifies our Master. Xander is a good example for any young man. He is a wonderful husband and will be an excellent father.*

Gabriel nodded. *I have recently thought that the Almighty knew exactly which angel to choose for this assignment. The Creator's wisdom is beyond comprehension. Neither you nor I would have done as well as our brother has.*

Michael's expression was serious. *You are right, brother. You would have been too easy, and I would have been too harsh. Xander was the perfect choice for Elizabeth.*

The angels maintained their constant vigil while the twilight fell and the room darkened, and the lovers remained embraced in slumber.

~~oo~~

"Xander," Elizabeth whispered. "Xander!" she said in a louder voice, wiggling against him.

As Xander came to consciousness, he saw that the room was dark, and he was lying on his side, holding his wife in his arms to prevent her from falling off the couch. He slowly sat up, careful to cradle her as he did so.

"Elizabeth? Are you hungry? We have slept through dinner time," he said as his stomach growled.

"I believe I'm in labor, but the pains are still about twenty minutes apart, I think. I want to walk. You should eat, but I can't," she answered, turning in his lap to put her feet on the floor.

"I should eat? While you are in labor?" He reached to turn on the lamp by the couch so that she could see.

As she clambered off his lap, he rose to his feet to help her stand.

Elizabeth watched him as he helped her up. "You must be stiff from staying in one position, holding me for so long," she said. "And yes, you must eat because I think we'll have to go to the hospital in a few hours. I can't eat because the doctor may need to use anesthesia." Her tone was reasonable.

He frowned, "Can you walk with me to the kitchen? I will not leave you alone."

Michael and Gabriel materialized, wearing jeans and Henleys.

"She will not be alone," said Michael.

Gabriel added, "We will certainly be here, in human form, to make Elizabeth more comfortable."

Elizabeth smiled as she looked at Michael and Gabriel. "You know, I will be safe with Uncle Michael and Uncle Gabriel, I know, but why don't we all go to the kitchen? I'm sure you won't eat unless you can see me."

Michael and Gabriel looked a little stunned, but Xander's lips twitched. "Good idea, love. Uncle Mike and Uncle Gabe can come with us. I will make myself an omelet if you insist that I must eat."

The little procession made its way into the adjoining kitchen, and Xander started assembling what he needed to cook. Michael and Gabriel took their stances on either side of Elizabeth as she stood before the sink, looking out of the window over the moonlit back yard. She rubbed her stomach with both hands, making large circles. Xander turned from the stove just in time to see her face contort in discomfort. *That was a strong one,* she thought. *Dear Lord, help me to bear it without crying out.*

He moved the pan to a cold burner and went to her.

"How long have you been having pains, Elizabeth? Why did you not wake me?" he asked.

"A couple of hours, and you needed to sleep. You'll probably be awake the rest of the night. Please, eat your omelet. There's nothing you can do right now, and I'm going to need you later," she replied as she stood on her tiptoes to kiss his cheek.

He frowned, but he realized that her reasoning was sound. He put the omelet on a plate and ate it quickly, watching her as she continued to stroke her stomach. Just as he finished, he saw her flinch again, and she leaned over the sink, grasping the edge of the counter. He practically threw the plate into the sink in his hurry to get to her.

"Elizabeth, the pains are not twenty minutes apart. There were fewer than ten minutes between the last one and this one. We should go to the hospital now," he said, pulling his brows together.

"Calm down, please. I've never seen you so upset," she soothed, turning her head to look at him. "Dr. Neal told me to call her when the pains are five minutes apart. My water hasn't broken. I'm fine, really."

Xander stood behind her, his hands over hers as they rubbed her stomach together. He had just begun to relax when he felt the muscles contract beneath his fingers and heard his wife grunt.

He could be inactive no longer. "Enough. I am calling Dr. Neal now. Gabriel, would you get her suitcase from upstairs? Her shoes are there by the bed, too." *Father, please help her. Please do not let her suffer.*

Gabriel was so quick that Xander had not finished punching the doctor's pre-programmed number before he was back with her shoes and case. The archangel knelt before her, sliding her shoes on her feet as she lifted one foot and then the other.

"Oh, no!" cried Elizabeth in embarrassment, feeling the warmth running down her legs.

Michael grabbed the drawer with the kitchen towels, pulling it completely out of the cabinet in his haste to get them. He took a huge handful, thrusting them at Elizabeth who used them to mop at the wetness. She dropped the soaked towels to the floor where the amniotic fluid had puddled between her feet, and Gabriel remained kneeling before her, mopping up the liquid.

Xander told the doctor they were on their way to the hospital, shoved the phone in his pocket, and scooped his wife up in his arms, heading for the door.

"I need to change clothes," she objected. "I'm wet."

He didn't slow down, calling over his shoulder as he went through the front door and down the steps, his voice assuming the tone of command. "Michael, bring some towels for her to sit on. Gabriel, get her suitcase. I want both of you to morph back into angelic form so that we can all be in the labor and delivery rooms with her. Elizabeth, it will take us ten minutes to get to the hospital. They will put you in a clean, dry gown there. I am sorry, but we cannot wait for you to change clothes now."

"But, Xander –" she began, and then stopped short when she looked at his determined face. *You are the Chief of the Guardians right now. I will let you do your job,* she thought wisely.

Hearing her thoughts, Xander realized that he was in command mode, but he could not help himself. He looked at her large eyes as he put her in the car. "Am I frightening you?" he asked.

Her smile was small. "A little," she admitted. "I've never seen you so focused before, and the whole 'large and in charge' thing is different, but it's growing on me. I kind of like this caveman side of you. Remember that for later," she laughed. Her laughter was short-lived as another contraction took her.

She instinctively reached for his hand and squeezed as she bent over and breathed through the pain. *Dear God, this hurts. Help me not to show it and upset my husband.* As soon as she loosened her grip, he started the car and backed out of the driveway, Michael and Gabriel flying overhead with the phalanx of warriors whom Michael had summoned.

Xander drove with his left hand so that his wife could grasp his right hand as the pains came. A nurse waited at the Emergency Room doors as he pulled the car up.

"Here you go, sweetie," said the nurse, helping Elizabeth into the wheelchair. "Mr. Xander, you can park the car while I take her inside."

"No," he said. "I do not want her out of my sight."

The nurse looked at him, quizzically. "We'll wait for you just inside the door."

Xander took a deep breath. "Thank you. I will hurry." *Michael and Gabriel, go with her.*

As Gabriel began to object that he should stay with his charge, Xander nearly growled. He clenched his teeth, working his jaw. *I said, go with Elizabeth. Leave a few warriors with me if you must.*

His brothers remained silent and did as they were told.

Trying to talk with him now is pointless, thought Michael.

Obviously, answered Gabriel.

As the nurse wheeled Elizabeth into the building, Xander parked in the nearest space, thankful that it was the middle of the night and the lot was nearly empty.

He reached into the back seat and grabbed Elizabeth's bag before he hurried into the building, relieved beyond measure to see her just inside the door with the nurse. Michael and Gabriel stood on either side of her, faces carefully neutral. Warriors surrounded the hospital and stood throughout the building.

Xander stepped to his wife's side, and Michael moved to follow them as the nurse pushed her into a room to be examined. Before the nurse could help Elizabeth from the chair, he had lifted her and placed her on the bed. The nurse lifted an eyebrow, but refrained from speaking.

Dr. Neal hurried in, her guardian Alexandra close behind her. "Mr. Xander, would you please step outside while I examine your wife?" she asked.

Good luck with that, thought the nurse.

She has your number, Xander, Michael thought.

Zip it, Michael, was Xander's curt response.

"I would prefer to stay with her, Dr. Neal," answered Xander, trying not to sound threatening.

Elizabeth quickly said, "I want him to stay, doctor. It's okay."

Dr. Neal looked surprised, but she acquiesced to the wishes of her patient. "Fine," she said, lifting Elizabeth's gown and putting her feet in the stirrups.

The doctor asked Elizabeth questions during the examination, stopping when Elizabeth had a contraction. When she was finished with her evaluation, she looked from Xander to Elizabeth, saying, "You are farther along than I thought, and your labor is progressing rapidly. I expect the baby will be born in a couple of hours. I have to see a few other patients, and then I'll be back to check on you."

As soon as the doctor left, Elizabeth asked her husband to call her parents.

He did as she requested, advising them that she would probably not deliver for at least two hours and there was no need to rush to the hospital. Lynne told him that they would call Janna and Chance, and then come as soon as they were dressed.

Xander remained by Elizabeth's side, encouraging her and sponging her face throughout her labor, and Michael and Gabriel took positions at the head of her bed, one at either corner. He obeyed the admonition in I Thessalonians 5:17 and prayed without ceasing, sometimes aloud and at other times in his mind.

A nurse entered periodically to check on her progress, and after an hour of watching his wife bear the painful contractions, Xander asked the nurse if she could bring Elizabeth something for pain.

The nurse looked at Elizabeth. "You're probably too far along for an epidural. I think you'll be ready to deliver within an hour. Do you want pain meds?"

He spoke into his wife's mind. *Please, love. You do not have to be a hero.*

Elizabeth looked at her worried husband, and then back at the nurse. "I'm tired. I've been up all night, and it's hard to concentrate on breathing through the contractions. Could I have some Demerol?"

The nurse nodded. "I'll check with Dr. Neal and be right back."

In a few minutes, the nurse returned and injected the drug into Elizabeth's IV. Xander listened to her thoughts and could tell that she had relaxed. The contractions were coming quickly, but in her mind, time was stretched, and she seemed to distance herself from the pain.

Thank you, Father. I cannot say all that is in my heart, prayed Xander.

Dr. Neal came in to check on Elizabeth and smiled at her. "I think you're ready to have this baby."

As another nurse came into the room, Michael and Gabriel moved to the head of Elizabeth's bed, and Xander put on the gloves which a nurse handed to him.

Everything happened so rapidly from that point on that it all blurred together in Xander's mind. As the baby's head crowned, Dr. Neal called for him to stand by her and told Elizabeth not to push during her next contraction. When the pain hit again, Dr. Neal told her to push, and as Elizabeth pushed a few more times, he watched in amazement as his wife delivered their child. Dr. Neal positioned the tiny boy on Elizabeth's stomach and handed Xander scissors, instructing him in how and where to cut the cord; he did as he was told. As the nurses wiped the tiny infant clean, Elizabeth lifted her head to see her two men.

"Is everything all right?" she asked, the exhaustion clear in her voice.

"Everything is perfect. You are wonderful, and our son is beautiful. Rest, love," answered Xander, looking at her with his heart in his eyes. *Thank you, Father, for my family. Thank you that Elizabeth is safely through this. Thank you for our healthy son. I love you, Lord.*

After a moment, the nurses took the baby to complete the required tests and finish cleaning him as Xander removed his gloves and went to Elizabeth's side, brushing her hair back from her damp forehead and kissing her cheek.

"I want to hold him," said Elizabeth, looking up at her husband.

"You're not quite finished, Elizabeth. When you feel another contraction, push again. You have to deliver the afterbirth," said Dr. Neal from the foot of the bed.

Xander held his wife's hand throughout the process, and when she was finished, Dr. Neal left to deliver another child as a nurse massaged Elizabeth's stomach.

Finally, one of the nurses handed the baby to Xander, and he stepped up beside Elizabeth, laying the child gently on her chest before he leaned over to kiss her cheek.

"You are a champion," he said, admiring her. "I am indescribably proud of you, my love. How do you like our son?"

"John David Xander is the second most important man in my life now," she said lifting her head to kiss her son's head of dark curls. She turned her gaze to her husband. "He is as beautiful as you are, Xander." *Thank you, Abba Father. My soul magnifies you, Lord. Help us to be good parents to this child.*

Xander straightened up when an orderly approached, saying, "Let's get her into the maternity ward for recovery." He, Michael, and Gabriel followed as the man rolled the bed into another room.

Little John David chose that moment to begin crying, his newborn wail like that of an angry kitten, displaying his dimples.

Elizabeth smiled at her husband. "He has your dimples, and he can already sing, too. I think that's an F sharp."

Michael and Gabriel smiled at each other from opposite sides of Elizabeth's bed.

That is my nephew, Michael thought into Elizabeth's mind. *You have done well.*

He will call me Uncle Gabriel, and we will sit on the floor together and play games, said Gabriel to his sister.

She smiled as Xander chuckled and thought, *Now you are happy to be Uncle Michael and Uncle Gabriel?*

Another Voice spoke to all of them at once. *I am well pleased. It is good. The child is a legacy.*

As husband and wife exchanged a solemn look, a warrior and a guardian joined them. The warrior, Cahal, was from the highest ranks, a commander of renown. Kenward, the guardian, was well-known to Xander. They had often worked in tandem, protecting husbands and wives. When Xander had guarded Abraham, Kenward had protected Sarah, and it had been the same with Moses and Kipporah, Jacob and Rebekah, King David and Bathsheba, and Queen Victoria and Prince Albert. He looked at Kenward and raised an eyebrow in question.

Kenward raised his palm in salute to his chief and answered his unspoken inquiry. *Cahal and I have been sent by the Master to guard your child together.*

Xander now knew why his son had not had a guardian from the moment of his conception. God had allowed him to wonder about it so that he would fiercely guard their secret. In doing so, he had uncovered the enemy's ability to read Amy's texts, hear her phone conversations, and intercept her e-mails. He briefly thought about how important that information could be in the Master's plan.

The Chief of Guardians looked at his wife and son as he prayed, *Father, thank You so much for Your love and protection. You are worthy of praise in all things, and You have blessed me beyond measure. I love you, Lord.*

~~oo~~

Senator Gregory Wickham and his wife Anne sat in an upscale restaurant in Washington, D.C. Several photographers stopped by their table and asked for pictures, and Gregory graciously granted their requests, leaning closer to his wife and smiling.

Across the room, Vice President Andrews was entertaining a group of his closest friends and their wives. Champagne flowed freely, and their laughter carried across the room. Earlier in the day, as President of the Senate, the fifty-year-old Vice President had cast a tie-breaking vote, defeating one of Senator Wickham's pet bills, and he was celebrating his victory. He had objected to the bill very publicly, calling it unconstitutional and an encroachment upon the rights of the people, and he was enjoying the feeling of power over Wickham, the darling of the media.

Andrews speared a large piece of steak and put it into his mouth, barely chewing it in his eagerness to return to the conversation. He swallowed it nearly whole, and it stuck in his throat. Within a few seconds, the others at the table had noticed that he was choking, and one of the men jumped up to hit him on the back. When that was ineffective, another tried the Heimlich maneuver without success. After five minutes, the Vice President blacked out, though patrons came from different parts of the restaurant, trying to help him.

Within ten minutes, an ambulance had pulled up to the front of the restaurant, and emergency personnel rushed to assist the choking man, but they were too late. Vice President Howard Andrews was dead.

Gregory had watched the entire scene, hiding his smirk behind his hand.

As the Vice President was wheeled from the crowded restaurant, Gregory stood respectfully, bowed his head, and held his wife's hand. The photographers captured an appropriately shocked and grieved expression on his handsome face.

By the next morning, Senator Gregory Wickham had been nominated by the President to be the new Vice President. There was no doubt that both the House and the Senate would confirm his nomination.

Chapter 16

"Now the serpent was more crafty than any beast of the field which the Lord God had made."
Genesis 3:1

Xander and Elizabeth settled into parenting joyously, taking little John David with them on the SoulFire USA tour in the summer of 2010. Because two of the members of Thorncrown were married and also had a baby, SoulFire Ministries had hired a young woman, Anna Armstrong, to travel with them and babysit the two infants during rehearsals and rallies. She fit so well with SoulFire that no one could imagine what it would be like without her; her guardian, Halvard, was also a welcome addition to the ranks.

Toward the end of the summer tour, Elizabeth began to notice that she was tiring more easily than was normal for her. Xander, holding their son, noticed the dark circles under her eyes following a rally one night and suggested that they forego their training session.

"I don't think we should skip training, my love. I really think I should keep working at developing my skills in light of what could be happening soon. I also think I'll feel better if I exercise. Besides, I'll get a better night's sleep," Elizabeth said to her concerned husband.

She is probably right, thought Michael. *We will know if she is overly fatigued.*

Gabriel added, *Training gives her a feeling of confidence, and she is becoming quite adept in her skills. There is a reason God gave you the idea to train her, and I think it might go beyond having to defend herself against Gregory before you married.*

Xander frowned slightly. He could not bear to think of Elizabeth truly fighting, having to protect herself against the dark ones. *We will always take care of her.*

He offered her a compromise. "If I agree to the workout, will you agree to let Anna keep John David tonight so that you can get a full night's sleep, uninterrupted?" he asked, kissing the baby and bouncing him in his arms.

The hotel had furnished them with cribs for both rooms, and Elizabeth had stopped breastfeeding him just before the tour had started. Anna's room had everything necessary for their child's comfort and care, just as theirs did.

She thought a moment. *I don't like to be separated from my baby.*

He is seven months old now. You are hardly abandoning him, my love, answered Xander. *He will be in the adjoining room, and Anna can get us quickly if we are needed.*

Elizabeth sighed and held out her arms. "Okay. Give him to me. I'll take him to Anna and ask her to put him down for the night."

Xander smiled at her. "Before he leaves us to go to sleep, we must pray with him." He kissed his son's forehead, and the boy's chubby fingers reached for his father's ears.

He laughed and knelt, holding his son close to his chest. Elizabeth went to her knees beside her husband and took his free hand, placing her other hand on her baby's shoulder. Michael and Gabriel stood on either side of their charges, their hands lightly touching Xander's and Elizabeth's heads, as John David's guardians stepped up behind them for the nightly ritual.

"Bow your head, John David," said Xander, looking into the serious blue eyes of his boy. John David put his head on his father's shoulder and closed his eyes.

"Dear Father, thank you for John David. I pray that You will keep him safe tonight and hold him close in Your hands. I pray that he will grow up to be a man who loves You and follows in Your ways. In Jesus' name. Amen," said Xander softly.

Elizabeth took her son in her arms and smiled as he gurgled at her, tangling his small hands in her hair. "I'm glad that he loves Anna. He won't mind sleeping in her room tonight."

Cahal and Kenward joined Halvard in Anna's room.

~~oo~~

Back in their room after their training session, Xander stood behind his wife as she faced the bathroom mirror and brushed her long hair. He took the brush from her and put his arms around her waist. As his hands covered her stomach, an idea took root in his mind.

"Elizabeth," he said, looking at her in the mirror, "have you missed a period?"

She turned in his arms to face him, looking up at him as she concentrated. It was obvious that she was doing the mental math. Suddenly she smiled. "Yes, I missed last month, and it's time for another one – which I show no signs of starting. Do you think I'm –"

He hugged her to his chest. "I do, but I cannot be certain. There is no guardian, but perhaps God will not supply one until the birth, just as He did with John David. The tour will be over in a week, and you can see Dr. Neal when we return home. The timing is perfect, as God's timing always is. You would deliver between the short fall Global Tour and the long one next summer."

She put her arms around his neck, drawing him down for a kiss. "I haven't felt sick like I did the last time, but Mom says that every pregnancy is different. Maybe I'll just skip the whole morning sickness routine with this baby."

He kissed her again, lightly. "Would you mind being pregnant again so soon?"

Elizabeth smiled and put her hands on either side of his face. "Not at all. I am glad, though, that we put off finishing our doctorates. We are just too busy, and I certainly wouldn't want us to shortchange our children. But, Xander, how do you feel about having a fat wife again? I haven't had my figure back but a few months."

He lowered his forehead to hers. "Have I ever acted as if I find you unattractive, Mrs. Xander?"

She laughed. "I believe the evidence speaks to the contrary, Mr. Xander."

He picked her up and carried her to the bed, holding her with one arm as he drew the covers down with his other hand. After gently laying her on the sheets, Xander knelt by the bed, turned his head toward her face, and placed his ear against her stomach.

She was watching him closely for his reaction.

He smiled at her broadly. "I hear the heartbeat. It is somewhat different from the way John David's sounded. Can you hear it through my mind?"

She listened intently as he projected the sound through his thoughts. Her joy was in her eyes as she heard the thudding of the tiny heart. "It does seem to be beating in double time, but it is very strong," she said.

Xander sat on the edge of the bed, turning to pull her into his arms. "We have done very well, my love. I think we are well on our way to that full quiver mentioned in Psalm 127:3-5. I can say with Solomon, 'Behold, children are a gift of the Lord; the fruit of the womb is a reward. Like arrows in the hand of a warrior, so are the children of one's youth. How blessed is the man whose quiver is full of them; they shall not be ashamed, when they speak with their enemies in the gate.'"

He kissed her deeply. *How can my love keep expanding this way? The more I love you and our children, the more love I have to give. I want to show you how much I love you, Elizabeth.*

"What about that rest that I need so badly?" she asked innocently.

"You said that you rest better after exercise. I am helping you in that respect – though, if you prefer, I can just rub your back until you fall asleep," he replied, a small smile playing about his lips as he held her in his arms.

Elizabeth kept her arms around his neck, drawing him beside her into the bed. "I'll never turn down a back rub, but if that leads to other things, we can sleep a little later in the morning, perhaps?"

In answer, Xander turned off the alarm and texted Jonathan that he and Elizabeth would be late for breakfast.

Michael and Gabriel faced the windows.

~~oo~~

Xander and Elizabeth entered the dining room with John David around ten the next morning, surprised to see Charlotte and Jonathan just sitting down to eat. Of further and more pressing interest to Xander, Michael, and Gabriel, however, was the extra guardian with the young couple. Alec lifted his palm in salute to his Chief, the Captain, and the archangel, and they nodded in acknowledgement. Cahal and Kenward saluted the newest addition to their group.

Lexus and Edward stood behind their charges.

Charlotte is with child? asked Michael, looking toward Lexus.

Lexus allowed himself a smile. *She is. The child was conceived after Xander sent his message to Jonathan. They also decided to 'sleep in.'*

Gabriel beamed beatifically. *That is wonderful news. It appears that Elizabeth is into her second month with another child as well. Our Master has abundantly blessed this team.*

Elizabeth, you cannot show any change of expression, but Charlotte is pregnant, too. I have just met the baby's guardian, said Xander into her mind.

Elizabeth hid her smiling face by kissing John David's cheek. *I am so excited! Charlotte and I will carry our children together. We can share this with each other. Don't worry; I'll keep the secret, but I can't pretend that it will be easy to do so. Fortunately, I won't have to keep it for long. She'll know within a couple of months. I should deliver in late February or early March, and she'll be a month or so behind me. This is wonderful! I'm really glad that she's already finished her Master's degree. It was very important to her, but I know how hectic her life is about to become.*

Xander and Elizabeth sat down with Jonathan and Charlotte, and Xander began a conversation about their plans for the day. Soon a waitress came to take their orders and bring them a highchair.

If Charlotte noticed that Elizabeth seemed a little more animated than was usual for her friend in the morning, she kept her observations to herself.

~~oo~~

The following night, in Washington, D.C., President Timothy Reeves slept soundly in his bed in the White House, secret service agents guarding the door. As his wife was in Florida taking a short vacation with their two children before school resumed, he was alone, except for the unseen dark ones lining the walls of his room.

The President had not rested well since the untimely death of his Vice President in January, and he had never trusted the man whom he was forced to nominate as his new Vice President. The cabal supporting Wickham had met with him the night of Howard Andrews's unfortunate demise, showing him "evidence" proving him to be a traitor. If he refused to nominate Wickham as Vice President, they threatened to start impeachment proceedings against him immediately, and knowing that his career would end in ignominy, he had capitulated quickly. He had worked too hard and too long to accept the infamy of impeachment or the trial that would surely follow resulting in his conviction, and he refused to resign.

As Reeves twisted and turned in the bed, Gregory Wickham's face invaded his nightmares.

Reeves was running, yet unable to move with any speed, his feet slogging through the muck of a swamp. The powerful men who had forced him to accept Wickham chased him through the darkness, Wickham at the front of them, waving the counterfeit evidence. He worked to escape, even knowing that evasion was impossible, but he could not outrun them. He tried to scream, but his screams were silent. His mouth opened over and over, but he could make no sound. The trees seemed to bend over him, grabbing at him, ghostly and bare.

The demons drank of his fear, reveling in his terror.

He heard a strange sound as Wickham finally reached him, pulling at him, forcing him to turn and face him. Reeves slowly looked behind him, and what he saw nearly stopped his heart. Wickham opened his mouth wide, hissing, displaying fangs, and his eyes glowed a brilliant crimson. The monster was deadly, but at the same time, beautiful. His forked tongue darted out, tasting the air, as he slowly lowered his head to Reeves's throat.

Reeves jolted to consciousness, drenched in sweat, shrieking at full volume while the demons danced around his bed. Within seconds, the agents were in his room and the lights were on. One of them shook the President until he awoke. Reeves stopped screaming and looked at the agent, terrified.

"What happened?" Reeves asked.

"Nothing, Mr. President. You had another nightmare," the man answered.

"Have you searched the room? Someone was here – I swear it," whispered Reeves.

The other agents had been carefully combing the room, and each of them answered, "All clear."

"Shall we stay with you, Mr. President?" asked one of the agents.

Reeves felt foolish. "No – no. That won't be necessary." *How can I tell them that it was Vice President Wickham, and that he had fangs?*

"Are you sure, Mr. President? Should we call your doctor for something to help you sleep?" the agent asked, genuinely concerned.

"No. Don't disturb him. I already have some sleeping pills he gave me earlier," Reeves answered, rising from the bed to change his pajamas and take the prescription medication. "I'll hit the panic button if I need you. Return to your posts."

The men nodded and left the room, resuming their seated positions outside the door, and the demons again surrounded the President's bed.

Reeves, clad in fresh pajamas, lay back down. He picked up the remote and turned on the television, thinking to distract himself with an old movie. After watching for a half hour, the pills did their work, and he drifted back off to sleep, leaving the television on, the noise lulling him to unconsciousness.

He began to dream again, and the nightmare picked up where he had awakened.

Wickham was there again, leaning over him, fangs extended.

President Reeves realized that he was dreaming, and he slowly opened his eyes.

Hovering above him was an enormous olive green snake, watching him with cold, dead eyes. *Am I still dreaming? I must be.*

He looked at the reptile coiled in his bed, and he calmed himself. *This is a dream. There is no way a snake could get in here. He must be more than ten feet long.*

The snake slowly lowered his head to the President's neck and bit him, delivering a full load of venom directly into his jugular vein as Dark Spirit spoke into the man's confused, medicated mind, *You are dreaming. Do not embarrass yourself by screaming again.*

Reeves thought, *I am dreaming. This is just a dream.*

The snake continued to bite him on his neck, face, and chest, flooding him with deadly poison. After each bite, the reptile stared into Reeves's eyes hypnotically, mesmerizing him, convincing him that nothing was real.

The demons bowed to Dark Spirit, worshipping him and chanting as he removed the obstacle to the Dark Prince's power.

The black mamba finally drew back, watching Reeves as the signs of severe neurotoxicity ensued. Within a few minutes, Reeves experienced difficulty breathing and his heart began to beat erratically. When his stomach began to twist and spasm in pain, he tried to reach for the panic button, but his arm would not obey his brain's commands. His paralysis was such that he could not make a sound. Reeves's eyes rolled back as he went into shock; cardiac arrest soon followed, and the President died before ten minutes had passed.

His work done, the snake slithered to the door and waited, surrounded by his admirers.

~~oo~~

When the President did not answer his wake up call the next morning, the agents opened the door to rouse him. Quickly the coiled snake struck, catching one of the agents on the hand and then racing down the hall in the aftermath of confusion. By the time anyone thought of chasing the reptile, it had disappeared, though it had been identified as a black mamba.

As one of the agents radioed for a doctor and made a tourniquet for the victim's hand from his tie, the others entered the room, finding a horrible scene.

Several doctors appeared nearly immediately, but none of them could help President Reeves. He had been dead for several hours, and the cause was obvious. The only question was how the snake had gotten into the President's room, and security footage of the hallways gave no answers.

Vice President Wickham was contacted, and within an hour, he took the Oath of Office administered by the Chief Justice of the Supreme Court. Gregory Wickham swore to preserve, protect, and defend the Constitution of the United States, his hand carefully hovering just above a Bible without touching it, and became President of the United States.

At thirty-six years old, the handsome young man was the youngest President in the history of the country, displacing John F. Kennedy from that position. He photographed beautifully, dressed impeccably, and spoke intelligently. While the American people grieved for the loss of President Reeves, they were quickly distracted from mourning by the vision of their virile, youthful leader and his lovely, accomplished wife. President Reeves was soon a distant memory, and President Wickham was hailed across the nation and around the globe as the leader for a new age.

President Wickham nominated one of his colleagues, Senator Hugh Dodge of North Carolina, to be Vice President, and he was confirmed by the Senate in record time. Dodge knew Wickham's family very well. In fact, he had helped to train his master's son.

There would be no need for secrecy between the new President and his Vice President, and there was a guarantee of absolute loyalty.

Lucifer was very pleased.

~~oo~~

Late July 2010

Xander and Elizabeth were shocked by President Reeves's sudden, horrible death, as were the rest of the SoulFire team. They had finished the tour, offering comfort to the stunned people in the rallies, and pointing them to the only true security, much more powerful than anything the world had to offer – placing their trust in God and accepting salvation through His Son. The summer had been truly amazing in its success. Americans were turning to God by the thousands, spurred to action by Jonathan's series of sermons on the end times. The media was talking of a revival surpassing the Great Awakening of the 1700's, led, interestingly enough, by Jonathan Edwards. Three or four such "awakenings" had been recognized in the history of the country, but none equaled the power and scope of the one beginning in the twenty-first century.

More than ever, Xander and the others were convinced that they were, indeed, seeing the fulfillment of Christ's six signs of the times from Matthew 24. The first sign, the proliferation of false teachers and false christs, was undeniable. David Icke, Jim Jones, David Koresh, Maria Devi Christos, Sergei Torrop, David Shayler, and several others had claimed to be the Messiah with disastrous results. The current crop of false religious leaders who tickled the ears of the public with promises of prosperity were gaining followers daily.

The second sign, wars and rumors of wars, was easy to prove. Wars abounded across the planet, skirmishes and full-fledged battles, killing more people than at any other time in history, and the potential for mass destruction continued to escalate.

Famines, the third sign, were widespread as a large percentage of the world's five billion people suffered from food shortages while drug lords replaced food crops with poppies, and well-intentioned politicians diverted corn which had previously fed the starving masses into bio-fuel production.

Earthquakes, the fourth sign, were occurring at a level higher than at any other time known to man with staggering numbers of seismic events happening daily throughout the world.

Worldwide attacks on Christians were the fifth sign, tribulation. In many nations, Christians were suffering great persecution and even death. The world watched apathetically as great churches were razed or converted to other uses. Countries allowing religious freedom were growing scarce, while the numbers of nations closing their borders to missionaries and ministers were increasing at an alarming rate.

SoulFire was actually helping to fulfill the sixth sign, the preaching of the gospel throughout the world, with their ministry. Other ministries continued to do so as well, using television, radio, missionaries, the internet, and multiple translations of the Bible.

As Xander mused over the events of the past two years, however, he realized something important.

During the short weeks between tours, Xander and Elizabeth employed Anna Armstrong to stay with them. As John David was down for a nap under Anna's watchful eye, Xander asked his wife if she would enjoy a walk with him. She agreed, so Cahal, Kenward, and Halvard remained with Anna and the baby while Michael and Gabriel followed Xander and Elizabeth as they began ambling through the trees behind their house. They drank in their peaceful surroundings and the hot summer weather, walking in silence, shaded by a canopy of leaves until Xander paused and turned to Elizabeth, taking both of her hands in his.

"Elizabeth, I have been thinking about Gregory," he said.

"Something I try to avoid as much as possible," she returned, smiling as she looked at their joined hands.

"You know that Gregory appears to be setting himself up as the Antichrist," he continued.

"Yes. You don't think he is anymore?" she asked, looking quickly up at her husband.

Michael and Gabriel listened closely, intensely interested.

"I think he wants to be the Antichrist, but I am no longer convinced that he truly will be," said Xander, dropping his hands to his sides.

"Why not? Didn't God tell you Gregory is the Antichrist?" she queried.

His perfect mind recalled the exact words of God: *Satan has a greater plan for Gregory after he eliminates Elizabeth; however, the time is not full. He cannot be allowed to force My hand.*

Xander paused for a moment. "Actually, I thought that is what He meant, but it may not be so. God said that the time is not full, and that Satan cannot be allowed to force His hand."

"What do you think that means?" Elizabeth asked.

Xander spoke deliberately. "I have been thinking about the Scriptural qualifications of the Antichrist, and Gregory does not meet all of them. He has not fulfilled all of the prophecies, and it appears that he is trying to make himself fit some of them. When he was shot on the steps of the Senate and seemed to come back from the dead, he was trying to fulfill Revelation 13:3 and 17:8, but he arranged that entire episode himself."

"That's true," replied Elizabeth. "And he also made himself answer the prophecy of Revelation 13:17-18 by having '666' tattooed behind his ear."

"The main consideration at this time is his origins," said Xander. "I do not see how he can make himself fit into Daniel, chapters 7, 8, and 11. He does not come from the race of the original Roman Empire, or that of Seleucus, who ruled the areas of Syria, Mesopotamia, and Persia. Neither is he of Middle Eastern descent. He was born in North Carolina to an American mother of Scots-Irish heritage and Lucifer. That is the material point."

"Then what could it all mean?" she asked.

"I believe that God wants us to stop Gregory and Lucifer from trying to 'force His hand' in attempting to hurry His timetable. I am not certain that Jehovah is ready for this to be the end of the age. He will select His own Antichrist, and Lucifer cannot put his choice in place of God's," Xander answered.

"So, God chooses the Antichrist? That's an odd thought," Elizabeth said, puzzled.

"Not exactly. I think that Lucifer always has an Antichrist ready for every age, but God will choose the time, and therefore, the Antichrist, Himself. Jesus said in Matthew 24:35-36, 'Heaven and earth will pass away, but My words shall not pass away. But of that day and hour no one knows, not even the angels of heaven, nor the Son, but the Father alone.' Lucifer wants to choose the time himself, and his choice for the Antichrist is Gregory." Xander paused for a moment, and then continued resolutely. "I think that God wants us to stop him," he explained. "That does not necessarily mean that we are not in the end times. The Almighty does not view time as we do. He may choose to rapture the church and begin the second coming of Christ in two years, five years, or twenty years. There is no way to predict when it will happen. However, we must live each day as if His coming is imminent."

"What should we do then?" she asked.

"We should continue what we have been doing, winning the world for Christ. I also think that we should begin to make people aware of Gregory's true nature. We must find a way to expose him for what he is – someone who is evil and bent on destruction, a person who is diametrically opposed to God and the things of God." He leaned his chin on Elizabeth's hair and hugged her to his chest. She turned her head so that her cheek rested against him.

When she finally spoke, her voice was quiet. "Everyone who opposes him dies."

Michael and Gabriel exchanged glances and stepped closer to their charges, placing their hands on the backs of Xander and Elizabeth.

"So far, no *believers* have openly opposed him. No *believers* have died yet, Elizabeth. God will protect us if it is in His will," Xander said, trying to keep the anguish he felt hidden from her. He knew that it was not always God's will that believers were protected from evil. There had been many, many martyrs for the cause of Christ, and he and Elizabeth could conceivably be among that number. But the blood of martyrs was never wasted; if God desired the ultimate sacrifice from him and his wife, there would be a purpose in it.

LEGACY

She knew him too well, and she understood what he could not say. She knew that it was possible that they would die fighting Gregory.

Elizabeth looked up at him with love in her eyes. "We are like Esther. God has preserved us 'for such a time as this.'"

"She was a very courageous woman. I enjoyed guarding her," said Xander.

Elizabeth tilted her head and smiled. "I remember now that you told me you guarded Esther."

"I did, and God preserved her. She took a risk to save God's people, and He protected all of them. Our lives are in the hands of the same God that Esther served. We must trust Him," he answered.

Michael and Gabriel stepped back from them and appeared in angelic form underneath the shelter of the trees.

Michael reached out and touched Elizabeth's arm. "I will fight for you until a death angel pushes me away. Do not fear. You will not go until God calls you home Himself."

Elizabeth stood up straighter and calmly faced her husband and his brothers. "I am not afraid. I will say what Job said in Job 13:15, 'Though He slay me, I will hope in Him,' and as Paul said in Philippians 1:21, 'For to me, to live is Christ, and to die is gain.' If I die, I will be with Him in glory. What could be better than that?"

Gabriel smiled at her. "I am happy to call you my sister and honored to call you my friend."

Xander took her hand and kissed it gently. "It appears that you have made friends in high places."

Michael's green eyes softened as he looked at his brother and sister. "Elizabeth, even when you cannot see us, remember that we are always there. The three of us would be unbodied before we would allow harm to come to you. Never doubt it."

She took a breath. "Promise me something," she said, looking at each of them in turn. "If there is ever a choice between saving my life or saving John David's, promise me that you will choose him."

"Do not ask that," said Michael quickly, the pain showing on his face. "You are my charge. I cannot make that choice."

"Please, Michael. Promise me," she said, her eyes begging him.

He turned his head away, but Gabriel touched her arm, saying, "Michael cannot promise that while you are his charge, Elizabeth. I will promise in his stead. Xander is well able to protect himself – at least most of the time. If Xander tells me to go to his son, I will do it."

She breathed more easily, and looked at her husband. "And you, Xander. Will you promise to choose our son over me?"

His voice was strangled, and he looked away. Tears filled his eyes as he said, "Please do not ask it of me, Elizabeth. I would die for either of you. I cannot choose between you. You are carrying our second child now. Would you split me three ways?"

She bit her lip, and then spoke softly. "Perhaps it *is* too much to ask of you, my love. I will trust you to make the best decision if the time comes. You will do what is right, just as you always have."

Dear Lord, he prayed, *please do not let it come to that.*

Chapter 17

"From the mouth of infants and nursing babes Thou has established strength, because of Thine adversaries, to make the enemy and the revengeful cease."
Psalm 8:2

August 2010

They had been back from the summer tour for a week and had a doctor's appointment scheduled for the afternoon. Though his wife suffered no morning sickness, Xander was a little anxious about her fatigue and the unusual heartbeat of the child. He had no wish, however, to alarm Elizabeth, so he had not pressured her to go to the doctor's office on the day they arrived home. Instead, he, along with Michael and Gabriel, had watched her very closely, fully prepared to rush her to the hospital at the first sign of trouble.

They had spent the week relaxing at home and playing with their energetic baby boy. He had reached each developmental milestone much earlier than was normal, but that was not wholly unexpected.

Xander, especially attuned to any sound from the nursery, located next to his and Elizabeth's bedroom, woke early to the sound of happy gurgling and a childish voice. "Dada. Dada."

Careful not to disturb his sleeping wife, he slid from the bed and pulled on the sweatpants and T-shirt he had left neatly folded on a chair nearby. Walking quietly, Xander, followed by Gabriel, went to John David's room. His son greeted him with a toothless grin, standing up holding onto the rail of his crib. Seeing his father, the little boy began to bounce, bending his knees.

Xander smiled with delight and reached for his sturdy son, holding him securely in his arms and looking into his eyes. "Are you calling me, John David? Did you say, 'Dada'?"

"Dada! Dada!" John David shouted, pulling on his father's ears. Looking over Xander's shoulder, the baby's eyes grew round. "Oooooo."

"What do you see, son?" asked Xander, looking behind him. Gabriel was there in angelic form, and Cahal and Kenward stood at either end of his crib. There was a mobile of butterflies hanging from the ceiling. "Do you see the pretty butterflies? Are they sparkly?" Xander turned to see what John David saw, and the baby twisted in his arms, keeping his eyes locked on Gabriel.

"Petty. Oooooo," he said, pointing to Gabriel. "Unca."

Xander heard his son's thoughts and looked into his mind to see what he was seeing.

Does he see me? Is it possible? asked Gabriel in astonishment.

"Do you see Uncle Gabriel, John David?" asked Xander. "Is he shiny? Is he pretty?"

The baby nodded his head vigorously, dark curls bouncing, and pointed again with his tiny finger. "Unca. Petty. Oooooo."

How can this be? Gabriel was bewildered.

Xander was thoughtful. *I do not know. Perhaps Elizabeth's and my children will have a foot in both worlds. I have noticed that since Elizabeth has become my wife, she sometimes sees the glow of angels and senses the presence of demons more acutely than she did before, and her sensitivity to the spiritual world seems to be increasing. Now that she knows you are there, she looks for you. Maybe our children will be born with those abilities, and seeing you will be natural for them from an early age.*

Gabriel reached out his hand to John David, and the baby placed his small hand in the much larger one offered to him, looking solemnly into the kind, dark blue eyes of his "uncle." The archangel smiled at the child he loved, but he was unable to speak for a moment.

Gabriel quickly assumed human form and took the baby from Xander, kissing his forehead. "You are precious." He turned to face Cahal and Kenward. "What do you see, John David? Do you see the big men?"

John David's blue eyes rested first on Cahal, and then on Kenward. He nodded his head, his blue eyes serious, as he pointed first at the guardian, and then at the warrior. "Uh huh."

Kenward smiled at him, but Cahal was uncomfortable and looked at the wall directly before him, all expression carefully kept from his handsome visage.

Xander placed his hands on either side of his son's face and looked into his sparkling eyes. "You must not tell anyone about the big men, John David. You must not talk about the shiny, pretty angels. Can you keep the secret?"

"Mama?" whispered the little boy, looking somberly into his father's eyes.

Taking his son from Gabriel Xander hugged him, whispering into his ear, "Mama knows. You can tell Mama, but not Anna. Do not tell anyone else but Mama. Do you understand?"

John David nodded slowly. "Mama."

Michael had heard the entire exchange from his position by the sleeping Elizabeth. He summoned Cahal and Kenward to watch her, nodded to them, and strode into the nursery.

As he entered the room, John David smiled at him like a ray of sunshine. "Unca Mike!"

Xander could tell from his brother's thoughts that he was overcome with the idea that John David was happy to see him and was not afraid. Elizabeth had been the only human in history who was comfortable in his presence in angelic form. Michael knew that Elizabeth loved him, but John David was delighted to see him. There was a difference in her love for and acceptance of him and in the child's happiness. Quite simply, no one had ever been that overjoyed to be with him. In that moment, something changed inside Michael. He had never felt any vulnerability before, but this child had touched his heart. He would unbody legions or even kill humans if it was necessary in order to protect Elizabeth, but he would cheerfully die himself for John David without any thought of his own safety.

Michael took human form and stood before the little boy. John David immediately reached out his arms for him, and the last remnant of any barrier in Michael's heart melted away.

The massive angel took the small child into his embrace and spoke into his mind words that he had never said before to any human being. *I love you.*

In answer, John David pulled on his uncle's blond hair and looked into his green eyes with a grin. He touched Michael's face with one small hand, patting his cheek gently, and replied with his first sentence, spoken directly into Michael's mind. *Love Unca Mike.*

He spoke his thoughts to me. He loves me. Michael looked helplessly at Xander and Gabriel.

Now you have some small understanding of how I feel about Elizabeth and John David, thought Xander.

How do you bear it? How can you live with knowing that they could sicken or die? asked Michael.

Xander spoke softly. *I bear it because I must, and I thank God for allowing me to love them in this way. I would not exchange loving them for going back to the time before I had these feelings. I am glad that you and Gabriel love my wife and my son. You will be even fiercer in your protection of them. Now, let us remember that John David can see us in angelic form and possibly hear our thoughts as well. Be careful of what you think and how you look until we know how far his gift extends. We know that he can speak into our minds, but we do not yet know if he can hear all of our thoughts.*

Elizabeth walked gracefully into the room, smiling at her husband and his brothers, a little surprised to see John David in Michael's arms rather than his father's. Cahal and Kenward followed behind her.

Xander watched his son closely. *I wonder if he can hear human thoughts and speak into human minds.*

John David reached for his mother immediately, opening and closing his hands. "Mama!" he crowed.

"Mama? You're talking now? My smart boy!" His developmental leaps had ceased to shock her. She took him, kissed him, and felt his diaper, and then she glanced at the three brothers, eyebrows raised. "What have you guys been doing? He's wet. There are three of you. Surely someone could have changed him."

Gabriel and Michael immediately morphed back into angelic form.

She crossed the room and laid him on the changing table, expertly replacing his wet diaper with a clean one. "Who's hungry? Auntie Anna is already downstairs cooking breakfast, and there is cereal and fruit for you, little man! Yum!"

As she picked up their son, pressing her lips to his soft cheek, Xander stepped up behind her, enveloping them both in his strong arms and kissing Elizabeth's ear. "I love you both so much. My heart overflows," he said, his voice husky with emotion.

She turned her face to catch his lips with hers. "My, my. So serious. What's been going on in here?"

John David grabbed her chin. "Eat!" he demanded. *Now!* he said loudly into his mother's mind.

Elizabeth caught her breath and looked at her husband in amazement. *Did he just do what I think he did?*

I suppose that answers one question, thought Michael.

Xander caught his wife off guard by lifting both her and their child up in his arms and heading for the door. "We will talk later. Our son is evidently hungry."

"Yum!" answered John David, laughing as his father bounced him and Elizabeth in his arms with each step.

Elizabeth cuddled closer to her two men, allowing herself to enjoy the warmth of their bonds of love.

Cahal and Kenward awaited them at the bottom of the stairs, and the archangels walked behind them, now even more mindful of their safety.

~~oo~~

Later that day, Anna took charge of John David after lunch while Xander and Elizabeth went to Dr. Neal's office. After a short wait, the nurse called them back to an examination room, and Michael and Gabriel stationed themselves at the head of Elizabeth's bed. Alexandra saluted them as she followed Dr. Neal into the room, and they nodded their acknowledgement. Because Dr. Neal knew that Xander would stay in the room during the visit, she had dismissed the nurse to tend another patient.

"Hello," said Dr. Neal, looking first at Xander, and then at Elizabeth. "How are you feeling today?"

Elizabeth started to say that she felt fine, but one look at her husband's face made her change her words. "I'm tired. I think I'm always tired, Dr. Neal."

The doctor continued to ask questions as she checked Elizabeth.

Knowing that the Darcys would be leaving for another Global Tour in a few weeks and that they would be gone for three months, the doctor had elected to do a transvaginal ultrasound. As the images appeared on the screen, Dr.

Neal looked closely at the pictures, and then reached for her Doppler instrument.

"I think you are far enough along to hear the heartbeat," she commented, running the device over Elizabeth's abdomen.

"Listen to that!" exclaimed the doctor.

The double thuds filled the room, and Xander could hold his tongue no longer. "Is anything wrong with the baby's heart, Dr. Neal?"

"No, both hearts are very healthy," she answered, glancing back at him and smiling.

Elizabeth's face registered her shock. "Our baby has two hearts? Can he live like that?"

"Your baby doesn't have two hearts," replied the doctor, chuckling. "Each of your babies has one heart. You have two babies, Elizabeth – twins."

Dr. Neal was the only one in the room whose mouth did not drop open. Had she been able to see the angels as well as the humans, she surely would have laughed aloud.

Xander stepped closer to the screen, peering at the tiny, moving images. "Two babies," he said in wonder. He looked at Elizabeth, his face wreathed in a breathtaking smile. "Elizabeth, we will have three children!"

His joy was tempered as he remembered that they would soon leave for an international tour with a grueling schedule. Xander straightened up and looked at the doctor. "Dr. Neal, will she be all right to travel?"

Elizabeth sighed audibly. "Xander, I am healthy, and this is a short tour. I have already had one baby, and I know what to expect. I will take care of myself. Please stop worrying. You will be gray before you're twenty-five at this rate."

Dr. Neal laid aside her instruments and looked at Elizabeth, asking, "You'll be back in mid-November?"

"Yes, a week before Thanksgiving," she answered.

"You're a little more than two months along now, so you'll be back before you begin your sixth month. You should be fine. I would like a copy of your travel schedule so that I can contact doctors and set up an appointment for each month you will be away, and I would like to have you back in here as soon as you return. Since you're carrying twins, no more touring between the time you return and their birth. Understood?" Dr. Neal replied sternly.

"Not even weekends?" asked Elizabeth. "Not even if we stay within a few hours of here?"

"Depending on how well you feel, you can travel two hours by car through the middle of January. After that, you will probably need to stay in the immediate area. If you carry to full term, you will be much larger with twins than you were with John David. You need to rest as much as is possible," said the doctor to Elizabeth. She then turned to Xander. "I suppose you will make certain that my instructions are followed?"

His smile was a determined one. "I will make arrangements as soon as we get back home. We will take no chances with her health or that of the babies. We will be at home most of the time after we return from this tour, and we will come back in the middle of it if there are any difficulties. I think it will work out well for everyone concerned," he replied, thinking of Charlotte and how she would also be nearing the end of her pregnancy by the time Elizabeth was unable to travel.

Very fortuitous that Charlotte and Elizabeth became with child so close together, thought Gabriel, smiling.

Our Master always has a plan, replied Michael.

"I can see how it will be," said Elizabeth, a little grumpily. "He will coddle me and fuss over me even more than usual."

Dr. Neal spoke kindly. "There are far worse things than being cared for by your husband, Elizabeth. You are very blessed."

"I know. I know. He's the best husband in the world, and I'm thankful for him. He's just so *good* at following doctor's orders, and he never lets me cheat at all." She laughed lightly and reached for his hand. "Rest assured, Dr. Neal, that we will do everything exactly as you have said."

"Excellent," replied the doctor.

~~oo~~

When Xander called Jonathan to tell him about the twins and discuss changes in the winter and spring schedules, Jonathan confided that Charlotte had performed a home pregnancy test after missing a period, and the test had been positive. They had an appointment scheduled with Dr. Neal for the following day. Jonathan was more than happy to hear Xander and Elizabeth's news, and he saw no problems in adjusting the schedule for a few months. He was also pleased to know that Elizabeth and Charlotte could visit the doctors together on the tour, and that Charlotte would have the benefit of Elizabeth's experience in traveling while pregnant.

The evangelist further suggested that he and Xander might do a few Saturday night rallies, leaving their wives at home together when they were no longer able to travel. Xander promised to consider the matter and call him back within a few hours. He was not at all sure that he could bring himself to leave her and their children while he traveled several hours away, and he was positive that he would not spend a night away from her. After careful thought, he decided that he could find a way to fly to and from the rallies in angelic form, thus reducing the amount of time he would be gone, and he could always return to her within seconds if she needed him.

When Xander discussed the matter with Elizabeth, she readily agreed, so he called Jonathan and agreed to his plan. Jonathan then contacted Dave Branard, instructing him to alert Amy to make the changes in the spring schedule.

~~oo~~

Xander looked at his watch as he, Elizabeth, Anna, and John David sat in the den after dinner. While Elizabeth held John David in her lap and read to him, Xander noted that it was nearly time for Dirk Horne's program, so he picked up the remote and turned on the television. Guardians and warriors stood at various places in the room, close to their charges.

Hundreds of miles away in New York, Dirk Horne sat impatiently in the wing chair on the office set of his cable news show as the makeup girl powdered a slight shine from his forehead.

As she finished and hurried away, his expression changed and he looked into the camera, exuding the very essence of confidence and trustworthiness.

When he received the signal, Horne began to speak persuasively. "Last evening, President Wickham signed an Executive Order giving him the power to implement martial law in the case of war or a national emergency in the United States. The National Defense Executive Order will give our President the power to commandeer the country's resources in a time of crisis or peace, including resources ranging from food, livestock, farming equipment, manufacturing, industry, transportation, defense, construction, hospitals, and health care facilities to sources of energy and water.

"Many critics of the Wickham Administration believe this is another effort at a power grab, but others argue that an Executive Order update is irrelevant."

As the camera panned, Horne turned to his guest, smiling amiably. "President Wickham, we are honored to have you in our studio today. How would you answer the concerns of those who think you are amassing too much control over our government?"

The camera shifted to President Gregory Wickham, whose distinguished, handsome features held just the right mixture of concern and understanding. "Dirk, let me begin by thanking you for the opportunity to explain my actions to the American people. First, citizens need to understand that martial law has been declared numerous times in the history of this great country to its great benefit. President Andrew Jackson imposed martial law in New Orleans during the War of 1812, and in 1892, the governor of Idaho declared martial law when mine workers blew up a mill and shot at workers who attempted to break a strike.

"Following the San Francisco earthquake of 1906, the troops stationed in the Presidio were pressed into martial law service. Troops were ordered to shoot looters of the dynamite used to prevent fires from spreading."

"In 1914, the governor of Colorado instituted martial law during the Coal Field Wars and the Colorado National Guard was called in. President Wilson finally sent in federal troops, ending the violence.

"In 1934, California Governor Frank Merriam placed the docks of San Francisco under martial law, citing rioting resulting from a dock worker's strike. The National Guard was called in to open the docks, and the guardsmen were empowered to make arrests and try detainees or turn them over to the civil courts.

The camera panned to include both men in the picture as Dirk Horne leaned toward President Wickham to ask a question. "Mr. President, has martial law been implemented in our country in more recent times?"

The President nodded. "I'm glad you asked that, Dirk. In fact, Hawaii was placed under martial law in 1941, after the attack on Pearl Harbor. On May 21, 1961, Alabama Governor Patterson declared martial law during the civil rights movement, and Attorney General Robert Kennedy sent in federal marshals because he was not certain that the governor could quell the violence and maintain the peace."

"Even more recently, in the wake of Hurricane Katrina in 2005, New Orleans was put under martial law after widespread flooding rendered civil authority ineffective. The state of Louisiana called it a state of public health emergency rather than martial law, but the order allowed the governor to suspend laws, order evacuations, and limit the sales of items such as alcohol and firearms.

Dirk smiled. "That's quite interesting, Mr. President. It seems that your proposal is more commonplace than some people think. Do you have an example of a revered President placing a large area of the country under martial law?" asked the anchorman.

President Wickham chuckled. "I am certain that most of my countrymen would agree that Abraham Lincoln was one of the greatest Presidents in the history of the United States, yet during his presidency, he was criticized for taking what were considered 'extra-constitutional measures.' However, the verdict of history is that Lincoln's use of power did not constitute abuse; every survey of historians ranks Lincoln as number one among the great Presidents.

"Would Lincoln have been better remembered if he had allowed the whole American experiment of a democratic Union to fail? If such a calamity had occurred, what benefit would have been gained by clinging to a fallen Constitution?

"According to historian James G. Randall: 'No president has carried the power of presidential edict and executive order (independently of Congress) so far as Lincoln did.... It would not be easy to state what Lincoln conceived to be the limit of his powers.'

"In 1861, Lincoln performed a whole series of highly controversial and important acts by his sheer assumption of presidential power. Without congressional approval, Lincoln called out the militia to 'suppress said combinations,' and he ordered citizens to return peacefully their homes. He increased the size of the Army and Navy, expended funds for the purchase of weapons, instituted a blockade (which in itself is an act of war) and suspended the writ of habeas corpus, which is the right to a hearing on lawful imprisonment, or by way of explanation, the supervision of law enforcement by the judiciary, all without congressional approval. Lincoln did all of this in the name of suppressing rebellion."

The camera zoomed in on Dirk Horne as he called for a commercial, promising that the President would continue to speak after the break.

Elizabeth had been watching the newscast with interest. "You know that I don't follow politics as avidly as you do. What exactly is martial law?"

Xander thought a moment to formulate his answer. "Martial law is the imposition of temporary military rule by military authorities over designated regions on an emergency basis when the civilian government or civilian authorities fail to maintain order and security and provide essential services, when there are extensive riots and protests, or when the disobedience of the law becomes widespread. The military is deployed to quiet the crowds, to secure government buildings and key or sensitive locations, and to maintain order. Military personnel replace civil authorities and perform some or all of their functions. Gregory is deliberately leaving out these facts because they are inconvenient and do not further his agenda."

Michael made a noise of disgust and paced closer to the television.

Both angels and humans returned their attention to the television as Dirk Horne reappeared to proudly announce his distinguished guest.

"It is my privilege tonight to welcome President Gregory Wickham to my program." He turned toward the President. "Mr. President, we have been discussing the history of martial law in the United States. Please explain to our audience why your Executive Order is not an unconstitutional assumption of power on your part."

The camera zoomed in on the President. "Dirk, everyone knows that only Congress is constitutionally empowered to declare war, but suppression of rebellion has long been recognized as an executive function, for which the prerogative of setting aside civil procedures has been placed in the President's hands.

"For example, at this very moment, our country is involved in a war with Iraq, yet the war has not been formally declared. Whereas Lincoln used the term 'suppression of rebellion,' our former President couched this effort as a movement to liberate Iraq's people from their dictator and to prevent acts of terrorism against both American citizens and the citizens of other countries."

Wickham paused dramatically and leaned forward. "In other words, my friends, I am following the precedents laid down by many of our most highly respected leaders on both sides of the political fence. I will do whatever is necessary to ensure the peace in this country and the safety of its citizens. Normally, Congress would have to approve the declaration of martial law because of the *Posse Comitatus Act* of 1878. I fear, however, that waiting to fight a battle with my detractors in the Senate and the House could result in a tragic loss of life, as well as vast destruction of our infrastructure, in the event of a natural disaster or a civil war. That is why I have taken the step of issuing an Executive Order giving me the right to impose martial law myself.

"There is no cause for alarm. Trust me to do what is in the best interests of our country should there be unrest or widespread violence. I want only what is best for the majority of our citizens. We should not allow a minority of dissenters to determine our course."

His spiel at an end, Wickham leaned back and crossed his legs, a smile gracing his beautiful face.

Dirk Horne looked empathetically at the President, reaching out to shake his hand. "Thank you, Mr. President, for taking the time to explain your actions to the American people. I know they join me in a feeling of relief that we have such a wise leader during these troubling times. I had not realized that martial law had been imposed so many times in our history."

Wickham nodded. "There is a sad dearth of those who are well-acquainted with the true history of this great nation, Dirk. The step I have taken to protect our people is not at all unprecedented, as some would have everyone believe. It is merely the action any good leader would take under the circumstances. As we have been recently reminded by a prominent evangelistic team, everywhere there are 'wars and rumors of wars,' and disasters are occurring around the globe on an escalating basis. We must be prepared for the worst, and I am in the position responsible for doing so in the United States. I will take care of the citizens of this country, and no one will stand in my way."

Xander made a sound of revulsion and clicked the remote, turning away from the darkened screen to look at his wife and son.

"He actually had the audacity to use SoulFire to support his audacious acquisition of more power. Can you believe it?" he asked.

She laughed darkly. "Are you really surprised? He will stop at nothing to get what he wants."

"And he wants everything," Xander agreed vehemently. "All Wickham has to do is stir up a war or declare a national emergency, and he can call out the military to enforce this Executive Order. He can then set curfews, and suspend civil law, civil rights, and habeas corpus. Furthermore, under martial law he can apply military law and military justice to civilians. Civilians defying martial law could be subjected to military tribunals for court martial. Military law is very different from civil law. Whereas civil laws are made to benefit all civilians or citizens of a nation, military laws control the army of that nation. Civil law protects the citizen; military law protects the military. Did you know that adultery is against military law? It is certainly difficult to prove and rarely prosecuted, but Wickham could have a field day with it. He could arrest most of Congress."

Elizabeth shivered and held her son more closely in her arms. Looking up at her husband, she was comforted by the faint glow at his side. In her mind, she heard a little voice. *No tell Anna, Mama. Petty angels. No tell Anna.*

Sensing her disquiet, John David put his arms around his mother's neck, and he kissed her cheek.

She bent her head to whisper into his ear, "Don't worry, darling. I won't tell."

Chapter 18

"And another angel, a third one, followed them, saying with a loud voice, 'If any one worships the beast and his image, and receives a mark on his forehead or upon his hand, he also will drink of the wine of the wrath of God, which is mixed in full strength in the cup of His anger; and he will be tormented with fire and brimstone in the presence of the holy angels and in the presence of the Lamb. And the smoke of their torment goes up forever and ever; and they have no rest day and night, those who worship the beast and his image, and whoever receives the mark of his name.'"
Revelation 14:9-11

March 2011

Xander, holding John David's hand as they followed Elizabeth down the stairs, was more than a little concerned about his wife. He had been anxious to the point of having to ask forgiveness for his lack of faith several times in the past forty-eight hours. Although he knew intellectually that God would take care of his wife and children, in his heart he had to keep committing them to His care, only to take them back whenever he saw her grimacing while she put her hands on the small of her back or watched her waddle slowly from room to room.

Elizabeth had been more and more restless when she tried to sleep, though she placed a pillow between her knees that was as long as she was tall in an effort to ease the pressure on her hips. She got up several times each night to visit the bathroom, and her lower legs and feet were swollen to the point that her ankle bones were no longer visible. Consequently, Xander had not had a full night's rest in a month. He awakened every time she stirred, and he got up each time she did.

As they reached the bottom of the stairs, guardians all around them, Xander spoke carefully, trying not to offend his increasingly sensitive wife. To his chagrin, he had reduced her to tears on several occasions by saying the most innocuous things as he attempted to express his worry for her.

"Elizabeth?" he asked tentatively. "Will you not lie down on the couch for a bit?"

"Why?" she asked in a petulant voice. "Maybe if I walk enough the babies will come a little early."

"If you lie on your side, I can rub your back. I know it hurts, though you seldom complain," he answered. "Please, love. Let me do something to help you." He put his hand on her shoulder and gently turned her around to face him and John David.

"Am I so pathetic?" Her lower lip began to quiver, and she rubbed her temples with her fingertips. "I'm huge. If I were on a beach, some well-meaning person would call Greenpeace! Activists would attempt a rescue and try to roll me back into the water – unless I was harpooned first! My name should be changed to Shamu," she wailed, drawing out the last syllable and hiccupping.

Though what she said was humorous, Xander had not felt less like laughing in two thousand years. Michael chuckled, and Xander glared at him. John David's blue eyes were enormous as he watched his uncles. Gabriel's face mirrored Xander's unhappiness, and he jabbed Michael in his ribs.

What? It was funny, thought Michael.

Have you never heard of dark humor? remonstrated Gabriel. *Elizabeth would be most offended by your amusement at her expense.*

Xander squatted down to look into his son's eyes, stroking the boy's hair as he spoke to him. "John David, Mommy is very tired from holding the babies inside of her. Uncle Michael and Uncle Gabriel will play with you until Auntie Anna gets back from the store. Be a good boy for me. Okay?"

"Okay!" said the sturdy one-year-old, heading unerringly toward his uncles, though they were still in angelic form. Michael and Gabriel morphed into human shapes just as he reached them, and Michael caught him under his arms and tossed him up in the air. John David squealed with delight, shrieking with laughter.

Gabriel tapped Michael's shoulder. "We should take him into the play room so that Elizabeth can rest in relative quiet. Cahal and Kenward can stay in here with Xander and our sister."

"Agreed," answered Michael, holding John David in his arms and walking quickly to the large room across the hall. French doors allowed a clear line of sight between the two rooms.

Xander stood and reached for Elizabeth's hand, guiding her to the sofa. As she sat down, she pulled him down by his hands until he was beside her. She brought his hand to her lips and kissed his knuckles.

Then she hung her head. "I'm so sorry, my love. I know I have been awful to live with for the last couple of months. You are too good to me. I just feel so ugly and miserable – and don't tell me that I'm beautiful, or I may actually scream."

He put his arm around her and drew her face to his shoulder, pushing her hair from her face, caressing her cheek with his fingers, thinking, *Proverbs 15:1, 'A gentle answer turns away wrath.'* "I guess you must scream then, my Elizabeth, because you are always beautiful to me." He dropped his hand to her distended belly and tenderly rubbed large, slow circles over his children. "How can you be anything but lovely to me when you are carrying our babies?"

As she relaxed, he moved further down the couch and laid her on her side, holding her head in his lap, stroking her hair with one hand and massaging her back with the other. She mumbled something, and he leaned over to catch her words. Her thoughts spoke to him. *That feels so good, my love. Sing to me.*

Xander continued to minister to her aching back as he sang softly to her. He sang old ballads like "Greensleeves" and "Oh, Danny Boy," as well as songs that were special to them, such as "Forever" and "My Angel's Kiss."

He leaned over to kiss her eyelids and her cheeks, resting his lips on her forehead, but her mind whispered, *More, love,* and so he kept singing, adding Christian love songs, including "Love You Forever," "Only God Could Love You More," and "When God Made You."

He could feel the tension leaving her muscles under the movements of his hand, so he kept singing, switching to secular love song, softly crooning "This I Promise You," "I Knew I Loved You," and "I Do Cherish You."

Xander smiled a little mischievously when he made up his own version of "I Believe I Can Fly," and her mouth turned up at the corners though her eyes remained closed.

Elizabeth lingered in the place between consciousness and sleep, listening to her husband's soothing voice, drinking in his words of love and affirmation. She was totally relaxed when he bent over her and kissed her cheek, and she turned her face to his and pulled his head down to hers, kissing him tenderly. Her eyes fluttered closed as he pulled away a few inches, and her breathing became slow and steady.

She had just drifted off to sleep when Anna arrived back home, laden with bags from the grocery store. Xander eased out from under his wife's head, carefully replacing his lap with a pillow, and went to help Anna get the rest of the bags from the car.

John David saw him as he walked past the doors of the play room, and the little boy ran to the windows of the French doors, pressing his nose against the panes and smiling at his father. Xander opened the door, putting his finger on his lips to indicate silence. *Mommy is sleeping. Be very quiet.*

John David nodded. *Mommy tired.* He reached his arms up to his father and was rewarded by Xander, who picked him up and took him out to the car with him, followed by Michael and Gabriel. Halvard nodded at them in passing as he kept close behind Anna.

By trial and error, Xander had established that John David could hear angelic "spoken" thoughts, but not those which were private. He could not yet hear human thoughts, but he could project his own thoughts into both human and angelic minds, and he seemed to understand instinctively how and when to do so.

Anna was making a return trip for more bags when Michael stopped her. "We will bring in the rest, Anna. I am sure that you have much to do."

"Elizabeth is asleep on the couch," said Xander, smiling as he passed her with a grinning John David bouncing in his arms.

Anna was accustomed to Xander's brothers dropping in at odd hours, so she was not surprised to see Michael and Gabriel. "Thanks, Michael. I'll start dinner. Will you and Gabriel eat with us?"

"No, thank you, Anna," replied Gabriel. "We have to leave soon. It is unfortunate, for you are an excellent cook."

That's funny. How would you know since you never stay to eat? she thought, smiling to herself. She continued on to the kitchen, walking lightly to avoid waking Elizabeth.

Eventually, you two will have to become accustomed to human food, thought Xander. *She is starting to notice.*

By that time they were at the van Xander had purchased to accommodate his growing family, trading in Elizabeth's car as they no longer needed it. There were already three car seats in the bench seat just behind the front captain's seats: John David's seat and those of his soon-to-arrive siblings.

Xander walked to the back of the van. The rear door was still opened, so he held John David with one arm and grabbed a few bags with his free hand. Michael and Gabriel gathered the rest of the items.

In addition to buying groceries, Anna had shopped for supplies for the new nursery which had been set up in the bedroom on the other side of Xander and Elizabeth's room, allowing them to be between John David's room and the new nursery. The cheerful room already held two of everything: cribs, changing tables, and dressers, as well as a double glider in which the young couple could sit together to rock their babies.

While Xander took his bags to the kitchen, Michael and Gabriel continued up the stairs with the huge boxes of diapers, baby wipes, and other items. They left their bags on the floor of the nursery, knowing that Anna would wish to put the things away herself.

They will be here soon, thought Michael with excitement, surveying the room.

Gabriel smiled. *It cannot be too soon to suit Elizabeth. Our sister is weary.*

Elizabeth is strong, and the babies are healthy. She will quickly be back to herself, answered Michael.

While I am happy about the babies, I cannot look forward to her pain. I hope it will be of short duration, thought Gabriel as they turned to leave and go back down the steps.

God is merciful, Michael replied. *Perhaps it will proceed rapidly.*

I hope so, thought Gabriel soberly.

~~oo~~

President Gregory Wickham was having an excellent day. He met reporters in the Rose Garden as he signed a stringent gun control measure into law. He knew that there would be a constitutional challenge to the controversial law which had passed Congress by slim margins and, even then, only through threats. The Supreme Court would likely overturn it in a year or so, but until that happened, the American citizenry was effectively disarmed. As things stood, the Court had four justices who would certainly vote against the law, four who would support it, and a swing voter; five of them had guardians. Michael had placed warriors around them as well, but the justices were aging. Eventually, they would sicken and retire or die. Then he would be able to do anything he wished.

Even Michael cannot stop the aging process, Gregory thought with glee.

Looking directly into the cameras with great sincerity, the President intoned, "This is a momentous day in the history of our country. The numbers of violent crimes will plummet as a result of this bill, and many Americans will live this year who otherwise would have died at the hands of armed criminals. I would like to take this opportunity to thank the dedicated, courageous members of Congress who fought to have this measure passed. We are all in your debt. I also want to remind all Americans to take their firearms to local police stations immediately and voluntarily. No one wants to send agents to your homes to confiscate the weapons, but rest assured that this law will be enforced. I will take any step necessary to secure the safety of every American."

He signed the bill with a flourish, handed out pens made especially for the occasion, and then, backed by his collection of bipartisan supporters, he looked up to smile for photographs.

What no one else could see were the demons surrounding them, chortling at the idea that criminals would agree to disarm. After all, they habitually broke laws, and there was no reason to believe that they would obey this one and surrender their weapons.

~~oo~~

Later that afternoon, the President met with the select group of senators and representatives who had pledged to further his agenda.

Everyone was standing as he entered the room, followed by his guards who had become part of his Secret Service detail.

President Wickham sat at the head of the table, staring levelly at each of the men and women in turn, and then he began to speak very deliberately.

"I am quite intrigued by some new technology which has been presented to me recently," he said while he held up a microchip. "As you can see, it is quite small, yet it can store a massive amount of information. A person's entire history can be transmitted to this chip, and it can be updated easily from many forms of smart technology. It also contains a GPS device that would allow us to track anyone who has it implanted. I want every American, as well as every person in the country who is not American, to be required to accept an identification chip by this time next year."

President Wickham placed the chip in front of him and folded his hands on the table.

One of the senators cleared his throat and spoke timidly. "Mr. President, your idea is a wonderful one, of course, but the implications of requiring such an invasive procedure are far-reaching and unprecedented. It will be declared unconstitutional."

The President's steely gaze impaled the man. "We will promote the chip to the people as a health product. Each person's healthcare records will be on the implant, readily accessible to every EMT, doctor, and hospital. In the case of an accident or medical emergency, all that will be required to have a complete medical history available is a simple scan by a handheld device similar to the innocuous technology available to every grocery store and department store in the country. Most Americans have already agreed to the palm scans in hospitals and doctors' offices. This will be considered a mere upgrade in technology. Citizens will receive a small tattoo of my design over the area containing the chip, and that tattoo will be scanned each time they buy or sell anything. They will be unable to buy food, gas, or goods of any sort if they do not receive the implant, and they will be unemployable. To encourage people to accept the device quickly, the government will give $2,000 to every person who submits to implantation within the first three months it is available. They will bring their children and wait in line for the money. The chip will be placed in the top of a person's right hand or in his forehead." He grinned maliciously. "I would not wish to take all choices away from the citizenry. My only unresolved issue is determining which department should handle this— homeland security or health and human services. Of course, the justice department stands ready to prosecute."

A representative waited a moment, and then spoke, her voice trembling. "Many people will refuse. What will happen to them? And where will the $2,000 come from? The economy is very unstable and the budget deficit is growing at alarming rates. Our national debt is the highest that it has ever been."

President Wickham waved his hand dismissively. "The money is not a problem. I know private individuals who will make donations to fund this project, and their participation will be untraceable. Failure to comply with this law will be a felony offense. As for those who refuse, they will have six months to comply or be arrested and submit to psychological counseling and treatment – attitude adjustments, if you will. If after six months, they still refuse, they will be arrested. They will go to prison until they agree to take their implant. Eventually, people who refuse the Mark – named for the tattoo – will be put to death for treason."

There was a unified gasp from every person seated around the table.

One senator spoke before he thought through his answer. "Put to death! My state is in the Bible belt, and a great many people there know what the Bible says about taking the Mark! They will never submit. Will you kill them all?"

The room went deadly silent. President Wickham leaned toward the man with a menacing smile as the others held their breath.

"Are you calling me the Beast? The Antichrist?" His eyes briefly flashed red, and he did not shut them to disguise it.

The senator gulped hard. "Certainly not, Mr. President." He shivered visibly and shifted uncomfortably in his seat. "We all know that you're acting in the best interests of the American people and those throughout the world." The man paused, and then continued, his voice barely audible. "You do realize that you will make martyrs of them, sir?"

President Wickham interlaced his fingers on the table before him, holding the eyes of the senator with his. "One of my favorite books is Foxe's *Book of Martyrs*, Senator. It is bedtime reading for me." He chuckled darkly. "Karl Marx said that religion is the opiate of the masses. I am simply going to cure them of that addiction. In time, they will be grateful to me for opening their eyes. Maybe they will erect a statue of me – preferably in Israel in a newly built temple. I have heard that plans are underway to rebuild it, and negotiations are underway to obtain the necessary land, though some people are being a bit difficult because their own sacred buildings are already there. It makes no difference to me who is inconvenienced. One religion is no better than another in my opinion. Having just one religion for everyone would be so much simpler. It occurs to me that if an earthquake were to clear the structures presently existing on that land, the problem would be solved."

The senator dropped his eyes to his hands which were clenched together in his lap. He mumbled to himself, "The abomination of desolation."

The President's voice dropped to a whisper, though his voice was clearly heard by everyone in the room. "Perhaps I *am* the Beast – the Messiah. I like the sound of that. And, remember, whatever I accomplish, all of you have helped me to do it. I will not forget that; no one will."

President Wickham stood to his full, impressive height, saying, "After I leave, my assistant will come in and give each of you a copy of the Mark bill. You may stay and decide among yourselves who will introduce the bill to Congress, but all of you will be co-sponsors of this. I require your complete commitment to the passage of this measure. It is vital."

No one spoke until he and his guards left the room, and even then, the only words spoken were the ones necessary to carry out the President's instructions.

~~oo~~

Xander felt Elizabeth shift beside him in the darkness of their room. He searched her mind and found that she was awake and in a great deal of pain.

He rolled toward her in their bed and put his hand over hers as she arched her back. She gripped his hand tightly, and he could hear her breathing in the short pants she had been taught to use while breathing during a contraction. After a few moments, she relaxed back into the bed.

"Elizabeth," he said softly. "How long have you been in labor?"

"I woke up just after midnight," she answered.

"It's about four o'clock now. I wish that you had awakened me, love. Do you know how far apart your pains are?" he asked, sitting up in the bed.

"Xander, there was no reason to wake you up. There was nothing you could do for me, and there was no need for both of us to be awake and tired. I think my pains are about ten minutes apart," she said, and then gripped his hand again.

He murmured encouragement and reached under her to rub her back with his free hand as she breathed through the long contraction. While one part of his mind talked to her, another part prayed.

As soon as her grip loosened, he said, "Elizabeth, you do not need to go through this alone. If nothing else, I could have been praying for you these four hours. I helped to create these children, and I want to be included in their lives, and yours, for everything. Please do not leave me out, even if you think you are doing what is best for me."

He looked at Michael and Gabriel kneeling on Elizabeth's side of the bed, touching her shoulders and whispering peace. "Why did you not awaken me?" he demanded of his brothers in a low voice.

They looked up at him in surprise.

Michael was the first to speak, and he spoke aloud so that she could hear him. "Elizabeth did not wish to have you awake, or she would have done it herself."

"She has been in pain all night and perhaps was not the best judge of what was good for her during those hours. You should have roused me," replied Xander tersely.

Gabriel's voice was gentle. "Brother, I am sorry. I did not think of going against what our sister wanted."

Xander replied with quiet force. "From now on, no matter what Elizabeth thinks she wants, if she is in pain or danger of any sort, tell me, no matter where I am or what I am doing. I always wish to know if my wife or my children are suffering or are in any danger, whether or not you think I can help them. Is that clear?"

Michael stood, assuming solid angelic form, arms crossed and green eyes flashing. "While I cannot like your tone of voice or choice of words, I agree with the sentiment expressed. If Elizabeth or the children are ever in pain or danger, I will tell you. Even if you cannot physically help them, you can intercede in prayer."

Gabriel followed Michael's example and materialized. "I agree as well."

Elizabeth rolled her eyes. "Hello! I'm here. Elizabeth can hear you discussing her. Don't I get any say in whether or not Xander needs to know if I have a headache?"

"No," answered the three brothers in unison.

She sniffed and released a sigh. "Well, I'm glad that's settled."

Immediately she gripped her husband's hand again, and he was surprised at her strength. Had he not had such strength and stature, it would have been painful. *Dear Lord, please help her through this. Please ease her suffering. Help her to bear it, Father.*

When her hand finally relaxed, he reached for his cell phone on the bedside table. "Hello, Dr. Neal? Elizabeth's pains are five minutes apart, and we are on our way to the hospital." Pause. "Yes." Pause. "No, not yet." Pause. "Thank you. We will be there shortly."

After their brief conversation, he left the bed and quickly pulled on his clothes, afterward coming around to her side of the bed to help her dress in between contractions.

Michael and Gabriel morphed back into their usual forms and followed the couple as Xander carried Elizabeth into the hall. He stopped at Anna's room and tapped on the door while Gabriel set Elizabeth's suitcase down so that it would not appear to be floating. Within a few moments, the door opened a few inches, and Xander saw her face.

"We are on our way to the hospital, and I will call you when we have news. Please take care of John David and pray for Elizabeth," he said.

After Anna nodded, Xander continued on his way, carrying his wife down the stairs, out of the house, and to the waiting van.

~~oo~~

By seven o'clock in the morning, a beaming Xander was holding Faith Marrilyn Xander while a happy, exhausted Elizabeth cuddled Alexander Bennet Xander. Their guardians, Kenelm and Reima, and warriors, Abner and Baron, joined the other angels as they surrounded the little family.

Because the babies were not large – only 6.5 and 6.8 pounds each – Elizabeth, though extremely tired, had been able to birth each of them without the intervention of invasive surgery, much to Xander's relief.

Within a month, Charlotte and Jonathan had added another tiny member to the SoulFire team, Elijah William Edwards, known affectionately as "Eli." Cenhelm, his guardian, was a welcome addition to the Edwards family's protective force.

By June, both the Edwards and Xander families were ready for the USA Summer SoulFire Tour, and God's blessings rained richly on them. Many thousands of people flooded into their rallies, disturbed by the direction in which their country seemed to be headed and eager to hear the gospel of hope.

The team did not water down their message, though it had become even more politically incorrect and was attracting the attention of Washington, D.C. They boldly proclaimed that all signs pointed to an imminent return of Christ, and they spoke to the laws being passed in Washington to reinforce that idea. SoulFire members were careful to say that they were not guaranteeing the Second Coming would happen within a certain timeframe, because no one except God Himself knew when He would come. They said instead that most of the prophecies had been fulfilled.

Near the end of the tour, Xander and Elizabeth were in their hotel room on the king-sized bed together, each of them feeding one of the twins while they watched an early morning program. John David was still asleep in Anna's room.

Abruptly, the light banter of the show's host and hostess was interrupted with a special news bulletin. Xander and Elizabeth watched in shock as graphic pictures of death and devastation flashed across the screen, and horrifying news was reported: a 6.6 magnitude earthquake had hit Israel in the previous hour, toppling buildings and leveling holy places in Jerusalem, including the original site of Solomon's temple.

Chapter 19

"And he will make a firm covenant with the many for one week, but in the middle of the week he will put a stop to sacrifice and grain; and on the wing of abominations will come one who makes desolate, even until a complete destruction, one that is decreed, is poured out on the one who makes desolate."
Daniel 9:27

Xander and Elizabeth, along with the rest of the world, spent the next few weeks with their eyes trained on the cable news networks. In the aftermath of the earthquake, chaos reigned in Israel, particularly in Jerusalem, as the fragile peace of the area completely disintegrated. Fighting in the streets as well as heated debates among the leadership of the different factions broke out daily over the division of land, and former agreements were no longer honored. The site of Solomon's ancient temple was a major point of contention. With the area covered in rubble, completely cleared of all former holy buildings, a clamor arose to rebuild the Jewish temple on its original land. Surrounding countries began to take sides, and a full-fledged war involving the entire Middle East seemed unavoidable. The rest of the world, fearing the devastating consequences of a nuclear confrontation, cried out for a peacemaker, and President Gregory Wickham appeared to be the only man capable of accomplishing the seemingly impossible.

At the request of the United Nations, President Wickham boarded Air Force One, flew to the area, and sat down with the leaders of the nations involved, meeting separately with each faction before having a conference with all of them together. The negotiations were closed to the news media, but when the week was done, the President emerged smiling, having brokered a deal for seven years of peace. No one except for the people in the private meetings knew what had been promised in exchange for cooperation, but the rebuilding of the temple would commence immediately, and the city of Jerusalem would be restored.

All that mattered to the world's population in general was that war had been avoided, and that peace was promised for the future. President Gregory Wickham was the man of the hour, certain of a Nobel Peace Prize and global adoration. His star had certainly risen in the East.

~~oo~~

Jonathan, Charlotte, and baby Eli arrived promptly at six for their engagement with the Darcys. A dinner meeting before their summer tour began was in order, and because Xander and Elizabeth had three children and Jonathan and Charlotte only one, the Xander house was the simplest choice. Mark, David, and Amy were already in the living room, and they rose to greet the family as they entered.

Anna had eaten earlier, and then had helped Xander feed John David and the twins while Elizabeth had finished cooking and putting the final touches on the table. Charlotte had fed Eli before leaving their house, so Anna took all the children in the play room while the others sat down to eat and discuss summer plans.

Guardians and warriors split into two groups, each remaining with their charges.

After Xander asked the Lord's blessing on the food, they began to pass the dishes of food family-style, filling their plates and chatting amiably, catching up on the latest news of their friends.

Finally, Jonathan broached the subject that was never far from any of their minds. "Xander, do you think that our President is the Antichrist? He has now made a pact for seven years of peace in the Middle East which fulfills the 'week' foretold in Daniel 10:2, and the temple is now being rebuilt in Jerusalem on the original site of Solomon's temple."

Xander spoke carefully. "The seven years of peace he negotiated would signal the beginning of the Tribulation if Gregory were the Antichrist. While he has fulfilled some of the remaining prophecies, I do not see evidence that we are living in the Tribulation. For one thing, we are still here."

Quiet laughter from everyone broke through the thick tension that had set in at the beginning of the conversation. Based on Scriptural context, Xander's comment certainly provided a momentary relief for their somber thoughts.

Charlotte spoke up. "Yes, if the Rapture has occurred, why haven't we gone to heaven? I'm certainly ready for a new body since having Eli."

Michael spoke into Xander's and Elizabeth's minds. *I have not been summoned either. If this were the beginning of the Second Coming of Christ, Daniel 12:1 would be in order. 'Now at that time, Michael, the great prince who stands guard over the sons of your people, will arise. And there will be a time of distress such as never occurred since there was a nation until that time; and at that time your people, everyone who is found written in the book, will be rescued.'*

Gabriel nodded. *Xander, you, Michael, and I would all know by now if the Second Coming were indeed taking place at this time.*

Jonathan looked at Xander. "Then what is happening? How can so many of the signs be there, and yet God has not taken us and the other believers into heaven?"

Xander answered, "Gregory does not meet all the requirements of the Antichrist. As I am sure you have already realized, he does not have the correct heritage. Neither does he fit Daniel 11:37, 'And he will show no regard for the gods of his fathers or for the desire of women, nor will he show regard for any other god; for he will magnify himself above them all.' While Gregory certainly magnifies himself above God and shows no regard for our Father, he does have a desire for women – even if that desire is not a proper one. He uses women for gratification only, to satisfy his lusts and need for dominance."

Elizabeth looked at Xander, her eyes sorrowful. "Yes, Char, and I have known Gregory for years. He definitely has a way with the ladies." Sudden thoughts of that terrible day when Gregory had tried to rape her flooded her mind, and she immediately felt sick to her stomach. *I'm so sorry, Xander. I was so stupid.*

Do not think of it, Elizabeth. It is past. It has absolutely no power over you, Xander thought into her mind, comforting her and squeezing her hand under the table.

Michael put his hand on Elizabeth's back. *All is well, my sister. Do not be anxious.*

Gabriel thought, *But what of the Mark?*

Xander looked around the table. "I have contacts in Washington, and they have told me some very disturbing news. Gregory's cabal has proposed the implantation of a microchip in everyone on U.S. soil by next March. The legislation is called the Mark bill, named after the tattoo to be placed over the site of the implant; that tattoo is a duplicate of the one behind Gregory's ear – three intertwined sixes. The official story will be that the chip will store the person's medical history."

Charlotte gasped, and Jonathan turned his head sharply, his eyes wide as he looked at Xander. "He is introducing the Mark of the Beast? Why would he do that if he is not the Antichrist?"

"I think that Gregory is Satan's instrument, Lucifer's choice to be the Antichrist. Gregory wants to be the Antichrist, the Son of Perdition, and he is trying to fulfill all the prophecies, but this is not God's time. Ultimately, God decides when He will return, not Lucifer. Satan always has someone ready to step into the role of the Beast, because he does not know when that time will come. But now, it appears that Lucifer wants to take that power to himself. He must believe that he can win now with Gregory at the helm," answered Xander.

Jonathan was silent for a moment. Then he spoke thoughtfully. "I have never considered it in that light. Even so, can we let people take the Mark ignorantly? What if the President actually turns out to be the Beast? He is certainly a man of sin. Shouldn't we warn people so that they can make an informed choice? Revelation 14:9 -10 says that anyone who takes the Mark cannot go to heaven. What if this chip is the Mark of the prophecy?"

Xander nodded. "I have thought of that already, Jonathan. The bill has been quietly introduced to both Houses of Congress with an absence of media coverage, and the penalties for refusing to take the chip and the Mark will be severe. In telling people to refuse the Mark, we will be advising people to go to jail, and I do not like that, but I think we must do so. If everything goes as Gregory has planned, we have fewer than nine full months to educate people about the dangers of submitting to this law. Whether or not Gregory is the Antichrist, the implant could still be the Mark of the Beast, and people need to know that to accept the Mark is to reject God. What if there is another person waiting to step into his place? No one can deny that many prophecies are coming to pass."

There was complete silence at the table as everyone thought about what could be coming.

Amy spoke up. "What will happen to us for speaking against the President and his plans?"

Xander looked at her with kindness and sympathy. "I will do all I can to protect the rest of you. I am willing to be the only one who will speak on this subject. Perhaps the rest of you will avoid arrest if you remain quiet."

Elizabeth interjected, "That will not matter, because I will refuse to take the chip and the tattoo in any case, and I know that we will never consent to have that thing put into our children. I will be arrested anyway, so I may as well make the most of it. You will not do this alone."

Michael spoke into her mind. *Neither of you will be alone.*

Each guardian placed their hands on the shoulders of their charges, speaking words of comfort to them, and the warriors stepped up closer behind the protectors.

Jonathan said with conviction, "No, you will not. Elizabeth is right. Those of us who speak for SoulFire will share this burden together." His eyes rested briefly on each one seated around the table. "There is no need for Amy, Mark, or Dave to say anything, and if any of you want to leave the team entirely, we will understand, but the four of us who speak at the rallies will stand united." Jonathan glanced at Charlotte, "If you agree, of course."

Charlotte smiled with determination. "You know me better than to think I will back down from Gregory and his goons, Jon. I will be beside you, El, and Xander."

Mark looked at the four of them. "I will prepare a written statement from SoulFire. As Elizabeth pointed out, I will be arrested for not taking the implant, so I might as well be fully on the side of right."

Dave nodded. "I agree. Even if this chip were not the Mark of the Beast, I don't trust our President. There is more to this than he's telling us. There's no way that our medical records are all that will be accessible through the device. Count me in."

Amy's voice was soft. "I am not particularly courageous, but I think forcing people to have an invasive procedure is against the freedoms guaranteed to all Americans." She paused, and then added thoughtfully, "I also agree with Dave, and I stand with the team. I'll bet the government will be able to track us with those chips."

Xander smiled grimly. "Yes, my sources tell me that the tattoo will be scanned anytime people buy or sell anything. No one will be able to buy food or anything else without the chip, and people who refuse it will lose their jobs. The government, meaning Gregory, will have access to everyone's personal information, and I do not doubt that the microchip will contain some sort of GPS."

Jonathan muttered, "Outrageous. First he forces young people into the military for two years, next he disarms all of us, and now this."

Elizabeth added, "What we haven't said is that everyone who takes the implant will get $2,000. In this economy, people will have their children take the Mark just to get the extra money. I wouldn't be surprised if Gregory doesn't eventually offer a reward to those who turn in the names of people who haven't lined up for the chip."

Xander tilted his head and looked at her with frank admiration. "That is exactly what he will do. He will turn neighbors and families against each other. People's loyalties will be to him first, and he will do it with money. He has unlimited resources."

Jonathan looked at the beloved faces around the table. "So, we are all agreed. We will stand against the President and speak out against his legislation. We will be putting targets on our heads, but suffering for Christ is an honor. We need to talk strategy now."

After much prayer and discussion, by the end of the evening the team had decided to cancel their International Tour planned for the fall and instead concentrate on the United States. If there was to be any hope of stopping

Gregory before the Mark Bill became law and was implemented, SoulFire would have to travel the country extensively.

~~oo~~

Xander helped Elizabeth clear the table and load the dishes into the dishwasher after their guests left so that they could put their children to bed together as was their custom. As John David sat on the floor of the babies' nursery, already dressed for bed and looking at a book, the couple sat side-by-side in a double glider rocker, each of them holding one of the twins and feeding them their final bottles for the night.

Michael and Gabriel smiled at the sight, as did Kenward, Kenelm, and Reima. Cahal, Abner, and Baron stood by the wall, backs turned to the little family, keeping watch out the windows and showing no change of expression.

Elizabeth folded her legs under her, cuddled her tiny, dark-haired daughter, and snuggled closer to her husband, sighing with contentment.

"This is my favorite time of the day," she said, turning her head to kiss her husband's strong shoulder.

Xander chuckled. "You say that about the morning and when we go to bed, too, my love."

"Don't be such a stickler for accuracy. Anytime I'm with you and my children is my favorite time," she retorted playfully.

He kissed the top of her head and held out an empty bottle. "I think Alex is finished, and he is asleep. How about Faith?"

Elizabeth sat up. "She's through, too." She put her daughter on her shoulder and patted her back. Xander followed her example with Alex, and both babies burped noisily.

John David looked up at the noise, giggling, and Elizabeth put a finger to her lips.

"Shhh," she said softly, looking at her little man.

"Shhh," he answered, smiling, mimicking her motion.

Xander and Elizabeth got up carefully and walked softly across the room with their babies, placing them gently in their cribs. Then Xander turned and picked up John David, laying his book aside and holding him so that their faces were level.

"John David, do you want to pray first tonight, or shall I?" he asked his son.

"I pray," the boy replied, reaching for his mother's hand.

Standing by the cribs, surrounded by their guardians, Xander's family bowed their heads.

"Thank you, Jesus, for Mommy, Daddy, Faith, and Alex," John David intoned in his childish voice. "Love you. Help me be good. Good night, God. Amen."

Elizabeth added, "Thank you for Xander, John David, Faith, and Alex, dear Lord. Please keep us safe tonight, and help us to sleep well. We love you. In Jesus' name. Amen."

"Father, we love you. Please bless my wife, John David, Faith, Alex, Nana and Papa, Aunt Janna and Uncle Chance, Matthew, and all of our loved ones. Thank you so much for giving me these people to love and help me never to take their love for granted. In Jesus' name. Amen."

Leaving the twins in the care of Abner, Kenelm, Baron, and Reima, Elizabeth turned off the overhead lights, leaving on a small lamp, and led the way as Xander carried John David to his room. Michael, Gabriel, Cahal, and Kenward followed them.

A night light glowed softly, illuminating the familiar shapes in John David's room. Both Elizabeth and Xander kissed their son, and Xander leaned over to put him in his crib. John David frowned as his father laid him down.

"I want bed," he said, though his eyes were closed and his voice was sleepy. "Me big boy."

Xander smiled and stroked his son's hair. "Yes, you are. But you are not yet two years old. When you have your second birthday, we will go buy a bed for you that is your size."

"Okay," John David answered and rolled over on his side. "Good night, Unca Mike and Unca Gabe."

"Good night, John David," they answered aloud in unison.

Elizabeth pulled the covers over him and rubbed his cheek. "He looks just like you, Xander, right down to the dimples," she whispered.

They held hands and walked quietly from the room. Xander stopped in the hallway and pulled Elizabeth to him, holding her face with one hand as he kissed her. When he moved back he replied, "I am happy that the twins have your beautiful eyes. Faith is my miniature Elizabeth."

He took her hand and led her into their bedroom. "Are you tired?" he asked.

Michael and Gabriel took up their posts by the windows.

"Well," she answered with a playful smile, "it has been a long day, but I could probably be talked into a back rub."

His lips twitched. "Back rubs are relaxing, but they often lead to other things. So, how tired are you?"

"Read my mind," she invited.

Xander smiled.

Michael and Gabriel turned to look out of the windows.

Hello, trees, thought Michael glumly.

Be quiet, answered Gabriel.

~~oo~~

Shortly after they had fallen asleep, Xander awoke to a bright Light streaming through the windows. He sat up quickly, noticing that Gabriel and Michael had moved to stand on either side of the bed.

Elizabeth, said a familiar Voice.

Gabriel and Michael dropped to their knees and bowed their heads, and Xander bowed his head in submission, moving to kneel on the bed.

She stirred and opened her eyes, squinting at the Light. Seeing that her husband was bowed, Elizabeth sat up. *Did you call me, Xander?* she thought. *Did you turn the light on?*

I called you, Elizabeth, My daughter, answered the Voice.

The Voice was all around her. There did not seem to be a point of origination. Elizabeth immediately left the bed and fell to her knees, her face on the floor. *Father, here am I. How can I serve You?*

Xander quickly joined her on the floor, kneeling beside her, prostrating himself.

The Voice was beautiful. *You have pleased Me, Elizabeth. I will ask you what I asked your husband several years ago. If you could have anything that you desired, what would you ask of Me?*

Tears filled her eyes. *I am happy that I have pleased You, Lord, but You have given me so much more than I ever thought I would have. I am complete. What more could I ask for?*

You do not desire power, fame, or wealth, Elizabeth? asked the Voice.

No, Father. I desire only to serve You and love my family, she answered.

If you could serve Me in a better way, would you want to do it? No matter the cost? The Voice was kind and loving.

Her tears flowed freely and a lump stuck in her throat as she thought of her beloved husband and her children. Would God ask her to give them up? He had given them to her, and they were His to take away if He chose to do so.

She struggled to control her mind. *I do not deserve all the blessings that You have graciously given me, Father. If You require that I give them up, I will do so if it is Your desire. I want to bring You glory. 'Naked I came from my mother's womb, and naked I shall return there. The Lord gives, and the Lord takes away. Blessed be the name of the Lord,'* she answered, paraphrasing from the book of Job.

You have been taught well. Again you please Me, Elizabeth, replied the Voice. *Will you ask for nothing?*

Her mind reached out to Him. *I ask only that Xander and my children would be unharmed. I request that You keep them safe. Whatever must happen, let it happen to me, but not to them.*

Xander grasped her hand, but he did not speak.

The Voice was filled with love. *Elizabeth, I love you more than you could ever imagine. As it is now, eventually, you will die and come to heaven to live with Me for eternity, but that will not happen for many years. Your husband has a dual nature; he is both an angel and a human. He will not die, but will transform back to an angel when his time on Earth is complete. He is My Chief Guardian, and I will require his service when this time is passed. I ask you again, My daughter, if you could have anything you desired, what would you ask of Me?*

Elizabeth tried to control her tears, but they gushed from her eyes at the thought of being separated from her husband. As she sobbed, she could feel Xander's hand jerk in hers, and she knew that he felt the same. She was in agony.

Oh, God! I am selfish, and I do not want to be separated from my beloved. I would bear anything to know that I could be with him and serve You for eternity at his side. My soul is tormented when I think of his leaving me. Is there an answer for this pain? She stretched out on the floor and wept, and her tears mingled with those of her husband.

Elizabeth, you are not selfish. I made you and Xander for each other, and I would not separate you. He would be grieved in My service without you, though he would try not to betray his unhappiness. He is both Xander and Xander, both angel and human, and, if you desire it, you will be Elizabeth, both human and angel, living your full number of days on the Earth, as he will. Upon your deaths, which will occur together if you agree, both of you will transform to angelic form for eternity. However, there is a price for this, Elizabeth, so consider it carefully. The Voice was low and kind.

Father, You are good, and You always work what is best for your children. I do not fear the price, for I know that Your yoke is easy and Your burden is light. What is the cost? she asked without looking up.

The Voice spoke gently. *Elizabeth, if I change you now, you will be able to assume angelic form just as your husband does, and you will be a guardian warrior as he is, but there will be no more children. You will fight beside him, for he has trained you well, but I cannot allow the two of you to reproduce angels. Angels are created beings, made only by Me, and I will close your womb. You will be barren. The three children that you have are extremely gifted, and half of their bloodline is pure. They will be powerful enough and will serve Me well. They are My legacy to the world. If you were to have children with Xander after I change you, they would be more angel than human. It would be an abomination. Are you willing to pay the price?*

Elizabeth did not answer immediately; she turned her head to look at her husband. *Father, my decision will affect my husband. May I ask him what he wishes?*

The Voice chuckled, and the angelic realm turned in unison to hear the sound. *You are a delight to Me, Elizabeth. Ask your husband, though I know what he will say.*

I know what I want, Xander, but what do you want? Will it sadden you to know that we can have no more children? You wanted a quiver full, and that is thirteen.

As Xander looked at her, his expression was tender and full of love. *My love, our children are blessings from our Father, but I would have been happy to have only you. To know that we would never be apart is more than I could ask or imagine. If you want this, know that I want it, too. Beloved, my quiver holds three by God's design, and that is enough.*

Elizabeth? asked the Voice, and all of creation stopped to hear her answer.

Her mind overflowed with joy. *Yes, Father. You have blessed us beyond measure, and I am Your handmaiden. Do to me as it seems fit to You.*

Then it is done. The Light rapidly withdrew, and suddenly it was as dark as it had been before.

Had she not still been on the floor, Elizabeth would have had difficulty in believing that the amazing events of the past half hour had ever happened.

"Xander," she whispered.

"Yes, Elizabeth?" he answered.

"Am I different now?" she asked.

"Let us stand and see," he replied, laughing quietly.

She stood. "How do I do this? How do I change?"

Xander looked at her quizzically. "Just think about it."

Michael and Gabriel stood, and she pointed at them, and then looked backed at Xander in amazement. "I can see them clearly! In the dark! They aren't hazy to me anymore. I really am different! I can hear all of your thoughts! Please, Xander, change forms now so that I can hear what your mind does."

Her husband transformed, and she allowed her mind to follow his.

His mind reeled as Elizabeth stood before him, glorious in her armor and tunic, even more beautiful with her sword at her waist and her shield suspended from her belt. She glowed softly, just as he did.

"Oh!" they said together as the holy angels looked on in amazement.

Smiling, Xander reached for her hand. "Come outside with me. Quietly, through the back door."

Michael and Gabriel followed them down the steps as they padded on the carpet, careful to make no noise.

When they came to the door, she stopped, waiting for Xander to open it for her, but he simply smiled at her and walked through it, gently pulling her hand so that she would follow him.

Once they stood in the back yard, Xander unfurled his wings.

Elizabeth smiled in understanding and spread her wings as well. She followed her husband into the sky, laughing and twirling, flying by his side, reading his thoughts to learn how to control her movements.

The couple, along with Michael and Gabriel, stayed in the immediate area, careful to remain close to the treetops, aware that it was possible that they were being watched.

After an hour or so, they returned to the trees behind their home. They settled to the ground, and Xander tucked his wings, drew her into his arms, and kissed her soundly.

"Now I have also kissed an angel," he proclaimed before he morphed back into human form.

She changed as he did, her eyes sparkling. "Will I have to give up the use of contractions now and speak in formal English?"

"Do not change anything about yourself, Elizabeth. You are perfect to me already," he answered.

As they walked back to their house, Elizabeth became serious.

"Now we know why you felt compelled to train me," she said.

"I have already thought of that," he answered in a whisper.

"I know," she answered in awestruck wonder. "Isn't that amazing? I know because I heard you. Praise God from Whom all blessings flow."

Her husband regarded her in profound reverence for their loving Father and said in a hushed and deliberate voice, "Praise Him above, ye heavenly host. Amen and amen."

Chapter 20

"Thus let all Thine enemies perish, O Lord; but let those who love Him be like the rising of the sun in its might."
Judges 5:31

February 2012

President Gregory Wickham was extremely agitated. He paced the carpets of the Oval Office, eyes flashing crimson, as Lucifer, dressed impeccably in a three-piece suit, lounged on a couch inspecting his fingernails. Demonic guards lined the room, hands clasped before them and heads bowed.

"SoulFire is thwarting all of my plans," Gregory spat angrily.

"My son," said Lucifer in a soothing voice, "why do you let them upset you? They can do nothing to prevent what has been set in motion."

Gregory turned and glared at his father. "They are running all over the country, speaking against me and instructing their followers not to accept the Mark when it becomes available. People are listening to them, and now there is a groundswell of opposition."

"You always knew that Christians would refuse the chip, Gregory. That is why we have built more prisons – to contain all those who fight against us," said Lucifer reasonably, fixing calm eyes on his son.

Gregory swore and replied acidly, "But they are convincing more and more people to become believers. Thousands are added to the enemy's camp daily. Do you not see the danger, Father?"

"Gregory, Gregory," replied Lucifer, shaking his head and smiling. "You are very young. I have seen periodic 'revivals' for thousands of years. These things go in cycles, and this time will be no different. Calm yourself. New believers quickly fall away when their lives become difficult, and in today's society, very few Christians will be willing to go to jail for their faith. Life has been too easy for them, and they have not the backbones of the martyrs." He smirked, distorting his beautiful features. "They will not suffer for Jesus as the apostles did. Trust me, and you will see that I am right."

Folding his arms and turning his face away to look at one of the portraits on the wall, Gregory spoke softly, though his glowing eyes betrayed his true feelings. "So you do not agree that we need to take action? You think SoulFire should be allowed to continue to mock me?"

"My son, let them do what they will. The people love you, and they will worship us when we put money in their pockets," answered Lucifer with confidence.

There was silence while Gregory appeared to be considering his father's words.

"I understand you perfectly. You always know what is best," said Gregory, keeping his eyes averted.

"There is nothing to be upset about, Gregory. All will be well," replied Lucifer cheerfully as he stood with easy grace. He walked to his son and placed his hand on the younger man's shoulder for a moment, and then exited the room with his guards.

No one looked at Lucifer twice as he strode the halls of the White House. After all, he had been there many times before, and he had been a close friend of a few other Presidents as well. If anyone wondered why the tall, striking man never seemed to age, they kept their questions to themselves. Each administration employed their own people, so no one really knew how long the stranger had been welcome in that building as he took care never to be photographed.

Gregory stood completely still, eyebrows drawn together, perfect lips pressed into a straight line, for fully five minutes before he suddenly wheeled around to face one of his trusted guards. "Bring Aborian to me immediately," he barked, his eyes flaming once again.

The demon instantly assumed his natural form and flew through the wall of the Oval Office, bent on completing his mission as quickly as possible.

No one heard Gregory muttering under his breath, "This shall not stand."

~~oo~~

The SoulFire team had been crisscrossing the country for months, rarely taking a break, knowing that March would soon be upon them, and with it, the implementation of the Mark Bill. All across the United States, centers dedicated solely to the implant procedure were ready to open on March 15. Court cases had been filed challenging the constitutionality of the law, but as yet, no judge had issued an injunction of any sort. Barring that, in less than a month's time, entire families would start lining up to receive their microchips, tattoos, and government checks.

Xander sat in his van in front of a grocery store in Bethel, watching his three children while Elizabeth ran in for a few items they needed. He looked at their innocent faces in the rearview mirror and thanked God for blessing his marriage in such a way.

His sons and daughter had fallen asleep during their drive back from an evening rally nearby, and Elizabeth had not wanted to wake them so that they could all go into the store together. Even though Michael was with Elizabeth, Xander stayed in constant contact with her mind. Lately, he had felt the presence of such overpowering evil continually building that he rarely allowed his wife or his children out of his sight, and he was never so far from Elizabeth that he could not hear her thoughts. The presence of Gabriel, along with the other guardians and warriors surrounding his vehicle reminded him that they were well protected, but he was never easy when he could not see both his wife and his children.

As he mused quietly over the seeming defeat that loomed before them, he saw a black truck whose doors were emblazoned with the Mark emblem pull up and park across from him. Three men in the familiar government-issued uniforms got out of the vehicle and headed for the store, laden with equipment. Xander had seen similar scenarios played out across the country, and he knew that the men were there to install the Mark equipment. Soon, store employees would begin to scan people before they would be allowed to purchase food. Those without implants would go hungry or be taken to jail. Some farmers might try to avoid the situation for a while by eating the produce they grew themselves, but eventually, they would need to buy seed, fertilizer, or equipment. There would come a time when they would have to choose either to take the Mark or be arrested.

Xander watched his beautiful wife come through the electronic doors carrying her bags with Michael close behind her. Elizabeth's long dark hair was swinging as she walked, her eyes lighting with a smile as she saw him, and he suddenly found himself very angry.

As Elizabeth got in the van, she felt his dark mood. She placed the bags at her feet and reached for her husband's hand. "What's wrong, my love?"

"The same thing that has been wrong since the beginning of last summer," he answered bitterly. "Did you not see those men who entered the store just before you left it? They are here to bring the grocery store up to government standards. Soon, we will not be able to buy food here, Elizabeth."

She tilted her head and saw the tension in his face. "We knew this was coming. Why are you suddenly upset?"

He thought a moment. "We have spent almost nine months traveling the country warning people not to submit to this law, but we really have not accomplished anything. We have not done anything to stop it, and in a little more than two weeks, people whom we have failed to reach for Christ will be permanently marked with the symbol of Satan. They will belong to him, choosing to take the Mark without fully realizing the consequences. We must do something," Xander said.

"We have done important work, my love. People are fighting against Gregory now. They will refuse to take the Mark," Elizabeth replied earnestly.

"And they will go to jail and lose their jobs," he answered. "We have done what we were supposed to do, but now it is time for action. I feel strongly that we must do more; we must stop this lunacy."

He released her hand and turned the key in the ignition, beginning the short drive to their home.

"What can we do?" she asked, looking back at her sleeping babies.

"God's timing is always perfect, Elizabeth. He changed you when He did for a reason. He said that you and I would fight side-by-side, and He also said that we would live for many more years."

She nodded. "Yes, He did. Do you think that means that you and I are supposed to stop Gregory ourselves? And that we will survive it?"

"While we traveled the country over the past few months, I have had peace that we were doing what God wanted us to do. Now, I know that the time is right for doing more. We have taught the people, explaining the Scriptures to them, and when we give them the chance to reject the Mark, they will do so, but it is up to us to give them that chance. I am the Chief Guardian. This bill is a direct threat to every believer in the United States, and we will deal with it as such."

Xander's anger evaporated quickly as a plan began to form in his mind. "To answer your questions, yes, I do think that we are supposed to put a halt to Gregory's plans. However, we will not be alone – far from it, in fact. And, yes, my love, we will survive."

Finally! exclaimed Michael, who had been ready to fight Gregory for many years. The warriors who flew by their Captain actually smiled.

Even I am eager for this confrontation, thought Gabriel.

"So I guess it is unanimous?" asked Elizabeth, hearing the thoughts of her brothers. "Suddenly, I feel the need for an intense training session."

"You are more prepared than you know, Elizabeth," said Xander. "Jehovah Himself said that you have done well, my guardian warrior wife." His blue eyes twinkled in spite of his serious mien.

"I suppose that you already have a plan in mind," she stated. Then, listening to his mind, she began to smile. "Excellent!"

~~oo~~

Aborian stood fidgeting before Gregory, awaiting his instructions and avoiding his eyes.

The President spoke. "It is time for us to use the information we glean from the woman who works with SoulFire. So far, we have only irritated them. That was well-played, Aborian, for they have no idea that we can intercept all of her messages. Now, we will use your work to destroy them. I want to know where they are at all times. Report directly to me and to no one else. Do you understand?"

Aborian understood very well. "I will tell no one else but you, my Prince."

~~oo~~

Xander and Elizabeth met the rest of the SoulFire team the next morning at Jonathan and Charlotte's home in Columbia, South Carolina, to plan their next tour. Amy, Dave, and Mark sat on a couch in the living room, while Charlotte and Jonathan were on the loveseat.

Both Jonathan and Charlotte noticed that Xander was uncharacteristically edgy.

Unwilling to leave his children so far from him, he had brought them with him and Elizabeth. Anna watched their three children, along with Eli, in Eli's nursery.

Guardians remained close to their charges as warriors stood vigil throughout the house.

Jonathan raised an eyebrow. "Xander, are you going to tell us what is wrong?"

Xander had been sitting on the edge of the couch, so tense that he had not leaned back into the furniture. At Jonathan's question, he rose and began to pace. He stopped at the mantel, turned, and faced the questioning expressions of his friends. Gabriel stood beside him.

"Elizabeth and I feel that we must take drastic action to stop people from being forced to take the Mark," he said quietly.

Elizabeth left the couch and stepped to her husband's side, reaching for his hand, as they listened to the others processing the information in their minds. Michael was at Elizabeth's side.

After a few moments, Jonathan asked, "What do you want us to do?"

Xander shook his head. "There is no 'us' in this, Jonathan. God has chosen this task for Elizabeth and me. The rest of you must stay together and pray while we meet Gregory."

Charlotte's face showed her fear for her closest friends. "You expect us to hide away while you meet Gregory and whatever army he brings with him? How can you ask that of us? And how do you even know Gregory himself will come?"

Xander visibly relaxed. "I can ask it because I know your prayers will be powerful and used by God to strengthen us and ensure our success. I know that Gregory will come, because I know how his mind works. We have been convincing people not to take his Mark, and he wants to kill us. We will stop Gregory from carrying out his plans, and we will be safe. You should not worry, Charlotte."

"Are you sure about this?" asked Jonathan, his eyes full of concern.

Xander and Elizabeth looked at each other. She smiled at him, and the confidence she displayed spoke to everyone else in the room.

Without moving her eyes from those of her husband, she replied, "We are confident that this is God's will."

He kissed her forehead, and then turned, looking at Amy.

"Amy, it is time to spring the trap we have been laying for three years," said Xander.

"Good," she said. "I've been ready for a new phone and laptop for at least a year now."

Her levity broke the somber mood of the room, and they chuckled in response.

Xander smiled. "Send everyone in this room a text and an e-mail saying that you have set up the secret meeting I requested for tonight at eleven. There's a big, open field well outside the city limits to the northwest with nothing for miles around."

He drew a paper from his pocket and handed it to Amy, saying, "I have written out the message for you, because you must be very specific about the location. While we meet Gregory and his followers there, all of you must gather a group of the strongest believers you know into the sanctuary of Northwoods Church and pray for us until we come to you after it is over. Tell them to bring their children with them, and do not let them out of your sight. I have already contacted Pastor Brooks, so he is expecting your call today, Jonathan. No one except for the people you contact can know of your meeting."

Jonathan looked unhappy. "What about your children?"

Elizabeth's face was serene. "We visited my parents last night. They, along with Chance, Janna, and Matthew, will be at Northwoods with our children and the rest of you."

Charlotte's eyes bored into Elizabeth's like laser beams. "You do not have to do this alone. Please, let Jonathan and me come with you and Xander."

Mark added, "You were there for me several years ago when the serpent came for me; please let me be there with you now. Don't try to take this on by yourselves."

Xander and Elizabeth spoke together. "We will not be alone."

Michael smiled with confidence and folded his arms, legs apart, while Gabriel's expression became unusually steely. Gone was the peacemaker, and in his place stood the undefeated warrior.

From his place behind Jonathan, Lexus looked at the archangels and spoke. *I would fight alongside you. Can you not send warriors to take my place?*

Edward's expression held a similar look of longing, and that expression was duplicated on every angelic face in the room.

Xander, the Chief of Guardians, answered, *You are needed to protect the rest of the team. I want the two of you, as well as the other guardians and warriors in this room, to be near my children, my friends, and the rest of my family while I fight. The warriors who are not assigned to be with you will be with us. When Gregory sees that Jonathan, Charlotte, and the other team members are not with us, he may send demonic warriors to look for them. He may even try to find our children, and you may have to battle for them tonight. Elizabeth and I will be more at peace knowing that you and the others are here, Lexus. It will be well.*

Xander spoke into the minds of the guardians and warriors in the room with them as well as those whom God had selected for his children, and who protected them in the nursery even as they listened to him. *Cahal, Kenward, Abner, Kenelm, Baron, and Reima will be with the rest of you – Elizabeth and I know that you, as well as the others, would battle for our children until you were unbodied.*

Every guardian and warrior in the room nodded solemnly at his statement. Through the might of Jehovah-Ganan, they would protect John David, Faith, and Alex. Such a mighty group had not been assembled in one place for two thousand years.

Charlotte searched Elizabeth's eyes, and then Xander's. She was satisfied and nodded at Jonathan.

Jonathan stood, and the four other members of the SoulFire team followed his example. Xander and Elizabeth stepped into the middle of their circle where five pairs of human hands were laid on them as Jonathan led the group in a prayer requesting protection for the Darcys. Guardians moved and reached to touch their charges as warriors hovered over them.

As soon as Jonathan said, "Amen," Amy sent her text messages and e-mails, and the rest of the group discussed what had to be done. They then said their goodbyes, hugged each other, and hurried to accomplish their tasks before the evening was upon them.

~~oo~~

By 10:30 that night, everyone was in place. Northwoods Church was filled with believers on their knees in intercessory prayer. Most of the children were asleep on the pews, and the few who were not, sensing the gravity of the situation, remained quietly by their parents. The only lights left shining in the building were those which were never turned off for security reasons. A storm threatened, but so far, the rain had not come. Distant lightning flashed occasionally, and the rumble of thunder could be heard from far away.

Guardians and warriors stood thickly throughout the sanctuary, remaining on full alert, every sense heightened.

David and Lynne bowed on their knees in a group with Jonathan and Charlotte at the front of the sanctuary. The twins and Eli slept in their baby seats while John David slumbered with his cousin Matthew on a blanket and pillows which had been placed on the floor for him by his grandmother. Charles and Janna knelt with Caroline and Anne Bingley behind the Bennets. The sanctuary was quiet except for the murmur of voices raised in intercessory prayer.

Niall and Roark stood alongside David and Lynne Bennet, their hands resting on the shoulders of their charges.

Niall looked at Roark, a question in his eyes. *Sometimes it is God's will that His people die. Do you think that Xander and Elizabeth will survive this?*

Roark lowered his head, hiding his expression. *If Jehovah takes them, it will serve His greater glory. It would mean that their deaths will accomplish more than their lives.*

Niall sighed. *That is true; however, I must admit that I will be glad when this night is over. I will rejoice to see my brother and my sister again, if it is His will.*

~~oo~~

Xander and Elizabeth drove to the meeting place, accompanied by Michael and Gabriel, as well as many other guardians and warriors. While they traveled, they listened to a radio news channel. None of them were surprised to hear the announcement that President Wickham, along with the governor of South Carolina, had declared martial law throughout the state. A curfew was in effect, and anyone who was outside of their homes after 11:00 would be arrested.

By 10:30, they had arrived at the designated area and parked in an area off the dirt access road in which their vehicle would be hidden. The couple left the van and traveled the short remaining distance on foot.

Michael had deployed scouts throughout the city and the outlying areas, and as they reported back periodically to him, he relayed information to all of the angelic beings both in Columbia and with him in the open area. Xander had summoned all un-assigned guardians, and Michael had called in many thousands of warriors. The Host stood at attention as they encircled the open field where they waited for the meeting.

At 10:45, scouts reported the movement of a large military force, transported by jeeps and trucks, headed for the field. President Wickham, surrounded by his guards and the Secret Service, rode in a covered vehicle with the state governor. Led by Commander Abigor and Underprince Tala, demonic warriors flew overhead in swarms, numbering in the thousands.

Xander took Elizabeth's hand as they walked in human form to the middle of the field – two lone humans surrounded by an unseen force of unparalleled power. Michael stood by Elizabeth, tensed for battle, and Gabriel took his stance by Xander.

Xander smiled as he smelled the foul odor of approaching evil. *He took the bait.*

Elizabeth squeezed his hand. *We have been heading for this battle from the moment I was born. We will do as instructed in James 4:7, 'Submit therefore to God. Resist the devil and he will flee from you.'*

Xander answered, *And since we have long ago submitted to God, we now take the first step in resisting the devil. We are standing fast and fighting. It will be interesting to see if Gregory comes without Lucifer. Gregory thinks he is smart, but Lucifer is the crafty one. He would flee in the face of the angelic Host. I doubt that Gregory will do so. He has deceived himself into believing that he can defeat us.*

Elizabeth answered with Psalm 144:1, *'Blessed be the Lord my Rock, who trains my hands for war, and my fingers for battle; my lovingkindness and my fortress, my stronghold and my deliverer, my shield and He in whom I take refuge; who subdues my people under me.'*

'For Thou art my lamp, O Lord; and the Lord illumines my darkness. For by Thee I can run upon a troop; by my God I can leap over a wall. As for God, His way is blameless; the word of the Lord is tested; He is a shield to all who take refuge in Him,' replied Xander, quoting II Samuel 22:29.

Elizabeth lifted her face to the moonless sky, raised her hands with her palms toward heaven, and quoted Psalm 16:8, *I have set the Lord continually before me; because He is at my right hand, I will not be shaken.*

Xander spoke aloud from I John 5:19-20. "We know that we are of God, and the whole world lies in the power of the evil one. And we know that the Son of God has come, and has given us understanding, in order that we might know Him Who is true, and we are in Him Who is true, in His Son Jesus Christ. This is the true God and eternal life."

As the minutes passed, the couple continued to quote Scripture and pray, and their strength grew. They felt the prayers of the saints, and they were anointed with the power of God Himself.

The air grew heavy with the smell of rain as the sounds of thunder grew louder, and eventually, the thunder mingled with the sounds of the approaching army.

Gregory's transport entered the huge clearing first and stopped at the edge of the woods. A guard opened his door, and President Wickham exited the vehicle and walked toward the couple, accompanied by troops of armed soldiers. A few guardians walked among the soldiers, whispering to their charges.

The state governor, as well as a military officer, walked by Wickham's side, and legions of dark ones fanned out around the Dark Prince, howling and shrieking as they danced and writhed. Demonic warriors formed a line to each side of President Wickham and stood in battle stances, Abigor and Tala taking their places on either side of him.

Elizabeth carefully controlled her features, unwilling to betray any hint of her feelings upon seeing the dark ones for the first time. Xander heard her mind recoil in revulsion at the sight of their distorted, evil beauty. He knew she fought the bile rising in her throat.

Gregory stopped about five feet from Xander and Elizabeth, glancing around the clearing. "So, you two are here alone. I am not surprised. You are aware, I suppose, that the governor of South Carolina is the Commander-in-Chief of the state's National Guard?"

Xander smiled and extended his hand to the unfortunate man. "Governor, I am Xander Darcy, and this is my wife, Elizabeth."

As the governor hesitated, and then reached out his hand toward Xander's, Gregory swore an ugly oath. The governor blinked and withdrew his hand.

"This is not a church picnic, Xander. We are here to arrest you and your wife," Gregory spat.

It was Elizabeth's turn to smile, focusing her full attention on her former friend. "Arrest us, Gregory? Whatever for?"

Gregory's eyes glowed dangerously. "Haven't you been going all over the country encouraging people to refuse the Mark? The Adjutant General, Major General Fields, is here as the head of the Military Department of this state. Under martial law, I could arrest you myself, but I am scrupulously observing all the correct protocols. The governor and the Major General will enforce the laws of South Carolina."

Xander raised an eyebrow. "What laws have we broken? We still have freedom of speech in this country, do we not?"

Gregory's eyes flashed. "You do not have freedom to preach against the laws of the land. You are an accessory before the fact and are accused of solicitation and incitement. It is illegal to encourage your followers to commit a crime by refusing to submit to the law. That is an inchoate offense, concerned with aiding, abetting, counseling, or procuring an offense to be committed. Counseling people to refuse the Mark is an active attempt to get them to commit an offending act. Your intent is clear."

Elizabeth smiled at him again. "It seems the law degree paid off, Gregory, but you are forgetting one tiny fact."

"And just what 'fact' have I forgotten, El?" Gregory asked with a sneer. "Enlighten me."

She laughed. "No one has yet refused the Mark."

The governor looked uncomfortable, and the Major General narrowed his eyes.

Gregory's temper was unleashed as he shouted at the two officials, "Arrest them! I order it!"

Michael and Gabriel stepped closer to their charges in response to the threat.

"Sir, with all respect, I cannot," replied the officer. "Mrs. Xander is correct. Once the law is implemented, if their followers refuse the Mark, we can arrest them. It was my understanding that this couple had already broken a law. If I had known this was not the case, we would not have come here."

The governor nodded in agreement. "Mr. President, I think the Major General is correct. I don't think we have grounds for their arrest as yet."

Gregory looked at his watch. "They have broken the curfew. Arrest them."

Xander calmly held up his hand. "We will leave immediately. Would that suit?"

"No!" thundered Gregory, looking at the governor. "I order you to arrest them. Under martial law, you must obey me."

A rumble sounded in the heavens, as if in answer to the Dark Prince.

"Mr. President, I don't think this will play well in the press. We have a small army here to take two people into custody. They aren't armed, and they aren't causing any problems that I can see. Let's wait until the Mark law goes into effect. We can take them to jail in two weeks just as well as we can tonight," said the governor reasonably.

"Then leave, cowards!" shouted Gregory, not even attempting to hide his flaming eyes and balled fists. "I'll handle this myself, but I promise that you will regret this!"

Seeing his loss of control and frightened by his erratic behavior, the governor and the Major General ordered the troops back to the transports, and then hurried to the nearest vehicle and got inside with the soldiers.

Gregory held to his fragile self-control until the human troops were clear of the area. When the sounds of the trucks faded, he swiftly changed into demonic form, and his followers spread into a battle formation.

Xander also morphed, fully arrayed in the battle gear provided to him by his Father, including his helmet and sandals. Gregory quickly drew his sword and, and the metallic shriek of thousands of weapons being unsheathed screamed through the night.

The dark forces rapidly attacked Xander, separating him from Elizabeth, as other strong demons advanced on Michael and Gabriel, covering them in darkness. Consequently, Xander, Michael, and Gabriel were immediately engaged in the thick of the battle, surrounded by demonic warriors, unable to help Elizabeth as Gregory lunged at her.

However, in the second before the Dark Prince could reach her, Elizabeth assumed her guardian warrior form, her armor a feminine version of Xander's, lifting her shield to fend off Gregory's expected blows.

Gregory's face registered his surprise, and he faltered for a moment before he was able to continue the fight. Elizabeth took full advantage of his hesitation and pressed her advantage, using her sword to drive him closer to her husband.

Light faced darkness across the field as the two sides engaged in fierce combat. Xander, Gabriel, and Michael slashed through the demons, working their way ever closer to Elizabeth and Gregory. As soon as Elizabeth had maneuvered Gregory into position, swinging and slashing her sword against his in figure-eight patterns, Elizabeth allowed him to think he had the upper hand, and she began to move backwards, as if he were pushing her.

Elizabeth's strategy was successful, and when she had lured Gregory near enough to Xander, Michael, and Gabriel, she fitted her back to theirs in a formation they had practiced many times. Michael was the point of the square, while Xander and Gabriel took the attack positions to his right and his left. Michael rapidly turned the formation, putting Elizabeth in the rear, facing the opposite direction of the Captain of the Host, while he directed their movements. Their thoughts linked together, and they fought as one, twirling and slashing through the heart of the demonic army as Gregory stayed with them.

The storm clouds moved in, obliterating the stars, and the battle raged in absolute darkness.

Michael concentrated on Gregory. *If we behead the snake, the body will be without direction*, he thought.

Gregory's guards tried to protect him, but in his pride, the halfling ordered them away.

Elizabeth held her own, using her sword skillfully, taking the heads of several fiends, breathing in their foul stench as they disintegrated before her.

When too many threatened her at once, Michael turned their formation, sometimes spinning the four of them rapidly as they twirled their bodies and slashed back and forth with their weapons.

Three things happened at once in the blackness of the night.

At the edge of the clearing, Michael pinned Gregory against a tree with his sword at the halfling's throat, and Lucifer's roar resounded through the clearing, calling a halt to the battle.

At the same time, every angelic being heard a deep Voice commanding, *Put away your instruments of war.*

Their orders were instantly obeyed. Both sides disarmed, a hiss rippling through the ranks as weapons were put away, and then there was silence.

Gregory, freed when Michael sheathed his sword, raised his own weapon to take advantage, but Michael blocked him with his shield.

When Gregory moved to the side to position himself for another strike at Michael, Lucifer, in full battle gear, landed between them, holding up his hand to his son.

You dare to defy me? I told you there was no need for action at this time, yet you engage Michael and the Host! Who do you think you are, infant? You worm! Your stupidity is destroying my army. I made you, and I will unmake you! the Prince of Demons screamed, drawing his sword and causing the ground to shake.

Gregory sneered at him. *You are old and useless. The only power you have kept has been through me! The people worship me, not you! You are a complete failure and an utter fool. Step aside and let the true Lord of Darkness reign. I will raise my throne above yours and God's.*

Lucifer, enraged beyond anything he had ever known before, leapt and slashed at his son, neatly severing him into two halves. As Gregory bled out on the ground, Lucifer kicked the upper half of his torso away from his legs. While the forces of light and evil watched, Gregory slowly melted away, and nothing was left except his hot blood, scorching the grass and soaking into the ground.

Rain began to fall, pelting the ground, washing away all evidence that Gregory had ever existed.

Lucifer stood over the fading remains of his son, eyes blazing while he muttered oaths. He looked up and saw Michael, standing a short distance away with his arms folded.

Lucifer smirked at the Captain of the Hosts. *You think this is over, old friend? Gregory was not the only way. I have another.*

Satan then fixed his flaming eyes on Xander and Elizabeth. *You are feeble and pitiful before me. You have won nothing. My time will come, and I will destroy both of you and your children myself.*

Xander replied, *The Lord rebuked you this time, and He will do so again by the Word of His mouth. It is written.*

Lucifer cursed and turned his back, facing his army. As if by silent command, the demonic ranks rose as one into the air, blocking the sky, making the night even darker as they scattered and flew off in different directions.

Xander and Elizabeth looked up, watching the darkness flee the clearing.

Elizabeth held her husband's eyes with hers. *It isn't over, is it?*

He smiled grimly. *For this moment it is; however, until the Almighty Himself decides that this age will end, we will continue to fight.*

~~oo~~

Anne Wickham sat in a rocking chair in the White House, smiling a secret smile as she looked at the small, distinct bulge of her belly, caressing it with both hands, rocking slowly. She began to sing a lullaby softly, and her mother entered the room.

"Ah, I used to sing that song to you when you were little." She paused. "Anne, it is finished, but there is no body to be found. Your husband has simply vanished as far as the world is concerned," she said, stroking her daughter's hair.

"I'm glad he's dead, and I hope it was painful. I suffered enough at his hand." She sighed. "I will live with you and Father until the baby is born, and then my father-in-law will have need of my son… and of me," answered Anne.

Her father stood in the open door, his Russian heritage plainly displayed by his accent. "He will have uses for all four of us, I would imagine."

Anne's mother laughed. "Gregory never realized that while he did not fulfill the prophecies, his child would. I would have loved to have told him myself that my mother was of Middle Eastern descent. His expression would have been most amusing, I think."

Anne glanced up at her father. "It's a good thing our Master told us to say you were dead, Papa. That accent would have given you away, and legally changing our last name years ago was brilliant, Mama. The Dark Lord had every detail planned from the beginning. When he presented me as a bride for his son, Gregory never suspected that he was merely a pawn, a way for this child to be conceived."

~~oo~~

After searching for several days, the governmental powers could no longer keep the disappearance of the President a secret. A statement was released detailing the President's sudden illness and consequent death. An unopened coffin stood in the rotunda of the Capitol Building while the Vice President, Hugh Dodge, was sworn in as President. His first official act was to lead the repeal of the controversial Mark bill. As the repeal wended its way through Congress, the Supreme Court agreed to hear a case challenging the constitutionality of the law, and they issued an injunction stopping the implementation of it until the case was decided.

Knowing that the bill would be struck down, Lucifer had decided that a retreat for the present was the wisest course of action.

~~oo~~

Xander and Elizabeth enjoyed time at home with their children, extended family, and friends for several months after the death of Gregory. SoulFire Ministries continued, but the pace was not as frantic as it had been. The couple continued to teach their children themselves, knowing that eventually, the three of them would need to be ready to live their unique destinies.

One afternoon as Xander sat at the piano, playing a Chopin etude to keep his skills sharp, three-year-old John David came up beside him.

"I can do that!" said the boy, confidently.

Xander and Gabriel shared a smile. Xander well remembered those words coming from Elizabeth's mouth when she was but five years old.

Cahal and Kenward stood on either side of the instrument.

"Elizabeth!" called Xander as he lifted his son to the bench and moved to stand behind him. "You may want to come in here and see this."

She hurried in, followed by Michael carrying a twin on each hip.

Abner, Kenelm, Baron, and Reima were close behind Michael.

There on the piano bench sat her eldest, John David, a small replica of his father, smiling at her brightly. He then turned to the piano, his short fingers flying over the keys as he played the etude perfectly.

Elizabeth put her hand over her mouth, and in her mind she heard two childish voices.

I play, too!

She walked over to the piano, ruffled her son's hair, and kissed her husband. "I think we may need to build another music room onto the house. It appears that we may need more than one piano."

"I think you are right, love," he said as he turned to take his wife into his arms. "I have been debating the idea of building our own recording studio on the land in the back of the property."

She stood on her tiptoes and kissed his nose. "You would like to keep us all here together, wouldn't you? You would be happy never to leave the house."

"And what is wrong with that?" he asked, smiling gently at her. "I love my family. We have to leave to tour and do a few other things, but otherwise, I would willingly stay right here with you and the children. Is that so terrible?" he asked, pulling her more tightly to him.

"No," she answered, putting her cheek to his chest and listening to his strong heart beat. "Nothing is wrong with that at all. It's a lovely idea. I've had enough excitement to last at least one lifetime, and I'm looking forward to being with you for eternity."

Xander looked over his wife's head at his brothers with his children, and his heart swelled with love. He was perfectly content. As he began to think of how much he had been blessed, Elizabeth's thoughts joined with his as they quoted Ephesians 4:20 and 21 together, *'Now to Him who is able to do exceeding abundantly beyond all that we ask or think, according to the power that works within us, to Him be the glory in the church and in Christ Jesus to all generations forever and ever. Amen.'*

"Amen!" sounded three little voices in unison.

END OF

THE GUARDIAN TRILOGY

NAMES OF GOD

Jehovah - The Lord - Exodus 6:2-3
Jehovah-Adon Kal Ha'arets- Lord of Earth - Josh 3:13
Jehovah-Bara - Lord Creator - Isaiah 40:28
Jehovah-Chatsahi - Lord my Strength - Psalm 27:1
Jehovah-Chereb - Lord the Sword - Deut. 33:29
Jehovah-Eli - Lord my God - Psalm 18:2
Jehovah-Elyon - Lord Most High - Psalm 38:2
Jehovah-Gador Milchamah - Mighty in Battle - Ps 24:8
Jehovah-Ganan - Lord Our Defense - Ps 89:18
Jehovah-Go'el - Lord My Redeemer - Is. 49:26, 60:16
Jehovah-Hamelech - Lord King - Psalm 98:6
Jehovah-Helech 'Olam - Lord King Forever - Ps 10:16
Jehovah-Hoshe'ah - Lord Saves - Psalm 20:9
Jehovah-Jireh - Provider - Gen. 22:14, I John 4:9, Philip 4:19
Jehovah-Kanna - Lord Jealous - Ex 34:14
Jehovah-Machsi - Lord my Refuge - Psalm 91:9
Jehovah-Magen - Lord my Shield - Deut. 33:29
Jehovah-Ma'oz - Lord my Fortress - Jer. 16:19
Jehovah-Mephalti - Lord my Deliverer - Psalm 18:2
Jehovah-Metshodhathi - Lord my Fortress - Psalm 18:2
Jehovah-Misqabbi - Lord my High Tower - Psalm 18:2
Jehovah-Naheh - Lord who Smites - Ezekiel 7:9
Jehovah-Nissi - Banner - I Chronicles 29:11-13
Jehovah-Rohi - Shepherd - Psalm 23
Jehovah-Rophe - Healer - Isaiah 53:4,5
Jehovah-Sabaoth - Lord of Hosts - I Sam 1:3
Jehovah-Shalom - Peace - Isaiah 9:6, Rom 8:31-35
Jehovah-Shammah - Present - Hebrews 13:5
Jehovah-Tsidkenu - Righteousness - I Cor 1:30
Jehovah-Tsori - Lord my Strength - Psalm 19:14
Jehovah-Yasha - Lord my Savior - Isaiah 49:26
Jehovah-'Ez-Lami - Lord my Strength - Ps 28:7
Jehovah-'Immeku - Lord Is With You - Judges 6:12
Jehovah-'Izoa Hakaboth - Lord Strong -Mighty - Ps 24:8
Jehovah-'Ori - Lord my Light - Psalm 27:1
Jehovah-'Uzam - Lord Strength in Trouble - Is 49:26

ABOUT THE AUTHOR

Robin Helm's books reflect her love of music, as well as her fascination with the paranormal and science fiction.

Published works include The Guardian Trilogy: *Guardian*, *SoulFire*, and *Legacy*), the Yours by Design series: *Accidentally Yours*, *Sincerely Yours*, and *Forever Yours* (Fitzwilliam Darcy switches places in time with his descendant, Will Darcy), and *Understanding Elizabeth* (Regency romance).

She contributed to *A Very Austen Christmas: Austen Anthologies, Book 1*, an anthology featuring like-minded authors, in 2017, and *A Very Austen Valentine: Austen Anthologies, Book 2* which was released on December 29, 2018.

Her newest release is *More to Love*, a standalone historical sweet romance dealing with body image. Coming in 2019: *Lawfully Innocent*, a historical U.S. Marshal romance book in the Lawkeepers series; *Maestro*, a historical sweet romance featuring a brilliant musician and his student; and *A Very Austen Romance: Austen Anthologies, Book 3*.

She lives in sunny South Carolina where she teaches piano and adores her one husband, two married daughters, and three grandchildren.

For updates on new releases, follow Robin Helm on her Amazon Author page at https://www.amazon.com/Robin-Helm/e/B005MLFMTG/

Robin Helm recommends books by Wendi Sotis, Laura Hile, and Mandy Cook.

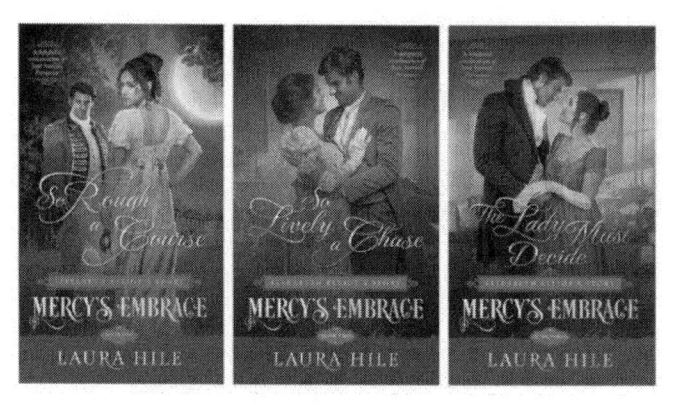

Our latest book -

A Very Austen Valentine: Austen Anthologies, Book 2

Six beloved authors deliver romantic Valentine novellas set in Jane Austen's Regency world. Robin Helm, Laura Hile, Wendi Sotis, and Barbara Cornthwaite, together with Susan Kaye and Mandy Cook, share variations of Pride and Prejudice, Persuasion, and Sense and Sensibility, featuring your favorite characters in sequels, adaptations, and spinoffs of Austen's adored novels.

Experience uplifting romance, laugh-out-loud humor, and poignant regret as these authors deftly tug on your heartstrings this Valentine's Day.

A Very Austen Valentine, the second book in the Austen Anthologies series, features six authors, all friends, who wished to share Austenesque variations, prequels, and sequels with their readers. Working together to produce the first book in the series (*A Very Austen Christmas*) was such an enjoyable experience, and the book was so well received, that we knew we had to do another one. Our four original authors invited two more to join us in the follow-up, and we plan to do at least five books in the series.

Most of our stories feature our own original characters, as well as the favorite characters of Austen. We strive to keep Austen's heroes and heroines within the confines she set for them herself. In other words, we do not have the characters act in ways she would not have written. The good guys remain good guys, and the bad guys remain bad guys. We also believe in happily-ever-afters. We want you to be happy at the end of each story.

All six of us are experienced writers with previously published books. I hope you enjoy this introduction to six authors, some of whom may be new to you. If you loved *Pride and Prejudice, Persuasion, Sense and Sensibility, Emma, Northanger Abbey,* or *Mansfield Park*, you will enjoy their books.

A Very Austen Valentine

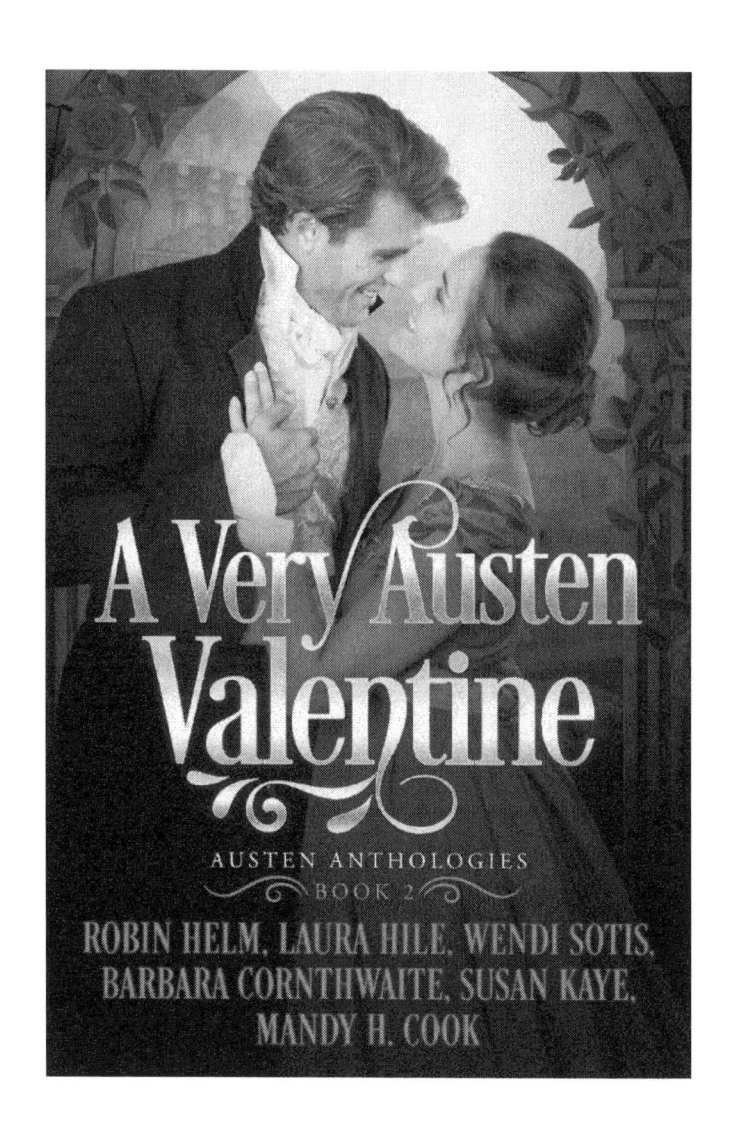

AUSTEN ANTHOLOGIES
BOOK 2

ROBIN HELM, LAURA HILE, WENDI SOTIS, BARBARA CORNTHWAITE, SUSAN KAYE, MANDY H. COOK

Made in the USA
Middletown, DE
29 March 2023